W9-BTE-126

The
Flanders
Panel

BY THE SAME AUTHOR

The Fencing Master

ARTURO PÉREZ-REVERTE

The Flanders Panel

Translated from the Spanish
by Margaret Jull Costa

HARCOURT BRACE & COMPANY
New York   San Diego   London

© 1990, Arturo Pérez-Reverte
© De esta edicion: 1990, Althea, Taurus, Alfaguara, S.A.
English translation copyright © 1990 by HarperCollins Publishers Ltd

All rights reserved. No part of this publication may
be reproduced or transmitted in any form or by any means,
electronic or mechanical, including photocopy, recording, or
any information storage and retrieval system, without
permission in writing from the publisher.

Requests for permission to make copies
of any part of the work should be mailed to:
Permissions Department, Harcourt Brace & Company,
6277 Sea Harbor Drive, Orlando, Florida 32887-6777.

This is a translation of *La Tabla de Flandes.*

Library of Congress Cataloging-in Publication Data
Pérez-Reverte, Arturo.
[Tabla de Flandes. English]
The flanders panel/Arturo Pérez-Reverte;
translated from the Spanish
by Margaret Jull Costa.—1st U.S. ed.
p.   cm.
0-15-148926-2
I. Title.
PQ6666. E765T3313   1994
863—dc20   93-14504

Printed in the United States of America
First United States edition
A B C D E

For Julio and Rosa, Devil's advocates
And for Cristiane Sánchez Azevedo

CONTENTS

I

The Secrets of Meister Van Huys

> God moves the player, he in turn the piece.
> But what god beyond God begins the round
> Of dust and time and sleep and agonies?
> *Jorge Luis Borges*

A SEALED ENVELOPE is an enigma containing further enigmas. This particular one was of the large, bulky manila variety with the name of the laboratory stamped in the lower left-hand corner. And, as she weighed it in her hand whilst scrabbling for a paper knife amongst the many brushes and bottles of paint and varnish, Julia could never have imagined the extent to which the gesture of slitting it open would change her life.

In fact, she already knew what the envelope contained. Or, as she discovered later, she thought she did. Perhaps that's why she felt no special sense of anticipation until she'd removed the prints from the envelope, spread them out on the table and looked at them, almost holding her breath. Only then did she realise that her work on *The Game of Chess* would be far from routine. Unexpected discoveries, in paintings, on furniture, even on the binding of antiquarian books, were commonplace in her profession. During her six years of restoring works of art, she'd uncovered her fair share of preliminary sketches and pentimenti, of retouching and repainting and even forgeries. But never had she come across an inscription concealed beneath the painted surface of a picture: three words revealed by X-ray photography.

She picked up her crumpled pack of unfiltered cigarettes and lit one, unable to take her eyes off the prints. Given the evidence of the 12 x 16 inch X-ray plates, there was no possible room for doubt. The painting was a fifteenth-century Flemish panel, and the original sketch, done in grisaille, was as clearly visible as the grain of the wood and the glued joints of the three pieces of oak that made up the panel on which, out of lines, brush strokes and layers of underpaint, the artist had gradually created his work. At the bottom of the painting, brought to light after five centuries, thanks to radiography, was the hidden phrase, its Gothic characters standing out in sharp contrast against the black and white of the plate.

QUIS NECAVIT EQUITEM

Julia knew enough Latin to be able to translate it without a dictionary: *Quis*, interrogative pronoun meaning "who", *necavit*, from *neco*, "to kill", and *equitem*, the accusative singular of *eques*, "knight". Who killed the knight? Adding a question mark, which, in Latin, the use of *quis* rendered redundant, lent the phrase an air of mystery.

WHO KILLED THE KNIGHT?

It was disconcerting. She took a long pull at her cigarette, holding it in her right hand whilst with her left she rearranged the X-ray photos on the table. Someone, possibly the painter himself, had planted a kind of puzzle in the picture and had then concealed it with a layer of paint. Or perhaps someone else had done so at a later date. That gave her approximately five hundred years to play with in dating the inscription. The notion pleased Julia. Solving the mystery shouldn't prove too difficult. After all, that was her job.

She picked up the photos and got to her feet. The grey light from the large window in the sloping ceiling fell directly on to the painting on the easel. *The Game of Chess*, oil on wood, painted in 1471 by Pieter Van Huys. She stood in front of it and looked at it for a long time. It was a domestic interior painted in minute fifteenth-century detail, the sort of scene with which the great Flemish masters, using oil for the first time, had laid the foundations of modern painting. The main subjects were two gentlemen of noble appearance, in their middle years, sitting on either side of a chessboard on which a game was in progress.

2

In the background to the right, next to a lancet window framing a landscape, a lady, dressed in black, was reading the book that lay in her lap. Completing the scene were the painstaking details typical of the Flemish school, recorded with a perfection that bordered on the obsessive: the furniture and decorations, the black-and-white tiled floor, the design on the carpet, a tiny crack in the wall, the shadow cast by a minuscule nail in one of the ceiling beams. The painting of the chess-board and chess pieces was executed with the same precision as the faces, hands and clothes of the people depicted, with a realism that contributed to the painting's extraordinarily fine finish, its colours still brilliant despite the inevitable darkening caused by the gradual oxidation of the original varnish.

Who killed the knight? Julia looked at the photo she was holding and then at the picture, where, to the naked eye, not a trace of the hidden inscription was visible. Even closer examination, using a binocular microscope x 7, revealed nothing. She lowered the blind over the large skylight, plunging the room into darkness, and near the easel placed a tripod on which was mounted an ultraviolet lamp. Under its rays all the oldest materials, paints and varnishes would show up as fluorescent, whereas more recent ones would appear dark or black, thus revealing any later repainting and retouching. In this case, however, the ultraviolet light revealed only a uniformly fluorescent surface, including the part concealing the inscription. This indicated that it had been painted over either by the artist himself or very soon after the painting was completed.

She switched off the lamp and raised the blind. The steely light of the autumn morning again spilled onto the easel and the painting; it filled the whole book-cluttered studio, its shelves overflowing with paints and brushes, varnishes and solvents, the floor a jumble of carpen-try tools, picture frames and precision instruments, antique sculptures, bronzes and wooden stretchers, pictures that rested, face to the wall, on the valuable but paint-stained Persian carpet. In a corner, on a Louis XV bureau, sat a hi-fi surrounded by piles of records: Don Cherry, Mozart, Miles Davis, Satie, Lester Bowie, Michael Edges, Vivaldi . . . On one wall a gold-framed Venetian mirror presented Julia with a slightly blurred image of herself: shoulder-length hair, faint shadows (from lack of sleep) under her large, dark and, as yet, unmade-up eyes. Whenever César saw her face framed in gold by that mirror, he used to say that she was as lovely as one of da Vinci's models, *ma più bella*. And although César could be considered more of an expert on young men than on madonnas, Julia knew that what he said was absolutely right. Even she enjoyed looking at herself in that gold-framed mirror, because it always gave her a sense of having suddenly emerged on the other side of a magic door, a door through which she'd leapfrogged time and space, and it returned to her an image of herself that had all the robustness of an Italian Renaissance beauty.

She smiled to think of César. She always smiled when she thought of him and had since she was a child. It was a smile of tenderness, often a smile of complicity. She put the X-ray photos down on the table, stubbed out her cigarette in the heavy bronze ashtray signed by Benlliure and sat down at her typewriter.

The Game of Chess

Oil on wood. Flemish school. Dated 1471.
Artist: Pieter Van Huys (1415–1481).
Base: Three fixed oak panels, joined by glue.
Dimensions: 60 x 87 cm (three identical panels of 20 x 87).
Thickness of panel: 4 cm.

State of preservation of base: No warping. No noticeable damage by woodworm.

State of preservation of the painted surface: Good adhesion and cohesion of the layer structure. No changes in colour. Some craquelure due to ageing, but no blistering or scaling.

State of preservation of surface film: No apparent traces of salt exudation or damp. Excessive darkening of the varnish due to oxidation; varnish removal and new varnish advisable.

The coffeepot was bubbling in the kitchen. Julia got up and poured herself a large cup, black, no sugar. She returned with the cup in one hand, drying the other on the baggy man-size sweater she was wearing over her pyjamas. A light touch of her index finger and the sounds of Vivaldi's *Concerto for lute and viola d'amore* burst upon the room, gliding on the grey morning light. She took a sip of thick, bitter coffee that burned the tip of her tongue. Then she sat down again, her feet bare on the carpet, and continued typing the report.

UV and X-ray examination: Detected no obvious major changes, alterations or subsequent repaints. The X-rays reveal a concealed inscription of the period, in Gothic lettering (see enclosed prints). This is not visible using conventional methods of examination. It could be uncovered without damage to the original by removing the layer of paint now covering the area.

She removed the sheet of paper from the typewriter and put it in an envelope with the X-ray photos, drank the rest of the coffee, which was still hot, and settled down to smoke another cigarette. Before her on the easel, in front of the lady by the window absorbed in her reading, the two chess players were engaged in a game that had been going on now for five centuries, a game depicted by Pieter Van Huys with such rigour and mastery that, like all the other objects in the picture, the chess pieces seemed to stand out in relief from the surface. The sense of realism was so intense that the painting effortlessly achieved the effect sought by the old Flemish masters: the integration of the spectator into the pictorial whole, persuading him that the space in which he stood was the same as that represented in the painting, as if the picture were a fragment of reality, or reality a fragment of the picture. Adding to this effect were the window on the right-hand side of the composition, showing a landscape *beyond* the central scene, and a round, convex mirror on the wall to the left, reflecting the foreshortened figures of the players and the chessboard, distorted according to the perspective of the spectator, who would be standing *facing* the scene. It thus achieved the astonishing feat of integrating three planes – window, room and mirror

– into one space. It was, thought Julia, as if the spectator were reflected between the two players, inside the painting.

She went over to the easel. Arms folded, she stood looking at the painting for a long time, utterly still, apart from drawing occasionally on her cigarette and screwing up her eyes against the smoke. One of the chess players, the one on the left, looked to be about thirty-five. His brown hair was shaved just above the ears in the medieval fashion; he had a strong, aquiline nose and a look of intense concentration. He was wearing a doublet painted in a vermilion that had admirably withstood both the passage of time and the oxidation of the varnish. Round his neck he wore the insigne of the Golden Fleece and near his right shoulder an exquisite brooch, whose filigree pattern was rendered in minute detail, right down to the tiny gleam of light on each precious stone. He was sitting with his left elbow and right hand resting on the table on either side of the board. Between the fingers of his right hand he was holding one of the chess pieces: a white knight. By his head there was an identifying inscription in Gothic lettering: *FERDI-NANDUS OST. D.*

The other player was thinner and about forty. He had a smooth forehead and almost black hair turning to grey at the temples, where the finest of white lead brush marks were just distinguishable. This, together with his expression and general air of composure, gave him a look of precocious maturity. His profile was serene and dignified. Unlike the other player, he was dressed not in sumptuous court clothes, but in a simple leather cuirass, with a gorget of burnished steel that gave him an unmistakably military air. He was leaning further over the chessboard than his opponent, as if concentrating hard on the game, apparently oblivious to his surroundings, his arms folded on the edge of the table. His concentration could be seen in the faint, vertical lines between his eyebrows. He was looking at the pieces as if they were confronting him with a particularly difficult problem whose solution required every ounce of intellectual energy. The inscription above his head read: *RUTGIER AR. PREUX.*

The lady sitting next to the window was set apart from the two players by the use of a sharp linear perspective that situated her on a higher plane within the picture. The black velvet of her dress, to which the skilled application of white and grey glazes added volume, seemed to

6

come out of the painting towards you. Its realism rivalled even the painstaking detail of the carpet border, the precision in the painting of the tiled floor, every knot, joint and grain of the ceiling beams. Leaning towards the painting to study these effects more closely, Julia felt a shiver of professional admiration run through her. Only a master like Van Huys could have used the black of a gown to such advantage, employing colour created out of the absence of colour to an extent few would have dared. Yet it was so real that Julia felt that at any moment she would hear the soft swish of velvet on the embossed leather of the low stool.

She looked at the woman's face. It was beautiful and, in the fashion of the time, extremely pale. Her thick blonde hair, carefully smoothed back from her temples, was caught up beneath a toque of white gauze. Her arms, sheathed in light grey damask, emerged from loose sleeves; her hands, long and slender, held a book of hours. The light from the window picked out the same metallic gleam on the open clasp of the book and on the single gold ring adorning her hand. Her eyelids were lowered, over what had to be blue eyes, in an expression of serene and modest virtue characteristic of female portraits of the period. The light came from two sources, the window and the mirror, at once connecting the woman with the two chess players and keeping her subtly separate, her figure more marked by foreshortening and shadows. Her inscription read: *BEATRIZ BURG. OST. D.*

Julia took a couple of steps back to view the painting as a whole. There was no doubt about it: it was a masterpiece, with documentation accredited by experts. That would mean a high price at the auction to be held by Claymore's in January. Perhaps the hidden inscription, together with the appropriate historical documentation, would increase the value of the painting. Ten per cent for Claymore's, five per cent for Menchu Roch, the rest for the owner. Less one per cent for insurance and her fee for restoring and cleaning it.

She took off her clothes and stepped into the shower, leaving the door open, so that Vivaldi's music could keep her company in the steam. Restoring *The Game of Chess* for its entry into the art market could bring her a sizeable amount. Within only a few years of finishing her degree, Julia had won for herself a solid reputation and become one of the art restorers most sought after by museums and antiquarians. Methodical

7

and disciplined, a painter of some talent in her spare time, she was known for the respect she showed the original work, an ethical position not always shared by her colleagues. In the difficult and often awkward spiritual relationship between any restorer and his or her job, in the bitter controversy between conservation and renovation, the young woman had the virtue of never losing sight of one fundamental principle: no work of art could ever be restored to its primitive state without sustaining serious damage. Julia believed that things like the ageing process, the patina, the way colours and varnishes changed, even flaws, repainting and retouching, became, with the passing of time, as integral a part of a work of art as the original work. Perhaps because of that, the paintings that passed through her hands never left them decked out in strange new, supposedly original colours and lights – "painted courtesans", César called them – but were treated with a delicacy that integrated the marks of time with the work.

She emerged from the bathroom wrapped in a bathrobe, her wet hair dripping onto her shoulders. Lighting yet another cigarette, she stood in front of the picture while she dressed: low-heeled shoes, a brown pleated skirt and a leather jacket. She gave a satisfied glance at herself in the Venetian mirror and then, turning to the two grave-faced chess players, she winked at them provocatively. *Who killed the knight?* As she put the photographs and her report into her bag, the phrase kept going round and round in her head as if it were a riddle. She switched on the electronic alarm and turned the key twice in the security lock. *Quis necavit equitem.* One way or another, it must mean something. She repeated the three words under her breath as she went down the stairs, sliding her fingers along the brass-trimmed banister. She was genuinely intrigued by the painting and its hidden inscription, but there was something else, too: She felt a strange sense of apprehension, the same feeling she'd had when she was a little girl and used to stand at the top of the stairs trying to screw up enough courage to peer into the dark attic.

"You've got to admit he's a beauty. Pure quattrocento."

Menchu Roch was not referring to one of the paintings on display in the gallery that bore her name. Her pale, heavily made-up eyes were trained on the broad shoulders of Max, who was talking to someone he knew at the bar of the café. Max was six foot tall, with the shoulders of a swimmer beneath his well-cut jacket. He wore his hair long and tied back in a brief ponytail with a dark silk ribbon and he moved with a kind of indolent flexibility. Menchu gave him a long, appreciative look and, with proprietorial satisfaction, sipped her martini. He was her latest lover.

"Pure quattrocento," she repeated, savouring both the words and her drink. "Doesn't he remind you of one of those marvellous Italian bronzes?"

Julia nodded half-heartedly. They were old friends, but the ease with which Menchu could lend suggestive overtones to even the most vaguely artistic remark never failed to surprise her.

"An Italian bronze, one of the originals, I mean, would work out a lot cheaper."

Menchu gave a short, cynical laugh.

"Cheaper than Max? I should say." She sighed ostentatiously and bit into the olive in her martini. "Michelangelo was lucky; he sculpted them in the nude. He didn't have to foot their clothes bill courtesy of American Express."

"No one forces you to pay his bills."

"That's the whole point, darling," Menchu said, batting her eyelids in a languid, theatrical manner. "That no one forces me to do it, I mean. So you see . . ."

She finished her drink, keeping one little finger carefully raised; she did this on purpose, purely to provoke. Menchu was nearer fifty than forty and was of the firm belief that sex was to be found everywhere, even in the most subtle nuances of a work of art. Perhaps that's why she was able to look at men with the same calculating, greedy eye she employed when assessing the potential of a painting. Amongst those who knew her, the owner of Gallery Roch had the reputation of never missing an opportunity to appropriate anything that aroused her interest, be it a painting, a man or a line of cocaine. She was still attractive, although her age made it increasingly difficult to overlook what César scathingly referred to as certain "aesthetic anachronisms". Menchu could not resign herself to growing old, largely because she didn't want to. And, perhaps as a kind of challenge to herself, she fought against it by adopting a calculated vulgarity in her choice of make-up, clothes and lovers. For the rest, in line with her belief that art dealers and antiquarians were little more than glorified rag-and-bone merchants, she pretended a lack of culture that was far from the truth, deliberately bungling artistic and literary references and openly mocking the rather select world in which she conducted her professional life. She boasted about all this with the same frankness with which she had once claimed to have experienced the best orgasm of her life masturbating in front of a catalogued and numbered reproduction of Donatello's *David*, an anecdote that César, with his refined, almost feminine brand of cruelty, always cited as the only example of genuine good taste that Menchu Roch had ever shown in her life.

"So what shall we do about the Van Huys?" asked Julia.

Menchu looked again at the X-ray photos lying on the table between her glass and her friend's coffee cup. She was wearing blue eye shadow and a blue dress that was much too short for her. Julia thought, quite without malice, that twenty years ago Menchu must have looked really pretty in blue.

"I'm not sure yet," said Menchu. "Claymore's have undertaken to auction the painting exactly as it stands . . . We'll have to see what effect the inscription has on its value."

"Just think what that could mean."

"I love it. You've hit the jackpot and you don't even realise it."

"Ask the owner what he wants to do."

Menchu put the prints back in the envelope and crossed her legs. Two young men drinking aperitifs at the next table cast furtive, interested glances at her bronzed thighs. Julia fidgeted, a touch irritated. She was usually amused by the blatant way Menchu contrived special effects for the benefit of her male audience, but sometimes the display struck her as unnecessary. She looked at the square-faced Omega watch she wore on the inside of her left wrist. It was much too early to be showing off one's best underwear.

"The owner's no problem," Menchu explained. "He's a delightful old chap in a wheelchair. And if the discovery of the inscription increases his profits, he'll be only too pleased . . . His niece and her husband are a pair of real bloodsuckers."

Max was still chatting at the bar but, ever-conscious of his duties, he turned round occasionally to bestow a dazzling smile on Julia and Menchu. Speaking of bloodsuckers, Julia said to herself, but decided against putting the thought into words. Not that Menchu would have minded – she showed an admirable cynicism when it came to men – but Julia had a strong sense of the proprieties which always stopped her from going too far.

Ignoring Max, she said: "It's only two months till the auction. That's not nearly enough time if I have to remove the varnish, uncover the inscription and then revarnish again. Besides, getting together the documentation on the painting and the people in it *and* writing a report will take time. It would be a good idea to get the owner's permission as soon as possible."

Menchu agreed. Her frivolity did not extend to her professional life, in which she moved with all the cunning of a trained rat. She was acting as intermediary in the transaction because the owner of the Van Huys knew nothing of the workings of the art market. It was she who had handled the negotiations for the auction with the Madrid branch of Claymore's.

"I'll phone him tomorrow. His name is Don Manuel Belmonte, he's seventy years old, and he's delighted, as he puts it, to be dealing with a pretty young woman with such a splendid head for business."

There was something else, Julia pointed out. If the uncovered inscription could be linked to the story of the people in the painting, Claymore's would be sure to play on that to up the asking price.

"Have you managed to get hold of any more useful documentation?"

"Very little," Menchu said, pursing her lips in her effort to remember. "I gave you all I had along with the painting. So you're going to have to find out for yourself."

Julia opened her handbag and took longer than necessary to find her cigarettes. At last, she slowly took one out and looked at her friend.

"We could ask Álvaro."

Menchu raised her eyebrows and said at once that the very idea left her petrified, or saltified or whatever the word was, like Noah's wife, or was it Lot's? Anyway, like the wife of that twit who got so fed up with life in Sodom.

"It's up to you, of course," she said, her voice growing hoarse with expectation. She could sense strong emotion in the air. "After all, you and Álvaro . . ."

She left the phrase hanging and adopted a look of exaggerated concern, as she did whenever the topic of conversation turned to the problems of others, whom she liked to think of as utterly defenceless when it came to affairs of the heart.

Julia held her gaze, unperturbed, and said only: "He's the best art historian we know. And this has nothing to do with me, but with the painting."

Menchu pretended to be considering the matter seriously and then nodded. It was up to Julia, of course. But if she was in Julia's shoes, she wouldn't do it. *In dubio pro reo*, as that old pedant César always said. Or was it *in pluvio*?

"I can assure you that as regards Álvaro, I'm completely cured."

"Some illnesses, sweetie, you never get over. And a year is nothing. As the song says."

Julia couldn't suppress a wry smile at her own expense. A year ago Álvaro and she had finished a long affair, and Menchu knew all about it. It had been Menchu who, quite unintentionally, had pronounced the final verdict, which went to the very heart of the matter, something along the lines of: In the end, my dear, a married man invariably finds in favour of his legal wife. All those years of washing underpants and giving birth always prove to be the deciding factor. "It's just the way they're made," she had concluded between sniffs, her nose glued to a narrow white line of cocaine. "Deep down, they're sickeningly loyal." Another sniff. "The bastards."

Julia exhaled a dense cloud of smoke and slowly drank the rest of her coffee, trying to keep the cup from dripping. That particular ending had been very painful, once the final words had been said and the door slammed shut. And it went on being painful afterwards. On the two or three occasions when Álvaro and she had met by chance at lectures or in museums, both had behaved with exemplary fortitude: "You're looking well." "Take care of yourself." After all, they both considered themselves to be civilised people who, quite apart from that fragment of their past, had a shared interest in the world of art. They were, to put it succinctly, mature people, adults.

She was aware of Menchu watching her with malicious interest,

12

gleefully anticipating the prospect of new amorous intrigues in which she could intervene as tactical adviser. She was forever complaining that since Julia had broken up with Álvaro her subsequent affairs had been so sporadic as to be hardly worth mentioning: "You're becoming a puritan, darling," she was always saying, "and that's deadly dull. What you need is a bit of passion, a return to the maelstrom." From that point of view, the mere mention of Álvaro seemed to offer interesting possibilities.

Julia realised all this without feeling the slightest irritation. Menchu was Menchu and always had been. You don't choose your friends, they choose you, and you either reject them or you accept them without reservations. That was something else she'd learned from César.

Her cigarette was nearly finished, so she stubbed it out in the ashtray and smiled wanly at Menchu.

"Álvaro's not important. What concerns me is the Van Huys." She hesitated, searching for the right words as she tried to clarify her idea. "There's something odd about that painting."

Menchu shrugged distractedly, as if she were thinking about something else.

"Don't get worked up about it, love. A picture is just canvas, wood, paint and varnish. What matters is how much it leaves in your pocket when it changes hands." She looked across at Max's broad shoulders and blinked smugly. "The rest is just fairy tales."

Throughout her time with Álvaro, Julia had thought of him as conforming to the most rigorous of professional stereotypes, a conformity that extended to his appearance and style of dress. He was pleasant-looking, fortyish, wore English tweed jackets and knitted ties, and, to top it all, smoked a pipe. When she saw him come into the lecture hall for the first time – his subject that day had been "Art and Man" – it had taken her a good quarter of an hour before she could actually listen to what he was saying, unable as she was to believe that anyone who looked so like a young professor actually *was* a professor. Afterwards, when Álvaro had dismissed them until the following week and everyone was streaming out into the corridor, she'd gone up to him as if it were the most natural thing in the world, knowing full well what would happen: the eternal repetition of a rather unoriginal story, the classic teacher-student plot, and Julia had simply assumed this, even before Álvaro, who was on his way out of the door, had turned round and smiled at her for the first time. There was something inevitable about the whole thing – or at least so it seemed to Julia as she weighed the pros and cons of the matter – a suggestion of a deliciously classical *fatum*, of paths laid by Destiny, a view she'd keenly espoused ever since her schooldays, when she'd translated the brilliant family dramas of that inspired Greek, Sophocles. She hadn't been able to bring herself to mention it to César until much later, and he, who had acted as her confidant in affairs of the heart for years – the first time, Julia had still been in short socks and pigtails – had simply shrugged and, in a calculatedly superficial tone, criticised the scant originality of a story that had provided the most sentimental plots, my dear, for at least three hundred novels and as many films, especially – and here he'd pulled a scornful face – French and American films: "And that, as I'm sure you'll agree, Princess, sheds a new and truly ghastly light on the whole subject." But that was all. César had never gone in for reproachful remarks or fatherly warnings, which, as they both well knew, would never have helped anyway. César had no children of his own, nor would he ever have, but he did possess a special flair when it came to tackling such situations. At some point in his life, César had realised that no one ever learns from anyone else's mistakes and, consequently, there was only one dignified and proper attitude to be taken by a guardian – which, after all, was what he was – and that consisted in sitting down next to his young ward, taking her by the hand and listening, with infinite kindness, to the evolving story of her loves and griefs, whilst nature took its own wise and inevitable course.

"In affairs of the heart, Princess," César used to say, "one should offer neither advice nor solutions . . . just a clean hanky when it seems appropriate."

And that was exactly what he'd done when it had all ended between her and Álvaro, that night when she'd turned up at César's apartment, like a sleepwalker, her hair still damp, and had fallen asleep with her head on his lap.

But that had happened long after that first encounter in the corridor at the university, when there were no notable deviations from the anticipated script. The ritual proceeded along well-trodden, predictable paths, which proved, nonetheless, unexpectedly satisfying. Julia had had other affairs, but never before – as she had on the afternoon when, for the first time, she and Álvaro lay down together in a narrow hotel bed – had she felt the need to say "I love you" in quite that painful, heart-wrenching way, hearing herself say the words with joyous amazement, words she'd always refused to say, in a voice she barely recognised as her own, more like a moan or a lament. And so, one morning when she woke up with her face buried in Álvaro's chest, she had carefully brushed the tousled hair from her own face and studied his sleeping profile for a long time, feeling the soft beat of his heart against her cheek, until he too had opened his eyes and smiled back at her. In that moment Julia knew, with absolute certainty, that she loved him, and she knew too that she would have other lovers but never again would she feel what she felt for him. Twenty-eight months later, months she had lived through and counted off almost day by day, the moment arrived for a painful awakening from that love, for her to ask César to get out his famous handkerchief. "The dreaded handkerchief," he'd called it, theatrical as ever, half in jest but perceptive as a Cassandra, "the handkerchief we wave when we say good-bye for ever." And that, in essence, had been their story.

A year had been enough to cauterise the wounds, but not the memories, memories that Julia had no intention of giving up anyway. She'd grown up quite fast, and that whole moral process had crystallised in the belief – unashamedly drawn from those professed by César – that life is like an expensive restaurant where, sooner or later, someone always hands you the bill, which is not to say that you should deny the joy and pleasure afforded by the dishes already eaten.

Julia was pondering this now, as she watched Álvaro at his desk, leafing through a book and making notes on white index cards. He'd hardly changed at all physically, apart from a few grey hairs. His eyes were still calm and intelligent. She'd loved those eyes once, as she had those long, slender hands with their smooth, round nails. She watched as his fingers turned the pages, held his pen, and she heard, much to her discomfort, a distant murmur of melancholy, which, after brief analysis, she decided to accept as perfectly normal. His hands did not provoke in her the same feelings now as then, but they had, nonetheless, once caressed her body. Even his smallest touch, its warmth, had remained imprinted on her skin; the traces had not been erased by other loves.

She tried to slow the pulse of her feelings. She hadn't the least intention of giving in to the temptations of memory. Besides, that was now a secondary consideration. She hadn't gone there in order to stir up nostalgic longings. So she forced herself to concentrate on her ex-lover's words and not on him. After the first awkward minutes, Álvaro had looked at her thoughtfully, as if trying to assess the importance of what had brought her there again after all this time. He smiled affectionately, like an old friend or colleague, relaxed and attentive, placing himself at her disposal with the quiet efficiency so familiar to her, full of silences and considered remarks uttered in that low voice of his. After the initial surprise, there was only a hint of perplexity in his eyes when Julia asked him about the painting, though not about the hidden inscription, which she and Menchu had decided to keep a secret. Álvaro confirmed that he knew the painter, his work and the historical period well, but that he hadn't known the painting was going to be auctioned or that Julia had been placed in charge of its restoration. In fact he had no need of the colour photographs Julia had brought, and he seemed familiar with the people in the painting. Running his forefinger down the page of an old volume on medieval history to check a date, he was intent on his task and apparently oblivious to the past intimacy which Julia sensed floating between them like the shroud of a ghost. But perhaps he feels the same, she thought. Perhaps from Álvaro's point of view, she too seemed oddly distant and indifferent.

"Here you are," he said, and Julia clung to the sound of his voice like a drowning woman to a piece of wood, knowing, with relief, that she couldn't do two things at once: remember him as he was then and listen to him now. With no regret, her feelings of nostalgia were immediately left behind, and the relief on her face must have been so patent that he looked at her, surprised, before turning his attention back to the page of the book.

Julia glanced at the title: *Switzerland, Burgundy and the Low Countries in the Fourteenth and Fifteenth Centuries*.

"Look." Álvaro was pointing at a name in the text. Then he transferred his finger to the photograph of the painting she had placed on the table.

"*FERDINANDUS OST. D.* is the identifying inscription of the chess player on the left, the man dressed in red. Van Huys painted *The Game of Chess* in 1471, so there's no doubt about it. It's Ferdinand Altenhoffen, the Duke of Ostenburg, *Ostenburguensis Dux*, born in 1435, died in . . . yes, that's right, in 1474. He was about thirty-five when he sat for the painter."

Julia had picked up a card from the table and was pointing at what was written there.

"Where *was* Ostenburg? . . . In Germany?"

Álvaro shook his head and opened a historical atlas.

"Ostenburg was a duchy that corresponded, more or less, to Charlemagne's Rodovingia . . . It was here, inside the Franco-German borders, between Luxembourg and Flanders. In the fifteenth and sixteenth centuries, the Ostenburg dukes tried to remain independent, but ended up being absorbed, first by Burgundy and then by Maximilian of Austria. In fact, the Altenhoffen dynasty died out with this particular Ferdinand. If you like, I can make you some photocopies."

"I'd be very grateful."

"It's no trouble." Álvaro sat back in his chair, took a tin of tobacco from a drawer in the desk and started filling his pipe. "Logically, the lady by the window, with the inscription *BEATRIX BURG. OST. D.* can only be Beatrice of Burgundy, the Duke's consort. See? Beatrice married Ferdinand Altenhoffen in 1464, when she was twenty-three."

"For love?" asked Julia with an enigmatic smile, looking at the photograph. Álvaro responded with a brief, rather forced smile of his own.

"As you know, very few marriages of this kind were love matches . . . The wedding was an attempt by Beatrice's uncle, Philip the Good, Duke of Burgundy, to create closer ties with Ostenburg in an alliance against France, which was trying to annex both duchies." Álvaro looked at the photograph and put his pipe between his teeth. "Ferdinand of Ostenburg was lucky though, because she was very beautiful. At least, according to what the most important chronicler of the time, Nicolas Flavin, said in his *Annales bourguignonnes*. Your Van Huys seems to have thought so too. It appears she'd been painted by him before, because there's a document, quoted by Pijoan, which states that Van Huys was for a time court painter at Ostenburg. In 1463, Ferdinand Altenhoffen assigned him a pension of £100 a year, payable half

17

at the feast of St John and the other half at Christmas. The same document contains the commission to paint a portrait, *bien au vif*, of Beatrice, who was then the Duke's fiancée."

"Are there any other references?"

"Loads. Van Huys became quite an important person." Álvaro took a file out of a cabinet. "Jean Lemaire, in his *Couronne Margaridique*, written in honour of Margaret of Austria, Governor of the Low Countries, mentions Pierre de Brugge (Van Huys), Hughes de Gand (Van der Goes) and Dieric de Louvain (Dietric Bouts), together with the person he dubs the king of Flemish painters, Johannes (Van Eyck). The actual words he uses in the poem are: 'Pierre de Brugge, qui tant eut les traits utez', which translates literally as 'he who drew such clean lines'. By the time that was written, Van Huys had been dead for twenty-five years." Álvaro carefully checked through some other cards. "And there are earlier mentions too. For example, inventories from the Kingdom of Valencia state that Alfonso V the Magnanimous owned works by Van Huys, Van Eyck and other painters, all of them now lost. Bartolomeo Fazio, a close relative of Alfonso V, also mentions him in his *De viribus illustribus liber*, describing him as 'Pietrus Husyus, insignis pictor'. Other authors, particularly Italians, call him 'Magistro Piero Van Hus, pictori in Bruggia'. There's a quote in 1470 in which Guido Rasofalco mentions one of his paintings, a Crucifixion, which again has not survived, as 'Opera buona di mano di un chiamato Piero di Juys, pictor famoso in Fiandra.' And another Italian author, anonymous this time, refers to a painting by Van Huys that has survived, *The Knight and the Devil*, stating that 'A magistro Pietrus Juisus magno et famoso flandesco fuit depictum.' He's also mentioned by Guicciardini and Van Mander in the sixteenth century and by James Weale in the nineteenth century in his books on great Flemish painters." He gathered up the cards and put them carefully back into the file, which he returned to the cabinet. Then he sat back in his chair and looked at Julia, smiling. "Satisfied?"

"Very." She'd noted everything down and was now taking stock. After a moment, she pushed her hair back and looked at Álvaro curiously: "Anyone would think you'd had it all prepared. I'm positively dazzled."

The professor's smile faded a little, and he avoided Julia's eyes. One of the cards on his desk seemed suddenly to require his attention.

"It's my job," he said. And she couldn't tell if his tone was simply distracted or evasive. Without quite knowing why, this made her feel vaguely uncomfortable.

"Well, all I can say is, you're still extremely good at it." She observed him with interest before returning to her notes. "We've got plenty of references to the painter and to two of the people in the painting." She leaned over the reproduction and placed a finger on the second player. "But nothing about him."

Álvaro was busy filling his pipe and didn't reply at once. He was frowning.

"It's difficult to say with any exactitude," he said between puffs. "The inscription *RUTGIER AR. PREUX* isn't very explicit. Although it's enough to come up with an hypothesis." He paused and stared at the bowl of his pipe as if hoping to find in it confirmation of his idea. "Rutgier could be Roger, Rogelio, Ruggiero, all of them possible forms – and there are at least ten variants – of a name common at the time. Preux could be a surname or a family name, in which case we'd come to a dead end, because there's no mention of any Preux whose deeds would have merited an entry in the chronicles. However, *preux* was also used in the high Middle Ages as an honorific adjective, even as a noun, with the sense of 'valiant', 'chivalrous'. The word is applied to Lancelot and Roland, to give you but two famous examples. In France and England, they would use the formula 'soyez preux' when knighting someone, that is, 'be loyal or brave'. It was a very exclusive title, used to distinguish the *crème de la crème* of the knighthood."

Unconsciously, out of professional habit, Álvaro had adopted the persuasive, almost pedagogical tone that he tended to slip into sooner or later whenever a conversation touched on aspects of his speciality. Julia noticed it with some alarm; it stirred up old memories, the forgotten embers of an affection that had occupied a place in time and space and in the formation of her character as it was now. The residue of another life and other feelings that a relentless war of attrition had succeeded in deadening and displacing, the way you relegate a book to a shelf to gather dust, with no intention of ever opening it again, but which is still there, despite everything.

Confronted by such feelings, she knew that she had to resort to other tactics: keep her mind on the matter in hand; talk, ask for further details, whether she needed to know them or not; lean over the desk, pretending to concentrate hard on taking notes; imagine she was standing before a different Álvaro, which, of course, she was; act, feel, as if the memories belonged not to them, but to two other people someone had once mentioned to her and whose fate was a matter of indifference.

Another solution was to light a cigarette, and Julia did so. The smoke filling her lungs helped reconcile her and lend her a small measure of detachment. She looked at Álvaro, ready to continue.

"What's your hypothesis then?" Her voice sounded quite normal and that made her feel much calmer. "As I see it, if Preux wasn't the surname, then the key might lie in the abbreviation *AR*."

Álvaro nodded. Half-closing his eyes against the smoke from his pipe, he leafed through the pages of another book until he found a name.

"Look at this. Roger de Arras, born in 1431, the same year in which the English burned Joan of Arc at the stake in Rouen. His family were related to the Valois, the reigning dynasty in France at the time, and he was born in the castle of Bellesang, very near the duchy of Ostenburg."

"Could he be the second chess player?"

"Possibly. *AR* would be exactly right for the abbreviation of Arras. And Roger de Arras appears in all the chronicles of the time. He fought in the Hundred Years' War alongside the King of France, Charles VII. See? He took part in the conquest of Normandy and Guyenne to win them back from the English. In 1450 he fought in the battle of Formigny and three years later at the battle of Castillon. Look at this engraving. He might well be one of those men; perhaps he's the knight with his visor down, offering his horse in the midst of the fray to the King of France, whose own horse has been killed, but who continues to fight on foot . . ."

"You amaze me, Professor," Julia said, looking at him with open astonishment. "I mean that picturesque image of the warrior in the battle. You were the one who always said that imagination is the cancer of historical rigour."

Álvaro burst out laughing.

"Consider it poetic licence, in your honour. How could I forget your fondness for going beyond the mere facts? I recall that when you and I . . ."

He fell silent, suddenly uncertain. His allusion to the past had caused Julia's face to darken. Recognising that memories were out of place just then, Álvaro hurriedly back-pedalled.

"I'm sorry," he said in a low voice.

"It doesn't matter," Julia replied, briskly stubbing out her cigarette in the ashtray and burning her fingers in the process. "It was my fault really." She looked at him more calmly. "So what have you got on our warrior, then?"

With visible relief, Álvaro plunged back into familiar terrain. Roger de Arras, he explained, had not only been a warrior, he'd been many other things besides. For example, he was a model of chivalry, the perfect medieval nobleman. In his spare time he'd been a poet and musician. He was much admired in the court of the Valois, his cousins. So the word "preux" fitted him like a glove.

"Did he have any links with chess?"

"There's no mention of any."

Julia was taking notes, caught up in the story, but she stopped suddenly and looked at Álvaro.

"What I don't understand," she said, chewing the end of her pen, "is what this Roger de Arras would be doing in a picture by Van Huys, playing chess with the Duke of Ostenburg."

Álvaro fidgeted in his seat with apparent embarrassment, as if suddenly gripped by doubt. He sucked on his pipe and stared at the wall behind Julia's head, with the air of someone waging an inner battle. Finally, he managed a cautious smile.

"I've no idea what he's doing there – apart from playing chess, that is." Julia was sure that he was looking at her with unusual wariness, as if he could not quite put into words an idea that was going round and round in his head. "What I do know," he added at last, "and I know this because it's mentioned in all the books on the subject, is that Roger de Arras didn't die in France, but in Ostenburg." After a slight hesitation, he pointed to the photograph of the painting. "Have you noticed the date of this painting?"

Puzzled, Julia said: "Yes, 1471. Why?"

Álvaro slowly exhaled some smoke and uttered something that sounded like an abrupt laugh. He was looking at Julia as if trying to read in her eyes the answer to a question he could not quite bring himself to ask.

"There's something not quite right there," he said finally. "That date is either incorrect or the chronicles are lying, or else that knight is not the Rutgier Ar. Preux of the painting." He picked up a mimeographed copy of the *Chronicle of the Dukes of Ostenburg* and, after leafing through it for a while, placed it in front of her. "This was written at the end of the fifteenth century by Guichard de Hainaut, a Frenchman and a contemporary of the events he describes, and it is based on eyewitness accounts. According to Hainaut, our man died at Epiphany in 1469, two years *before* Pieter Van Huys painted *The Game of Chess*. Do you understand, Julia? Roger de Arras could never have posed for that picture, because by the time it was painted, he was already dead."

He walked her to the university car park and handed her the file containing the photocopies. Almost everything was in there, he said: historical references, an update on the catalogued works of Van Huys, a bibliography . . . He promised to send a chronological account and a few other papers to her as soon as he had a free moment. He stood looking at her, his pipe in his mouth and his hands in his jacket pockets, as if he still had something to say but was unsure whether or not to do so. He hoped, he added after a short pause, that he'd been of some help.

Julia nodded, feeling perplexed. The details of the story she'd just learned were still whirling round in her head. And there was something else.

"I'm impressed, Professor. In less than an hour you've completely reconstructed the lives of the people depicted in a painting you've never studied before."

Álvaro looked away, letting his gaze wander over the campus. Then he made a wry face.

"The painting wasn't entirely unfamiliar to me," he said. Julia thought she detected a tremor of doubt in his voice, and it troubled her. She listened extra carefully to his words. "Apart from anything else, there's a photograph in a 1917 Prado catalogue. *The Game of Chess* used to be exhibited there. It was on loan for about twenty years, from the turn of the century until 1923, when the heirs asked for it back."

22

"I didn't know that."

"Well, now you do." He concentrated on his pipe again, which seemed about to go out. Julia looked at him out of the corner of her eye. She knew him, or, rather, she had known him once, too well not to sense that something important was preying on his mind, something he couldn't bring himself to say.

"What is it you haven't told me, Álvaro?"

He didn't move, just stood there sucking on his pipe, staring into space. Then he he turned slowly towards her.

"I don't know what you mean."

"I just mean that everything to do with this painting is important." She looked at him gravely. "I'm staking a lot on this."

She noticed that Álvaro was chewing indecisively on the stem of his pipe. He sketched an ambivalent gesture in the air.

"You're putting me in a very awkward position. Your Van Huys seems to have become rather fashionable of late."

"Fashionable?" She became tense, alert, as if the earth might suddenly shift beneath her feet. "Do you mean that someone else has already talked to you about him, before I did?"

Álvaro was smiling uncertainly now, as if regretting having said too much.

"They might have."

"Who?"

"That's the problem. I'm not allowed to tell you."

"Don't be ridiculous."

"I'm not. It's true." He looked at her imploringly.

Julia sighed deeply, trying to fill the strange emptiness she felt in her stomach; somewhere an alarm bell was ringing. But Álvaro was talking again, so she remained attentive, searching for some sign. He'd like, he said, to have a look at the painting, if Julia didn't mind, of course. He'd like to see her, too.

"I can explain everything," he concluded, "when the time is right."

It could be a trick, she thought. He was quite capable of creating the whole drama as a pretext for seeing her again. She bit her lower lip. Inside her, the painting was now jockeying for position with feelings and memories that had nothing whatever to do with it.

"How's your wife?" she asked casually, giving in to a dark impulse.

23

She looked up, mischievously, and saw that Álvaro had stiffened and seemed suddenly uncomfortable.

"She's fine," was all he said. He was staring hard at the pipe in his hand, as if he didn't recognise it. "She's in New York, setting up an exhibition."

A memory flitted into Julia's head: an attractive blonde woman in a brown tailored suit, getting out of a car. Just fifteen seconds of a rather blurred image that she could only barely recall, but which had marked the end of her youth, as cleanly as a cut with a scalpel. She seemed to remember that his wife worked for some official organisation, something to do with the Ministry of Arts, with exhibitions and travelling. For a time, that had facilitated matters. Álvaro never talked about her, nor did Julia, but they felt her presence between them, like a ghost. And that ghost, fifteen seconds of a face glimpsed purely by chance, had ended up winning the game.

"I hope things are going well for you both."

"They're not too bad. I mean not entirely bad."

"Good."

They walked on a little in silence, not looking at each other. At last, Julia clicked her tongue, put her head on one side and smiled into the empty air.

"Anyway, it doesn't much matter now," she said and stopped in front of him, her hands on her hips and a roguish smile on her lips. "How do you think I'm looking these days?"

He looked her up and down, uncertainly, his eyes half-closed.

"You look great. Really."

"And how do you feel?"

"A bit confused." He gave a melancholy smile and looked contrite. "I keep wondering if I made the right decision a year ago."

"That's something you'll never find out."

"You never know."

He was still attractive, Julia thought, with a pang of anxiety and irritation that made her stomach clench. She looked at his hands and eyes, knowing that she was walking along the edge of something that simultaneously repelled and attracted her.

"I've got the painting at home," she said in a cautious, noncommittal way, trying to put her ideas in order. She wanted to reassure herself of her painfully acquired resolution, but she sensed the risks and the need to remain on guard. Besides – indeed above all else – she had the Van Huys to think about.

That line of argument helped at least to clarify her thinking. So she shook the hand he held out to her, sensing in that contact the clumsiness of someone unsure of how the land lies. That cheered her up, provoking in her a malicious, subterranean joy. On an impulse that was at once calculated and unconscious, she kissed him quickly on the mouth – an advance on account, to inspire confidence – before opening the car door and getting into her little white Fiat.

"If you want to have a look at the painting, come and see me," she said, with equivocal nonchalance, as she started the car. "Tomorrow afternoon. And thanks."

She knew that, with him, she need say no more. She watched him receding in her rear-view mirror, as he stood waving, looking thoughtful and perplexed, the campus and the brick faculty building looming behind him. She smiled as she drove through a red light. You'll take the bait, Professor, she was thinking. I don't know why, but someone, somewhere, is trying to play a dirty trick on me. And you're going to tell me who it is, or my name's not Julia.

On the little table, within easy reach, the ashtray was piled high with cigarette ends. Lying on the sofa, she read until late into the night. The story of the painting, the painter and his subjects was gradually taking shape. She was reading avidly, alert to the smallest clue, driven on by her desire to find the key to the mysterious game of chess that was still being played out on the easel opposite the sofa, in the semidarkness of the studio, amongst the shadows:

> ... Released from vassalage to France in 1453, the Dukes of Ostenburg struggled to maintain a difficult equilibrium between France, Germany and Burgundy. Ostenburg's policy aroused the suspicions of Charles VII of France, who feared that the duchy might become absorbed by powerful Burgundy, which was trying to establish itself as an independent kingdom. In that whirl of palace intrigue, political alliances

and secret pacts, French fears grew with the marriage, in 1464, between Ferdinand, the son and heir of Duke Wilhelmus of Ostenburg, and Beatrice of Burgundy, niece of Philip the Good and cousin of the future Burgundian duke Charles the Bold.

Thus, during those years, which were crucial for the future of Europe, two irreconcilable factions were lined up face to face in the court of Ostenburg: the Burgundy faction, in favour of integrating with the neighbouring duchy, and the French faction, plotting for reunification with France. Right up until his death in 1474, the turbulent government of Ferdinand of Ostenburg was characterised by confrontation between those two forces.

She placed the file on the floor and sat up, her arms round her knees. The silence was absolute. For a while she remained motionless, then she got to her feet and went over to the painting. *QUIS NECAVIT EQUITEM*. Without actually touching the surface, she passed a finger over the hidden inscription, covered by the successive layers of green pigment that Van Huys had used to represent the cloth covering the table. Who killed the knight? With the facts Álvaro had given her, the phrase took on a dimension which here, in the painting only dimly lit by a small lamp, seemed sinister. She placed her face as close as possible to that of *RUTGIER AR. PREUX*. Regardless of whether or not he was Roger de Arras, Julia was convinced that the inscription referred to him. It was obviously a kind of riddle, but she was puzzled by the role the chess game played. *Played*. Perhaps that's all it was, a game.

She had an unpleasant sense of exasperation, like the feeling she got when she had to resort to the scalpel to remove a stubborn layer of varnish, and she clasped her fingers behind the back of her neck and closed her eyes. When she opened them, there was the profile of the unknown knight, intent on the game, frowning in grave concentration. He had clearly been an attractive man. He had a noble demeanour, an aura of dignity cleverly suggested by the colours the artist had chosen to surround him. Furthermore, his head was placed exactly at the inter-section of lines known in painting as the golden section, the law of pictorial composition that classical painters from the time of Vitruvius

26

onwards had used as a guide to the proportions of figures in a painting. The discovery startled her. According to the rules, if Van Huys had intended, when painting the picture, to highlight the figure of Duke Ferdinand of Ostenburg – who, given his rank, undoubtedly deserved this honour – he would have placed *him* at the intersecting point of the golden section, not to the left. The same could be said of Beatrice of Burgundy, who had in fact been relegated to the background next to the window, at the right. It was reasonable to suppose, therefore, that the person presiding over that mysterious game of chess was not the Duke or the Duchess but *RUTGIER AR. PREUX*, who just might be Roger de Arras. Except that Roger de Arras was dead.

Keeping her eyes on the painting, looking at it over her shoulder as if fearing that someone in it might move the moment she turned her back, she went over to one of the book-crammed shelves. Bloody Pieter Van Huys, she muttered, setting riddles that were keeping her from her bed five hundred years later. She picked up Amparo Ibañez's *Historia del Arte*, the volume on Flemish painting, and sat down on the sofa with the book on her lap. Van Huys, Pieter. Bruges 1415–Ghent 1481.

. . . While Van Huys does not wholly reject the embroidery, jewellery and marble of the court painter, the family atmos- phere of his paintings and his eye for the telling detail mark him as an essentially bourgeois artist. Although influenced by Jan Van Eyck, and above all by his own teacher Robert Campin (Van Huys makes clever use of both these artists' tech- niques), his is a serene analysis of reality, his way of looking at the world a very calm Flemish one. But he was always inter- ested in symbolism, and his paintings are packed with parallel readings (the sealed glass bottle or the door in the wall as signs of Mary's virginity in his *Virgin of the Chapel*, the interplay of shadows in the interior depicted in *The Family of Lucas Bremer*, for example). Van Huys's mastery lies in his incisive delin- eation of both people and objects and in his approach to the most testing problems in painting at the time, such as the plas- tic organisation of surface, the seamless contrast between dom- estic half-light and bright daylight, the way shadows change according to the nature of the material on which they fall.

Surviving works: *Portrait of the Goldsmith Guillermo Walhuus* (1448), Metropolitan Museum, New York. *The Family of Lucas Bremer* (1452), Uffizi Gallery, Florence. *The Virgin of the Chapel* (c. 1455) Prado Museum, Madrid. *The Money Changer of Louvain* (1457), private collection, New York. *Portrait of the Merchant Matteo Conzini and His Wife* (1458), private collection, Zurich. *The Antwerp Altarpiece* (c. 1461), Pinacoteca, Vienna. *The Knight and the Devil* (1462), Rijksmuseum, Amsterdam. *The Game of Chess* (1471), private collection, Madrid. *The Ghent Descent from the Cross* (c. 1478), St Bavon Cathedral, Ghent.

By four in the morning, her mouth rough from too much coffee and too many cigarettes, Julia had finished her reading. The story of the painter, the painting and its subjects were at last becoming almost tangible. They were no longer just images on an oak panel, but living beings who had once occupied a particular time and space in the interval between life and death. Pieter Van Huys, painter, Ferdinand Altenhoffen and his wife, Beatrice of Burgundy. And Roger de Arras. For Julia had come up with proof that the knight in the painting, the chess player studying the position of the chess pieces with the silent intensity of one whose life depends upon it, was indeed Roger de Arras, born in 1431, died in 1469, in Ostenburg. She was absolutely convinced of that, just as she was sure that the painting, made two years after his death, was the mysterious link that bound him to the two other people and to the painter. A detailed description of that death lay on her lap, on a page photocopied from Guichard de Hainaut's *Chronical*:

And so it was, at the Epiphany of the Holy Kings in the year of our Lord fourteen hundred and sixty-nine, that when Master Ruggier was taking his customary walk along the fosse known as that of the East Gate, a crossbowman posted there did shoot him straight through the heart with an arrow. Master Ruggier remained in that place crying out for his confession to be heard, but by the time help came, his soul had already slipped free through the gaping mouth of his wound. The death of Master Ruggier, a model of chivalry and a consummate gentleman, was sorely felt by the French

28

faction in Ostenburg, the faction he was said to favour. That tragic fact led to many voices being raised in accusation against those who favoured the house of Burgundy. Others attributed the vile deed to some affair of the heart, to which the unfortunate Ruggier was much given. Some even said that Duke Ferdinand himself was the hidden hand behind the blow, carried out by some third party, because Master Ruggier had dared to declare his love for the Duchess Beatrice. The suspicion of such a stain pursued the Duke to his grave. And thus the sad case was concluded without the assassins ever being found, though it was murmured in porches and in gossip shops that they had escaped under the protection of some powerful hand. And so it was left to God to dispense justice. And Master Ruggier was handsome of form and face, despite the wars fought in the service of the King of France, before he came to Ostenburg to serve Duke Ferdinand, with whom he had been brought up in his youth. And he was mourned by many ladies. And when he was killed, he was in his thirty-eighth year and at the height of his powers . . .

Julia switched off the light, and as she sat in the dark with her head resting on the back of the sofa, she watched the glowing tip of the cigarette in her hand. She couldn't see the picture opposite, nor did she need to. Every last detail of it was engraved on her retina and on her brain. She could see it in the dark.

She yawned, rubbing her face with the palms of her hands. She felt a mixture of weariness and euphoria, an odd sense of partial but exhilarating triumph, like the presentiment you get in the middle of a long race that it is still possible to reach the finishing post. She'd managed to lift one corner of the veil and, though there were still many more things to find out, one thing was clear as day: there was nothing capricious or random in that painting. It was the careful execution of a well-thought-out plan, the aim of which was summed up in the question *Who killed the knight?*, a question that someone, out of expediency or fear, had covered up or ordered to be covered up. And whoever that person was, Julia was going to find out. At that moment, sitting in the dark, dazed from tiredness and lack of sleep, her head full of medieval images and intersecting lines beneath which whistled arrows from crossbows shot from behind as night fell, Julia's mind was no longer on restoring the picture, but on reconstructing its secret. It would be rather amusing, she thought as she was about to surrender to sleep, if when all the protagonists of that story were no more than skeletons turned to dust in their graves, she were to find the answer to the question asked by a Flemish painter called Pieter Van Huys across the silence of five centuries, like an enigma demanding to be solved.

II

⁂

Lucinda, Octavio, Scaramouche

"I declare it's marked out just like
a large chessboard!" Alice said at last.
Lewis Carroll

THE BELL ABOVE THE DOOR tinkled as Julia went into the antiques shop. She had only to step inside to find herself immediately enveloped by a sense of warmth and familiar peace. Her first memories were suffused by the gentle golden light that fell on the antique furniture, the baroque carvings and columns, the heavy walnut cabinets, the ivories, tapestries, porcelain, and the paintings, grown dark with age, of grave-faced personages in permanent mourning, who, years before, had watched over her childhood games. Many objects had been sold since then and been replaced by others, but the effect of those motley rooms and of the light gleaming on the antique pieces arranged there in harmonious disorder remained unalterable. Like the colours of the delicate porcelain commedia dell'arte figures signed by Bustelli: a Lucinda, an Octavio and a Scaramouche, which, as well as being Julia's favourite playthings when she was a child, were César's pride and joy. Perhaps that was why he never wanted to get rid of them and kept them in a glass case at the back, next to the stained-glass window that opened onto the inner courtyard of the shop, where he used to sit reading – Stendhal, Mann, Sabatini, Dumas, Conrad – waiting for the bell announcing the arrival of a customer.

"Hello, César."

"Hello, Princess."

César was over fifty – Julia had never managed to extract a confession from him as to his exact age – and he had the smiling, mocking blue eyes of a mischievous child whose greatest pleasure lies in defying the world in which he has been forced to live. He had white, immaculately waved hair – she suspected he'd been dyeing it for years now – and he was still in excellent shape, apart from a slight thickening about the hips. He always wore beautifully cut suits, of which the only criticism might be that they were, strictly speaking, a little daring for a man his age. He never wore a tie, not even on the most select social occasions, opting instead for magnificent Italian cravats knotted at the open neck of a shirt, invariably silk, that bore his entwined initials embroidered in blue or white just below his heart. He had a breadth and degree of culture Julia had never met elsewhere and was the most perfect embodiment of the saying that amongst the upper classes extreme politeness is merely the most highly refined expression of one's scorn for others. Within César's social milieu, a concept that might have been expanded to include Humanity as a whole, Julia was the only person who enjoyed that politeness, knowing that she was safe from his scorn. Ever since she'd been able to think for herself, César had been for her an odd mixture of father, confidant, friend and confessor, without ever being exactly any of those things.

"I've got a problem, César."

"Excuse me, but in that case, *we* have a problem. Tell me all about it."

And Julia told him, omitting nothing, not even the hidden inscription, a fact that César acknowledged with a slight lift of his eyebrows. They were sitting by the stained-glass window, and César was leaning slightly towards her, his right leg crossed over his left, one hand, on which gleamed a valuable topaz set in gold, draped nonchalantly over the Patek Philippe watch he wore on his other wrist. It was that distinguished pose of his, by no means calculated (although it may once have been), that so effortlessly captivated the troubled young men in search of exquisite sensations, the painters, sculptors, fledgling artists whom César took under his wing with a devotion and constancy which, it must be said, lasted much longer than his sentimental relationships.

"Life is short and beauty transient, Princess." Whenever César adopted his confidential tone, dropping his voice almost to a whisper, the words were always touched with a wry melancholy. "And it would be wrong to possess it for ever. The beauty lies in teaching a young sparrow to fly, because implicit in his freedom is your relinquishment

32

of him. Do you see the subtle point I'm making with this parable?"

As she'd openly acknowledged once before when César, half-flattered and half-amused, had accused her of making a jealous scene, Julia felt inexplicably irritated by all those little sparrows fluttering around César, and only her affection for him and her rational awareness that he had every right to lead his own kind of life, prevented her giving voice to it. As Menchu used to say, with her usual lack of tact: "What you've got, dear, is an Electra complex dressed up as an Oedipus complex, or vice versa . . ." Menchu's parables, unlike César's, tended to be all too explicit.

When Julia had finished recounting the story of the painting, César remained silent, pondering what she'd said. He didn't seem surprised – in matters of art, especially at his age, very little surprised him – but the mocking gleam in his eyes had given way to a flicker of interest.

"Fascinating," he said at last, and Julia knew at once that she would be able to count on him. Ever since she was a child that word had been an incitement to complicity and adventure on the trail of some secret: the pirate treasure hidden in the drawer of the Isabelline bureau – which he sold to the Museo Romántico – and the story he invented about the portrait of the lady in the lace dress, attributed to Ingres, whose lover, an officer in the hussars, died at Waterloo, calling out her name as the cavalry charged. With César holding her hand, Julia had lived through a hundred such adventures in a hundred different lives, and, invariably, in each of them what she'd learned from him was to value beauty, self-denial and tenderness, as well as the delicate and intense pleasure to be gained from the contemplation of a work of art, from the translucent surface of a piece of porcelain to the humble reflection of a ray of sunlight on a wall broken up by a pure crystal into its whole exquisite spectrum of colours.

"The first thing I need to do," César was saying, "is to have a good look at the painting. I can be at your apartment tomorrow evening, at about half past seven."

"Fine," she said, eyeing him cautiously. "It's just possible that Álvaro will be there too."

If César was surprised, he didn't say so. He merely made a cruel face with pursed lips.

"How delightful. I haven't seen the swine for ages, so I'd be thrilled to have an opportunity to send a few poisoned darts his way, wrapped up, of course, in delicate periphrases."

"Please, César."

"Don't worry, my dear, I'll be kind . . . given the circumstances. My hand may wound, but no blood will be spilled on your Persian carpet . . . which, incidentally, could do with a good cleaning."

She looked at him tenderly, and put her hands over his.

"I love you, César."

"I know. It's only natural. Almost everyone does."

"Why do you hate Álvaro so much?"

It was a stupid question, and he gave her a look of mild censure.

"Because he made you suffer," he replied gravely. "I would, with your permission, pluck out his eyes and feed them to the dogs along the dusty roads of Thebes. All very classical. You could be the chorus. I can see you now, looking divine, raising your bare arms up to Olympus, where the gods would be snoring, drunk as lords."

"Marry me, César. Right now."

César took one of her hands and kissed it, brushed it with his lips.

"When you grow up, Princess."

"But I have."

"No, you haven't. Not yet. But when you have, Your Highness, I will dare to tell you that I loved you. And that the gods, when they woke, did not take everything from me. Only my kingdom." He seemed to ponder that before adding, "Which, after all, is a mere bagatelle."

It was a very private dialogue, full of memories, of shared references, as old as their friendship. They sat in silence, accompanied by the ticking of the ancient clocks that continued to measure out the passage of time while they awaited a buyer.

"To sum up," said César, "if I've understood you correctly, it's a question of solving a murder."

Julia looked at him, surprised.

"It's odd you should say that."

"Why? That's more or less what it is. The fact that it happened in the fifteenth century doesn't change anything."

"Right. But that word 'murder' throws a much more sinister light on it all." She smiled anxiously at César. "Maybe I was too tired last night to see it that way, but up till now I've treated it all as a game, like

34

deciphering a hieroglyph . . . a personal matter, in a way. A matter of personal pride."

"And now?"

"Well, as if it was the most natural thing in the world, you talk about solving a *real* murder, and I suddenly understand . . ." She stopped, her mouth open, feeling as if she were leaning over the edge of an abyss. "Do you see? On the sixth of January 1469, someone murdered Roger de Arras, or had him murdered, and the identity of the murderer lies in the painting." She sat up straight, carried along by excitement. "We could solve a five-hundred-year-old enigma. Perhaps find the reason why one small event in European history happened one way and not another. Imagine the price *The Game of Chess* could reach at the auction if we managed to do that!"

"Millions, my dear," César confirmed, with a sigh dragged from him by the sheer weight of evidence. "Many millions." He considered the idea, convinced now. "With the right publicity, Claymore's could increase the opening price three or four times. It's a gold mine, that painting of yours."

"We must go and see Menchu. Now."

César shook his head with an air of sulky reserve.

"Oh no. Anything but that. Out of the question. You're not going to involve me in any of your friend Menchu's shenanigans. Though I'm quite happy to stand behind the barriers, as bullfighter's assistant."

"Don't be difficult. I need you."

"I'm entirely at your disposal, my dear. But don't force me to rub shoulders with that resprayed Nefertiti and her ever-changing crew of panders or, if you want it in the vernacular, pimps. That friend of yours gives me a migraine" – he pressed one temple – "right here. See?"

"César . . ."

"All right, I give in. *Vae victis*. I'll see Menchu."

She planted a resounding kiss on his well-shaven cheek, conscious of the smell of myrrh. César bought his perfume in Paris and his cravats in Rome.

"I love you, César. Very much."

"Don't you soft-soap me. Fancy trying to get round me like that. At my age too."

*　　*　　*

Menchu bought her perfume in Paris too, but it was rather less discreet than César's. She arrived, in a hurry and without Max, and in a cloud of Balenciaga's Rumba, which preceded her, like an advance party, across the foyer of the Palace Hotel.

"I've got some news," she said, tapping her nose with one finger and sniffing repeatedly before sitting down. She had obviously just made a pit stop in the Ladies, and a few tiny specks of white dust still clung to her upper lip. That, Julia thought, explained why she was so bright-eyed and bushy-tailed.

"Don Manuel is expecting us at his house to discuss the matter," she said.

"Don Manuel?"

"The owner of the painting. Are you being dense? You know, my charming little old man."

They ordered mild cocktails, and Julia brought her friend up to date on the results of her research. Menchu opened her eyes wide as she rapidly worked out percentages in her head.

"That really changes things." On the linen cloth that covered the low table between them she was busily etching calculations with a blood-red fingernail. "My five per cent is far too little. So I'm going to suggest a deal with the people at Claymore's: of the fifteen-per-cent commission on the price the painting reaches at auction, they get seven and a half and I get seven and a half."

"They'll never agree. It's way below their usual profit margin."

Menchu burst out laughing. It would be that or nothing. Sotheby's and Christie's were just around the corner, and they'd howl with pleasure at the prospect of making off with the Van Huys. It would be a question of take it or leave it.

"And the owner? Your little old man might have something to say about it. What if he decides to deal directly with Claymore's? Or with someone else."

Menchu gave her an astute look.

"He can't. He signed a piece of paper." She pointed to her short skirt, which revealed a generous amount of leg sheathed in dark stockings. "Besides, as you see, I'm dressed for battle. If my Don Manuel doesn't fall into line, I'll take the veil." As if trying out the effect, she crossed and uncrossed her legs for the benefit of the male customers in the hotel. Satisfied with the results, she turned her attention back to her cocktail. "As for you . . ."

"I want one and a half of your seven and a half per cent."

Menchu gave a pained yelp. That was a lot of money, she said, scandalised. Three or four times the fee they'd agreed on for the restoration work. Julia allowed her to protest while she took a pack of cigarettes from her bag and lit one.

"You don't understand," she explained, as she exhaled. "The fee for my work will be deducted directly from your Don Manuel, from the price the painting gets at auction. The other percentage is in addition to that, to be deducted from the profit that you make. If the painting sells for one hundred million pesetas, Claymore's will get seven and a half, you'll get six and I'll get one and a half."

"Who'd have thought it?" said Menchu, shaking her head in disbelief. "You seemed such a nice girl, with your little brushes and varnishes. So inoffensive."

"Well, there you are. God said we should be kind to our fellow man, but he didn't say anything about letting him rip us off."

"You shock me, you really do. I've been nurturing a serpent in my left bosom, like Aïda. Or was it Cleopatra? I had no idea you knew about percentages."

"Put yourself in my place. After all, I was the one who made the discovery." She waggled her fingers in front of her friend's nose. "With my own fair hands."

"You're taking advantage of my tender heart, you little snake."

"Come off it. You're as tough as old boots."

Menchu heaved a melodramatic sigh. It was taking the bread out of her Max's mouth, but she was sure they could come to some agreement. Friendship was friendship, after all. She glanced towards the door and put on a conspiratorial look. "Talk of the devil . . ."

"Do you mean Max?"

"Don't be nasty. Max is no devil, he's a sweetie." She gave a sideways flick of her eyes, inviting Julia to sneak a look. "Paco Montegrifo, from Claymore's, has just come in. And he's seen us."

Montegrifo was the director of the Madrid branch of Claymore's. He was in his forties, tall and attractive, and he dressed with the strict elegance of an Italian prince. His hair parting was as immaculate as his tie, and when he smiled he revealed a lot of teeth, too perfect to be real.

"Good afternoon, ladies. What a happy coincidence!"

He remained standing while Menchu made the introductions.

"I've seen some of your work," he said to Julia when he learned that it was she who would be working on the Van Huys, "and I have only one word for it: perfection."

"Thank you."

"I'm sure your work on *The Game of Chess* will be of the same high standard." He showed his white teeth again in a professional smile. "We have great hopes for that painting."

"So have we," said Menchu. "More than you might think."

Montegrifo must have noticed the edge she gave to that remark, because his brown eyes became suddenly alert. He's no fool, thought Julia as he gestured towards an empty chair. Some people were expecting him, he said, but they wouldn't mind waiting a few minutes.

"May I?"

He indicated to an approaching waiter that he didn't want anything and sat down opposite Menchu. His cordiality remained undented, but there was a measure of cautious expectation, as if he were straining to hear a distant note of discord.

"Is there some problem?" he asked calmly.

Menchu shook her head. No problem, not really. Nothing to worry about. Montegrifo didn't seem in the least worried, just politely interested.

"Perhaps," Menchu suggested after a moment or two, "we should renegotiate the conditions of our agreement."

There was an embarrassing silence. Montegrifo was looking at her as he might at a client unable to control his excitement in the heat of the bidding.

"My dear lady, Claymore's is a serious establishment."

"I don't doubt it," replied Menchu resolutely. "But research on the Van Huys has uncovered some important facts that alter the value of the painting."

"Our appraisers did not find anything."

"The research was carried out after your people's examination. The findings . . ." – Menchu seemed to hesitate, and this did not go un-remarked – "are not immediately apparent."

Montegrifo turned to Julia, looking thoughtful. His eyes were cold as ice.

"What have you found?" he asked gently, like a confessor inviting someone to unburden their conscience.

Julia looked uncertainly at Menchu.

"I don't think I . . ."

"We're not authorised to say," Menchu intervened, coming to her rescue. "At least not today. We have to await instructions from my client."

Montegrifo shook his head pensively and, with the languid mien of a man of the world, rose slowly.

"I'll see what I can do. Forgive me . . ."

He didn't seem worried. He merely expressed a hope – without once taking his eyes off Julia, although his words were addressed to Menchu – that the "findings" would do nothing to alter their present agreement. With a cordial good-bye, he threaded his way amongst the tables and sat down at the other end of the room.

Menchu stared into her glass with a contrite look on her face.

"I put my foot in it."

"What do you mean? He'd have to find out sooner or later."

"Yes, but you don't know Paco Montegrifo." She studied the auction-eer over her glass. "You might not think so to look at him, with his nice manners and good looks, but if he knew Don Manuel, he'd be over there like a shot to find out what's going on and to cut us out of the deal."

"Do you think so?"

Menchu gave a sarcastic little laugh. Paco Montegrifo's curriculum vitae held no secrets for her.

"He's got the gift of the gab and he has class. Moreover, he's got no scruples and he can smell a deal thirty miles away." She clicked her tongue in admiration. "They also say that he's involved in illegally exporting works of art and that he's a real artist when it comes to bribing country priests."

"Even so, he makes a good impression."

"That's how he makes his living."

39

"What I don't understand is why, if he's got such a bad track record, you didn't go to another auctioneer."

Menchu shrugged. The life and works of Paco Montegrifo had nothing to do with it. Claymore's itself was an impeccable organisation.

"Have you been to bed with him?"

"With Montegrifo?" Menchu roared with laughter. "No, dear. He's not my type at all."

"I think he's attractive."

"It's your age, dear. I prefer them a bit rougher, like Max, the sort that always look as if they're about to thump you one. They're better in bed and they work out much cheaper in the long run."

"Naturally, you're both too young to remember."

They were sitting drinking coffee round a small Chinese lacquer table next to a balcony full of leafy green plants. Bach's *Musical Offering* was playing on an old record player. Occasionally Don Manuel Belmonte would break off as if certain passages had caught his attention. After listening for a while, he would drum a light accompaniment with his fingers on the metal arm of his wheelchair. His forehead and hands were flecked with the brown stains of old age. Plump veins, blue and knotted, stood out along his wrists and neck.

"It must have been about 1940," he continued, and his dry, cracked lips curved into a sad smile. "Times were hard, and we sold off nearly all the paintings. I particularly remember a Muñoz Degrain and a Murillo. My poor Ana, God rest her soul, never got over losing the Murillo. It was a lovely little virgin, very like the ones in the Prado." He half-closed his eyes, as if trying to conjure up that painting from his memory. "An army officer who later became a minister bought it. García Pontejos, his name was, I think. He really took advantage of our situation, the scoundrel. He paid us a pittance."

"It must have been painful losing all that." Menchu adopted a suitably understanding tone of voice. She was sitting opposite Belmonte, affording him a generous view of her legs. The invalid gave a resigned nod, a gesture that dated from years back, the gesture of those who only learn at the expense of their own illusions.

"There was no alternative. Even friends and my wife's family turned

40

their backs on us after the war, when I was sacked as conductor of the Madrid orchestra. At that time, if you weren't for them, you were against them. And I certainly wasn't for them."

He paused for a moment and his attention seemed to drift back to the music playing in one corner of the room, amongst the piles of old records that were presided over by engravings, in matching frames, of the heads of Schubert, Verdi, Beethoven and Mozart. A moment later, he was looking once again at Julia and Menchu with a blink of surprise, as if he were returning from somewhere far off and had not expected to find them still there.

"Then I had a stroke, and things got even more complicated. Luckily we still had my wife's inheritance, which no one could take away from her. And we managed to keep this house, a few pieces of furniture and two or three good paintings, amongst them *The Game of Chess.*" He looked sadly at the space on the wall, at the bare nail, the rectangular mark left on the wallpaper, and he stroked his chin, on which a few white hairs had escaped his razor. "That painting was always my favourite."

"Who did you inherit the painting from?"

"From another branch of the family, the Moncadas. A great-uncle. Moncada was Ana's second family name. One of her ancestors, Luis Moncada, was a quartermaster general under Alejandro Farnesio, around 1500 or so . . . He must have been something of an art enthusiast."

Julia consulted the documentation that was lying on the table.

" 'Acquired in 1585', it says here, 'possibly in Antwerp, at the time of the surrender of Flanders and Brabant . . .' "

The old man nodded, almost as if he'd been witness to the event himself.

"Yes, that's right. It may have been part of the spoils of war from the sacking of the city. The troops of the regiment my wife's ancestor was in charge of were not the kind of people to knock at the door and sign a receipt."

Julia was leafing through the documents.

"There are no references to the painting before that," she remarked. "Do you remember any family stories about it, any oral tradition? Any information you have would help us."

Belmonte shook his head.

"No, I don't know of anything else. My wife's family always referred to the painting as the *Flanders* or *Farnesio Panel*, doubtless so as not to remember the manner of its acquisition. It appeared under those names for the twenty-odd years it was on loan to the Prado, until my wife's father recovered it in 1923, thanks to Primo de Rivera, who was a friend of the family. My father-in-law always held the Van Huys in great esteem, because he was a keen chess player. That's why, when it passed into his daughter's hands, she didn't want to sell it."

"And now?" asked Menchu.

The old man remained silent for a while, staring into his coffee cup as if he hadn't heard the question.

"Now, things are different," he said at last. He seemed almost to be making fun of himself. "I'm a real old crock now; that much is obvious." And he slapped his half-useless legs. "My niece Lola and her husband take care of me, and I should repay them in some way, don't you think?"

Menchu mumbled an apology. She hadn't meant to be indiscreet. That was a matter for the family, naturally.

"There's no reason to apologise," said Belmonte, raising his hand, as if offering absolution. "It's perfectly natural. That picture is worth a lot of money and it serves no real purpose just hanging in the house. My niece and her husband say that they could do with some help. Lola has her father's pension, but her husband, Alfonso . . ." He looked at Menchu as if appealing for her understanding. "Well, you know what he's like: he's never worked in his life. As for me . . ." The sardonic smile returned to his lips. "If I told you how much I have to pay in taxes every year just to hang on to this house and live in it, you'd be horrified."

"It's a good area," Julia said. "And a good house."

"Yes, but my pension is tiny. That's why I've gradually been selling off little souvenirs. The painting will give me a breathing space."

He remained thoughtful, nodding slowly, although he didn't seem particularly downcast. On the contrary, he seemed to find the whole thing amusing, as if there were humorous aspects to it that only he could appreciate. Perhaps what at first sight seemed only vulgar pillaging on the part of an unscrupulous niece and her husband was, for him, an odd kind of experiment in family greed: it's always "uncle this and uncle that", here we are at your beck and call, and your pension only just covers the costs; you'd be better off in a home with people the same

42

age as you; it's a shame, all these pictures hanging on the walls for no purpose. Now, with the Van Huys as bait, Belmonte must have felt safe. He could regain the initiative after long years of humiliation. Thanks to the painting, he could finally settle his account with his niece and her husband.

Julia offered him a cigarette, and he gave a grateful smile but hesitated.

"I shouldn't really," he said. "Lola allows me only one milky coffee and one cigarette a day."

"Forget Lola," Julia replied, with a spontaneity that surprised her. Menchu looked startled, but the old man didn't seem bothered in the least. He gave Julia a look in which she thought she caught a glimmer of complicity, instantly extinguished, and reached out his thin fingers. Leaning over the table to light the cigarette, Julia said: "About the painting . . . Something unexpected has come up."

The old man took a pleasurable gulp of smoke, held it in his lungs as long as possible and half closed his eyes.

"Unexpected in a good way or a bad way?"

"In a good way. We've discovered an original inscription underneath the paint. Uncovering it would increase the value of the painting." She sat back in her chair, smiling. "It's up to you what we do."

Belmonte looked at Menchu and then at Julia, as if making some private comparison or as if torn between two loyalties. At last he seemed to decide. Taking another long pull on his cigarette, he rested his hands on his knees with a look of satisfaction.

"You're not only pretty, but you're obviously bright as well," he said to Julia. "I bet you even like Bach."

"I love Bach."

"Please, tell me what the inscription says."

And Julia told him.

"Who'd have thought it!" Belmonte, incredulous, was still shaking his head after a long silence. "All those years of looking at that picture and I never once imagined . . ." He glanced briefly at the empty space left by the Van Huys, and his eyes half-closed in a contented smile. "So the painter was fond of riddles."

"So it would seem," Julia said.

Belmonte pointed to the record player in the corner.

"He's not the only one," he said. "Works of art containing games and hidden clues used to be commonplace. Take Bach, for example. The ten canons that make up his *Musical Offering* are the most perfect thing he composed, and yet not one of them was written out in full, from start to finish. He did that deliberately, as if the piece were a series of riddles he was setting Frederick of Prussia. It was a common musical stratagem of the day. It consisted in writing a theme, accompanied by more or less enigmatic instructions, and leaving the canon based on that theme to be discovered by another musician or interpreter; or by another player, since it was in fact a game."

"How interesting!" said Menchu.

"You don't know just how interesting. Like many artists, Bach was a joker. He was always coming up with devices to fool the audience. He used tricks employing notes and letters, ingenious variations, bizarre fugues. For example, into one of his compositions for six voices, he slyly slipped his own name, shared between two of the highest voices. And such things didn't happen only in music. Lewis Carroll, who was a mathematician and a keen chess player as well as a writer, used to introduce acrostics into his poems. There are some very clever ways of hiding things in music, in poems and in paintings."

"Absolutely," said Julia. "Symbols and hidden clues often appear in art. Even in modern art. The problem is that we don't always have the right keys to decipher those messages, especially the more ancient ones." Now it was her turn to stare pensively at the space on the wall. "But with *The Game of Chess* we at least have something to go on. We can make an attempt at a solution."

Belmonte leaned back in his wheelchair, his mocking eyes fixed on Julia.

"Well, keep me informed," he said. "I can assure you that nothing would give me greater pleasure."

They were saying good-bye in the hallway when the niece and her husband arrived. Lola was a scrawny woman, well over thirty, with reddish hair and small rapacious eyes. Her right arm, encased in the sleeve of her fur coat, was firmly gripping her husband's left arm. He was dark and slim, slightly younger, his premature baldness mitigated by a deep tan. Even without the old man's remark about him, Julia would have guessed that he had won a place in the ranks of those who prefer to do as little as possible to earn their living. His features, to which the slight puffiness under his eyes lent an air of dissipation, wore a sullen, rather cynical look, which his large, almost vulpine mouth did nothing to belie. He was wearing a gold-buttoned blue blazer and no tie, and he had the unmistakable look of someone who divides his considerable leisure time between drinking aperitifs in expensive bars and frequenting fashionable nightclubs, although he was clearly no stranger either to roulette and card games.

"My niece, Lola, and her husband, Alfonso," said Belmonte, and they exchanged greetings, unenthusiastically on the part of the niece, but with evident interest on the part of Alfonso, who held on to Julia's hand rather longer than necessary, looking her up and down with an expert eye. Then he turned to Menchu, whom he greeted by name, as if they were old acquaintances.

"They've come about the painting," Belmonte explained.

Alfonso clicked his tongue.

"Of course, the painting. Your famous painting."

Belmonte brought them up to date on the new situation. Alfonso stood with his hands in his pockets, smiling and looking at Julia.

"If it means the value of the painting will go up," he said, "it strikes me as excellent news. You can come back whenever you like if you're going to bring us surprises like that. We love surprises."

The niece didn't immediately share her husband's satisfaction.

"We'll have to discuss it," she said. "What guarantee is there that they won't just ruin the painting?"

"That would be unforgivable," chimed in Alfonso. "But I can't imagine that this young lady would be capable of doing such a thing."

Lola gave her husband an impatient look.

"You keep out of this. This is *my* business."

"That's where you're wrong, darling." Alfonso's smile grew broader. "We share everything."

"I've told you: keep out of it."

Alfonso turned slowly towards her. His features grew harder and more obviously foxlike, and his smile seemed like the blade of a knife.

45

Julia thought that he was not perhaps as inoffensive as he at first sight seemed. It would be unwise to have any unsettled business with a man capable of a smile like that.

"Don't be ridiculous . . . darling."

That "darling" was anything but tender, and Lola seemed more aware of that than anyone. They watched her struggle to conceal her humiliation and her rancour. Menchu took a step forward, determined to enter the fray.

"We've already talked to Don Manuel about it," she announced. "And he's agreed."

The invalid, his hands folded in his lap, had observed the skirmish from his wheelchair like a spectator who has chosen to remain on the sidelines but watches with malicious fascination.

What strange people! thought Julia.

"That's right," confirmed the old man to no one in particular. "I have agreed. In principle."

The niece was wringing her hands, and the bracelets on her wrists jingled loudly. She seemed to be in a state of anguish – either that or just plain furious. Perhaps she was both things at once.

"Uncle, this is something that has to be discussed. I don't doubt the good will of these two ladies . . ."

"Young ladies," put in her husband, smiling at Julia.

"Young ladies then." Lola was having difficulty getting her words out, hampered by her own irritation. "But they should have consulted us too."

"As far as I'm concerned," said her husband, "they have my blessing."

Menchu was studying Alfonso quite openly and seemed about to say something. But she chose not to and looked at the niece.

"You heard what your husband said."

"I don't care. I'm the legal heir."

Belmonte raised one thin hand in an ironic gesture, as if asking permission to intervene.

"I am still alive, Lola. You'll receive your inheritance in due course."

"Amen," said Alfonso.

The niece pointed her bony chin, in the most venomous fashion, straight at Menchu, and for a moment Julia thought she was about to hurl herself on them. With her long nails and that predatory, birdlike

46

quality, there was something dangerous about her. Julia prepared herself for a confrontation, her heart pumping. When she was a child, César had taught her a few dirty tricks, useful when it came to killing pirates. Fortunately, the niece's violence found expression only in her glance and in the way she turned on her heel and flounced out of the room.

"You'll be hearing from me," she said. And the furious tapping of her heels disappeared down the corridor.

Hands in his pockets, Alfonso wore a quietly serene smile.

"Don't mind her," he said, and turned to Belmonte. "Right, Uncle? You'd never think it, but Lolita has a heart of gold really. She's a real sweetie."

Belmonte nodded, distracted. He was clearly thinking about something else. His gaze seemed drawn to the empty rectangle on the wall as if it contained mysterious signs that only he, with his weary eyes, was capable of reading.

"So you've met Alfonso before," said Julia as soon as they were out in the street.

Menchu, who was looking in a shop window, nodded.

"Yes, some time ago," she said, bending down to see the price of some shoes. "Three or four years ago, I think."

"Now I understand about the painting. It wasn't the old man who approached you; it was Alfonso."

Menchu gave a crooked smile.

"First prize for guessing, dear. You're quite right. We had what *you* would demurely call an 'affair'. That was ages ago, but when the Van Huys thing came up, he was kind enough to think of me."

"Why didn't he choose to deal directly?"

"Because no one trusts him, including Don Manuel." She burst out laughing. "Alfonsito Lapeña, the well-known gambler and playboy, owes money even to the bootblack. A few months back he narrowly escaped going to prison. Something to do with bad cheques."

"So how does he live?"

"Off his wife, by scrounging off the unwary, and off his complete and utter lack of shame."

"And he's relying on the Van Huys to get him out of trouble?"

47

"Right. He can't wait to convert it into little piles of chips on smooth green baize."

"He strikes me as a nasty piece of work."

"Oh, he is. But I have a soft spot for low-lifers, and I like Alfonso." She remained thoughtful for a moment. "Although, as I recall, his technique certainly wouldn't have won him any medals. He's . . . how can I put it . . . ?" She groped for the right word. "Rather unimaginative. No comparison with Max. Monotonous, you know: the wham, bang and thank-you-ma'am type. But you can have a good laugh with him. He knows some really filthy jokes."

"Does his wife know about you and him?"

"I imagine she senses something, because she's certainly not stupid. That's why she gave me that look, the rotten cow."

III

❦

A Chess Problem

The noble game has its depths
in which many a fine and gentle soul,
alas, has vanished.
An old German master

"I THINK," SAID CÉSAR, "that we're dealing here with a chess problem."

They'd been discussing the painting for half an hour. César was leaning against the wall, a glass of gin-and-lemon held delicately between thumb and forefinger, Menchu was poised languidly on the sofa and Julia was sitting on the carpet with the ashtray between her legs, chewing on a fingernail. All three of them were staring at the painting as if they were watching a television screen. The colours of the Van Huys were darkening before their eyes as the last glow of evening faded from the skylight.

"Do you think someone could put a light on?" suggested Menchu. "I feel as if I'm slowly going blind."

César flicked the switch behind him, and the indirect light, reflected from the walls, returned life and colour to Roger de Arras and the Duke and Duchess of Ostenburg. Almost simultaneously the clock on the wall struck eight in time to the swing of the long brass pendulum. Julia turned her head, listening for the noise of non-existent footsteps on the stairs.

"Álvaro's late," she said, and saw César grimace.

"However late that philistine arrives," he murmured, "it'll never be late enough for me."

Julia gave him a reproachful look.

"You promised to behave. Don't forget."

"I won't, Princess. I'll suppress my homicidal impulses, but only out of devotion for you."

"I'd be eternally grateful."

"I should hope so." He looked at his wristwatch as if he didn't trust the clock on the wall, an old present of his. "But the swine isn't exactly punctual, is he?"

"César."

"All right, my dear. I won't say another word."

"No, go on talking." Julia indicated the painting. "You were saying it was something to do with a chess problem."

César nodded. He made a theatrical pause to moisten his lips with a sip of gin, then dry them on an immaculate white handkerchief he drew from his pocket.

"Let me explain" – he looked at Menchu and gave a slight sigh – "to both of you. There's a detail in the inscription we haven't noticed until now, or at least I hadn't. *Quis necavit equitem* can indeed be translated as 'Who killed the knight?' And that, according to the facts at our disposal, can be interpreted as a riddle about the death or murder of Roger de Arras. However, that phrase could be translated in another way." He looked thoughtfully at the painting, assessing the soundness of his argument. "Reformulated in chess terms, perhaps the question is not 'Who killed the knight' but 'Who *captured*, or *took*, the knight?' "

No one spoke. At last Menchu broke the silence, her face betraying her disappointment.

"So much for all our high hopes. We've based this whole story on a piece of nonsense."

Julia, who was looking hard at César, was shaking her head.

"Not at all; the mystery's still there. Isn't that right, César? Roger de Arras was murdered *before* the picture was painted." She got up and pointed to the corner of the painting. "See? The date the painting was finished is here: *Petrus Van Huys fecit me, anno MCDLXXI*. Two years after Roger de Arras was murdered, Van Huys chose to employ an ingenious play on words in order to paint a picture in which both victim and executioner appear." She paused, because another idea had just occurred to her. "And, possibly, the motive for the crime: Beatrice of Burgundy."

Menchu was puzzled, but excited. She'd shifted to the edge of the sofa and was looking at the Flemish painting as if she were seeing it for the first time.

"Go on. I'm on tenterhooks."

"According to what we know, there are several reasons why Roger de Arras could have been killed, and one of them would have been the supposed romance between him and the Duchess Beatrice, the woman dressed in black, sitting by the window reading."

"Are you trying to say that the Duke killed him out of jealousy?"

Julia made an evasive gesture.

"I'm not trying to say anything. I'm simply suggesting a possibility." She indicated the pile of books, documents and photocopies on the table. "Perhaps the painter wanted to call attention to the crime. Maybe that's what made him decide to paint the picture, or perhaps he was commissioned to do it." She shrugged. "We'll never know for certain, but one thing is clear: the picture contains the key to Roger de Arras's murder. The inscription proves it."

"The *hidden* inscription," César corrected her.

"That gives further support to my argument."

"What if the painter was simply afraid he'd been too explicit?" Menchu asked. "Even in the fifteenth century you couldn't go around accusing people just like that."

Julia looked at the picture.

"It might be that Van Huys was frightened he'd depicted the situation *too* clearly."

"Or else someone painted it over at a later date," Menchu suggested.

"No. I thought of that too and, as well as looking at it under ultra-violet light, I prepared a cross section of a tiny sample to study under the microscope." She picked up a piece of paper. "There you are, layer by layer: oak base, a very thin preparation made from calcium carbonate and animal glue, white lead and oil as imprimatura, and three layers containing white lead, vermilion and ivory black, white lead and copper resinate, varnish, and so on. All identical to the rest: the same mixtures, the same pigments. It was Van Huys himself who painted over the inscription, shortly after having written it. There's no doubt about that."

"So?"

"Bearing in mind that we're walking a tightrope of five centuries, I agree with César. It's very likely that the key does lie in the chess game. As for '*necavit*' meaning 'took' as well as 'killed', that never occurred to me." She looked at César. "What do you think?"

César sat down at the other end of the sofa, and, after taking a small sip of gin, crossed his legs.

"I think the same as you, love. I think that by directing our attention from the human knight to the chess knight, the painter is giving us the first clue." He delicately drank the contents of his glass and placed it, tinkling with ice, on the small table at his side. "By asking who took the knight, he forces us to study the game. That devious old man, Van Huys, who I'm beginning to think had a distinctly odd sense of humour, is inviting us to play chess."

Julia's eyes lit up.

"Let's play, then," she exclaimed, turning to the painting. Those words elicited another sigh from César.

"I'd love to, but I'm afraid that's beyond my capabilities."

"Come on, César, you must know how to play chess."

"A frivolous supposition on your part, my dear. Have you ever actually seen me play?"

"Never. But everyone has a vague idea how to play."

"In this case, you need something more than a vague idea about how to move the pieces. Have you had a good look at the board? The positions are very complicated." He sat back melodramatically, as if exhausted. "Even I have certain rather irritating limitations, love. No one's perfect."

At that moment someone rang her bell.

"It must be Álvaro," said Julia, and ran to the door.

It wasn't Álvaro. She came back with an envelope delivered by a messenger. It contained several photocopies and a typed chronology.

"Look. It seems he's decided not to come, but he's sent us this."

"As rude as ever," mumbled César, scornfully. "He could have phoned to make his excuses, the rat." He shrugged. "Mind you, deep down, I'm glad. What's the rotter sent us?"

"Don't be nasty about him," Julia said. "It took a lot of work to put this information together."

And she started reading out loud.

Pieter Van Huys and the Characters Portrayed in "The Game of Chess":

1415: Pieter Van Huys born in Bruges, Flanders, present-day Belgium.

1431: Roger de Arras born in the castle of Bellesang, in Ostenburg. His father, Fulk de Arras, is a vassal of the King of France and is related to the reigning dynasty of the Valois. His mother, whose name is not known, belonged to the ducal family of Ostenburg, the Altenhoffens.

1435: Burgundy and Ostenburg break their vassalage to France. Ferdinand Altenhoffen is born, future Duke of Ostenburg.

1437: Roger de Arras brought up at the Ostenburg court as companion in play and studies to the future Duke Ferdinand. When he turns seventeen, he accompanies his father, Fulk de Arras, to the war that Charles VII of France is waging against England.

1441: Beatrice, niece of Philip the Good, Duke of Burgundy, is born.

1442: Around this time Pieter Van Huys painted his first works after having been apprenticed to the Van Eyck brothers in Bruges and Robert Campin in Tournai. No work by him from this period remains extant until . . .

1448: Van Huys paints *Portrait of the Goldsmith Guillermo Walhuus*.

1449: Roger de Arras distinguishes himself in battle against the English during the conquest of Normandy and Guyenne.

1450: Roger de Arras fights in the battle of Formigny.

1452: Van Huys paints *The Family of Lucas Bremer*. (His finest surviving work.)

1453: Roger de Arras fights in the battle of Castillon. The same year he publishes his *Poem of the Rose and the Knight* in Nuremberg. (A copy can be found in the Bibliothèque National in Paris.)

1455: Van Huys paints *Virgin of the Chapel*. (Undated, but experts place it at around this period.)

1457: Wilhelmus Altenhoffen, Duke of Ostenburg, dies. He is succeeded by his son Ferdinand, who has just turned twenty-two. One of his first acts would have been to call Roger de Arras to his side. The latter is probably still at the court of France, bound to King Charles VII by an oath of fealty.

1457: Van Huys paints *The Money Changer of Louvain*.

1458: Van Huys paints *Portrait of the Merchant Matteo Conzini and His Wife*.

1461: Death of Charles VII of France.

Presumably freed from his oath to the French monarch, Roger de Arras returns to Ostenburg. Around the same time, Pieter Van Huys finishes the Antwerp retable and settles in the Ostenburg court.

1462: Van Huys paints *The Knight and the Devil*. Photographs of the original (in the Rijksmuseum, Amsterdam) suggest that the knight who posed for this portrait could have been Roger de Arras, although the resemblance between the character in this painting and that in *The Game of Chess* is not particularly marked.

1463: Official engagement of Ferdinand of Ostenburg to Beatrice of Burgundy. Amongst the embassy sent to the Burgundy court are Roger de Arras and Pieter Van Huys, the latter sent to paint Beatrice's portrait, which he does this year. (The portrait, mentioned in the chronicle of the nuptials and in an inventory of 1474, has not survived.)

1464: The Duke's wedding. Roger de Arras leads the party bringing the bride from Burgundy to Ostenburg.

1467: Philip the Good dies and his son, Charles the Bold, Beatrice's cousin, takes over the duchy of Burgundy. French and Burgundian pressure intensifies the intrigues within the Ostenburg court. Ferdinand Altenhoffen tries to keep a difficult balance. The pro-French party back Roger de Arras, who has great influence over Duke Ferdinand. The Burgundian party relies on the influence of Duchess Beatrice.

1469: Roger de Arras is murdered. Unofficially, the blame is laid at the door of the Burgundy faction. Other rumours allude to an affair between Roger de Arras and Beatrice of Burgundy. There is no proof that Ferdinand of Ostenburg was involved.

1471: Two years after the murder of Roger de Arras, Van Huys paints *The Game of Chess*. It is not known whether the painter was still living in Ostenburg at this time.

1474: Ferdinand Altenhoffen dies without issue. Louis XI of France tries to exercise his dynasty's former rights over the duchy. This only worsens the already tense relations between France and Burgundy. Charles the Bold invades the duchy, defeating the French at the battle of Looven. Burgundy annexes Ostenburg.

1477: Charles the Bold dies at the battle of Nancy. Maximilian I of Austria makes off with the Burgundian inheritance, which will pass to his nephew Charles (the future Emperor Charles V) and ultimately belong to the Spanish Habsburg monarchy.

1481: Pieter Van Huys dies in Ghent, whilst working on a triptych intended for the cathedral of St Bavon, depicting the Descent from the Cross.

1485: Beatrice of Ostenburg dies in a convent in Lièges.

For a long while, no one dared speak. They looked from one to the other and then at the painting. After a silence that seemed to last forever, César shook his head and said in a low voice, "I must confess I'm impressed."

"We all are," added Menchu.

Julia put the documents down on the table and leaned on it.

"Van Huys obviously knew Roger de Arras well," she said, pointing to the papers. "Perhaps they were friends."

"And by painting that picture, he was settling a score with the murderer," said César. "All the pieces fit."

Julia walked over to her library, consisting of two walls covered with wooden shelves buckling beneath the weight of untidy rows of books. She stood there for a moment, hands on hips, before selecting a fat illustrated tome, which she leafed through rapidly. Then she sat down between Menchu and César with the book, *The Rijksmuseum of Amsterdam*, open on her knees. It wasn't a very large reproduction, but a knight could clearly be seen, armour-clad, head bare, riding along the foot of a hill on top of which stood a walled city. Next to the knight, engaged in friendly conversation, rode the Devil, mounted on a scrawny black horse, pointing with his right hand at the city towards which they seemed to be travelling.

"It could be him," said Menchu, comparing the features of the knight in the book with those of the chess player in the painting.

"And it could just as easily not be," said César. "Although, of course, there is a certain resemblance." He turned to Julia. "What's the date of this painting?"

"1462."

"That's nine years before *The Game of Chess* was painted. That could explain it. The horseman accompanied by the Devil is much younger."

Julia said nothing. She was studying the reproduction.

"What's wrong?" César asked.

Julia shook her head slowly, as if afraid that any sudden move would frighten away elusive spirits that might prove difficult to summon up again.

"Yes," she said, in the tone of one who has no alternative but to acknowledge the obvious. "It's too much of a coincidence." And she pointed at the page.

"I can't see anything unusual," said Menchu.

"No?" Julia was smiling. "Look at the knight's shield. In the Middle Ages, every nobleman decorated his shield with his particular emblem. Tell me what you think, César. What's painted on that shield?"

César sighed as he drew a hand across his forehead. He was as amazed as Julia.

"Squares," he said unhesitatingly. "Black and white squares." He looked up at the Flemish painting, and his voice seemed to tremble. "Like those on a chessboard."

Leaving the book open on the sofa, Julia stood up.

"It's no coincidence," she said, picking up a powerful magnifying glass before going over to the painting. "If the knight Van Huys painted in 1462 accompanied by the Devil is Roger de Arras, that means that, nine years later, the artist chose the theme of his coat of arms as the main clue in a painting in which, supposedly, he represented his death. Even the floor of the room in which he placed his subjects is chequered in black and white. That, as well as the symbolic nature of the painting, confirms that the chess player in the centre is Roger de Arras. And the whole plot does, indeed, revolve around chess."

She knelt down in front of the painting and peered through the magnifying glass at the chess pieces on the board and on the table. She also looked carefully at the round convex mirror on the wall in the upper left-hand corner of the painting, which reflected the board and the foreshortened figures of both players, distorted by perspective.

"César."

"Yes, love."

"How many pieces are there in a game of chess?"

"Um . . . two times eight, so that's sixteen of each colour, which, if I'm not mistaken, makes thirty-two."

Julia counted with one finger.

"The thirty-two pieces are all there. You can see them really clearly: pawns, kings, queens and knights . . . Some on the board, others on the table."

"Those will be the pieces that have already been taken." César had knelt down by her and was pointing to one of the pieces not on the board, the one Ferdinand of Ostenburg was holding between his fingers. "One knight's been taken; only one. A white knight. The other three, one white and two black, are still in the game. So the *Quis necavit equitem* must refer to that one."

"But who took it?"

César frowned.

"That, my dear, is the crux of the matter," he said, smiling exactly as he used to when she was a little girl sitting on his knee. "We've already found out a lot of things: who plucked the chicken and who cooked it. But we still don't know who the villain was who ate it."

"You haven't answered my question."

"I don't always have brilliant answers to hand."

"You used to."

"Ah, but then I could lie." He looked at her tenderly. "You've grown up now and are not so easily deceived."

Julia put a hand on his shoulder, as she used to when, fifteen years before, she'd ask him to invent for her the story of a painting or a piece of porcelain. There was an echo of childish supplication in her voice.

"But I need to know, César."

"The auction's in less than two months," said Menchu. "There's not much time."

"To hell with the auction," said Julia. She was looking at César as if he held the solution in his hands. César gave another slow sigh and brushed lightly at the carpet before sitting down on it, folding his hands on his knees. His brow was furrowed and he was biting the tip of his tongue, as he always did when he was thinking hard.

"We have some clues to begin with," he said after a while. "But having the clues isn't enough; what's important is how we use them." He looked at the convex mirror in the painting, in which both the players and the board were reflected. "We're used to believing that any object and its mirror image contain the same reality, but it's not true." He pointed at the painted mirror. "See? We can tell at a glance that the image has been reversed. The meaning of the game on the chessboard is also reversed, and that's how it appears in the mirror as well."

"You're giving me a terrible headache," moaned Menchu. "This is all too complex for my feeble encephalogram. I'm going to get myself a drink." She poured herself a generous measure of Julia's vodka, but before picking up the glass, she took out of her pocket a smooth polished piece of onyx, a silver tube and a small box, and set about preparing a thin line of cocaine. "The pharmacy's open. Anyone interested?"

No one answered. César seemed absorbed in the painting, indifferent to everything else, and Julia merely gave a disapproving frown. With a shrug, Menchu bent over and took two short, sharp sniffs. She was smiling when she stood up, and the blue of her eyes seemed more luminous and absent.

César moved closer to the Van Huys, taking Julia by the arm, as if advising her to ignore Menchu.

"We've already fallen into the trap," he said, as if only he and Julia were in the room, "of thinking that one thing in the picture could be real, whereas another might not be. The people and the board appear in the picture twice, once in a way that is somehow *less real* than the other. Do you understand? Accepting that fact forces us to place

58

ourselves inside the room, to blur the boundaries between what is real and what is painted. The only way of avoiding that would be to distance ourselves enough to see only areas of colour and chessmen. But there are too many inversions in between."

Julia looked at the painting and then, turning round, pointed to the Venetian mirror hanging on the wall on the other side of the studio.

"Not necessarily," she replied. "If we use another mirror to look at the painting, perhaps we can reconstruct the original image."

César gave her a long look, silently considering her suggestion.

"That's very true," he said at last, and his approval was translated into a smile of relief. "But I fear, Princess, that both paintings and mirrors create worlds that contain too many inconsistencies. They're amusing perhaps to look at from the outside, but not at all comfortable to inhabit. For that we need a specialist; someone capable of seeing the picture differently from us. And I think I know where to find him."

The following morning, Julia telephoned Álvaro, but there was no answer. She had no luck when she tried to phone him at home either, so she put on a Lester Bowie record, started the coffee, stood under the shower for a long time and then smoked a couple of cigarettes. With her hair still wet and wearing only an old sweater, she drank the coffee and set to work on the painting.

The first phase of restoration involved removing the original layer of varnish. The painter, no doubt anxious to protect his work from the damp of cold northern winters, had used a greasy varnish, dissolved in linseed oil. It was the correct solution, but over a period of five hundred years no one, not even a master like Pieter Van Huys, could have prevented it from yellowing and thereby dimming the brilliance of the original colours.

Julia, who had tested several solvents in one corner of the painting, prepared a mixture and concentrated on the task of softening the varnish by using saturated plugs of cotton wool held between tweezers. With great care, she began working where the paint was thickest, leaving until last the lighter and more delicate areas. She paused frequently to check for traces of colour on the cotton wool, to make sure that she wasn't removing any of the painted surface beneath the varnish. She worked all morning without a break, stopping for a few moments every now and then to look at the painting through half-closed eyes to judge how things were progressing. Gradually, as the old varnish disappeared, the painting began to recover the magic of its original pigments, most of which were almost exactly like those the old Flemish master had mixed on his palette: sienna, copper green, white lead, ultramarine . . . With reverential respect, as if the most intimate mystery of art and life were being revealed to her, Julia watched as the marvellous work came to life again beneath her fingers.

At midday, she phoned César, and they arranged to meet that evening. Julia took advantage of the interruption to heat a pizza. She made more coffee and ate sitting on the sofa, looking closely at the craquelure that the ageing process, exposure to light and movement of the wooden support had inevitably inflicted on the painted surface. It was particularly noticeable in the flesh tints and in the white-lead colours, less obvious in the darker tones and the blacks. That was especially true of Beatrice of Burgundy's dress, which seemed so real Julia felt that, if she ran her finger over it, it would have the softness of velvet.

It was odd, she thought, how quickly modern paintings became criss-crossed with cracks, often soon after they were finished, the craquelure and blistering being caused by the use of modern materials or artificial drying methods, whereas the work of the old masters, who took almost obsessive care, using skilled techniques of preservation, resisted the passage of the centuries with far greater dignity and beauty. At that moment, Julia felt intense sympathy for old, conscientious Pieter Van Huys, whom she imagined in his medieval studio, mixing clays and experimenting with oils, in search of the exact shade he needed for a glaze, driven by the desire to set the seal of eternity on his work, beyond his own death and the death of those he depicted on that modest oak panel.

After lunch, she continued removing the varnish from the lower portion of the painting, the part concealing the inscription. She worked with enormous care, trying not to damage the copper green, which was mixed with resin to prevent darkening with age. Van Huys had used it to paint the cloth covering the table, the cloth whose folds he'd later extended, using the same colour, to hide the Latin inscription. As Julia well knew, quite apart from any normal technical difficulties, this posed an ethical problem too. If one wanted to respect the spirit of the painting, was it legitimate to uncover an inscription that the painter himself had decided to cover up? To what extent should a restorer be allowed to betray the desires of an artist, desires made evident in his work with the formality of a last will and testament? And then there was the value of the painting; once the existence of the inscription had been established by X-ray and the fact made public, would the price be higher with the words covered or uncovered?

Fortunately, she concluded, she was only a hireling. The decision lay with the owner, with Menchu and the man from Claymore's, Paco Montegrifo. She would do whatever they decided. Although, when she thought about it, given the choice, she would prefer to leave things as they were. The inscription existed, they knew what it said, and it was therefore unnecessary to reveal it. After all, the layer of paint that had covered it for five centuries was part of the painting's history too.

The notes from Lester Bowie's saxophone filled the studio, cutting her off from everything else. Gently she ran the solvent-soaked cotton wool along Roger de Arras's profile, near his nose and mouth, and once more she immersed herself in her scrutiny of those lowered eyelids, the fine lines betraying slight wrinkles near his eyes, their gaze intent on the game. She gave her imagination free rein to pursue the echo of the ill-fated knight's thoughts. The scent of love and death hung over them, the way the steps of Fate hovered over the mysterious ballet performed by the black and white pieces on the squares of the chessboard, on his own coat of arms, pierced by an arrow from a crossbow. And in the half-light a tear glinted, a tear shed by a woman apparently absorbed in reading a book of hours (or was it the *Poem of the Rose and the Knight*?), a tear shed by a silent shadow next to the window, recollecting days of sunlight and youth, of burnished metal and tapestries, recalling the firm footsteps on the flagstones of the Burgundy court of the noble-browed warrior, with his helmet under his arm, at the height of his strength and fame, the haughty ambassador from that other man, whom she was advised, for reasons of state, to marry. And the murmur of court ladies and the grave faces of courtiers, her own face blushing when his calm eyes met hers and when she heard his voice, tempered in many

61

battles, full of that singular assurance found only in those who know what it is to cry out the name of God, their king or their lady as they ride into battle against an enemy. And the secret that lay in her heart in the years that followed. And the Silent Friend, her Final Companion, patiently sharpening his scythe, standing near the moat by the East Gate preparing to fire his crossbow.

The colours, the painting, the studio, the sombre music of the saxophone filling the room seemed to circle her. She stopped working and sat with her eyes closed, feeling dizzy, trying to breathe deeply, steadily, to shake off the momentary panic that had run through her when, confused by the perspective in the picture, she began to feel that she was actually inside the painting. It was as if the table and the players had suddenly shifted to her left and she had been thrust forward across the room reproduced in the painting, towards the window next to which Beatrice of Burgundy sat reading; as if she had only to lean out a little over the window ledge to see what lay below, at the bottom of the wall: the moat at the East Gate, where Roger de Arras had been shot in the back by an arrow.

It took her a while to regain her composure, and she only really did so when she lit a match and held it to the cigarette she had in her mouth. She found it hard to hold the match steady, for her hand was trembling as if she'd just touched the face of Death.

"It's a chess club," César said as they went up the steps. "The Capablanca Club."

"Capablanca?" Julia looked warily through the open door. She could see tables inside with men leaning over and spectators grouped around them.

"José Raúl Capablanca," César said, by way of explanation, clasping his walking stick beneath one arm as he removed his hat and gloves. "Some people say he was the best player ever. There are clubs and tournaments named after him all over the world."

They went in. The club consisted of three large rooms, filled by a dozen tables, at almost every one of which a game was in progress. There was an odd buzz, neither noise nor silence, but a sort of gentle, contained murmur, slightly solemn, like the sound of people filling a church. A few players and spectators looked at Julia with incredulity or disapproval. The membership was exclusively male. The place smelled of cigarette smoke and old wood.

"Don't women ever play chess?" asked Julia.

César offered her his arm before they went in.

"I hadn't really thought about it, to be honest," he said. "But they obviously don't play here. Perhaps they play at home, between the darning and the cooking."

"Male chauvinist!"

"Hardly an appropriate epithet in my case, my dear. Anyway, don't be horrid."

They were welcomed in the hallway by a friendly, talkative gentleman of a certain age, with a bald, domed head and a carefully trimmed moustache. César introduced him to Julia as Señor Cifuentes, the director of the José Raúl Capablanca Recreational Club.

"We have five hundred members on our books," he told them proudly, pointing out the trophies, certificates and photographs adorning the walls. "We also sponsor a nationwide tournament." He paused before a glass case containing a display of various chess sets, old rather than antique. "Nice, eh? Although here, of course, we use only the Staunton set."

He had turned to César as if expecting his approval, and the latter felt obliged to adopt an appropriately serious expression.

"Of course," he said, and Cifuentes rewarded him with a friendly smile.

"Wood, you know," he added. "No plastic."

"I should hope not."

Cifuentes turned to Julia.

"You should see it here on a Saturday afternoon." He looked around contentedly, like a mother hen inspecting her chicks. "It's a fairly average day today: keen players who leave work early, pensioners who spend the whole afternoon playing. And, as you've no doubt noticed, there's a pleasant atmosphere here. Very . . ."

"Edifying," said Julia, without thinking. But Cifuentes seemed to find the adjective appropriate.

"Yes, that's it, edifying. As you can see, there are a number of younger men. That one over there, for example, is quite remarkable. He's only nineteen but he's already written a hundred-page study on the four lines of the Nimzo-Indian Defence."

"Really? Nimzo-Indian? It sounds very . . ." – Julia searched desperately for the right word – "definitive."

"Well, I don't know about definitive," Cifuentes replied honestly. "But it's certainly significant."

Julia looked to César for help, but he merely arched an eyebrow, as if expressing a polite interest in the conversation. He was leaning towards Cifuentes, his hands behind his back holding both stick and hat, apparently enjoying himself hugely.

"Some years ago," added Cifuentes, pointing at the top button of his waistcoat with his thumb, "I added my own little grain of sand."

"Really?" said César, and Julia gave him a worried look.

"Yes, believe it or not," Cifuentes said, with false modesty. "A subvariant of the Caro-Kann Defence, using two knights. You know the one: knight three bishop queen. The Cifuentes variant, it's called," he added, looking hopefully at César. "Perhaps you've heard of it?"

"Naturally," replied César with great aplomb.

Cifuentes smiled gratefully.

"I can assure you it would be no exaggeration to say that in this club, or recreational society, as I prefer to call it, you'll find the best players in Madrid, and possibly in all Spain." Then he seemed to remember something. "By the way, I've found the man you need." He scanned the room, and his face lit up. "Ah, there he is. Come with me, please."

They followed him through one of the rooms, towards the rear.

"It wasn't easy," said Cifuentes as they approached. "I've spent all day turning it over in my mind. But then," he half-turned towards César with an apologetic gesture, "you did ask me to recommend our best player."

They stopped a short distance from a table at which two men were playing, watched by half a dozen others. One of the players was softly drumming his fingers at the side of the board over which he was leaning with, thought Julia, the same serious expression Van Huys had given to the chess players in the painting. Opposite him, apparently untroubled by his opponent's drumming, the other player sat utterly still, leaning slightly back in his wooden chair, his hands in his trouser pockets, his chin sunk on his chest. It was impossible to tell whether his eyes, fixed on the board, were concentrating on that or were absorbed in something else entirely.

The spectators maintained a reverential silence, as if what was being decided was a matter of life and death. There were only a few pieces left on the board, so intermingled that it was impossible, at least for new arrivals, to work out who was White and who was Black. After a couple of minutes, the man drumming his fingers used the same hand to move a white bishop, placing it between his king and a black rook. Having done that, he glanced briefly at his opponent and returned to his contemplation of the board and to his gentle drumming.

The move was accompanied by a lot of murmuring amongst the spectators. Julia went closer and saw that the other player, who hadn't changed his posture at all when his opponent made his move, was staring intently at the intervening white bishop. He stayed like that for a while, when, with a gesture so slow it was impossible to tell until the last moment which piece he was reaching for, he moved a black knight.

"Check," he said and returned to his former state of immobility, indifferent to the buzz of approval that rose about him.

Though no one said anything, Julia knew that he was the man Cifuentes had recommended to César. She therefore watched him closely. He must have been just over forty, he was very thin and most likely of medium height. His hair was brushed straight back, with no parting, and was receding at the temples. He had large ears, a slightly aquiline nose, and his dark eyes were set deep in their sockets, as if viewing the world with distrust. He completely lacked the air of intelligence Julia now believed essential in a chess player; instead, his expression was one of indolent apathy, a kind of deep-seated weariness that left him utterly indifferent to his surroundings. Julia, disappointed, thought he had the look of a man who expects very little from himself, apart from making the correct moves on a chessboard.

Nevertheless – or perhaps precisely because of that, because of the look of infinite tedium written on his impassive features – when his opponent moved his king one square back and he then slowly stretched out his right hand towards the remaining pieces, the silence in that corner of the room became absolute. Julia, perhaps because she didn't understand what was going on, realised that the spectators did not like him, that they felt not the least warmth towards him. She read in their

65

faces a grudging acceptance of his superiority at the chessboard, for, as enthusiasts of the game, they could not help but see the slow, precise, implacable advance of the pieces he was moving.

"Check," he said again. He'd made an apparently simple move, merely advancing a modest pawn one square. But his opponent stopped his drumming and rested his fingers instead on his temples, as if to calm a troublesome throbbing. Then he moved the white king diagonally back another square. He seemed to have three squares on which he would be safe, but, for some reason that escaped Julia, he chose that one. An admiring whisper round him seemed to suggest that the move had been an opportune one, but his opponent did not react.

"That would have been checkmate," he said, and there wasn't the slightest hint of triumph in his voice; he was merely informing his opponent of an objective fact. There was no pity there either. He pronounced those words before making another move, as if he felt it unnecessary to accompany them with a practical demonstration. And then, almost reluctantly, without appearing in the least affected by the incredulous look on the face of his opponent and on the faces of a good many spectators, he made a diagonal move with his bishop right across the board, bringing it, as it were, from some far distant place, and setting it down near the enemy king, but not near enough to constitute any immediate threat. Amidst the rumble of remarks that burst out around the table, Julia looked at the board in some bewilderment. She didn't know much about chess, but enough to know that checkmate involved a direct threat to the king. And the white king appeared to be safe. Hoping for clarification, she looked first at César and then at Cifuentes. The latter was smiling good-naturedly, shaking his head in admiration.

"It would, in fact, have been mate in three," he told Julia. "Whatever he did, the white king had no escape."

"Then I don't understand," said Julia. "What happened?"

Cifuentes gave a short laugh.

"That black bishop was the piece that could have delivered the *coup de grâce*, although, until he moved it, none of us could see that. What happened, though, was that this gentleman, despite knowing exactly which move to make, chose to take it no further. He moved the bishop to show us what would have been the correct move, but he deliberately placed it on the wrong square, thus rendering it completely harmless."

"I still don't understand," said Julia. "Doesn't he want to win the game?"

"That's the odd thing. He's been coming here for five years now, and he's the best chess player I know, but I've never once seen him win."

At that moment, the chess player looked up, and his eyes met Julia's. All his poise, all the confidence he'd shown during the game, seemed to have vanished. It was as if, when the game was over and he once more looked at the world around him, he found himself stripped of the gifts that ensured him the envy and respect of others. Only then did Julia notice his cheap tie, the brown jacket creased at the back and baggy at the elbows, the stubbly chin that had been shaved at five or six in the morning before catching the metro or the bus to go to work. Even the light in his eyes had gone out, leaving them grey, opaque.

Cifuentes said: "May I introduce Señor Muñoz, chess player."

IV

❧

The Third Player

"So, Watson," continued Holmes with a chuckle,
"is it not amusing how it sometimes happens
that to know the past, one must first
know the future?"   *Raymond Smullyan*

"IT'S A REAL GAME," said Muñoz. "A bit strange, but perfectly logical. Black was the last to move."

"Are you sure?" asked Julia.

"Yes, I'm sure."

"How do you know?"

"I just do."

They were in Julia's studio, in front of the picture, which was lit by every available light in the room. César was on the sofa, Julia was sitting at the table and Muñoz was standing before the Van Huys, perplexed.

"Would you like a drink?"

"No."

"A cigarette?"

"No. I don't smoke."

A certain embarrassment floated in the air. Muñoz seemed ill at ease. He was wearing a crumpled raincoat and had kept it firmly buttoned up, as if reserving the right to leave at any moment, with no explanation. He remained shy, mistrustful. It hadn't been easy to get him there. When César and Julia first put their proposition to him, the expression on Muñoz's face had required no commentary; he took them for a couple of lunatics. Then he became suspicious, defensive. They must forgive him if he seemed rude, but this whole story about medieval murders and a game of chess painted in a picture was just too bizarre.

68

And even if what they told him were true, he didn't really understand what it could possibly have to do with him. After all, he kept saying, as if that way he could establish the necessary social distinctions, he was just an accounts clerk, an office worker.

"But you play chess," César had said with his most seductive smile. They had gone across the street to a bar and were sitting next to a fruit machine that deafened them at intervals with its monotonous jingle designed to ensnare the unwary.

"So?" There was no defiance in the reply, only indifference. "So do a lot of other people. And I don't see why I . . ."

"They say you're the best."

Muñoz gave César an indefinable look. Julia interpreted it as meaning: Perhaps I am, but that has nothing to do with it. Being the best has no meaning. You could be the best, just as you could be blond or have flat feet, without feeling obliged to prove it to everyone.

"If that were true," he replied after a moment, "I'd go in for tournaments and such. But I don't."

"Why not?"

Muñoz glanced at his empty coffee cup and then shrugged his shoulders.

"Because I don't. You have to want to do that kind of thing. I mean, you have to want to win . . ." He looked at them as if he wasn't sure whether or not they would understand what he said. "And I don't care whether I win or not."

"So, you're a theoretician," remarked César, with a gravity in which Julia detected a hidden irony.

Muñoz held his gaze thoughtfully, as if struggling to find a suitable reply.

"Perhaps," he said at last. "That's why I don't think I would be much use to you."

He started to get up, but was prevented by Julia's reaching out her hand and placing it on his arm. It was only the briefest of contacts, but it was invested with anxious urgency. Later, when they were alone, César, arching one eyebrow, described it as "supremely feminine, darling; the damsel asking for help, though without overstating her case, and ensuring that the bird doesn't fly the coop." He himself could not have done it better; except that he would have uttered a little cry of alarm not at all appropriate in the circumstances. As it was, Muñoz had looked down fleetingly at the hand Julia was already withdrawing and let his eyes slide over the table and come to rest on his own hands, with their rather grubby nails, which lay quite still on either side of his cup.

"We need your help," Julia said in a low voice. "It really is important, I can assure you, important to me and to my work."

Muñoz put his head on one side and looked at her, or, rather, at her chin, as if he feared that looking directly into her eyes would establish between them a commitment he was not prepared to make.

"I really don't think it would interest me," he said at last.

Julia leaned over the table.

"Think of it as a game that would be different from any game you've played before. A game which, this time, would be worth winning."

César was growing impatient.

"I must admit, my friend," he said, his irritation evident in the way he kept twisting the topaz ring on his right hand, "that I find your peculiar apathy incomprehensible. Why do you bother to play chess?"

Muñoz thought for a while. Then he looked straight into César's eyes.

"Perhaps," he said calmly, "for the same reason that you are homosexual."

It was as if an icy blast had blown over them. Julia hurriedly lit a cigarette, terrified by the tactless remark, which Muñoz had uttered unemphatically and without a hint of aggression. On the contrary, he was looking at César with a kind of polite attention, as if, in the course of a perfectly normal dialogue, he was awaiting the response of a worthy conversational partner. There was a complete lack of malice in that look, Julia thought, even a certain innocence, like that of a tourist who, with the ineptness of the foreigner, unwittingly offends against local custom.

César merely leaned a little towards Muñoz, with an interested look on his face and an amused smile on his pale, thin lips.

"My dear friend," he said gently, "from your tone of voice and the expression on your face, I deduce that you have nothing against what your humble servant here might or might not represent. Just as, I imagine, you had nothing against the white king or against the man you were playing a short while ago at the club. Isn't that right?"

"More or less."

70

César turned to Julia.

"You see, Princess? Everything's fine; no need to be alarmed. This charming man merely wished to explain that the reason he plays chess is because the game is part of his very nature." César's smile grew brighter, kinder. "Something deeply bound up with problems, combinations, illusions. What's a prosaic checkmate beside all that?" He sat back in his chair and looked at Muñoz, who was still observing him impassively. "I'll tell you: Nothing." He held out his hands palms uppermost, as if inviting Julia and Muñoz to verify the truth of his words. "Isn't that so, my friend? Just a desolate full stop, an enforced return to reality." He wrinkled his nose. "To real life, to the routine of the commonplace and the everyday."

Muñoz remained silent for a while.

"It's funny," he said at last, screwing up his eyes in a suggestion of a smile that never quite reached his lips, "but I suppose that's exactly what it is. It's just that I've never heard anyone put it into words before."

"Well, I'm delighted to be the one to initiate you into the matter," replied César, not without a certain malice, and with a little laugh that earned him a reproving look from Julia.

Muñoz seemed somewhat disconcerted.

"Do you play chess too?"

César gave a short laugh. He was being unbearably theatrical today, thought Julia, as he always was when he had the right audience.

"Like everyone else, I know how to move the pieces. But as a game I can take it or leave it." He gave Muñoz a look of sudden seriousness. "What I play at, my esteemed friend, and it is no small thing, is getting out of the everyday checkmates of life." He gestured towards both of them with one delicate hand. "And like you, like everyone, I have my own little ways of getting by."

Still confused, Muñoz glanced at the door. The lighting in the bar made him look weary and accentuated the shadows under his eyes, making them appear even more deeply sunk. With his large ears, sticking out above the collar of his raincoat, his big nose and his gaunt face, he looked like a thin, ungainly dog.

"All right," he said. "Let's go and see this painting."

And there they were, awaiting Muñoz's verdict. His initial discomfort at finding himself in a strange place in the presence of a pretty young woman, an antiquarian of uncertain proclivities and a painting of equivocal appearance seemed to disappear as the game of chess in the painting took hold of his attention. For the first few minutes he had studied it without saying a word, standing quite still, his hands behind his back, in exactly the same posture, thought Julia, as that adopted by the spectators at the Capablanca Club as they watched other people's games unfold. And, of course, that was exactly what he was doing. After some time, during which no one said a word, he asked for paper and pencil, and after a further brief period of reflection, he leaned on the table in order to make a sketch of the game, looking up every now and then to check the position of the pieces.

"What century was it painted in?" he asked. He'd drawn a square on which he'd traced a grid of vertical and horizontal lines that divided it into sixty-four smaller squares.

"Late fifteenth," said Julia.

Muñoz frowned.

"Knowing the date is important. By then, the rules of chess were almost the same as they are now. But up to that point, the way some of the pieces could be moved was different. The queen, for example, used to be able to move only diagonally into a neighbouring square, and then, later on, to jump three squares. And castling was unknown until the Middle Ages." He left his drawing for a moment to take a closer look at the painting. "If the person who worked out the game did so using modern rules, we might be able to resolve it. If not, it will be difficult."

"It was painted in what is now Belgium," César said, "around 1470."

"I don't think there'll be any problem then. Nothing insoluble at any rate."

Julia got up from the table and went over to the painting to look at the position of the painted chess pieces.

"How do you know that Black has just moved?"

"It's obvious. You just have to look at the position of the pieces. Or at the players." Muñoz pointed to Ferdinand of Ostenburg. "The one on the left, the one playing Black and looking towards the painter, or towards us, is more relaxed, even distracted, as if his attention were directed at the spectators rather than at the board." He pointed to Roger de Arras. "The other man, however, is studying a move his opponent has just made. Can't you see the concentration on his face?" He returned to his sketch. "There's another way of checking it; in fact, it's the method to use. It's called retrograde analysis."

"*What* kind of analysis?"

"Retrograde. It involves taking a certain position on the board as your starting point and then reconstructing the game backwards in order to work out how it got to that position. A sort of chess in reverse, if you like. It's all done by induction. You begin with the end result and work backwards to the causes."

"Like Sherlock Holmes," remarked César, visibly interested.

"Something like that."

Julia had turned towards Muñoz, impressed. Until now, chess had been only a game for her, a game with rules marginally more complex than those for Parcheesi or dominoes and requiring greater concentration and intelligence. But from Muñoz's reaction to the Van Huys it was evident that the planes represented in the painting: mirror, room, window – the backdrop to the moment recorded there by Pieter Van Huys, a space in which she herself had experienced the dizzying effects of the optical illusion created by the artist's skill – presented no difficulties at all for Muñoz, who knew almost nothing about the picture and hardly anything about its disquieting connotations. For him, it was a familiar space beyond time and personalities. It was a space in which he appeared to move easily, as if, by making everything else an abstraction, he was able at once to take in the position of the pieces and integrate himself into the game. The more he concentrated on *The Game of Chess*, the more he shed the perplexity, reticence and awkwardness he'd shown in the bar, and revealed himself as the confident, impassive player she had thought him to be when she saw him at the Capablanca Club. It was as if this shy, grey, hesitant man needed only the presence of a chessboard to recover his confidence and self-assurance.

"You mean it's possible to play the game of chess in the painting backwards, right back to the beginning?"

Muñoz made one of his noncommittal gestures.

"I don't know about going right back to the beginning . . . but I imagine we could reconstruct a fair number of moves." He looked at the painting again as if he'd just seen it in a new light and, addressing César, he said: "I suppose that was exactly what the painter intended."

"That's what you have to find out," replied César. "The tricky question is: Who took the knight?"

"You mean the white knight," said Muñoz. "There's only one left on the board."

"Elementary," said César, adding with a smile, "my dear Watson."

Muñoz ignored this; humour was evidently not one of his strong points. Julia went over to the sofa and sat down next to César, as enthralled as a little girl watching some thrilling performance. Muñoz had finished his sketch now and he showed it to them.

"This," he explained, "is the position of the pieces as they are in the painting."

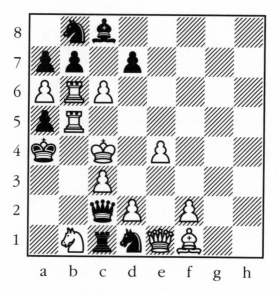

"As you see, I've given each square a coordinate, to make locating the pieces easier for you. So, seen from the perspective of the player on the right . . ."

"Roger de Arras," said Julia.

"Yes, Roger de Arras. Looking at the board from that position, we number the squares on the vertical from one to eight and assign a letter, from a to h, to each of the squares on the horizontal," he said, pointing to them with his pencil. "There are other more technical classifications, but that might just confuse you."

"And each symbol corresponds to a chess piece?"

"That's right. They're conventional symbols, some black, some white. I've made a note, below, of what each one means."

KING   QUEEN

BISHOP KNIGHT

ROOK   PAWN

"That way, even if you know very little about chess, it's easy to see that the black king, for example, is on square a4, and that on f1, for example, there's a white bishop. Do you understand?"

"Perfectly."

Muñoz went on to show them some further symbols he'd drawn.

"Now, we've looked at the pieces actually on the board, but in order to analyse the game, it's essential to know which ones are off the board too, the pieces that have already been taken." He looked at the picture. "What's the player on the left called?"

"Ferdinand of Ostenburg."

"Well, Ferdinand of Ostenburg, who's playing Black, has taken the following white pieces."

"That is: a bishop, a knight and two pawns. For his part, Roger de Arras has taken the following pieces from his rival."

"That's four pawns, one rook and a bishop." Muñoz looked thoughtfully at the sketch. "When you look at the game from that point of view, White would seem to have an advantage over his opponent. But, if I've understood correctly, that's not the problem. The question is who took the white knight. Clearly it must have been one of the black pieces, which may seem to be stating the obvious, but we have to go step by step here, right from the beginning." He looked at César and Julia as if what he'd said required some apology. "There's nothing more mislead-ing than an obvious fact. That's a principle from logic which is equally applicable in chess: what seems obvious doesn't always turn out to be what really happened or what is about to happen. To sum up: this means that we have to find out which of the black pieces on or off the board took the white knight."

"Or killed him," added Julia.

Muñoz made an evasive gesture.

"That's not my business, Señorita."

"You can call me Julia, if you like."

"Well, Julia, it's still not my business." He looked hard at the paper containing the sketch as if written on it was the script of a conversation of which he'd lost the thread. "I believe you brought me here to tell you which chess piece took the white knight. If by finding that out, the two of you are able to draw certain conclusions or decipher some hieroglyph, that's fine." He looked at them with more assurance, as often happened when he'd concluded a technical exegesis, as if he drew some measure of confidence from his knowledge. "That's up to you. I'm just a chess player."

César found this reasonable.

"I can't see anything wrong with that," he said, looking at Julia. "He makes the moves and we interpret them. Teamwork, my dear."

Julia was too interested in the whole problem to bother with details about method. She put her hand on César's, feeling the soft, regular beat of his pulse beneath the skin on his wrist.

"How long will it take to solve?"

Muñoz scratched his ill-shaven chin.

"I don't know. Half an hour, a week. It depends."

"On what?"

"On a lot of things. On how well I manage to concentrate. And on luck."

"Can you start right now?"

"Of course. I already have."

"Go on then."

But at that moment the phone rang, and the game of chess had to be postponed.

∗   ∗   ∗

76

Much later, Julia said she'd known at once what it was about, but she herself acknowledged how easy it is to say such things *a posteriori*. She also said that it was then she realised how terribly complicated everything was becoming. In fact, as she soon found out, the complications had started long before, tying themselves into solid knots, although at that point the most unpleasant aspects of the affair had not yet emerged. To be strictly accurate, it could be said that the complications began in 1469, when that man with a crossbow, an obscure pawn whose name is lost to posterity, positioned himself by the moat of Ostenburg Castle to wait, with the patience of a hunter, for the man to pass whose death had been bought with the gold coins jingling in his pocket.

At first the policeman didn't seem too unpleasant, given the circumstances and given that he was a policeman, although the fact that he belonged to the Art Investigation Squad didn't seem to mark him out much from his colleagues. His professional relationship with the world in which he worked had left him with, at most, a certain affectation in the way he said "Good morning" or "Sit down", and in the way he knotted his tie. He spoke very slowly and unemphatically and kept nodding unnecessarily. Julia could not decide if it was a professional tic intended to inspire confidence or was part of the pretence that he knew exactly what was going on. He was short and fat, sported a strange Mexican-style moustache and was dressed entirely in brown. As regards art, Inspector Feijoo considered himself, modestly, to be an enthusiast: he was a collector of antique knives.

Julia learned all this in an office in the police station on Paseo del Prado after Feijoo's description of some of the details of Álvaro's death. The fact that Professor Ortega had been found in his bathtub with a broken neck, presumably from slipping while taking a shower, was most regrettable. The body had been discovered by the cleaner. But the distressing part – and Feijoo weighed his words carefully before giving Julia a sorrowful look, as if inviting her to consider the tragedy of the human condition – was that the forensic examination had revealed certain disquieting details, and it was impossible to determine with any exactitude whether the death had been accidental or provoked. In other words, there was the possibility – the Inspector repeated the word "possibility" twice – that the fracture at the base of the skull had been caused by a blow from a solid object other than the edge of the bathtub.

"You mean," Julia said, leaning on the table, "that someone might have killed him while he was taking a shower?"

The policeman adopted an expression doubtless intended to dissuade her from going too far.

"I only mention that as a possibility. The initial inspection and the first autopsy, generally speaking, confirm the theory of accidental death."

"Generally speaking? What are you trying to say?"

"I'm trying to tell you the facts. There are certain details, such as the type of fracture, the position of the body – technical details I would prefer not to go into – which give rise to some perplexity, to certain reasonable doubts."

"That's ridiculous."

"I'm almost inclined to agree with you," he said, the Mexican moustache taking on the form of a sympathetic circumflex. "But if those doubts were confirmed, the situation would look very different: Professor Ortega would have been killed by a blow to the back of the neck. Then, after undressing him, someone could have put him under the shower and turned on the taps, to make it look like an accident. A new forensic study is being carried out to look into the possibility that the dead man was struck twice, not once; a first blow to knock him out and a second to make sure he was dead." He sat back in his chair, folded his hands and looked at her placidly. "Naturally, that's only a hypothesis."

Julia stared at him, like someone who believes herself to be the butt of a practical joke. She couldn't take in what she'd heard; she was unable to establish a link between Álvaro and what Feijoo was suggesting. A voice deep inside her was whispering that this was obviously a case of the wrong roles being given to the wrong people; he must be talking about someone else entirely. It was absurd to imagine Álvaro, the Álvaro she had known, murdered, like a rabbit, by a blow to the back of the neck, lying naked, his eyes wide open, beneath a shower of icy water. It was stupid, grotesque.

"Let's assume for a moment," she said, "that the death wasn't accidental. Who would have wanted to kill him?"

"That, as they say in the films, is a very good question." The policeman bit his lower lip in a gesture of professional caution. "To be honest, I haven't the slightest idea." He paused and adopted an air intended to convey that he was placing all his cards on the table. "In fact, I'm relying on your help to clear up the matter."

"On my help? Why?"

The Inspector looked Julia up and down with deliberate slowness. He was no longer being nice, and his look revealed a certain crude self-interest, as if he were trying to establish some kind of obscure complicity between them.

"You had a relationship with the dead man . . . Forgive me, but mine is an unpleasant job," he said, although, judging by the self-satisfied smile that appeared beneath the moustache, he didn't seem to be finding his job particularly unpleasant. He put his hand in his pocket and drew out a box of matches bearing the name of a four-star restaurant and, with a gesture intended to be gallant, lit the cigarette Julia had just placed between her lips. "I mean an . . . um . . . affair. Is that correct?"

"That's correct." Julia exhaled, half-closing her eyes, embarrassed and angry. An affair, the policeman had just said, summing up with great simplicity a piece of her life whose scars were still raw. And no doubt, she thought, that fat, vulgar man, with his ridiculous moustache, was weighing up the quality of the goods. The victim's girlfriend's a nice bit of stuff, he'd tell his colleagues when he went down to the canteen for a beer. I wouldn't mind doing her the odd favour.

But she was more concerned about other aspects of her situation. Álvaro was dead, possibly murdered. Absurd as it might seem, she was in a police station, and there were too many unknowns. And not understanding certain things could prove dangerous.

Her whole body was tense, alert, on the defensive. She looked at Feijoo, who was now neither compassionate nor kindly. It was a question of tactics, she said to herself. Trying to remain calm, she decided that there really wasn't any reason the Inspector should be considerate towards her. He was just a policeman, as clumsy and coarse as the next one, merely doing his job. Anyway, she thought, as she tried to see the situation from his point of view: she was all he had, the only lead, the dead man's ex-girlfriend.

"But that's ancient history," she said, letting the ash from her cigarette fall into the pristine ashtray full of paper clips that Feijoo had on his desk. "We stopped seeing each other over a year ago . . . as I'm sure you know."

79

The Inspector put his elbows on the desk and leaned towards her.

"Yes," he said, almost confidentially, as if his tone were irrefutable proof that they were old acquaintances now and that he was entirely on her side. "But you did have a meeting with him three days ago."

Julia managed to conceal her surprise and merely looked at the policeman with the expression of someone who's just heard an exceptionally foolish remark. Naturally, Feijoo had been making enquiries at the university. Any secretary or porter could have told him. But neither was it something she needed to hide.

"I went to ask for his help on a painting I'm restoring." She found it odd that the policeman wasn't taking notes, but assumed that was part of his method: people speak more freely when they think their words are disappearing into thin air. "As you are apparently well aware, we talked for nearly an hour in his office. We even arranged to meet later, but I never saw him again."

Feijoo was turning the box of matches round and round.

"What did you talk about, if you don't mind my asking? I'm sure you'll understand and forgive such an . . . um . . . personal question. I assure you it's purely routine."

Julia regarded him in silence while she pulled on her cigarette and then she shook her head slowly.

"You seem to take me for some kind of idiot."

The policeman looked at her through lowered eyelids but he sat a little straighter.

"I'm sorry, I don't know what you mean."

"I'll tell you what I mean," she said and stubbed out her cigarette hard in the little pile of paper clips, indifferent to the pained look with which he followed her gesture. "I have no objection whatsoever to answering your questions. But, before we go on, I want you to tell me if Álvaro slipped in the bath or not."

Feijoo seemed to be caught off guard. "I have no firm evidence . . ."

"Then this conversation is unnecessary. If you think there is something suspicious about his death and you're trying to get me to talk, I want to know right now whether I'm being questioned as a possible suspect. Because, in that case, either I leave this police station at once or I get a lawyer."

The policeman raised his hands in conciliatory fashion.

"That would be a bit premature." With a lopsided smile, he shuffled in his seat as if he were once again looking for the right words. "The official line, as of this moment, is that Professor Ortega had an accident."

"And what if your marvellous pathologists decide otherwise?"

"In that case" – Feijoo waved his hand vaguely – "you will be considered no more suspicious than any of the other people who knew the deceased. You can imagine the list of candidates . . ."

"That's the problem. I can't imagine anyone wanting to kill Álvaro."

"Well, that's your opinion. I see it differently: suspended students, jealous colleagues, angry lovers, intransigent husbands . . ." He ticked these off with one thumb on the fingers of the other hand and stopped when he ran out of fingers. "No. The thing is, and I'm sure you'll be the first to recognise this, your testimony will be extremely valuable."

"Why? Are you putting me in the category of angry lovers?"

"I wouldn't go that far, Señorita. But you did see him only hours before he, or someone else, fractured his skull."

"Hours?" This time Julia really was disconcerted. "When did he die?"

"Three days ago. On Wednesday, between two in the afternoon and midnight."

"That's impossible. There must be a mistake."

"A mistake?" the Inspector's expression had changed. He was looking at Julia with open distrust now. "Certainly not. That's the pathologist's verdict."

"There *must* be a mistake. An error of twenty-four hours."

"Why do you think that?"

"Because on Thursday evening, the day after my conversation with him, he sent me some documents I'd asked him for."

"What sort of documents?"

"About the history of the painting I'm working on."

"Did you receive them by post?"

"No, by messenger, that same evening."

"Do you remember the name of the company?"

"Yes. Urbexpress. And it was on Thursday, around eight o'clock. How do you explain that?"

The policeman emitted a sceptical sigh from beneath his moustache.

"I can't. By Thursday evening, Álvaro Ortega had already been dead for twenty-four hours, so he couldn't have sent them. Someone . . ."

81

– Feijoo paused briefly to allow Julia time to take in the idea – "someone must have done it for him."

"Someone? But who?"

"The person who killed him, if he was killed that is. The hypothetical murderer. Or murderess." He looked at Julia with some curiosity. "I don't know why we always immediately assume it was a man who committed a crime." Then he had an idea. "Was there a letter or a note accompanying the documents supposedly sent by Álvaro Ortega?"

"No, just the documents. But it is logical to think he sent them. I'm sure there's been some mistake."

"There's no mistake. He died on Wednesday, and you received the documents on Thursday. Unless the company delayed delivery . . ."

"No, I'm sure about that. It was dated the same day."

"Was there anyone with you that evening?"

"Two people: Menchu Roch and César Ortiz de Pozas."

The policeman seemed genuinely surprised.

"Don César? The antiques dealer on Calle del Prado?"

"The same. Do you know him?"

Feijoo hesitated before nodding. He knew him, he said, through his work. But he did not know that Julia and César were friends.

"Well, now you know."

"Yes, now I know."

The policeman tapped his pen on the desk, suddenly uncomfortable, and with good reason. As Julia learned the following day from César, Inspector Casimiro Feijoo was far from being a model police officer. His professional relationship with the world of art and antiques allowed him to supplement his police salary at the end of each month. From time to time, when a consignment of stolen goods was recovered, some of it would disappear through the back door. Certain trusted intermediaries participated in these operations and gave him a percentage of the profits. And, it being a small world, César was one of them.

"Anyway," said Julia, who still knew nothing of Feijoo's background, "I suppose having two witnesses proves nothing. I could have sent the documents to myself."

Feijoo merely nodded, but his eyes betrayed a greater degree of caution, as well as a new respect, which, as Julia understood later on, had a purely practical basis.

"The truth is," he said at last, "this whole business seems very odd."

Julia was staring into space. From her point of view, it was no longer merely odd; it was beginning to take on a sinister edge.

"What I don't understand is who could possibly be interested in whether I got those documents or not."

Biting his lower lip again, Feijoo took a notebook from a drawer. His moustache appeared flaccid and preoccupied. He was obviously less than enthusiastic to find himself embroiled in this matter.

"That," he murmured, reluctantly making his first notes, "that, Señorita, is another very good question."

She stood on the steps of the police station, aware that the uniformed man guarding the door was watching her with some curiosity. Beyond the trees on the other side of the Paseo, the neoclassical façade of the Prado Museum was lit by powerful spotlights concealed in the nearby gardens, amongst the stone benches, statues and fountains. It was raining, a barely perceptible drizzle, but enough for the lights of the cars and the relentless green-to-amber-to-red of the traffic lights to be reflected on the asphalt surface of the road.

Julia turned up the collar of her leather jacket and walked along listening to her footsteps echoing in the empty doorways. There wasn't much traffic; only now and then did the headlights of a car illuminate her from behind, casting a long, narrow shadow that stretched out ahead of her and then shifted to one side, became shorter, faltering and fitful, as the noise of the car overtook her, leaving her shadow crushed and annihilated against the wall, whilst the car, reduced to two red dots and their mirror image on the wet asphalt, disappeared.

She stopped at a traffic light. Waiting for it to change to green, she searched the night for other greens and found them in the fleeting signs of taxis, in other winking traffic lights along the avenue, in the distant blue, green and yellow neon sign on the roof of a glass skyscraper whose topmost windows were still lit, where someone was cleaning or perhaps still working even at that late hour. The light changed to green and Julia crossed over and began looking for reds, easier to find at night in a big city. But the blue flash of a police car passing in the distance interposed itself, so far off that Julia couldn't hear the siren. Red car lights, green traffic lights, blue neon, blue flash . . . that, she thought, would be the range of colours you'd need to paint this strange landscape, the right palette to execute a painting she could entitle, ironically, *Nocturne*, to be exhibited at the Roch Gallery even though Menchu would doubtless have to have the title explained to her. Everything would have to be in appropriately sombre tones: black night, black shadows, black fear, black solitude.

Was she really afraid? In other circumstances, the question would have been a good topic for academic discussion, in the pleasant company of friends, in a warm, comfortable room, in front of a fire, with a bottle of wine. Fear as the unexpected factor, fear as the sudden, shattering discovery of a reality which, though only revealed at that precise moment, has always been there. Fear as the crushing end to ignorance or as the disruption of a state of grace. Fear as sin.

However, as she walked amongst the colours of the night, Julia was quite incapable of considering her present feeling an academic question. She had, of course, experienced other minor manifestations of the same thing. The speedometer needle pushing up beyond the limit, whilst the landscape glides rapidly by to left and right and the intermittent white line down the middle of the road looks like a swift succession of tracer bullets, as in war films, being swallowed up by the voracious belly of the car. Or the sense of emptiness, of bottomless blue depths when you dive off the deck of a boat into the deep sea and swim, feeling the water slip over your bare skin and knowing with unpleasant certainty that your feet are far from any kind of terra firma. Even those intangible fears that form part of oneself during sleep and set up capricious duels between reason and the imagination, fears which a single act of will is almost always enough to reduce to memory or forgetting merely by opening one's eyes to the familiar shadows of the bedroom.

But this new fear, which Julia had only just discovered, was different. New, unfamiliar, unknown until now, touched by the shadow of Evil with a capital E, the initial letter of everything that lies at the root of suffering and pain. The kind of Evil that was capable of turning on a shower tap over the face of a murdered man. The Evil that can only be painted in the dark colours of black night, black shadows and black solitude. Evil with a capital E, Fear with a capital F and Murder with a capital M.

Murder. It was only a hypothesis, she said to herself as she watched her shadow. People do slip in bathtubs, fall downstairs, jump traffic lights and die. Pathologists and policemen were sometimes too clever by half; it was an occupational hazard. Yes, that was all true. But it was also true that someone had sent her Álvaro's report when he'd already been dead for twenty-four hours. That was no hypothesis; the documents were in her apartment, in a drawer. And that *was* real.

She shuddered and looked behind to see if anyone was following her. And although she didn't really expect to, she did in fact see someone. It was hard to ascertain whether he was following her or not, but someone was walking along some fifty yards behind her, a silhouette illuminated at intervals as it crossed the pools of light that spilled through the leaves of the trees and blazed on the museum façade.

Julia looked straight ahead as she continued on her way. Every muscle was filled by the imperious need to run, the feeling she had as a child when she crossed the dark entryway of her building, before bounding up the stairs and ringing the doorbell. But the logic of a mind accustomed to normality intervened. Running away simply because someone was walking in the same direction, fifty yards behind her, was not only unreasonable, but ridiculous. Even so, she thought, walking calmly along a badly lit street with, at her back, a potential assassin, however hypothetical, was not just unreasonable; it was suicidal. The debate between these ideas occupied her mind for a few moments, during which she relegated fear to a reasonable place in the middle distance and decided that her imagination might be playing tricks on her. She breathed deeply, looking back out of the corner of her eye and making fun of her own fear. And at that moment she saw that the distance between her and the stranger had grown a few yards shorter. She felt afraid again. Perhaps Álvaro really had been murdered, and it was the person who killed him who had later sent her the documents on the painting. That would establish a link between *The Game of Chess*, Álvaro, Julia and the presumed or possible killer. You're up to your neck in this, she said to herself, and could no longer find any reason to laugh at her own disquiet. She looked about for someone she could approach for help, or simply link arms with and ask him to take her away from there. She also considered going back to the police station, but that presented a problem: the stranger stood in her way. A taxi, perhaps.

But no little green for-hire sign, no green of hope, appeared. She noticed how dry her mouth was, so dry her tongue kept sticking to the roof of her mouth. Keep calm, she told herself, keep calm, you idiot, or you really will be in trouble. And she did manage to regain some composure, just enough to start running.

The shriek of a trumpet, heart-rending and solitary. Miles Davis on the record player and the room in darkness apart from the light shed by a small table lamp placed on the floor to illuminate the painting. The ticking of the clock on the wall and the slight metallic click each time the pendulum reached its farthest point to the right. Next to the sofa, on the carpet, was a smoking ashtray and a glass containing the last drops of ice and vodka, and on the sofa sat Julia, hugging her knees, a lock of hair falling over her face. She was looking straight ahead, her pupils dilated, staring at the painting without really seeing it, focused on some imaginary point beyond the surface, between the surface and the landscape glimpsed in the background, halfway between the two chess players and the lady sitting next to the window.

She'd lost all notion of time, feeling the music drift slowly through her brain with the fumes from the vodka and conscious of the warmth of her bare thighs and knees against her arms. Sometimes a trumpet note would rise up amongst the shadows and she would move her head slowly from side to side, following the rhythm. Ah, trumpet, I love you. Tonight, you are my one companion, faint and nostalgic as the sadness seeping from my soul. The sound floated through the dark room and through that other brightly lit room, where the two chess players continued their game, and out through Julia's window, open to the gleam of the lamps lighting the street below. Down to where someone, in the shadow cast by a tree or a doorway, was perhaps gazing up, listening to the music emanating from that other window too, the one painted in the picture, out into the landscape of soft greens and ochres in which you could just see, painted with the finest of brushes, the minuscule grey spire of a distant belfry.

V

The Mystery of the Black Lady

I knew by now that I had visited
his evil homeland, but I did not know
the rules of combat.   *G. Kasparov*

IN RESPECTFUL SILENCE and perfect stillness, Octavio, Lucinda
and Scaramouche were watching them with painted porcelain eyes from
behind the glass of their case. César's velvet jacket was dappled with
harlequin diamonds of coloured light from the stained-glass window.
Julia had never seen her friend so silent and so still, so like one of the
statues, in bronze, terracotta and marble, scattered here and there
amongst the paintings, glass figures and tapestries in his shop. In a way,
both César and Julia seemed to blend with the décor, which was more
suited to the motley scenery of a baroque farce than to the real world
in which they spent most of their lives. César looked especially distinguished – a dark red silk cravat at his neck, a long ivory cigarette holder
between his fingers – and he had assumed, in the multicoloured light,
a particularly classical, almost Goethian pose, his legs crossed, one hand
resting with studied negligence over the hand holding his cigarette, his
hair white and silky in the halo of red, blue and golden light pouring
through the window. Julia was wearing a black blouse with a lace collar,
and her Venetian profile was reflected in a large mirror along with
jumbled ranks of mahogany furniture and mother-of-pearl chests,
Gobelin tapestries and canvases, twisted columns supporting chipped
Gothic carvings and the blank, resigned face of a naked bronze gladiator, his weapons beside him, raising himself up on one elbow while he
awaited the verdict, the thumbs up or thumbs down, of some invisible,
omnipotent emperor.

87

"I'm frightened," Julia said, and César responded with a gesture that was half-solicitous, half-impotent, a small sign of magnanimous and futile solidarity, of a love conscious of its limitations, the kind of elegant, expressive gesture an eighteenth-century courtier might make to a lady whom he worships at the precise moment that he sees, at the end of the street along which both are being carried in a funeral cart, the shadow of the guillotine.

"Are you sure you're not exaggerating, my dear? Or being a bit premature? No one has yet proved that Álvaro didn't just slip in the bath."

"What about the documents?"

"That, I must admit, I can't explain."

Julia put her head to one side, and her hair brushed her shoulder. Her mind was full of disquieting images.

"This morning when I woke up I prayed that it was all just a dreadful mistake."

"Perhaps it is," said César. "As far as I know, it's only in films that policemen and pathologists are honourable and infallible. In fact, I believe they're not that even in films any more."

He gave a sour, reluctant smile. Julia was looking at him without really listening to what he was saying.

"Álvaro, murdered . . . Can you believe it?"

"Don't torment yourself, Princess. That's just some far-fetched hypothesis the police have come up with. Besides, you shouldn't think about him so much. It's over; he's gone. He left a long time ago."

"Not like this he didn't."

"It doesn't make any difference how it happened. He's gone and that's that."

"It's just so horrible."

"I know. But you gain nothing by going over it in your mind."

"No? Álvaro dies, the police interrogate me, I think someone interested in my work on *The Game of Chess* may be following me . . . and you wonder why I keep going over it again and again. What else can I do?"

"It's very simple, my dear. If it's really getting to you, you can give the painting back to Menchu. If you believe Álvaro's death wasn't an accident, then go away somewhere. We could spend two or three weeks in Paris; I've got loads to do there. The important thing is to go away until it's all over."

"But what's going on?"

"I don't know, and that's the worst of it . . . not having the slightest idea what's happening, I mean. Like you, I wouldn't be so worried about what happened to Álvaro if it wasn't for this business with the documents." He looked at her, smiling awkwardly. "And I have to admit that I'm worried, because I'm not the hero type . . . It may be that one of us unwittingly opened some sort of Pandora's box."

"The painting," said Julia, shuddering. "The hidden inscription."

"I'm afraid so. That, it would seem, is where it all began."

She turned towards her reflection in the mirror and looked at herself long and hard, as if she didn't recognise the dark-haired young woman looking silently back at her from large, dark eyes, the pale skin over her cheekbones bearing the faint, shadowy traces of sleepless nights.

"Perhaps they want to kill me too, César."

His fingers gripped the ivory cigarette holder.

"Not while I'm alive," he said, revealing an aggressive determination behind the exquisite, ambivalent exterior. His voice had a sharp, almost feminine edge to it. "I might be frightened out of my wits, or even worse than that, but nobody's going to hurt you if I have anything to do with it."

Julia couldn't help but smile, touched by his concern.

"But what can we do?" she asked, after a silence.

César bowed his head, seriously considering the problem.

"It seems a bit premature to do anything. We still don't know if Álvaro's death was an accident or not."

"And the documents?"

"I'm sure that someone, somewhere, has the answer to that. The question, I suppose, is whether the person who sent them to you is the same one who was responsible for Álvaro's death, or if the two things are entirely unrelated."

"What if our worst suspicions are confirmed?"

It was a while before César replied.

"In that case, I see only two options, the classic ones, Princess: you either run away or you stay and face the music. If I was in that situation, I suppose I'd vote in favour of running away; not that that means much.

If I put my mind to it, I can be a terrible coward, as you know."

Julia clasped her hands behind her head.

"Would you really run away, without waiting to find out what it's all about?"

"Of course I would. Remember, it was curiosity that killed the cat."

"What about what you taught me when I was a child? Never leave a room without looking in all the drawers."

"Ah, yes. But then people weren't falling over in bathtubs."

"Hypocrite. Deep down you're dying to know what this is all about."

César looked reproachful.

"To say that I'm *dying* to do so, my dear, is in the worst possible taste, given the circumstances. Dying is exactly what I don't want to do, now that I'm nearly an old man and have all these adorable young men to comfort me in my old age. And I don't want you to die either."

"What if I decide to go ahead and find out what's really behind this business with the picture?"

César pursed his lips and let his gaze drift as if he'd never even considered the possibility.

"Why would you do that? Give me one good reason."

"For Álvaro's sake."

"That's not enough reason for me. I know you well enough to know that Álvaro wasn't important any more. Besides, according to what you've told me, he wasn't entirely honest with you about the matter."

"All right then, I'd do it for my own sake." Julia crossed her arms defiantly. "After all, it is my painting."

"Listen, I thought you were afraid. That's what you said before."

"I still am. I'm truly terrified."

"I understand," said César, resting his chin on his clasped hands, on one of which gleamed the topaz ring. "In practice," he added, after a brief pause for reflection, "it's like a treasure hunt. Isn't that what you're trying to say? Just like the old days, when you were a stubborn little girl."

"Just like the old days."

"How awful! You mean, you and me?"

"You and me."

"You're forgetting Muñoz. We've enlisted him now."

"You're right. Of course, Muñoz, you and me."

César frowned, but there was an amused gleam in his eyes.

"We'd better teach him the pirates' song then. I doubt very much if he knows it."

"I shouldn't think so."

"We're mad, my girl." César was looking hard at Julia. "You do know that, don't you."

"So?"

"This isn't a game, my dear. Not this time."

She held his gaze, unperturbed. She really was very beautiful with that gleam of resolve that the mirror reflected in her dark eyes.

"So?" she repeated in a low voice.

César shook his head indulgently. Then he got up, and the diamonds of coloured light slid down his back to the floor and spread themselves at Julia's feet. He went to the corner where his office was and for some minutes fiddled about in the safe built into the wall, concealed behind an old tapestry of little value, a bad copy of *The Lady and the Unicorn*. When he came back, he was carrying a bundle in his hands.

"Here, Princess, this is for you. A present."

"A present?"

"That's what I said. Happy unbirthday."

Surprised, Julia removed the plastic wrapping and the oily cloth and weighed in her hand a small pistol of chromium-plated metal with a mother-of-pearl handle.

"It's an antique derringer, so you won't need a licence," César explained. "But it's as good as new, and it takes .45-calibre bullets. It's not at all bulky, so you can carry it around in your pocket. If anyone approaches you or comes snooping round your building in the next few days," he said, looking at her fixedly, without the least trace of humour in his weary eyes, "I'd be most grateful if you would pick up this little thing and blow his head off. Remember? As if it was Captain Hook himself."

Julia had three phone calls within half an hour of getting home. The first was from Menchu, who'd read the news in the papers and was worried. According to her, no one had suggested it might have been anything other than an accident. Julia realised that her friend cared nothing about Álvaro's death, what concerned her were possible complications affecting her agreement with Belmonte.

The second call surprised her. It was an invitation from Paco Montegrifo to have dinner that night to talk about business. Julia accepted, and they arranged to meet at nine at Sabatini's. After hanging up, she remained thoughtful for a while, searching for some reason for his sudden interest. If it had to do with the Van Huys, the correct thing would have been for him to talk to Menchu, or to meet them both. She'd said as much during the conversation, but Montegrifo made it quite clear that it was something of interest to her alone.

She sat down in front of the painting to continue her work of removing the old varnish. Just as she was applying the first dabs of solvent with the cotton wool the phone rang for the third time.

She tugged at the cable to pull the phone, which was on the floor, towards her and picked up the receiver. For the next fifteen or twenty seconds she heard absolutely nothing, despite the vain "Hello"s she uttered with growing exasperation. Intimidated, she kept quiet, holding her breath, for a few seconds longer, and then hung up, as a feeling of dark, irrational panic washed over her like an unexpected wave. She looked at the phone, sitting on the carpet as if it were a poisonous beast, black and shining, and she shuddered involuntarily, knocking over the bottle of turpentine with her elbow.

This call did nothing to calm her spirits. So when the doorbell rang, she remained quite still, staring at the closed door until the third ring forced her to pull herself together. Several times since leaving the antiques shop that morning, Julia had smiled wryly whenever she imagined herself making the movement she now made. But she felt not the slightest desire to laugh when she stopped before going to open the door, long enough to take the small derringer out of her bag, cock it and slip it into her pocket. No one was going to leave her to soak in a bathtub.

Muñoz shook the rain off his coat and stood awkwardly in the hallway. The rain had plastered his hair to his skull and was still dripping down his forehead and off the tip of his nose. In his pocket, wrapped in a bag from one of the big stores, he was carrying a chess set.

"Have you solved it?" asked Julia as soon as she'd closed the door.

Muñoz hung his head, half-apologetic and half-timid. He was clearly still uncomfortable in someone else's, especially Julia's, apartment.

"Not yet," he said, looking apologetically at the little pool of water forming at his feet. "I've just got out of work and we arranged yesterday to meet here now." He took two steps and stopped, as if wondering whether to remove his raincoat. He did so when Julia reached out a hand to take it, and he followed her through to the studio.

"What's the problem?" she asked.

"There's none in principle." As before, Muñoz showed no curiosity when he looked around the studio. He seemed instead to be searching for some hint about how to behave. "It's just a question of investing thought and time. And all I do is think about it."

He was standing in the middle of the room with the chess set in his hands. Julia didn't need to follow the direction of his gaze to know what he was looking at. His expression had changed, switching from elusive to fascinated intensity, like a hypnotist surprised by his own eyes in the mirror.

Muñoz left the chess set on the table and went nearer to the painting, focusing only on the part depicting the chessboard and the chess pieces. He leaned closer to look much more intensely than he had the previous day. And Julia realised that he was not exaggerating in the least when he said, "All I do is think about it." He was a man intent on resolving something more than just her problem.

He studied the painting for a long time before turning to Julia.

"This morning I reconstructed the two previous moves," he said, without a trace of boastfulness. "Then I ran into a problem. Something to do with the unusual position of the pawns." He pointed to the chess pieces in the picture. "We're not dealing with a conventional game here."

Julia was disappointed. When she'd opened the door and seen Muñoz standing there, she'd almost believed that the answer was within reach. Naturally, Muñoz had no idea of the urgency of the matter, nor of the implications the story now had. But she was not the person to explain it to him, at least not yet.

"The other moves don't matter," she said. "We just have to find out who took the white knight."

Muñoz shook his head.

"I'm spending all the time I can on it." He hesitated, as if his next remark were almost a confidence. "I've got the moves in my head, and I play them backwards and forwards." He paused again and curved his lips into a pained, distant half-smile. "But there's something odd about this game."

"It's not only the game," she said. "The thing is, César and I saw it as the central part of the painting, because we couldn't see anything else." Julia reflected on what she'd just said. "But it may be that the rest of the painting simply complements the game."

Muñoz nodded slightly, and Julia had the impression that he took for ever to do so. Those slow movements, as if he spent much more time on them than was strictly necessary, seemed to be an extension of his mode of reasoning.

"You're wrong to say that you see nothing else. You see everything, although you may not be able to interpret it." Muñoz didn't budge from where he was; he merely indicated the painting with a movement of his chin. "I think it comes down to points of view. What we have here are different levels, which are contained within each other: the painting contains a floor that is a chessboard which, in turn, contains people. Those people are sitting at a chessboard that contains chess pieces. The whole thing is contained in that round mirror to the left. And to complicate things further, another level can be added: ours, where we stand to contemplate the scene or the successive scenes. And beyond that there's the level on which the painter imagined us, the spectators of his work."

He'd spoken without passion, an absent look on his face, as if he were reciting a monotonous description whose importance he considered to be, at best, relative and over which he lingered only to please others. Dazed, Julia gave a low whistle.

"It's odd you should see it like that."

Impassive, Muñoz again shook his head, without taking his eyes off the painting.

"I don't know why you find it odd. I see a chess game. Not just one game, but several, which are all basically the same one."

"That's too complex for me."

"Not at all. At the moment, we're operating on a level from which we can obtain a lot of information: the level of the chess game. Once that's resolved, we can apply any conclusions we reach to the rest of the painting. It's simply a question of logic, of mathematical logic."

"I never thought mathematics would have anything to do with this."

"It has to do with everything. Any imaginable world, like this picture, for example, is governed by the same rules as the real world."

"Even chess?"

"Especially chess. But a real chess player's thoughts move on a different plane from those of the amateur. His logic doesn't allow him to see possible but inappropriate moves, because he discounts them automatically. The same way a talented mathematician never studies the false pathways to the theorem he's seeking, whereas that's exactly what less gifted people have to do, plodding forwards from error to error."

"Don't you ever make mistakes?"

Muñoz slowly shifted his eyes from the painting to Julia. The suggestion of a smile hovering on his lips was utterly without humour.

"Not in chess."

"How do you know?"

"When you play, you're confronted by an infinite number of possible situations. Sometimes they can be resolved by using simple rules and sometimes you need other rules in order to decide which of the simple rules you should apply. Or completely unfamiliar situations arise and you've got to imagine new rules that either include or discount the previous ones. The only time you make mistakes is in choosing one rule over another, when you're deciding which option to take. And I only make a move after I've discounted all the rules that don't apply."

"I find such confidence astonishing."

"I don't know why. That's precisely why you chose me."

The doorbell rang, announcing the arrival of César with a dripping umbrella and sodden shoes, cursing the season and the rain.

"I hate the autumn, my dear, I really do. Season of mists and all that rubbish." He sighed and shook Muñoz's hand. "After a certain age, some seasons seem horribly like a parody of oneself. Can I pour myself a drink? Silly me, of course I can."

He served himself a large measure of gin, ice and lemon, and a few minutes later joined them, just as Muñoz was setting out his chess set.

"Although I haven't got as far as the move involving the white

95

knight," he explained, "I think you'll be interested to know what progress I've made so far." With the small wooden pieces, he reconstructed the positions depicted in the painting. Julia noticed that he did so from memory, without looking at the Van Huys or at the sketch he'd made the night before, which he now took out of his pocket and placed to one side on the table. "If you like, I can explain the reverse reasoning process I've followed so far."

"Retrograde analysis," said César, sipping his drink.

"That's right," said Muñoz. "And we'll use the same system of notation that I explained yesterday." He leaned towards Julia with the

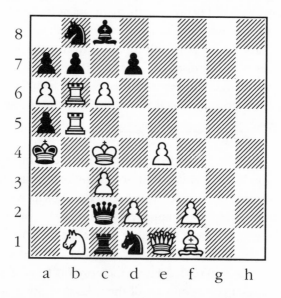

sketch in his hand, indicating to her the situation on the board.

"According to the way the pieces are distributed," Muñoz went on, "and bearing in mind that Black has just moved, the first thing to find out is which of the black pieces made that last move." He pointed at the painting with a pencil, then at the sketch and finally at the situation reproduced on the real board. "The easiest way to do that is to discount the black pieces that could not have been moved because they're blocked or because of the particular position they're in. It's clear that none of the three black pawns, on a7, b7 or d7 could have moved, because they're all in the position they occupied at the start of the game. The fourth and last pawn, on a5, couldn't have moved either, because it's between a white pawn and its own black king. We can also discount the black bishop on c8, still in its initial position, because the bishop moves diagonally and both of his two possible diagonal paths are blocked by the black pawns that have not as yet been moved. As for the black knight on b8, that wasn't moved either, because it could only have got there from a6, c6 or d7 and those three squares are already occupied by other pieces. Do you understand?"

"Perfectly," said Julia, who was leaning over the board following his explanation. "That means that six out of the ten pieces could not have moved."

"More than six. The black rook on c1 couldn't move, since it only moves in a straight line and its three surrounding squares are all blocked. So none of those seven black pieces could have made the last move. And we can also discount the black knight on d1."

"Why?" asked César. "It could have come from squares b2 or e3."

"No, it couldn't. On either of those squares, that knight would have had the white king on c4 in check; in retrograde chess that's what we might call an imaginary check. And no knight, or any other chess piece for that matter, with a king in check is going to abandon that position voluntarily; that's simply impossible. Instead of withdrawing, it would capture the enemy king, thus ending the game. Since such a situation is impossible, we can deduce that the knight on d1 could not have moved either."

"That," said Julia, who had kept her eyes glued to the board, "reduces the possibilities to two pieces then, doesn't it?" She put a finger on each of them. "The king and the queen."

"Right. That last move could have been made only by the king or the queen." Muñoz studied the board and gestured in the direction of the black king, without actually touching it. "First, let's analyse the position of the king, which can move one square in any direction. That means he could have arrived at his present position on a4 from b4, b3 or a3 . . . in theory."

"Even I can see what you mean about b4 and b3," remarked César. "No king can be on a square next to another king. Isn't that right?"

"Right. On b4 the black king would have been in check to the white rook, king and pawn. And on b3, he'd have been in check to rook and king. Both of which are impossible positions."

"Couldn't he have come from below, from a3?"

"No, never. It would then be in check to the white knight on b1, which, given its position, is clearly not a recent arrival, but must have got there several moves ago." Muñoz looked at them both. "So it's another case of imaginary check showing us that it wasn't the king that moved."

"Therefore the last move," said Julia, "was made by the black queen."

The chess player looked noncommittal.

"That, in principle, is what we must assume," he said. "In terms of pure logic, once we've eliminated the impossible, what remains, however improbable or difficult it may seem, must be right. Moreover, in this case we can prove it."

Julia looked at him with new respect.

"This is incredible. Like something out of a detective novel."

César pursed his lips.

"I'm afraid, my dear, that's exactly what it is." He looked at Muñoz. "Go on, Holmes," he added with a friendly smile. "We're on tenterhooks."

One corner of Muñoz's mouth twitched humourlessly, a mere polite reflex action. It was clear that all his attention was taken up by the chessboard. His eyes seemed even more deeply sunk in their sockets and there was a feverish gleam in them: the expression of someone absorbed in contemplating imaginary, abstract spaces that only he could see.

"Now," he suggested, "let's look at the possible moves the queen could have made, positioned as she is on square c2. I don't know if you're aware, Julia, that the queen is the most powerful piece in the game. She can move across any number of squares, in any direction, imitating the movement of all the other pieces except for the knight. As we can see, the black queen could have come from four possible squares: a2, b2, b3 and d3. By now, you can see for yourself why she couldn't have come from b3, right?"

"I think so." Julia frowned in concentration. "I presume she would never have left a position where she had the white king in check."

"Exactly. Another case of imaginary check, which discounts b3 as her possible origin. And what about d3? Do you think the queen could

98

have come from there, for example, to avoid the threat from the white bishop on f1?"

Julia considered that possibility for a while. At last her face lit up.

"No, she couldn't, for the same reason as before," she exclaimed, surprised to have reached that conclusion on her own. "On d3, the black queen would have been holding the white king in another one of those imaginary checks, right? That's why she couldn't have come from there." She turned to César. "Isn't this fantastic? I've never played chess in my life."

Muñoz was pointing his pencil at square a2 now.

"It would be another case of imaginary check if the queen had been here, and so we can discount that square too."

"Then it could obviously only have come from b2," said César.

"That's possible."

"What do you mean 'possible'?" César was confused and intrigued at the same time. "It looks obvious to me."

"In chess," replied Muñoz, "very few things can be termed 'obvious'. Look at the white pieces along line b. What would have happened if the queen had been on b2?"

César stroked his chin thoughtfully.

"She would have been under threat by the white rook on b5. That's probably why she moved to c2, to escape the rook."

"Not bad," conceded Muñoz. "But that's only a possibility. Anyway, the reason she moved isn't important to us at the moment. Do you remember what I told you before? Once the impossible has been eliminated, what remains must, of necessity, be right. To sum up, (a) Black has just moved, (b) nine of the ten black pieces on the board could not have moved, (c) the only piece that could have moved was the queen, (d) three of the four hypothetical moves by the queen are impossible. Therefore, the black queen made the only possible move: it moved from b2 to c2, *perhaps* fleeing from the threat of the white rooks on b5 and b6. Is that clear?"

"Very," said Julia, and César agreed.

"That means," Muñoz went on, "that we've managed to take the first step in this reverse chess game that we're playing. The subsequent position, or rather, the previous position, since we're working backwards, would be this."

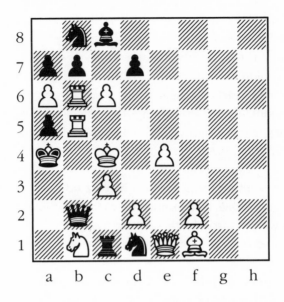

"Do you see? The black queen is still on b2, before its move to c2. So now we have to find out what move White made that obliged the queen to do that."

"It must have been the white rook," said César. "The one on b5. The treacherous devil could have come from any square along row 5."

"Possibly," replied Muñoz. "But that doesn't entirely justify the queen's flight."

César blinked, surprised.

"Why not?" His eyes went from the board to Muñoz and back to the board again. "The queen was obviously fleeing the threat from the rook. You yourself said so a moment ago."

"I said that *perhaps* she was fleeing from the white rooks, but at no point did I say that it was the white rook on b5 that caused the queen to flee."

"I'm lost," confessed César.

"Look closely at the board. It doesn't matter what the white rook now on b5 did, because the other white rook, the one on b6, *would already have been holding the black queen in check*. Do you see?"

César studied the game again, this time for quite a long time.

"I still don't get it," he said at last, demoralised. He'd drained his gin and lemon to the last drop, while, at his side, Julia was smoking cigarette after cigarette. "If it wasn't the white rook that moved to b5, then all your reasoning collapses. Wherever the piece was, that nasty queen had to move first, because she was in check before . . ."

"No," said Muñoz. "Not necessarily. The rook could, for example, have taken another black piece on b5."

Encouraged by that possibility, César and Julia studied the game with new heart. After a few more minutes, César glanced up and gave Muñoz a respectful glance.

"That's right," he said, astonished. "Don't you see, Julia? A black piece on b5 was protecting the queen from the threat posed by the white rook on b6. When that black piece was captured by the white rook, the queen was under direct threat." He looked back at Muñoz for confirmation. "That must be it. There's no other possibility." He looked at the board again, doubtfully. "There isn't, is there?"

"I don't know," Muñoz replied honestly and, when she heard that, Julia uttered a desperate "Good God!"

"You've just formulated a hypothesis," he continued, "and when you do that, you always run the risk of distorting the facts to fit the theory, instead of finding a theory that fits the facts."

"What then?"

"Well, that's just it. So far we can only consider as a hypothesis the idea that the white rook took a black piece on b5. We still have to ascertain if there are any other variants and, if so, discount all the impossible ones." The gleam in his eyes grew dim. He seemed more tired and grey as he sketched an indefinable gesture in the air, which was part justification and part uncertainty. The confidence he'd displayed in explaining the moves had disappeared; now he seemed shy and awkward. "That's what I meant," he said, avoiding Julia's eyes, "when I told you I'd run into problems."

"What's the next step then?" asked Julia.

Muñoz regarded the pieces with a resigned air.

"A long, painstaking examination of the six black pieces that are off the board. I'll try to find out how and where each one was taken."

"That could take days," said Julia.

"Or minutes, it depends. Sometimes, luck or intuition lend a hand." He gave a long look at the board and then at the Van Huys. "But there's one thing I'm sure of," he said after a moment's thought.

"Whoever painted this picture or thought up the problem, had a very peculiar way of playing chess."

"How would you describe him?" asked Julia.

"Who?"

"The absent player. The one you just mentioned."

Muñoz looked first at the carpet and then at the painting. There was something like admiration in his eyes, Julia thought. Perhaps the instinctive respect a chess player always feels for a master.

"I don't know," he said in a low voice, as if unwilling to be pinned down. "Whoever it was, he was very devious. All the best players are, but this one had something else: a particular talent for laying false trails, for setting all kinds of traps. And he enjoyed doing it."

"Is that possible?" asked César. "Can you really judge the character of a person by the way he behaves when playing?"

"I think you can," replied Muñoz.

"In that case, what do you think of the person who thought up this game, bearing in mind that he did so in the fifteenth century?"

"I'd say" – Muñoz was looking at the painting, absorbed – "I'd say there was something 'diabolical' about the way he played chess."

VI

Of Chessboards and Mirrors

And where is the end?
You'll find that out when you get there.
Ballad of the Old Man of Leningrad

SINCE THEY WERE DOUBLE-PARKED, Menchu had moved over into the driver's seat by the time Julia got back to the car. Julia opened the door of the small Fiat and dropped into the seat.

"What did they say?" Menchu asked.

Julia didn't reply at first; she still had too many things to think about. Staring into the traffic flowing down the street, she took a cigarette out of her handbag, put it to her lips and pressed the automatic lighter in the dashboard.

"There were two policemen here yesterday," she said at last, "asking the same questions as me." When the lighter clicked out, she held it to her cigarette. "According to the man in charge, the envelope was delivered to them that Thursday, first thing in the afternoon."

Menchu's hands were gripping the wheel hard, her knuckles white amongst the glittering rings.

"Who delivered it?"

Julia slowly exhaled.

"According to him, it was a woman."

"A woman?"

"That's what he said."

"What woman?"

"Middle-aged, well-dressed, blonde. Wearing a raincoat and sunglasses." She turned to her friend. "It could have been you."

"That's not funny."

"No, I know it isn't." Julia let out a long sigh. "But it could have been anyone. She didn't give her name or her address, she just gave Álvaro's details as sender. She asked for the fast delivery service. And that was it."

They joined the rest of the traffic. It looked like it was going to rain again and a few tiny drops were already spattering the windscreen. Menchu crunched the gears and wrinkled her nose with displeasure.

"You know, Agatha Christie could have made a blockbuster out of this."

Julia gave a humourless smile.

"Yes. But it has a real death in it." She imagined Álvaro naked and wet. If there was one thing worse than dying, she thought, it was dying grotesquely, with people coming to look at you.

"Poor devil," she said out loud.

They stopped at a pedestrian crossing. Menchu cast a glance at her friend. She was worried, she said, about Julia's being embroiled in such a situation. She too felt uneasy, so much so that she'd broken one of her golden rules and installed Max in her home until things were clearer. Julia should do the same.

"What, install Max in my apartment? No thanks. I'd rather go to rack and ruin on my own."

"Don't start that again. And don't be obtuse." The light changed to green, and Menchu shifted gear and accelerated. "You know perfectly well I didn't mean him. Besides, he's a sweetheart."

"A bloodsucker."

"Well, at least it isn't just my blood he sucks."

"Don't be vulgar."

"Oh, so now it's Sister Julia of the Holy Sacrament."

"And proud of it."

"Look. Maybe Max is what you say he is, but he's also so gorgeous that I get dizzy every time I look at him. The way Madame Butterfly felt about Lieutenant Pinkerton . . . in between coughing fits. Or was it Armand Duval?" She swore at a pedestrian crossing the road and, honking indignantly, skidded into a tiny space between a taxi and a bus belching fumes. "But, seriously, I don't think it's a good idea for you to be alone. What if there really is a murderer and he decides to get you?"

Julia shrugged irritably.

"What do you want me to do about it?"

"I don't know. Move in with someone else. I'll make the ultimate sacrifice, if you like. I'll send Max away and you can come and stay with me."

"What about the painting?"

"You can bring it with you and continue working on it at my place. I'll get in plenty of tinned food, coke, dirty videos and booze and we can hole up there, the two of us, like in *Fort Apache*, until we can get rid of the painting. Oh, and two other things. First, I've taken out extra insurance, just in case."

"What do you mean, just in case? The Van Huys is perfectly safe in my apartment, under lock and key. The security system cost me a fortune to install, remember? It's like Fort Knox, without the gold."

"You never know." It was starting to rain harder, and Menchu switched on the wipers. "The second thing is: don't say a word about all this to Don Manuel."

"Why not?"

"Are you mad? It's just what his little niece, Lola, needs in order to ruin this whole deal for me."

"So far no one has linked the painting with Álvaro."

"Heaven forbid. But the police aren't exactly tactful and they might have got in touch with my client. Or with his bitch of a niece. Oh, well. It's getting horribly complicated. I'm tempted to hand the whole problem over to Claymore's and just take my commission and run."

The rain created a procession of blurred grey images through the windows, so the car seemed surrounded by a strange, unreal landscape. Julia looked at her friend.

"By the way," she said, "I'm having supper with Montegrifo tonight."

"What!"

"You heard. He's got some business he wants to talk to me about."

"Business? He'll probably want to play mummies and daddies too."

"I'll phone and tell you all about it."

"I won't get a wink of sleep until you do. He's obviously guessed that something's going on. I'd stake the virginity of my next three reincarnations on it."

"I told you not to be vulgar."

"And don't you go betraying me. I'm your friend, remember. Your best friend."

"Trust me, and don't drive so fast."

"I'll stab you to death if you do. Like José in Mérimée's *Carmen*."

"OK. Look, you went through a red light just then. And since the car is mine, I'll have to pay any fines you get."

She glanced in the rear-view mirror and saw that another car, a blue Ford with smoked-glass windows, had jumped the light with them, but it soon disappeared off to the right. She seemed to remember seeing that same car parked – double-parked like them – on the other side of the street when she came out of the courier service. But it was difficult to say for sure, what with the traffic and the rain.

Paco Montegrifo was the sort of man who decides, as soon as he's old enough to make such decisions, that black socks are strictly for chauffeurs and waiters and opts instead for socks of only the darkest navy blue. He was dressed in a made-to-measure suit of dark and impeccable grey, a suit that could have walked straight off the pages of a high-fashion magazine for men. This perfect appearance was topped off by a shirt with a Windsor collar, a silk tie and, peeping discreetly out of his top pocket, a handkerchief. He got up from an armchair in the foyer to greet Julia.

"My word," he said as he shook her hand, his white teeth gleaming in agreeable contrast to his tanned skin, "you look absolutely gorgeous."

That introduction set the tone for the first part of the meal. And he'd expressed his unqualified admiration for the close-fitting black velvet dress Julia was wearing even before they'd sat down at the table reserved for them by the window with a panoramic night-time view of the Palacio Real. From then on, he deployed a repertoire of looks – which managed to be intense but never impertinent – and seductive smiles. After the aperitifs, and while the waiter was preparing the hors d'oeuvres, he began plying Julia with questions that prompted intelligent replies to which he listened with his chin resting on his clasped fingers, his lips slightly parted, and a gratifyingly absorbed expression, which at the same time permitted little gleams of light from the candle flames to sparkle on his perfect teeth.

The only reference he made to the Van Huys before dessert was his careful choice of a white Burgundy to accompany the fish. To art, he said, with a vague look of complicity, and that gave him the opportunity to launch into a brief discourse on French wines.

"Oddly enough," he explained, while waiters were still bustling round the table, "it seems to be something that changes as you get older. You start off as a staunch supporter of white or red Burgundy: the best companion until you're into your thirties. But then, though without renouncing Burgundy completely, it's time to move on to Bordeaux: a wine for adults, serious and even-tempered. Only in your forties can you bring yourself to pay out a fortune for a crate of Petrus or Château d'Yquem."

He tasted the wine, signalling his approval with a lift of his eyebrows, and Julia sat back and enjoyed the show, quite happy to play along with him. She even liked the supper and the banal conversation, concluding that, in different circumstances, Montegrifo would have been agreeable company, with his low voice, his tanned hands and the discreet smell of eau de cologne, fine leather and good tobacco that wafted about him, and despite his habit of stroking his right eyebrow with his index finger and snatching sly glances at his reflection in the window.

They continued to talk about everything but the painting. When she'd finished her slice of salmon à la Royale, he was still busy, using only a silver fork, with his sea bass Sabatini. A real gentleman, he explained, with a smile that emphasised that the remark was not to be taken totally seriously, would never use a fish knife.

"But how do you remove the bones?" Julia asked.

The auctioneer held her gaze unflinchingly.

"I never go to restaurants where they serve fish with bones."

After dessert, and before coffee, which, like her, he ordered black and very strong, Montegrifo took out a silver cigarette case and carefully selected an English cigarette. Then he leaned towards her.

"I'd like you to come and work for me," he said in a low voice, as if afraid that someone in the Palacio Real might overhear.

Julia, who was raising one of her own untipped cigarettes to her lips, looked into his brown eyes as he held out his lighter to her.

"Why?" she asked, with apparent disinterest, as if he were talking about someone else.

"For several reasons." Montegrifo had placed the gold lighter on top of the cigarette case, aligning them carefully dead centre. "The main reason is because I've heard nothing but good things about you."

"I'm pleased to hear it."

"I'm being serious. As you can imagine, I've asked around. I know the work you've done for the Prado and for private galleries. Do you still work at the museum?"

"Yes, three days a week. I'm working on a recent acquisition at the moment, a Duccio di Buoninsegna."

"I've heard about the painting. A difficult job. I know they always give you the important commissions."

"Sometimes they do."

"Even at Claymore's we've had the honour of auctioning a couple of works that you've restored. That Madrazo in the Ochoa collection, for example. Your work on that meant we could up the auction price by a third. And there was another one, last spring. *Concierto* by López de Ayala, wasn't it?"

"It was *Woman Playing the Piano* by Rogelio Egusquiza."

"That's right, that's right, forgive me. *Woman Playing the Piano*, of course. It had been badly affected by damp, and you did a wonderful job on it." He smiled, and their hands almost touched as they dropped the ash of their respective cigarettes into the ashtray. "Are you happy with the way things are going? I mean, just working on whatever comes up." He flashed his teeth again. "As a freelance."

"I've no complaints," said Julia, studying her companion through the cigarette smoke. "My friends take care of me, they find me things. And besides, it means I'm independent."

Montegrifo looked at her intently.

"In everything?"

"In everything."

"You're a fortunate young woman then."

"Maybe I am. But I work hard too."

"Claymore's has a large number of projects requiring the expertise of someone like you. What do you think?"

"I don't see any harm in talking about it."

"Wonderful. We could have another, more formal chat in a few days' time."

"As you wish." Julia gave Montegrifo a long look. She felt unable to suppress the mocking smile on her lips. "Now you can talk to me about the Van Huys."

"I'm sorry?"

Julia stubbed out her cigarette and leaned slightly towards Montegrifo.

"The Van Huys," she repeated, carefully enunciating the words. "Unless, of course, you intend taking my hand in yours and telling me I'm the loveliest woman you've ever met, or something equally charming."

Montegrifo took a split second to recompose his smile but he did so with perfect aplomb.

"I'd love to, but I never say that until after coffee. Even if I may be thinking it," he explained. "It's a question of tactics."

"Let's talk about the Van Huys then."

"Let's." He looked at her for a long time, and she saw that, although his lips were smiling, his brown eyes were not; they held a glint of extreme caution. "I've heard certain rumours – you know how it is. It's a real gossip shop, this little world of ours, where everyone knows everyone else." He sighed, as if he disapproved of the world he'd just described. "I understand you've discovered something in the painting. According to what I've heard, it's something that could considerably increase its value."

Julia kept an absolutely straight face, aware that she would have to do more than that to deceive Montegrifo.

"And who's been telling you this nonsense?"

"A little bird." The auctioneer stroked his right eyebrow thoughtfully. "But that's the least of it. What matters is that your friend, Señorita Roch, intends to blackmail me in some way."

"I don't know what you're talking about."

"I'm sure you don't." Montegrifo's smile was undimmed. "Your friend wants to reduce Claymore's percentage of the commission and increase hers." He tried to look impartial. "The truth is that legally there's nothing to stop her doing that, since ours is only a verbal agreement. She can easily break it and go to our competitors in search of a better percentage."

"I'm glad to see you're so understanding about it."

109

"Naturally I am. But that doesn't mean I won't be looking out for the interests of my own company."

"I should hope not."

"I won't conceal from you the fact that I've already located the owner of the Van Huys; an elderly gentleman. Or, to be exact, I've been in touch with his niece and her husband. My intention, and I won't conceal this from you either, was to get the family to dispense with your friend as intermediary and deal directly with me. Do you understand?"

"Perfectly. You've been trying to put one over on Menchu."

"That's one way of putting it, yes. I suppose you could call it that." A shadow crossed his tanned forehead, giving a slightly pained expression to his features, the look of someone wrongly accused. "The unfortunate thing is that your friend, a very prudent woman, got the owner to sign an agreement, which invalidates any deal I might make. What do you think?"

"You have my deepest sympathy. Better luck next time."

"Thank you." Montegrifo lit another cigarette. "But it may be that all is not quite lost. You're a close friend of Señorita Roch. Perhaps she could be persuaded to come to some amicable agreement. If we all work together, we could make a fortune out of that painting, from which you, your friend, Claymore's and I would all profit. What do you think?"

"Very likely. But why tell me all this rather than talk to Menchu? It would have saved you a supper."

Montegrifo composed his features into an expression of genuine hurt.

"I like you, and I don't mean just as a restorer. I like you a lot, to be honest. You strike me as being a reasonable and intelligent woman, as well as being extremely attractive. I'd rather trust in your mediation than go directly to your friend, whom, I'm afraid, I consider a little frivolous."

"In other words," said Julia, "you want me to convince her."

"If you could, it would be" – the auctioneer hesitated, carefully seeking the right word – "marvellous."

"And what do I get out of it?"

"My company's gratitude, of course. Now and in the future. As regards any immediate advantage, I won't ask you how much you were hoping to earn for your work on the Van Huys, but I can guarantee you double that figure. As an advance on the two per cent of the final price *The Game of Chess* reaches at auction, of course. I'm also in a position to offer you a contract to head the restoration department at Claymore's here in Madrid. How would you feel about that?"

"It's very tempting. Are you really expecting to make that much on the painting?"

"There are already interested buyers in London and New York. With the right publicity, this could turn into the biggest event in the art world since Christie's auctioned Tutankhamun's treasures. Given the situation, as I'm sure you'll understand, your friend's wanting to go halves with us really is too much. All she's done is find a restorer and offer us the picture. We do everything else."

Julia considered what he'd said without the least show of surprise; what could and could not surprise her had changed a lot over the last few days. She looked at Montegrifo's right hand, which lay on the tablecloth very close to hers, and she tried to calculate how far it had progressed in the last five minutes. Far enough to call an end to the supper.

"I'll try," she said, picking up her handbag. "But I can't guarantee anything."

Montegrifo stroked one eyebrow.

"Do try." His brown eyes looked at her with liquid, velvety tenderness. "It will be to everyone's advantage; I'm sure you'll manage it."

There wasn't a trace of menace in his voice, only a tone of affectionate entreaty, so friendly, so perfect, it could almost have been sincere. He took Julia's hand and planted a gentle kiss on it, barely brushing it with his lips.

"I don't know if I've mentioned it before," he added in a low voice, "but you really are an extraordinarily beautiful woman."

She asked him to drop her near Stephan's and walked the rest of the way. After midnight the place opened its doors to a distinguished clientele whose level of distinction was regulated by the high prices and a rigorously applied admissions policy. Everyone who was anyone in the Madrid art world gathered there, from agents working for foreign auctioneers, who were just passing through on the lookout for a reredos or a private collection for sale, to gallery owners, researchers, impresarios, specialist journalists and fashionable painters.

She left her coat in the cloakroom and, after saying hello to a few acquaintances, walked to the sofa at the far end where César usually sat. And there he was, legs crossed, a glass in one hand, immersed in intimate conversation with a handsome, blond young man. Julia knew the special contempt César felt for clubs popular exclusively with homosexuals. He considered it a simple matter of good taste not to frequent the claustrophobic, exhibitionist, often aggressive atmosphere of such places, where, as he would explain with a mocking look on his face, it was hard, my dear, not to feel like some old queen mincing around at a stud farm. César was a lone hunter – ambiguity refined to its elegant essence – who was at ease in the world of heterosexuals, where he felt perfectly free to cultivate friendships and make conquests, usually of artistic young bloods whom he would guide towards a discovery of their true sensibility, which the divine young things did not, *a priori*, know. He enjoyed playing at being both Maecenas and Socrates to his exquisite boys. After suitable honeymoons that always had Venice, Marrakesh or Cairo as their backdrop, each affair would follow its natural and distinctive course. César's long and intense life had, Julia knew, been shaped by a succession of confusions, disappointments and betrayals, but also by fidelities which, in private moments, she'd heard him describe with great delicacy, in that ironic and somewhat distant tone in which, out of personal modesty, he tended to veil any expression of his intimate longings.

He smiled at her from afar. My favourite girl, his lips said, moving silently as, placing his glass on the table, he uncrossed his legs, stood, and held out his hands to her.

"How did the supper go, Princess? Ghastly, I imagine. Sabatini's isn't what it was." He pursed his lips and there was a malicious gleam in his blue eyes. "All those executives and parvenu bankers with their credit cards and restaurant accounts chargeable to their companies will be the ruin of everything. By the way, have you met Sergio?"

Julia *had* met Sergio and, as always with César's friends, she sensed the confusion he felt in her presence, unable quite to grasp the real nature of the ties that bound the antiquarian and that calmly beautiful young woman. She could tell at a glance that the relationship was not serious, at least not that night and not on Sergio's part. The young man, sensitive and intelligent, wasn't jealous. They'd met on other occasions. Julia's presence merely intimidated him.

"Montegrifo wanted to make me an offer."

"How kind of him." César seemed to be considering the matter seriously as they all sat down. "But allow me, like old Cicero, to ask: *Cui bono*? For whose benefit?"

"His, I suppose. In fact, he wanted to bribe me."

"Good for Montegrifo. And did you let yourself be bribed?" He touched Julia's mouth with the tips of his fingers. "No, don't tell me yet, my dear; allow me to savour that marvellous uncertainty just a little longer . . . I hope his offer was at least reasonable."

"It wasn't bad. He seemed to be including himself in it too."

César licked his lips with expectant glee.

"That's just like him, wanting to kill two birds with one stone. He always was very practical." César half-turned towards his blond companion, as if warning him not to listen to such worldly improprieties. Then he looked back at Julia with mischievous expectation, almost trembling with anticipatory pleasure. "And what did you say?"

"That I would think about it."

"Perfect. Never burn your boats. Do you hear that, Sergio, my dear? Never."

The young man gave Julia a sideways glance and took a long sip of his champagne cocktail. Quite innocently, Julia imagined him naked, in the half-light of César's bedroom, beautiful and silent as a marble statue, his blond hair fallen over his face, with what César termed, using a euphemism Julia believed he'd stolen from Cocteau, the golden sceptre, erect and ready to be tempered in the *antrum amoris* of his mature companion, or perhaps it would be the other way round, the mature man busy with the young man's *antrum*. Julia had never taken her friendship with César so far as to ask him for a detailed description of such matters, about which, nevertheless, she occasionally felt a slightly morbid curiosity. She looked quickly at César. He was immaculate and elegant in his dark suit, white linen shirt and blue silk cravat with the red polka dots, the hair behind his ears and at the back of his neck slightly waved, and Julia asked herself again what the special charm of the man was, a man capable, even at fifty, of seducing young men like Sergio. It must be the ironic gleam in his blue eyes, the elegance distilled through generations of fine breeding and the easy assumption of world-weary wisdom, tolerant and infinite, to which he never gave complete expression – he rarely took himself entirely seriously – but which was nonetheless there in every word he uttered.

"You must see his latest painting," César was saying, and it took Julia a moment to realise he meant Sergio. "It's really remarkable, my dear." His hand hovered over the young man's arm, almost but not quite touching it. "Light in its purest state, spilling out over the canvas. Absolutely beautiful."

Julia smiled, accepting César's opinion as a cast-iron guarantee. Sergio, simultaneously touched and embarrassed, half-closed his blond-lashed eyes, like a cat receiving a caress.

"Of course," César went on, "talent isn't enough in itself to make one's way in the world. You do understand that, don't you, young man? All the great art forms require a certain knowledge of the world, a deep experience of human relations. It's quite another matter with abstract activities, in which talent is of the essence and experience merely a complement. By that I mean music, mathematics . . . chess."

"Chess," said Julia. They looked at each other, and Sergio's eyes flicked anxiously from one to the other.

"Yes, chess." César leaned over to take a long drink from his glass. His pupils had shrunk, absorbed in the mystery they were contemplating. "Have you noticed how Muñoz looks at *The Game of Chess*?"

"Yes. He looks at it differently somehow."

"Exactly. Differently from the way you, or indeed I, could look at it. Muñoz sees things in the painting that other people don't."

Sergio, who was listening, frowned and deliberately brushed against César's shoulder; he appeared to be feeling left out. César looked at him benevolently.

"We're discussing things that are much too sinister for your ears, my dear." He slid his index finger across Julia's knuckles, lifted his hand slightly, as if hesitating over a choice between two desires, and placed that hand between Julia's, but directed his words to the young man. "Guard your innocence, my friend. Develop your talent and don't complicate your life."

He blew Sergio a kiss just as Menchu, all mink coat and legs, made her entrance with Max and demanded news of Montegrifo.

"The bastard," she said when Julia had finished telling her about it. "I'll talk to Don Manuel tomorrow. We must fight back."

Sergio drew back from the tide of words issuing from Menchu, who was rushing from Montegrifo to the Van Huys, from the Van Huys to assorted platitudes, and from a second to a third drink, which she held in an increasingly unsteady hand. Max was silently smoking by her side, with the poise of a dark, sleek stallion put out to stud. Wearing a distant smile, César sipped his gin-and-lemon and dried his lips on the handkerchief from his top jacket pocket. From time to time he blinked, as if returning from some far-off place, and distractedly stroked Julia's hand.

"There are two sorts of people in this business, darling," Menchu was saying to Sergio, "those who paint and those who pocket the money. And they're rarely the same ones." She sighed loudly, touched by the boy's youth. "And all you young, blond artists, sweetheart." She gave César a poisonous sideways glance. "So utterly delicious."

César felt obliged to make a reluctant return from his remote thoughts.

"Pay no heed, my young friend, to voices poisoning your golden spirit," he said in a slow, lugubrious voice, as if he were offering Sergio condolences rather than advice. "This woman speaks with forked tongue, as do all women." He looked at Julia, bent to kiss her hand, and swiftly recovered his composure. "Forgive me. As do *nearly* all women."

"Look who's talking." Menchu grimaced. "If it isn't our own private Sophocles. Or do I mean Seneca? I mean the one who used to touch up young men as he sipped his hemlock."

César leaned his head back and closed his eyes melodramatically.

"The path the artist must follow, and I'm talking to you, my young Alcibiades, or Patroclus, or perhaps even Sergio . . . the path involves dodging obstacle after obstacle until finally you're able to peer deep inside yourself. A difficult task if you have no Virgil by your side to guide you. Do you understand the subtle point I'm making, young man? Thus the artist at last comes to drink deep of the sweetest of pleasures. His life becomes one of pure creation and he no longer needs miserable external things. He is far, far above the rest of his despicable fellow men. And growth and maturity build their nests in him."

This was greeted by a certain amount of mocking applause. Sergio looked at them, smiling but disconcerted. Julia burst out laughing.

"Take no notice of him. I bet he stole that from someone else. He always was a crook."

César opened one eye.

"I'm a bored Socrates. And I indignantly deny your accusation that I steal other people's words."

"He's really quite witty, isn't he?" Menchu was talking to Max, who had been listening with furrowed brow, while she helped herself to one of his cigarettes. "Give me a light, *condottiere mio.*"

The epithet caught César's malicious ear.

"*Cave canem*, sturdy youth," he said to Max, and Julia was possibly the only other person present who knew that in Latin *canem* can be both masculine and feminine. "According to the history books, the people the *condottieri* really had to watch were those they served." He looked at Julia and made an ironic bow; drink was beginning to have its effect on him too. "Burckhardt," he explained.

"Don't worry, Max," said Menchu, although Max did not seem in the least upset. "See? It wasn't even his idea. He crowns himself with other people's bay leaves . . . or is it laurels?"

"You mean acanthus," said Julia, laughing.

César gave her a hurt look.

"*Et tu, Bruta?*" He turned to Sergio. "Do you understand the tragic nature of the matter, Patroclus?" After another long drink of gin-and-lemon, he looked dramatically about, as if searching for a friendly face. "I really don't know what you've got against other people's laurels, my dears. In truth," he added after thinking about it, "no laurels can be said to belong to just one person. I'm sorry to be the bearer of bad news, but pure creation simply doesn't exist. We are not, or, rather, you are not, since I am not a creator . . . Nor are you, Menchu, my sweet. Perhaps you, Max . . . Now don't look at me like that, my handsome *condottiere feroce.* Perhaps you are the only person here who truly does create something." He sketched a weary, elegant gesture, expressive of profound tedium, brought on perhaps by his own line of argument, his hand coming to rest, apparently by chance, close to Sergio's knee. "Picasso – and I regret having to mention that old fraud – is Monet, is Ingres, is Zurbarán, is Brueghel, is Pieter Van Huys . . . Even our friend

Muñoz, who doubtless at this very moment is bent over a chessboard somewhere, trying to exorcise his demons, at the same time freeing us from ours, is not himself, but Kasparov and Karpov. He's Fischer and Capablanca and Paul Morphy and that medieval master, Ruy López . . . Everything is merely a phase of the same history, or perhaps the same history constantly repeating itself; I'm not altogether sure about that. And you, my lovely Julia, have you ever stopped to think, when you're standing before our famous painting, just exactly where you are, whether inside it or outside? I'm sure you have, because I know you, Princess. And I know too that you haven't found an answer." He gave a short, humourless laugh and looked at them one by one. "In fact, my children, parishioners all, we make up a motley crew. We have the cheek to pursue secrets that, deep down, are nothing but the enigmas of our own lives." He raised his glass in a kind of toast addressed to no one in particular. "And that, when you think about it, is not without its risks. It's like smashing the mirror to find out what lies behind the mercury. Doesn't that, my friends, send a little shiver of fear down your spine?"

It was two in the morning by the time Julia got home. César and Sergio had walked her to her street door. They wanted to accompany her up the three flights to her apartment but she wouldn't let them and kissed each of them good-bye before going up the stairs. She walked up slowly, looking about anxiously. And when she took the keys from her pocket, her fingers brushed reassuringly against the cold metal of the gun.

As she turned the key in the lock, she thought with surprise that, despite everything, she was taking it calmly. She felt a pure, precise fear, which she could evaluate without recourse to any talent for abstraction, as César would have said, parodying Muñoz. But that fear did not provoke in her any humiliating feelings of torment or a desire to run away. On the contrary, it was percolated by an intense curiosity, in which there was a strong dash of personal pride and defiance. It was like a dangerous, exciting game, like killing pirates in Never-Never-Land.

Killing pirates. She'd grown familiar with death at an early age. Her first childhood memory was of her father lying utterly still, with his eyes closed, on the mattress in the bedroom, surrounded by dark, sad people talking in low voices, as if they were afraid to wake him. She was six at the time and that image, incomprehensible and solemn, remained for ever linked with that of her mother, all in black and less approachable than ever, whom, even then, she never saw shed a single tear; and with that of her mother's dry, imperious hand on hers as she forced Julia to plant a final kiss on the dead man's forehead. It was César, a César whom she remembered as much younger, who had picked her up in his arms and taken her away from there. Sitting on his knee, Julia had stared at the door behind which the undertakers' men were preparing the coffin.

"It doesn't look like him, César," she'd said, trying not to cry. You must never ever cry, her mother used to say. It was the only lesson she could recall having learned from her. "Papa doesn't look the same."

"Well, no. It isn't Papa any more," came the answer. "He's gone somewhere else."

"Where?"

"That doesn't matter now, Princess. But he won't be coming back."

"Never?"

"Never."

Julia gave a childish frown and remained thoughtful.

"I don't want to kiss him again. His skin is cold."

César had looked at her in silence for a while, then hugged her hard. Julia could remember the warmth of his embrace, the subtle smell of his skin and his clothes.

"Well, you can come and kiss *me* any time you like."

Julia could never remember the exact moment when she'd discovered that César was homosexual. Perhaps she came to the realisation little by little, from minor details, intuition. But one day, when she'd just turned twelve, she went into his shop after school and found César touching a young man's cheek. That was all; he just brushed the youth's cheek with his fingertips. The young man walked past Julia, smiled at her and left. César, who was lighting a cigarette, gave her a long look, then set to work winding the clocks.

Some days later, while she was playing with the Bustelli figurines, Julia formulated the question:

"César, do you like girls?"

He was sitting at his desk, going over his accounts. At first he seemed not to have heard. Only after some moments did he raise his head and let his blue eyes rest calmly on Julia's.

"The only girl I like is you, Princess."

"What about the others?"

"What others?"

That was the last either of them said about it. But that night, as she went to sleep, Julia had thought about César's words and felt happy. No one was going to take him away from her; there was no danger. He would never go far away from her, as her father had, to that place from which there is no return.

Then came the times of long tales told in the golden light of the antiques shop; César's youth, Paris and Rome all mixed up with history, art, books and adventures. And there were the shared myths and *Treasure Island* read chapter by chapter amongst the old chests and rusty weapons. The poor sentimental pirates who, on moonlit Caribbean nights, felt their stony hearts melt when they thought of their old mothers. Because pirates had mothers too, even such refined riffraff as Captain Hook, who revealed his true self in his vile behaviour, but who at the end of every month despatched a few doubloons of Spanish gold to ease the old age of the woman who gave him life. And between stories César would take a pair of old sabres from a trunk and show her how the filibusters used to fight – on guard and retreat, the aim is to scar, not to slit your opponent's throat – and the best way to throw a grappling iron. He'd get out the sextant and teach her how to navigate by the stars. There was the stiletto with the silver handle, made by Benvenuto Cellini, who, in addition to being a goldsmith, had killed the Constable of Bourbon with a shot from his harquebus at the time of the sack of Rome; and the terrible dagger of mercy, long and sinister, that the Black Prince's page used to pierce the helmets of the French knights fallen at Crécy . . .

The years passed, and Julia's character began to come to life. Now it was César's turn to be silent, while he listened to her confidences. First love at fourteen. First lover at seventeen. He listened without passing judgment. He would simply smile, just once, when she finished speaking.

Tonight Julia would have given anything to see that smile, a smile that instilled courage in her and at the same time made things seem less important, cutting them down to their real size in the great scheme of things and in the inevitable course of one's life. But César wasn't there, and she had to fend for herself. As he would have said, we can't always choose our companions or our fate.

She busied herself preparing a vodka-on-the-rocks and suddenly smiled in the dark as she stood in front of the Van Huys. She had the odd feeling that if anything bad was going to happen, it would happen to someone else. Nothing bad ever happened to the hero, she remembered as she drank her vodka and felt the ice clink against her teeth. Only other people died, secondary characters, like Álvaro. Still vivid in her memory were the hundreds of such adventures she had experienced and from which she had always emerged unscathed, praise God. How did that other expression go? God's teeth!

She looked at herself in the Venetian mirror, just a shadow amongst other shadows, the slightly paler smudge of her face, the vague profile, two large, dark eyes, Alice through the looking glass. She looked at herself in the Van Huys too, in the painted mirror reflecting another mirror, the Venetian one, reflection on reflection on reflection. And she felt the same dizziness she'd felt before. The thought occurred to her that at that time of night, mirrors and paintings and chessboards can play strange tricks on the imagination. Or perhaps it was just that concepts like time and space were, after all, becoming so relative as to be barely worth worrying about. She took another sip of her drink and again felt the ice clink against her teeth. She thought that if she stretched out her hand, she would be able to set the glass down on the table covered by green cloth, on the very spot where the hidden inscription lay, between Roger de Arras's unmoving hand and the chessboard.

She moved closer to the painting. Beatrice of Ostenburg was seated near the lancet window, her eyes lowered, absorbed in the book that lay in her lap. She reminded Julia of the virgins painted by the early Flemish masters: fair hair sleeked back, caught up beneath the almost transparent toque. White skin. Solemn and distant in that black dress, so different from the usual cloaks of crimson wool, the cloth of Flanders, more precious than silk or brocade. Black, Julia realised with sudden clarity, was the symbol of mourning, and the black widow's weeds in which the Duchess had been dressed by Pieter Van Huys, the genius who so loved symbols and paradoxes, were not for her husband, but for her murdered lover.

The oval of her face was delicate, perfect, and every nuance, every detail, reinforced the resemblance to Renaissance virgins. Not a virgin like the Italian women honoured by Giotto, who were maids and nursemaids, even mistresses, nor like the Frenchwomen who posed as virgins but were often mothers or queens, but a bourgeois virgin, the wife of a municipal representative or of a noble landowner ruling over undulating plains scattered with castles, mansions, streams and belfries like the one painted there in the landscape outside the window. This one looked rather haughty and impassive, serene and cold, the embodiment of that northern beauty *a la maniera ponentina* that enjoyed such success in the countries of the south, in Spain and Italy. And the blue eyes – at least it could be assumed they were blue – their gaze turned away from the onlooker, apparently intent on her book, were nonetheless alert and penetrating, like the eyes of all the Flemish women depicted by Van Huys, Van der Weyden and Van Eyck. Enigmatic eyes that never revealed what they were looking at or wanted to look at, what they were thinking or feeling.

Julia pushed back her hair and touched the surface of the painting with her fingers, tracing the outline of Roger de Arras' lips. In the golden light that surrounded the knight like an aura, the steel gorget almost had the gleam of highly polished metal. He was resting his chin on the thumb of his right hand, which was slightly tinged by the surrounding glow, and his gaze was fixed on the chessboard that symbolised both his life and his death. Judging by his profile, like a profile stamped on an ancient medal, Roger de Arras appeared unaware of the presence of the woman sitting reading behind him. But perhaps his thoughts were not of chess at all; perhaps they flew to that Beatrice of Burgundy at whom he did not look, out of pride, prudence or possibly merely out of respect for his master. In that case, only his thoughts were free to devote themselves to her. At that same moment, perhaps the lady's thoughts were unaware of the pages of the book she held in her hands and her eyes were contemplating, with no need actually to look in their direction, the knight's broad back, his calm, elegant features, the memory of his hands and his skin, or merely the echo of contained silence, the melancholy, impotent gaze she once aroused in his loving eyes.

The Venetian mirror and the painted mirror framed Julia in an imaginary space, blurring the boundaries between the two surfaces. The golden light wrapped itself about her too as, very slowly, almost resting one hand on the green cloth of the painted table and taking great care not to upset the chess pieces laid out on the board, she leaned towards Roger de Arras and kissed him gently on the cold corner of his mouth. And when she turned, she caught a gleam, the insigne of the Golden Fleece on the vermilion velvet doublet of the other player, Ferdinand Altenhoffen, the Duke of Ostenburg, whose eyes were staring at her, dark and unfathomable.

By the time the clock on the wall struck three, the ashtray was full of cigarette ends and her cup and the coffeepot stood almost empty among sundry books and papers. Julia sat back in her chair and stared up at the ceiling, trying to put her ideas in order. To banish the ghosts encircling her, she'd turned on all the lights, and the boundaries of reality were slowly returning, gradually fitting back again into time and space.

There were, she concluded, other, more practical, ways of asking the question; there was another point of view, doubtless the correct one, if Julia bore in mind that she was more of a grown-up Wendy than an Alice. In order to approach things from that angle, all she had to do was close her eyes and open them again, look at the Van Huys as she would at any other picture painted five centuries ago and then pick up pencil and paper. And that's what she did, after drinking down the last of the now cold coffee. At that time of night, she thought, not feeling in the least sleepy and more afraid of sliding down the slippery slope of unreason than of anything else, it would be no bad thing to set about reordering her ideas in the light of recent events. So she began to write:

I. Painting dated 1471. Game of chess. The mystery: What really happened between Ferdinand Altenhoffen, Beatrice of Burgundy and Roger de Arras? Who ordered the death of the knight? What has chess got to do with this? Why did Van Huys paint the picture? Why, after painting the inscription *Quis necavit equitem*, did he paint over it? Was he afraid they might murder him too?

II. I tell Menchu about my discovery. I go to Álvaro. He

already knows all about the painting; someone has consulted him about it. Who?

III. Álvaro is dead. Dead or murdered? Obvious link with the painting, or perhaps with my visit and my research. Is there something somebody doesn't want me to know? Did Álvaro find out something important I don't know about?

IV. An unknown person (possibly the murderer or murderess) sends me the documents compiled by Álvaro. What was it that Álvaro knew that other people believe to be dangerous? What does that other person (or persons) want me to know, and what does he or she not want me to know?

V. A blonde woman takes the envelope to Urbexpress. Is she linked with Álvaro's death or merely an intermediary?

VI. Although we are both investigating the same thing, Álvaro dies and I (for the moment) do not. Does the person want to facilitate my work, or guide it towards something, and if so, what? Does it concern the painting's monetary value? Or my restoration work? Or the inscription? Or the chess problem? Or is it a matter of finding out or not finding out certain historical facts? What possible link can there be between someone in the twentieth century and someone in the fifteenth?

VII. Fundamental question (for the present): Would a hypothetical murderer benefit by an increase in the price of the painting at auction? Is there more to the painting than I have so far uncovered?

VIII. Is there a possibility that the whole thing has nothing to do with the value of the painting, but with the mystery of the chess game it depicts? Muñoz's work. Chess problem. How can that possibly cause a death five centuries later? That's not only ridiculous; it's stupid. (I think.)

IX. Am I in danger? Perhaps someone is waiting for me to find out a bit more. Perhaps I'm working for him without realising it. Perhaps I'm still alive because he still needs me.

She remembered something Muñoz had said the first time he saw the Van Huys, and she began to reconstruct it on paper. He'd talked about the different levels in the painting. An explanation of one of them might help her understand the whole thing.

123

Level 1. The scene within the painting. A floor in the form of a chessboard on which the people are placed.

Level 2. The people in the painting: Ferdinand, Beatrice, Roger.

Level 3. The chessboard on which two people are playing a game.

Level 4. The chess pieces that symbolise the three people.

Level 5. The mirror that reflects a reverse image of the game and of the people.

She looked at the result, drawing lines between the different levels and managing only to establish disquieting links. The fifth level contained the four previous levels, the first was linked to the third, the second to the fourth. It formed a strange figure turned in upon itself.

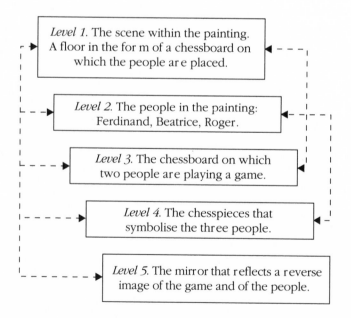

In fact, she said to herself while studying the curious diagram, it seemed a complete and utter waste of time. The only thing those links demonstrated was that the painter who created the picture had a brilliantly devious mind. It did nothing to help clear up Álvaro's death. Five hundred years after *The Game of Chess* had been painted, he had either slipped in the bath or someone else had made him slip. Whatever the result of all those arrows and boxes, neither Álvaro nor she could be contained in the Van Huys, whose creator could not possibly have foreseen their existence. Or could he? A disquieting question surfaced in her mind. Confronted by a collection of symbols, like that painting, was it up to the viewer to attribute meanings to it, or were the meanings there already, from the very moment of its creation?

She was still drawing arrows and boxes when the phone rang. She jumped, startled, looking at the phone on the carpet, unsure whether to answer it or not. Who could be phoning her at half past three in the morning? None of the possible replies to that question set her mind at rest, and the phone rang four more times before she moved. She went slowly over to it, suddenly feeling that it would be much worse if it were to stop ringing before she found out who was calling. She imagined herself spending the rest of the night curled up on the sofa, looking in terror at the phone, waiting for it to ring again. She hurled herself on it with something approaching fury.

"Hello?"

The sigh of relief that escaped her must have been audible to Muñoz, who interrupted his explanations to ask if she was all right. He was terribly sorry to phone her so late but he felt he was justified in waking her. He himself was quite excited about it; that's why he'd taken the liberty of calling. What? Yes, exactly. Five minutes ago the problem suddenly . . . Hello? Was she still there? He was telling her that it was now possible to ascertain, absolutely, which piece had taken the knight.

VII

Who Killed the Knight?

> The white pieces and the black pieces
> seemed to represent Manichean divisions
> between light and dark, good and evil,
> in the very spirit of man himself.
>
> *G. Kasparov*

"I COULDN'T SLEEP for thinking about it . . . I suddenly realised that what I was analysing was the only possible move." Muñoz put his pocket chess set down on the table, smoothed out his original sketch, now crumpled and heavily annotated, and placed it beside the set. "Even then, I couldn't believe it. It took me an hour to go over it all again, from start to finish."

They were in an all-night bar-cum-supermarket, sitting by a large window that gave them a clear view of the broad, empty avenue. There was hardly anyone there, a few actors from a nearby theatre and half a dozen night birds, male and female. A security guard in paramilitary uniform was standing next to the electronic security gates at the entrance, yawning and looking at his watch.

"Now," said the chess player, pointing first at the sketch and then at the small chessboard, "have a look at this. We managed to reconstruct the last move made by the black queen, from b2 to c2, but we didn't know what the previous move by White was that forced her to do that . . . Remember? When we looked at the threat from the two white rooks, we decided that the rook on b5 could have come from any of the squares on 5; but that couldn't explain why the black queen fled, since she would already be in check by another white rook, the one on b6. Maybe, we said, the rook had captured another black piece on b5. But which piece? That's where we got stuck."

"And which piece was it?" Julia was studying the board. Its geometrical black-and-white design was no longer unfamiliar, but one in which she could move about as if in familiar territory. "You said you could find out which it was by studying the pieces off the board."

"And that's what I did. I studied the pieces one by one, and I reached a surprising conclusion.

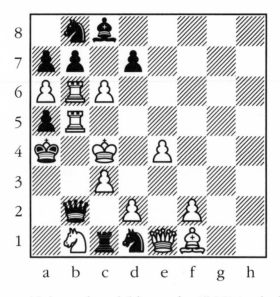

"Which piece could the rook on b5 have taken?" Muñoz looked at the board with his insomniac eyes, as if he genuinely didn't know the answer. "It wasn't a black knight, since both are still on the board. It wasn't the bishop either, because square b5 is white and the black bishop that can move along the white diagonal hasn't as yet left its original position. It's still there on c8 with its two escape routes blocked by pawns that have not yet come into play."

"Perhaps it was a black pawn," suggested Julia. Muñoz shook his head.

"That took me longer to reject as a possibility, because the position of the pawns is the most confusing thing about this game. But it couldn't have been any of the black pawns because the one on a5 came from c7. As you know, pawns capture by moving one square diagonally forwards, and that one presumably captured two white pieces on b6 and a5. As regards the other four black pawns, they were obviously miles away when they were captured. They would never have been anywhere near b5."

"Then it must have been the black rook. The white rook must have taken it on b5."

"No, that's impossible. Given the arrangement of the pieces around a8, it's obvious that the black rook was captured there, on its original square, without ever having moved. It was taken by a white knight – although in this case it doesn't much matter which piece it was captured by."

Julia looked up from the board, disoriented.

"I don't get it. That discounts all the black pieces. Which piece did the white rook take on b5 then?"

Muñoz gave a half-smile, which was not in the least bit smug; he merely seemed amused by Julia's question, or perhaps by the answer he was about to give.

"The fact is it didn't take any. Now don't look at me like that. Your painter Van Huys was also a master when it came to laying false trails. It turns out that nothing was captured on square b5." He crossed his arms and leaned over the small board, suddenly silent. Then he looked at Julia and laid one finger on the black queen. "If the last move by White wasn't a threat to the black queen by the rook, that means that a white piece must have moved and thus discovered the check by the white rook on the black queen. I mean a white piece that was either on square b4 or b3. Van Huys must have had a good laugh, knowing that anyone trying to solve the riddle was bound to be fooled by that ruse with the two rooks."

Julia nodded slowly. A few words from Muñoz were all it took to make a corner of the board, apparently static and unimportant, suddenly fill with infinite possibilities. There was something truly magical about his ability to guide other people through the complex black-and-white labyrinth to which he possessed the hidden keys. It was as if he were able to orient himself by means of a network of connections flowing beneath the board and giving rise to impossible, unsuspected combinations which he had only to mention for them to come to life, to become so obvious that you were amazed not to have noticed them before.

"I see," she said, after a few seconds. "That white piece was protecting the black queen from the rook. And, by moving away, it left the black queen in check."

"Exactly."

"And which piece was it?"

"Perhaps you can work it out for yourself."

"A white pawn?"

"No. One was captured on a5 or b6 and the other one is too far away. It couldn't have been any of the others either."

"Well, frankly, I haven't got a clue then."

"Have a good look at the board. I could have told you right at the start, but that would deprive you of a pleasure which, I suppose, you deserve. Take your time." He made a gesture encompassing the bar, the deserted street and the coffee cups on the table. "We're in no hurry."

Julia concentrated on the board. Soon, without taking her eyes off the game, she got out a cigarette, and a slight, indefinable smile appeared on her face.

"I think I may have got it," she said cautiously.

"OK, what do you think?"

"The bishop that can move diagonally along the white squares is on f1, intact, and hasn't had time to move there from his only possible original position, b3, since b4 is a black square." She looked at Muñoz for confirmation before going on. "I mean, it would have taken at least" – she counted with her finger on the board – "three moves to get from b3 to its present position. That means that it wasn't a move by the bishop that left the black queen in check to the rook. Am I right?"

"Absolutely. Go on."

"It couldn't have been the white queen, now on e1, that discovered the check either. Nor the white king. As for the white bishop that can move on the black squares, and is now off the board because it was taken, that could never have been on b3."

"Very good," said Muñoz. "Why not?"

"Because b3 is a white square. Anyway, if that bishop had moved diagonally along the black squares from b4, it would still be there on the board, and it isn't. I imagine it was taken some time before, during an earlier stage of the game."

"Correct. So what are we left with then?"

Julia looked at the board and a slight shiver crept down her spine and down her arms, as if someone had just run the blade of a knife over her skin. There was only one piece they had not yet mentioned.

"The only piece left is the knight," she said, swallowing hard, her voice involuntarily low. "The white knight."

Muñoz leaned towards her gravely.

"That's right, the white knight." He remained silent for a while, not looking at the board now but at Julia. "It was the white knight that moved from b4 to c2, thus uncovering the black queen and placing her in danger. And it was there, on c2, that the queen, in order both to protect herself from the rook and to gain another piece, took the knight." Muñoz fell silent again, checking that he hadn't left out anything of importance. Then the gleam in his eyes went out, as abruptly as if someone had switched it off. He looked away from Julia as he picked up the pieces in one hand and folded the board with the other, apparently signalling the end of his intervention in the matter.

"The black queen," she repeated in astonishment, feeling, indeed almost hearing, the rapid workings of her mind.

"Yes," said Muñoz with a shrug, "it was the black queen who took or killed the knight. Whatever that means."

"It means," she murmured, still stunned by the revelation, "that Ferdinand Altenhoffen was innocent." She gave a short laugh, reached out her hand to the sketch and placed her forefinger on square c2, the moat at the East Gate of the citadel of Ostenburg, where Roger de Arras had been murdered. "It means," she added, trembling, "that it was Beatrice of Burgundy who had the knight killed."

"Beatrice of Burgundy?"

Julia nodded. It seemed so clear to her now, so obvious, that she could kick herself for not having realised it before. Everything was there in the game *and* in the painting, crying out to be seen. Van Huys had recorded it all so carefully, down to the tiniest detail.

"Who else could it have been?" she said. "The black queen, of course: Beatrice, Duchess of Ostenburg." She hesitated, searching for the right word. "The bitch."

She saw it now with perfect clarity: the untidy studio smelling of oil and turpentine, the painter moving about amongst the shadows, by the light of tallow candles placed near the painting. He was mixing copper pigment with resin to produce a stable green that would withstand the passage of time. He applied it slowly, in successive layers, filling in the folds of the cloth on the table until he'd covered the inscription *Quis necavit equitem*, which he'd painted a few weeks before, in orpiment. It was done in beautiful Gothic lettering and it pained him to have to cover it, doubtless for ever. But Duke Ferdinand was right: "It's too obvious, Master Van Huys."

That must have been what happened, more or less, and no doubt the old man muttered to himself as he wielded the brush, applying slow swathes of green to the painting, whose colours, newly painted in oils, gleamed in the candlelight. Perhaps he rubbed his weary eyes and shook his head. His eyesight wasn't what it was, and hadn't been for some time now; the years did not pass unnoticed. They even gnawed away at his powers of concentration, which he needed for the only pleasure that could take his mind off painting during the enforced leisure of winter, when the days were short and there was little light to paint by. That pleasure was chess, a passion he shared with the much-mourned Master Roger, who, when alive, was his protector and his friend, and who, despite his status and position, never minded getting paint on his clothes when he visited the studio for a game amongst the oils, clays, brushes and half-finished paintings. He was quite unlike anyone else, as happy doing battle on the chessboard as he was indulging in long conversations about art, love and war, and about that strange idea of his, so often repeated, that now seemed like a terrible premonition: the idea of chess as a game for those who take an insolent pleasure in walking perilously close to the Devil's maw.

The painting was finished. When he was younger, Pieter Van Huys used to say a brief prayer as he applied the last brush stroke, thanking God for bringing a new work to a happy conclusion; but the years had closed his lips, just as it had made his eyes dry and his hair grey. He simply gave a short affirmative nod, placed the brush in an earthenware pot of solvent and wiped his fingers on his worn leather apron. Picking up a candlestick, he stepped back. God forgive him but it was impossible not to feel a sense of pride. *The Game of Chess* went far beyond the commission given him by his master, the Duke. Because it was all there: life, beauty, love, death, betrayal. The painting was a work of art that

131

would survive him and all the people represented in it. The old Flemish master felt in his heart the warm breath of immortality.

She saw Beatrice of Burgundy, Duchess of Ostenburg, sitting by the window, reading the *Poem of the Rose and the Knight*, a ray of sunlight falling obliquely over her shoulder, lighting up the illuminated pages. She saw Beatrice's hand, pale as ivory, the light glinting on the gold ring. She saw the hand tremble slightly, like a leaf on a tree in the gentlest of breezes. Perhaps she had been in love and was unhappy because her pride could not bear rejection by that man who had dared to deny her what even Lancelot had not denied Queen Guinevere. Perhaps the hired crossbowman was merely revenge for her despair after the death of an old passion, a final kiss and a cruel farewell. Clouds drifted over the countryside in the background, across the blue sky of Flanders, and the lady remained immersed in reading the book on her lap. No, that was impossible. Ferdinand Altenhoffen would never have paid homage to a betrayal, nor would Pieter Van Huys have poured all his art and skill into such a painting. Julia preferred to believe that Beatrice's eyes remained lowered because they hid a tear, that the black velvet was a symbol of mourning for her own heart, pierced by the same crossbow arrow that had whistled over the moat; a heart that had bowed to reasons of state, to the coded message from her cousin, Duke Charles of Burgundy: the many-folded sheet of parchment with its broken seal, which, dumb with grief, she had crumpled in her hands before burning it in the flame of a candle. A confidential message, delivered by secret agents. Intrigues and spider's webs woven about the duchy and its future, which was also Europe's future. The French faction and the Burgundy faction. A secret war between ministers, as pitiless as the bloodiest battle, with no heroes, only executioners who wore clothes trimmed with lace and whose chosen weapons were the dagger, poison and the crossbow. The voice of blood ties, the duty demanded by family, required nothing of her that could not be eased afterwards by a good confession. All that was needed was her presence, on a particular day and at a particular time, at the window of the tower above the East Gate, where every evening she sat to have her hair brushed by her maid, the window beneath which Roger de Arras walked alone each day at the same hour, meditating upon his impossible love and his regrets.

Yes, perhaps the lady in black kept her eyes lowered, fixed on the book in her lap, not because she was reading but because she was crying. But it might also have been because she dared not meet the painter's eye, which, after all, embodied the lucid gaze of Eternity and History.

She saw the unfortunate prince, Ferdinand Altenhoffen, besieged by winds from east and west, in a Europe that was changing much too fast for his taste. She saw him resigned and impotent, a prisoner of his own self and of his century, slapping at his silken breeches with his soft leather gloves, trembling with rage and grief, unable to punish the murderer of the only friend he had ever had in his life. She saw him leaning against a pillar in the room hung with tapestries and flags, recalling the years of their youth, their shared dreams, his admiration for the young nobleman who went off to war and returned scarred but glorious. His laughter, his calm, wise voice, his grave remarks, his graceful compliments to the court ladies, his prompt advice, the very sound and warmth of his friendship still echoed round the room. But he was no longer there. He had gone to some darker place.

And the worst thing, Master Van Huys, the worst, old friend, old painter, you who loved him almost as much as I did, the worst is that there is no room for vengeance. For she, like me and even he himself, was just the plaything of more powerful people, of those who, because they have the money and the might, can simply decide that the centuries will erase Ostenburg from the maps drawn up by the cartographers. There is no one person I can have beheaded upon my friend's tomb – and even if there was, I wouldn't do it. She alone knew and chose to remain silent. She killed him with her silence, letting him appear, as he did every evening – oh, yes, I too have my spies – near the moat at the East Gate, drawn by the silent siren song that drags all men to their fate, a fate that seems asleep or even blind until the day it opens its eyes and looks directly at us.

133

As you see, Master Van Huys, there is no possible vengeance. I put my faith in your hands and in your genius, and no one will ever pay you the price I will pay you for this painting. I want justice, even if it is only for me, even if it is only so that she knows that I know, and so that when we too are gone to ashes, like Roger de Arras, someone else other than God might also know it. So paint the picture, Master Van Huys, for God's sake, paint it. I want you to leave out nothing, and let it be your best, your most terrible work. Paint it, and then may the Devil, whom you once painted riding at his side, carry us off.

And finally, she saw the knight. Both his slashed tunic and his hose were the colour of amaranth; he wore a gold chain round his neck and a useless dagger hanging from his belt. He was walking through the twilight along the moat at the East Gate, alone, no page with him to interrupt his thoughts. She saw him raise his eyes to the lancet window and saw him smile. It was barely the suggestion of a smile, distant and melancholy, the sort of smile that speaks of memories, of past loves and dangers, and seems to have some inkling of its own fate. And perhaps Roger de Arras senses, on the other side of the crumbling battlements, from between whose stones gnarled bushes spring, the presence of the hidden crossbowman, who pulls the string of his bow taut and aims at his victim. Suddenly he understands that his whole life, the long road walked, the battles he fought, hoarse and sweating, in creaking armour, the women's bodies he has known, the thirty-eight years he carries on his back like a heavy burden, all will end here, in this precise place and at this precise moment, and that after he feels the blow there will be nothing more. He is filled by a profound sense of grief, because it seems to him unjust that he should die like this at twilight, pierced by an arrow like a wild boar. And he raises one delicate, beautiful hand, a manly hand, the kind of hand that immediately brings to mind the sword it must once have wielded, the reins it held, the skin it caressed, the quill it dipped into an inkwell before scratching words on parchment, he raises that hand by way of protest, though he knows it is in vain, for, amongst other things, he is not even sure to whom he should protest. He wants to shout out, but remembers the decorum he owes himself. So he reaches with his other hand for his dagger, thinking that at least with a steel blade in his hand, even if it is only that dagger, his death will be one more suited to a knight. He hears the thump of the crossbow and thinks fleetingly that he should move out of the path of the arrow, but he knows that an arrow moves faster than any man. He feels his soul slowly dissolving in a bitter lament for itself, whilst he searches desperately in his memory for a God to whom to offer up his repentance. And he discovers with surprise that he repents of nothing, although it is not clear either, as night closes in, that there is any God prepared to hear him. Then he feels the blow. He has suffered other blows, where now he bears the scars, but he knows that this will leave no scars. It does not even hurt, his soul seems simply to slip out of his mouth. Endless night falls, but before finally plunging into it, he understands that this time it will be for ever. And when Roger de Arras cries out, he can longer hear his own voice.

VIII

The Fourth Player

The chess pieces were merciless. They held
and absorbed him. There was horror in this,
but in this also was the sole harmony.
Because what else exists in the world besides chess?
Vladimir Nabokov

MUÑOZ HALF-SMILED, in that mechanical, distant way that seemed to commit him to nothing, not even to an attempt to inspire sympathy.

"So that's what it was all about," he said in a low voice, matching his step to Julia's.

"Yes." She was walking along with her head bent, absorbed in thought. Taking her hand out of the pocket of her leather jacket she brushed her hair from her face. "Now you know the whole story. You have every right to, I suppose. You've earned it."

He looked straight ahead, reflecting on that recently acquired right. "I see," he murmured.

They walked unhurriedly, side by side. It was cold. The narrower, more enclosed streets still lay in darkness and the light from the street lamps illuminated only segments of the wet asphalt, making it gleam like fresh varnish. Gradually the shadows grew less intense as a leaden dawn broke slowly at the far end of the avenue where the outlines of the buildings, silhouetted against the light, were shading from black into grey.

"Is there any particular reason," asked Muñoz, "why you've kept this part of the story from me until now?"

She looked at him out of the corner of her eye before replying. He seemed interested, in a vague way, but not offended. He was gazing absently at the empty street ahead of them, his hands in his raincoat pockets and his collar turned up.

"I thought you might prefer not to get involved."

"I see."

As they turned the corner they were greeted by a noisily churning refuse collector, and Muñoz helped her squeeze past the empty bins.

"What do you think you'll do now?" he asked.

"I don't know. Finish the restoration work, I suppose. And write a long report about its history. Thanks to you, I might even get to be a bit famous."

Muñoz was listening distractedly, as if his thoughts were elsewhere.

"What's happening with the police investigation?"

"Assuming there was a murderer, they'll find him eventually. They always do."

"Do you suspect anyone?"

Julia burst out laughing.

"Good heavens, no!" She frowned as she considered the possibility. "At least I hope not." She looked at Muñoz. "I imagine that investigating a crime that might not be a crime is very like what you did with the picture."

Muñoz's lips curved into a half-smile.

"It's all a question of logic, I suppose," he replied. "And that might be something that's common to both chess players and detectives." Julia couldn't tell if he was serious or only joking. "Apparently Sherlock Holmes played chess."

"Do you read detective novels?"

"No. Although the books I do read are somewhat like that."

"What for example?"

"Books on chess, of course. As well as books on mathematical puzzles, logic problems, things like that."

They crossed the deserted avenue. When they reached the opposite pavement, Julia gave her companion another furtive glance. He didn't look like a man of extraordinary intelligence, and she doubted that things had gone well for him in life. Walking along with his hands in his pockets, his rumpled shirt collar showing and his large ears protruding above his old raincoat, he looked exactly like what he was, an obscure office worker, whose only escape from mediocrity was what chess offered him, a world of combinations, problems and solutions. The oddest thing about him was the gleam in his eyes that was quite simply extinguished the moment he looked away from a chessboard, and his way of bowing his head as if he had a heavy weight on the back of his neck, tilting his head forwards, perhaps to allow the outside world to slip by without encroaching on him any more than was absolutely necessary. He reminded her a little of the pictures of prisoners of war she'd seen in old documentaries, trudging along with their heads down. He had the unmistakable air of someone defeated before the battle has even started, of someone who, when he opens his eyes each morning, awakens only to failure.

Yet there was something else. When Muñoz was explaining a move, following the twisted thread of the plot, there was in him a fleeting spark of something solid, even brilliant. As if, appearances to the contrary, there was in him the pulse of some extraordinary talent, logical, mathematical or whatever, that lent a certain assurance and undeniable authority to his words and gestures.

She realised that she knew nothing about him except that he played chess and was an accounts clerk. But it was too late now to get to know him better. His task was over and they would be unlikely to meet again.

"We've had an odd sort of relationship," she said.

"In chess terms, it's been a perfectly normal relationship," he replied. "Two people, you and me, brought together for the duration of a game." He smiled again in that diffuse way that meant nothing. "Call me if you ever want another game."

"You baffle me," she said spontaneously, "you really do."

He looked at her, surprised, not smiling any more.

"I don't understand."

"Neither do I." Julia hesitated slightly, unsure of her ground. "You seem to be two different people, so shy and withdrawn sometimes, with a kind of touching awkwardness. But as soon as anything to do with chess comes up, you're astonishingly assured."

"So?" His face inexpressive, Muñoz seemed to be waiting for the rest of her argument.

"Well, that's it really," she stammered, a bit embarrassed by her lack of discretion. "I suppose all this is slightly absurd at this hour of the morning. I'm sorry."

He had a prominent Adam's apple, visible above the unbuttoned neck of his shirt, and he was in need of a good shave. His head was tilted slightly to the left, as if he were considering what she'd just said. But he didn't seem in the least bewildered.

"I see," he said, and made a movement with his chin as if to indicate that he had understood, although Julia was unable to establish exactly what he had understood. He looked past her as if hoping that someone would approach, bringing a forgotten word. And then he did something that Julia would always remember with astonishment. Right there, in half a dozen phrases, uttered as dispassionately and coldly as if he were discussing some third party, he summarised his whole life for her, or that's what Julia thought he did, without pauses or inflections and with the same precision he employed when commenting on moves in a chess game. And only when he'd finished and fallen silent did the vague smile return to his lips, in apparent gentle mockery of himself, of the man he had just described and for whom, deep down, he felt neither compassion nor disdain, only a kind of disillusioned, sympathetic solidarity.

Julia just stood there, not knowing what to say, asking herself how the devil a man of so few words had been capable of explaining everything about himself so clearly. She had learned of a child who used to play chess in his head, staring up at his bedroom ceiling, whenever his father punished him for neglecting his studies; and about women capable of dissecting, with the meticulous skill of a watchmaker, the inner mechanisms that drive a man; and of the solitude that came in the wake of failure and the absence of hope. Julia had no time to take it in, and at the end, which was almost the beginning, she wasn't sure how much of it he'd actually told her and how much of it she'd imagined for herself, supposing that Muñoz had done anything more than just bow his head and smile like a weary gladiator, indifferent about the direction, up or down, of the thumb that would decide his fate. When he stopped talking – if, that is, he ever really spoke – and the grey light of dawn lit half his face, Julia knew with total clarity just what that small area of sixty-four black and white squares meant to this man: a miniature battlefield on which was played out the mystery of life itself, of success and failure, of the terrible, hidden forces that rule the fates of men.

She understood this, as well as the meaning of that smile that never quite settled on his lips. She slowly bowed her head, while he looked up at the sky and remarked how cold it was. She offered her pack of cigarettes; he accepted, and that was the first and almost the last time she saw Muñoz smoke. They walked on until they reached Julia's building. At that point it seemed that Muñoz would depart for good. He held out his hand to shake hers and say good-bye, but Julia had seen a small envelope, about the size of a visiting card, stuck in the little grid next to her bell. When she opened it and looked at the card it contained, she knew that Muñoz could not leave, not just yet, that a few other things, none of them good, would have to happen before they could let him do so.

"I don't like it," said César, and Julia noticed that the fingers holding his ivory cigarette holder were trembling slightly. "I really don't like the idea that there's some madman out there, playing at being the Phantom of the Opera."

As if those words were a signal, all the clocks in the shop started to chime, one after the other or simultaneously, in tones that varied from a gentle murmur to the grave bass of the heavy wall clocks. But the coincidence failed to make Julia smile. She looked at the Bustelli figure of Lucinda, absolutely still inside the glass case, and felt as fragile as it looked.

"I don't like it either. But I'm not sure we have any choice."

She looked away from the porcelain figure and across at the Regency table on which Muñoz had set out his pocket chess set, once again reproducing the positions of the pieces in Van Huys's chess game.

"If I ever get my hands on the swine . . ." César muttered, casting a distrustful eye at the card Muñoz was holding by one corner, as if it were a pawn he was not yet sure where to place. "It's beyond a joke."

"It's no joke," said Julia. "Have you forgotten about poor Álvaro?"

"Forgotten him?" César put the cigarette holder to his lips and blew out smoke in short, nervous puffs. "I wish I could!"

"And yet," said Muñoz, "it does make sense."

They looked at him. Muñoz, unaware of the effect of his words, remained leaning on the table over the chessboard, with the card between his fingers. He hadn't taken his raincoat off, and the light coming through the stained-glass window lent a blue tone to his unshaven chin and emphasised the dark circles under his weary eyes.

"My friend," said César, in a tone that was somewhere between polite incredulity and ironic respect, "I'm glad *you* can make some sense out of all this."

Muñoz shrugged, ignoring César's comment. He was clearly concentrating on the new problem, on the hieroglyphics on the small card:

$$Rb3? \ldots Pd7 - d5+$$

Muñoz looked at them for a moment longer, comparing them with the position of the pieces on the board.

"It seems that someone" – and with that word "someone" Julia shivered, as if, nearby, an invisible door had been opened – "is interested in the game of chess being played in the picture." He half-closed his eyes and nodded, as though in some obscure way he could intuit the motives of the mystery player. "Whoever he is, he knows the state of the game and knows too, or thinks he does, that we've successfully solved its secret by means of retrograde analysis. Because he proposes playing on, continuing the game from the current position of the pieces as they stand in the picture."

"You're joking," said César.

There was an uncomfortable silence, during which Muñoz glared at César.

"I never joke," he said at last, as if he'd been considering whether or not this was worth explaining. "And certainly not about chess." He flicked the card with his index finger. "That, I can assure you, is exactly what he's doing: continuing the game from the point where the painter left off. Look at the board."

"See," said Muñoz, pointing to the card. "That Rb3 means that White should move the rook currently on b5 to b3. I take the question mark to mean that he's suggesting we make this move. So we can deduce from that that we're playing White and our opponent is Black."

"How appropriate," remarked César. "Suitably sinister."

"I don't know whether it's sinister or not, but it's what he's doing. He's saying to us: 'I'm playing Black and I'm inviting you to move that rook to b3.' Do you understand? If we agree to play, we have to move as he suggests, although we could choose a better move. For example, we could take that black pawn on b7 with the white pawn on a6. Or

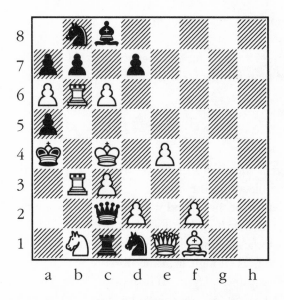

the white rook on b6 . . ." He stopped, absorbed, his mind plunged automatically into considering the various possibilities offered by the move he'd just mentioned. Then he blinked and returned with a visible effort to the real situation. "Our opponent takes it as read that we accept his challenge and that we've moved our white rook to b3, to protect our white king from a possible sideways move to the left by the black queen and, at the same time, with that rook backed up by the other rook and the white knight, threatening the black king on a4 with check. I deduce from this that he likes taking risks."

Julia, who was following Muñoz's explanations on the board, felt sure she detected in his words a hint of admiration for the unknown player.

"What makes you say that? How can you know what he does or doesn't like?"

Muñoz shrugged and bit his lower lip.

"I don't know," he replied after a brief hesitation. "Every person plays chess according to who he is. I believe I explained that once before." He placed the card on the table next to the chessboard. "Pd7 – d5+ means that Black now chooses to play by advancing the pawn he has on d7 to d5, thus threatening the white king with check. That little cross next to the figure means check. In other words, we're in danger, a danger we can avoid by taking their pawn with the white pawn on e4."

"Right," said César. "That's fine as far as the moves go. But I don't see what all this has to do with us. What relationship is there between those moves and reality?"

Muñoz looked noncommittal, as if they were asking too much of him. Julia noticed that his eyes again sought hers, only to slide away a second later.

"I don't know exactly what the relationship is. Perhaps it's a prompt, a warning. I have no way of knowing. But the next logical move by Black, after losing his pawn on d5, would be to put the white king in check again by moving the black knight on d1 to b2. In that case, there would be only one move White could make to avoid check whilst at the same time maintaining his siege of the black king, and that's to take the black knight with the white rook. The rook on b3 takes the knight on b2. Now look at the position on the board."

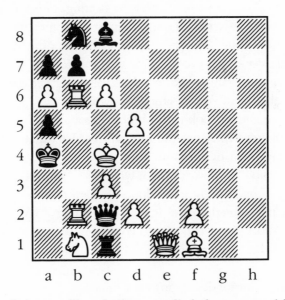

The three of them, still and silent, studied the new positions of the pieces. Julia would remark later that it was at that moment, long before she understood the meaning of the hieroglyphics, that she sensed the board had ceased to be simply a succession of black and white squares and become instead a real space depicting the course of her own life.

And, almost as if the board had become a mirror, she found something familiar about the piece of wood representing the white queen on e1, so pathetically vulnerable to the threatening proximity of the black chessmen.

But it was César who was the first to understand.

"My God," he said. And those words sounded so strange on his agnostic lips that Julia looked at him in alarm. He was staring fixedly at the board, the hand that held the cigarette holder apparently frozen a few inches from his mouth, as if the realisation had been so sudden it had paralysed a gesture only barely begun.

She looked again at the board, feeling the blood beating silently in her wrists and temples. She could see only the defenceless white queen, but she felt the danger like a dead weight on her back. She looked across at Muñoz, asking for help, and saw that he was shaking his head thoughtfully, the furrow between his eyebrows deepening. Then the vague smile she'd noticed on other occasions flickered briefly and humourlessly across his lips. It was the fleeting, rather resentful smile of someone who finds himself obliged, most reluctantly, to acknowledge his opponent's talent. And Julia felt an explosion of intense, dark fear, for she understood that even Muñoz was impressed.

"What's wrong?" she asked, barely recognising her own voice. The squares on the board swam before her eyes.

Exchanging a grave look with Muñoz, César said: "It means that the white rook's move threatens the black queen. Isn't that right?"

Muñoz gave a lift of his chin.

"Yes," he said. "The black queen, who before was safe, is now under threat." He stopped. Venturing along the path of non-chess interpretations was not something he felt at ease doing. "That might mean that the invisible player is trying to communicate something to us: his certainty that the mystery of the painting has been resolved. The black queen . . ."

"Beatrice of Burgundy," murmured Julia.

"Yes, Beatrice of Burgundy, the black queen, who, it would seem, has already killed once."

Muñoz's last words hung in the air without expectation of any response. César reached out a hand and, with the meticulousness of someone who desperately needs to do something in order to remain in touch with reality, delicately flicked the ash from his cigarette into an ashtray. Then he looked around as if he might find the answer to the questions they were all asking themselves in one of the pieces of furniture, one of the pictures or objects in his shop.

"You know, my dears, it really is an absolutely incredible coincidence. This just can't be real."

He raised his hands and let them fall in a gesture of impotence. Muñoz merely gave a gloomy shrug of his shoulders.

"This is no coincidence. Whoever planned this is a master."

"And what about the white queen?" asked Julia.

Muñoz moved one hand towards the board where it hovered over the piece in question, as if not daring to touch it. He pointed to the black rook on c1.

"There's a chance she could be taken," he said calmly.

"I see." Julia felt disappointed. She thought she would have felt more of a shock if someone had confirmed her fears out loud. "If I've understood you correctly, the fact of having discovered the picture's secret, that is, the lady in black's guilt, is reflected in that move of the rook to b2. And if the white queen is in danger, it's because she should have withdrawn to a safe place instead of wandering around making life difficult for herself. Is that the moral of the message, Señor Muñoz?"

"More or less."

"But it all happened five hundred years ago," protested César. "Only the mind of a madman . . ."

"Perhaps we're dealing with a madman," said Muñoz with equanimity. "But he played, or plays, damned fine chess."

"And he might have killed again," added Julia. "Now, a few days ago, in the twentieth century. He might have killed Álvaro."

César, scandalised, raised a hand, almost as if she'd made an improper remark.

"Now, hang on, Princess. We're getting ourselves tied in knots here. No murderer can survive for five hundred years. And a painting can't kill."

"That depends on how you look at it."

"Don't talk nonsense. And stop mixing things up. On the one hand there's a painting and a crime committed five hundred years ago . . . On the other hand there's Álvaro, dead."

145

"And the sending of the documents."

"But no one has yet proved that the person who sent the documents also killed Álvaro. It's even possible that the wretched man cracked his own head open in the bath." César raised three fingers. "Third, we have someone who wants to play chess. That's all. There's nothing that proves there's any link among the three things."

"The painting."

"That's not proof. It's just a hypothesis." César turned to Muñoz. "Isn't that right?"

Muñoz said nothing, refusing to take sides, and César gave him a resentful look. Julia pointed to the card on the table next to the chessboard.

"You want proof, do you?" she said suddenly, for she'd just realised what the card was. "Here's a direct link between Álvaro's death and the mystery player. I know these cards all too well. They're the ones Álvaro used in his work." She paused to take in the significance of her own words. "Whoever killed him could have taken a handful of his cards." The irrational sense of panic she'd felt only minutes before was already ebbing away, to be replaced by a more precise, more clearly defined feeling of apprehension. She said to herself, by way of explanation, that the fear of fear, of something dark and undefined, was not the same as the concrete fear of dying at the hands of a real human being. Perhaps the memory of Álvaro, of his death in broad daylight with the taps turned on, helped to clarify her mind and free her of superfluous fears. She had quite enough on her plate as it was.

She put a cigarette to her lips and lit it, hoping the men would interpret this as a display of self-control. She exhaled the first mouthful of smoke and swallowed. Her throat felt unpleasantly dry. She urgently needed a vodka. Or half a dozen vodkas. Or a strong, silent, good-looking man, with whom she could find oblivion in sex.

"Now what do we do?" she asked, mustering all the calm she could.

César was looking at Muñoz and Muñoz at Julia. She saw that Muñoz's eyes had become opaque again, devoid of life, as if he'd lost all interest until the next move claimed his attention.

"We wait," said Muñoz, indicating the board. "It's Black's turn to move."

*   *   *

146

Menchu was very excited, but not about the mystery chess player. As Julia told her what had happened, Menchu's eyes grew round, and if you listened carefully, you could have heard the clatter of a cash register ringing up totals. The fact is that, when it came to money, Menchu was always greedy. And at that moment, happily calculating future profits, she most definitely was greedy. And foolish, added Julia to herself, for Menchu had seemed almost unconcerned by the possible existence of a murderer with a taste for chess. True to her nature, her favourite method of dealing with problems was to act as if they didn't exist. Disinclined to give her attention to anything concrete for any length of time, perhaps bored with having Max in her home in his role as bodyguard – thus making other sexual encounters difficult – Menchu had decided to look at the whole business from a different angle. For her, it was now just an odd series of coincidences, or a strange, possibly harmless joke, thought up by someone with a peculiar sense of humour, whose motives were too ingenious for her to grasp. It was the most reassuring version of events, especially when there was so much to be gained along the way. As for Álvaro's death, hadn't Julia ever heard of judicial errors? Like the murder of Zola by that chap Dreyfus, or was it the other way round? And Lee Harvey Oswald and other such blunders. Besides, slipping in the bath could happen to anyone. Or almost anyone.

"As for the Van Huys, you'll see: we're going to make a pile of money out of it."

"And what do we do about Montegrifo?"

There were only a few customers in the gallery: a couple of elderly ladies chatting in front of a large classical seascape in oils, and a gentleman in dark clothes who was flipping through the portfolio of engravings. Menchu placed one hand on her hip as if it were the butt of a revolver and said in a low voice, theatrically fluttering her eyelashes:

"He'll fall into line, sweetie."

"You think so?"

"Take my word for it. Either he accepts or we go over to the enemy." She smiled, sure of herself. "With your track record and this whole fabulous story about the Duke of Ostenburg and his harpy of a wife, Sotheby's or Christie's would welcome us with open arms. And Paco Montegrifo is no fool." She seemed suddenly to remember something.

"By the way, we're meeting him for coffee this afternoon. Make yourself pretty."

"*We're* meeting him?"

"Yes, you and me. He phoned this morning, all sweetness and light. That bastard's got an amazing sixth sense when it comes to business."

"Look, don't drag me into this."

"I'm not. He insisted that you come too. I can't think what he sees in you, darling. You're nothing but skin and bones."

Menchu's high heels – the shoes were handmade, extremely expensive, but the heels were just half an inch higher than strictly necessary – left painful marks in the beige carpet. In her gallery, amongst all the indirect lighting, pale colours and large open spaces, there was a predominance of what César used to call "barbarian art". The dominant note was provided by acrylics and gouaches combined with collages, reliefs made from bits of sacking and rusty monkey wrenches or plastic tubing and steering wheels painted sky blue. Occasionally, relegated to some far corner, you would find a more conventional portrait or landscape, like an awkward guest, embarrassing but necessary to justify the supposedly catholic tastes of a snobbish hostess. Nevertheless, Menchu made money from the gallery; even César had (reluctantly) to recognise that, at the same time nostalgically recalling the days when every boardroom would have contained at least one highly respectable painting, suitably mellowed by age, set off by a heavy gilt wood frame, not the post-industrial nightmares so in keeping with the spirit – plastic money, plastic furniture, plastic art – of the new generations who now occupied those same offices, décor courtesy of the trendiest and most expensive interior designers.

As it happened, Menchu and Julia were at that moment contemplating a strange amalgam of reds and greens that answered to the portentous title *Feelings*. It had sprung only weeks before from the palette of Sergio, César's latest romantic folly, whom César had recommended, although he had at least had the decency to keep his eyes modestly averted when he mentioned the matter.

"I'll sell it somehow," said Menchu, with a resigned sigh, after they'd both looked at it for a while. "In fact, incredible though it may seem, everything gets sold in the end."

"César's very grateful," said Julia. "And so am I."

Menchu wrinkled her nose reprovingly.

"That's what bothers me. That you justify your friend the antiquarian's silly games. It's time the old queen started acting his age."

Julia brandished a threatening fist in front of her friend's nose.

"You leave him alone. You know that, as far as I'm concerned, César's sacred."

"Don't I just. For as long as I've known you, it's always been César this and César that." She looked irritably at Sergio's painting. "You ought to take your case to a psychoanalyst; he'd blow a fuse. I can just see you lying down together on the couch, giving him that old Freudian sob story. 'You see, doctor, I never wanted to screw my father, I just wanted to dance the waltz with César. He's gay, by the way, but he absolutely adores me.' A real can of worms, darling."

Julia looked at her friend without a trace of amusement on her face.

"That's utter rubbish. You know perfectly well the kind of relationship we have."

"Do I indeed?"

"Oh, go to hell. You know very well . . ." She stopped and snorted, irritated with herself. "This is absurd. Every time you talk about César, I end up trying to justify myself."

"Because, darling, there *is* something murky about your relationship. Remember, even when you were with Álvaro . . ."

"Now don't start in on Álvaro. You've got Max to worry about."

"At least Max gives me what I need . . . By the way, how's that chess player you're keeping so quiet about? I'm dying to get a look at him."

"Muñoz?" Julia couldn't help smiling. "You'd be very disappointed. He's not your type. Or mine, for that matter." She thought for a moment, since it had never occurred to her to consider how she would describe him. "He looks like an office worker in some old black-and-white film."

"But he solved the Van Huys problem for you." Menchu fluttered her eyelashes in mock admiration, in homage to the chess player. "He must have some talent."

"He can be brilliant, in his own way. But not always. One moment he seems very sure of himself, reasoning things out like a machine, the next he just switches off, right before your eyes. You find yourself noticing the frayed shirt collar, how ordinary he looks, and you think, I bet he's one of those men whose socks smell."

"Is he married?"

Julia shrugged. She was looking out at the street, beyond the window display consisting of a couple of pictures and some painted ceramics.

"I don't know. He's not much given to confidences." She considered what she'd just said and discovered that she hadn't even thought about it before. Muñoz had interested her less as a human being and more as a way of solving the problem. Only the day before, shortly before finding the card, when they were about to say good-bye, only then had she caught a glimpse of his life. "I imagine he's married. Or was . . . He seems damaged in the way that only we women can damage men."

"And what does César think of him?"

"He likes him. I imagine he finds him amusing as a character. He treats him with somewhat ironic courtesy. It's as if César feels a pang of jealousy every time Muñoz makes some particularly brilliant analysis of a move. But as soon as Muñoz takes his eyes off the board, he's ordinary again, and César feels better."

She stopped talking, puzzled. She'd just noticed, on the other side of the street, parked by the kerb, a car that seemed familiar. Where had she seen it before?

A bus passed, hiding the car from view. Menchu saw the look of anxiety on her face.

"Is something wrong?"

Disconcerted, Julia shook her head. The bus was followed by a delivery van that stopped at the light, making it impossible to see if the car was still there or not. But she had seen it. It was a Ford.

"What's up?"

Menchu looked uncomprehendingly from Julia to the street and back. Julia had a hollow feeling in the pit of her stomach, an uncomfortable feeling she'd come to know all too well over the last few days. She stood absolutely still, concentrating, as if her eyes, through sheer force of will, could be capable of seeing straight through the van to the car. A blue Ford.

She was afraid. She felt the fear creep gently through her body, felt it beating in her wrists and temples. After all, it was quite possible that someone was following her. That they'd been doing so for days, ever since Álvaro and she . . . A blue Ford with smoked-glass windows.

Then she remembered: it was double-parked opposite the offices of the messenger service and had jumped a red light behind them that rainy morning. Why shouldn't it be the same car?

"Julia." Menchu seemed genuinely worried now. "You've gone quite pale."

The van was still there, stopped at the light. Perhaps it was only coincidence. The world was full of blue cars with smoked-glass windows. She took a step towards the gallery door, putting her hand into the leather bag she wore slung over her shoulder. Álvaro in the bath, with the taps full on. She scrabbled in the bag, disregarding cigarettes, lighter, powder compact. She touched the butt of the derringer with a sort of jubilant sense of comfort, of exalted hatred for that car, hidden now, that represented the naked shadow of fear. Bastard, she thought, and the hand holding the weapon inside the bag began to tremble with a mixture of fear and rage. Whoever you are, you bastard, even if it is Black's turn to move, I'm going to show *you* how to play chess. And to Menchu's astonishment, Julia went out into the street, her jaw set, her eyes fixed on the van hiding the car. She walked between two other cars parked on the pavement just as the light was changing to green. She dodged a car bumper, ignored a horn sounding immediately behind her and, in her impatience for the van to pass, was on the point of taking out her derringer when, at last, in a cloud of diesel fumes, she reached the other side of the street just in time to see a blue Ford with smoked-glass windows and a numberplate ending in the letters TH disappearing into the traffic ahead.

IX

The Moat at the East Gate

ACHILLES: What happens if you then find a picture
inside the picture which you have already entered . . . ?
TORTOISE: Just what you would expect: you wind up
inside that picture-in-a-picture.
                                                    Douglas R. Hofstadter

"THAT REALLY WAS a bit over the top, my dear." César was winding
his spaghetti round his fork. "Can you imagine it? A worthy citizen
happens to stop at a traffic light, at the wheel of his car, which just
happens to be blue, when a pretty young woman transformed into a
basilisk appears, quite without warning, and tries to shoot him." He
turned to Muñoz, as if seeking the support of a voice of reason. "It's
enough to give anyone a nasty turn."

Muñoz stopped playing with the ball of bread he was rolling about
on the tablecloth, but he didn't look up.

"She didn't actually get that far. I mean, she didn't shoot him," he
said in a calm, low voice. "The car drove off first."

"Of course it did." César reached for his glass of rosé wine. "The
light had changed to green."

Julia dropped her knife and fork on her barely touched plate of
lasagne, making a noise that earned her a pained look from César over
the top of his wine glass.

"Listen, stupid. The car was already parked there before the light
turned red, when the street was empty . . . Right opposite the gallery."

"There are hundreds of cars like that." César put his glass gently down
on the table, dabbed at his lips and composed a sweet smile before
adding, in a voice lowered to a sibylline whisper, "It might well have
been one of your virtuous friend Menchu's admirers. Some heavily
muscled would-be pimp, hoping to oust Max."

Julia felt a profound sense of irritation. At moments of crisis César always slid into his vicious viper mode, aggressively slanderous. But she didn't want to give way to her ill humour by arguing with him, least of all in front of Muñoz.

"It might also," she replied, feigning patience after mentally counting to ten, "have been someone who, on seeing me come out of the gallery, decided to make himself scarce."

"It seems very unlikely to me, my dear. Really it does."

"You probably would have thought it unlikely that Álvaro would turn up with his neck broken, but he did."

César pursed his lips as if he found the allusion an unfortunate one, at the same time indicating Julia's plate.

"Your lasagne is getting cold."

"I don't give a damn about the lasagne. I want to know what you think. And I want the truth."

César looked at Muñoz, but the latter, utterly inscrutable, was still kneading his ball of bread. César rested his wrists symmetrically on either side of his plate, and stared at the vase containing two carnations, one white, one red, that adorned the centre of the tablecloth.

"Maybe you're right." He arched his eyebrows as if the sincerity demanded of him and the affection he felt for Julia were waging a hard-fought battle. "Is that what you wanted to hear? Well, there you are; I've said it." His blue eyes looked at her calmly, tenderly, stripped of the sardonic mask they'd worn before. "I must admit that the car's being there does worry me."

Julia threw him a furious look.

"May I know then why you've spent the last half-hour playing the fool?" She rapped impatiently on the table with her knuckles. "No, don't tell me. I know already. Daddy didn't want his little girl to worry, right? I'd be far better off with my head buried in the sand like an ostrich. Or like Menchu."

"You won't solve anything by hurling yourself on people who just happen to look suspicious. Besides, if your fears are justified, it might even be dangerous. Dangerous for you, I mean."

"I had your pistol."

"I hope I don't come to regret giving you that derringer. This isn't a game, you know. In real life, the baddies have pistols too. And they play chess."

As if Muñoz were doing a stereotyped impression of himself, the word "chess" seemed to breach his apparent apathy.

"After all," he murmured to no one in particular, "chess is essentially a combination of hostile impulses."

César and Julia looked at him in surprise. What he'd just said had nothing to do with the conversation. Muñoz was staring into space, as if he'd not quite returned from some long journey to remote places.

"My dear friend," said César, somewhat peeved by the interruption, "far be it from me to doubt the blazing truth of your words, but we'd be most grateful if you could be more explicit."

Muñoz continued rolling the ball of bread round and round in his fingers. Today he was wearing an old-fashioned blue jacket and a dark green tie, but the ends of his shirt collar, crumpled and none too clean, curled upwards as usual.

"I don't know what to say." He rubbed his chin with the back of his fingers. "I've spent the past few days going over and over it all." He hesitated for a moment, as if searching for the right words. "Thinking about our opponent."

"As has Julia, I imagine. As have I. We've all been thinking about the wretch."

"It's not the same thing. Calling him a 'wretch' presupposes a subjective judgment . . . That won't help us at all, and it could even divert our attention from what is really important. I try to think about him through the only perspective we have at the moment: his chess moves. I mean . . ." He passed a finger over the misted surface of his wine glass, from which he had drunk nothing, as if the gesture had made him lose the thread of his brief speech. "The style of play reflects the personality of the player. I think I've said that to you before."

Julia leaned towards him, interested.

"You mean that you've spent the past few days seriously studying the murderer's *personality*? Do you think you know him better now?"

The vague smile appeared, fleetingly, on Muñoz's lips. But Julia saw that he was deeply serious. He was never ironic.

"There are many different types of player." His eyes were looking at something in the distance, a familiar world beyond the walls of the restaurant. "Apart from style of play, each player has his own peculiarities, characteristics that distinguish him from other players: Steinitz used to hum Wagner while he played; Morphy never looked at his opponent until the final moment of the game . . . Others mutter in Latin or in some invented language. It's a way of dispelling tension, of keeping alert. A player might do it before or after moving a piece. Almost everyone does something."

"Do you?" asked Julia.

Muñoz hesitated, embarrassed.

"I suppose I do."

"And what's your peculiarity as a player?"

Muñoz looked at his fingers, still kneading the ball of bread.

"*We're off to Penjamo, one j no aitches.*"

"*We're off to Penjamo, one j no aitches?*"

"Yes."

"And what does '*We're off to Penjamo, one j no aitches*' mean?"

"It doesn't mean anything. It's just something I say under my breath, or else think, whenever I make an important move, just before I actually pick up the chess piece."

"But that's completely irrational."

"I know. But however irrational your gestures or idiosyncrasies are, they reflect your way of playing. They tell you about the character of your opponent too. When it comes to analysing a style or a player, any scrap of information is useful. Petrosian, for example, was a very defensive player, with a great instinct for danger. He would spend the whole game preparing defences against possible attacks, before his opponents had even thought up such attacks."

"He was probably paranoid," said Julia.

"You see how easy it is? The way someone plays might reveal egotism, aggression, megalomania. Just look at the case of Steinitz. When he was sixty, he was convinced he was in direct communication with God and that he could beat Him, even if he gave away a pawn and let Him play White."

"And our invisible player?" asked César, who was listening attentively, his glass halfway to his lips.

"He's good," replied Muñoz without hesitation, "and good players are often complicated people. A chess master develops a special intuitive feel for the right move and a sense of danger about the wrong move. It's a sort of instinct that you can't explain in words. When he looks at the chessboard he doesn't see something static; he sees a field crisscrossed by a multitude of magnetic forces, including the forces he himself contains." He looked at the ball of bread on the tablecloth for some seconds before moving it carefully to one side, as if it were a tiny pawn on an imaginary board. "He's aggressive and he enjoys taking risks. For example, the fact that he didn't use his queen to protect the king. The brilliant use of the black pawn and then the black knight to keep up the pressure on the white king, leaving the tantalising possibility of an exchange of queens. I mean that this man . . ."

"Or woman," put in Julia.

Muñoz looked at her uncertainly.

"I don't know about that. There are women who play chess well, but not many. In this case, the moves made by our opponent, male or female, show a certain cruelty and, I would say, an almost sadistic curiosity. Like a cat playing with a mouse."

"So, summing up," Julia said, ticking the points off on her fingers, "our opponent is very probably a man and far less probably a woman, someone with plenty of self-confidence, aggressive and cruel by nature and a kind of sadistic voyeur. Is that right?"

"Yes, I think so. And he enjoys danger. That much is obvious from his rejection of the classic approach whereby Black is always relegated to a defensive role. What's more he has a good intuitive sense of what his opponent's moves might be. He's able to put himself in someone else's shoes."

César puckered his lips, gave a silent whistle of admiration and looked at Muñoz with renewed respect. The latter now had a distant air, as if his thoughts had again drifted far away.

"What are you thinking about?" asked Julia.

Muñoz took a while to answer.

"Nothing special. On a chessboard, the battle isn't between two schools of chess, but between two philosophies, between two world-views."

"White and Black, isn't that it?" César said, as if he were reciting lines from an old poem. "Good and evil, heaven and hell, and all those other delightful antitheses."

"Possibly."

Muñoz shrugged. Julia looked at his broad forehead and at the dark shadows under his eyes. Burning in those weary eyes was the little light that so fascinated her and she wondered how long it would be before it flickered out again, as it had on other occasions. When that light was there, she felt a genuine desire to delve into his inner life, to know the taciturn man sitting opposite her.

"And what school do you belong to?"

He seemed surprised by the question. His hand moved towards his wine glass but stopped halfway and lay motionless on the tablecloth. His glass had remained untouched since the beginning of the meal.

"I don't think I belong to any school," he replied quietly. He gave the impression that talking about himself represented an intolerable violation of his sense of modesty. "I suppose I'm one of those who sees chess as a form of therapy. Sometimes I wonder what people like you, people who don't play chess, do to escape from depression and madness. As I told you once before, there are people who play to win, like Alekhine, Lasker and Kasparov, like nearly all the grand masters. Like our invisible player, I suppose. Others, like Steinitz and Przepiorka, concentrate on demonstrating their theories and making brilliant moves."

"And you?" asked Julia.

"Me? I'm neither aggressive nor a risk-taker."

"Is that why you never win?"

"Inside, I believe that I can win, that if I decided to win, I wouldn't lose a single game. But I'm my own worst enemy." He touched the end of his nose, tilting his head slightly to one side. "I read something once: man was not born to solve the problem of the world, merely to discover where the problem lies. Perhaps that's why I don't attempt to solve anything. I immerse myself in the game for the game's sake and some-times when I look as if I were studying the board, I'm actually day-dreaming. I'm pondering different moves, with different pieces, or I go six, seven or more moves ahead of the move my opponent is con-sidering."

"Chess in its purest state," said César, who seemed genuinely, albeit reluctantly, impressed.

"I don't know about that," Muñoz said. "But the same thing happens

157

to many other people I know. The games can last for hours, during which time, family, problems, work, all get left behind, pushed to one side. That's common to everyone. What happens is that while some see it as a battle they have to win, others, like myself, see it as an arena rich in fantasy and spatial combinations, where victory and defeat are meaningless words."

"But before, when you were talking to us about a battle between two philosophies, you were talking about the murderer, about our mystery player," said Julia. "This time it seems that you *are* interested in winning. Is that right?"

Muñoz's gaze again drifted off to some indeterminate point in space.

"I suppose it is. Yes, this time I do want to win."

"Why?"

"Instinct. I'm a chess player, a good one. Someone is trying to provoke me, and that forces me to pay close attention to the moves he makes. The truth is, I have no choice."

César smiled mockingly, lighting one of his special gold-filter cigarettes.

"Sing, O Muse," he recited, in a tone of festive parody, "of the fury of our grieving Muñoz, who, at last, has resolved to leave his tent. Our friend is finally going to war. Until now he has acted only as an outside observer, so I'm pleased at last to see him swear allegiance to the flag. A hero *malgré lui*, but a hero for all that. It's just a shame," a shadow crossed his smooth, pale brow, "that it's such a devilishly subtle war."

Muñoz looked at César with interest.

"It's odd you should say that."

"Why?"

"Because chess is, in fact, a substitute for war and for something else as well. I mean for patricide." He looked at them uncertainly, as if asking them not to take his words too seriously. "Chess is all about getting the king into check, you see. It's about killing the father. I would say that chess has more to do with the art of murder than it does with the art of war."

An icy silence chilled the air around the table. César was looking at Muñoz's now sealed lips, screwing up his eyes a little, as if troubled by the smoke from his cigarette. His look was one of frank admiration, as if Muñoz had just opened a door that hinted at unfathomable mysteries contained within.

"Amazing," he murmured.

Julia seemed equally mesmerised by Muñoz. However mediocre and insignificant he might appear, this man with his large ears and his timid, rumpled air knew exactly what he was talking about. In the mysterious labyrinth, even the idea of which made men tremble with impotence and fear, Muñoz was the only one who knew how to interpret the signs, the only one who possessed the keys that allowed him to come and go without being devoured by the Minotaur. And there, sitting before the remains of her barely touched lasagne, Julia knew with a mathematical, almost a chess player's certainty that, in his way, this man was the strongest of the three of them. His judgment was not dimmed by prejudices about his opponent, the mystery player and potential murderer. He considered the enigma with the same egotistical, scientific coldness that Sherlock Holmes used to solve the problems set him by the sinister Professor Moriarty. Muñoz would not play that game to the end out of a sense of justice; his motive was not ethical, but logical. He would do it simply because he was a player whom chance had placed on this side of the chessboard, just as – and Julia shuddered at the thought – it could have placed him on the other side. Whether he played White or Black, she realised, was a matter of complete indifference to him. All that mattered to him was that, for the first time in his life, he was interested in playing a game to the end.

Her eyes met César's and she knew he was thinking the same thing. It was he who spoke first, in a low voice, as if fearing, as she did, to extinguish the light in Muñoz's eyes.

"Killing the king . . ." César put the cigarette holder slowly to his lips and inhaled a precise amount of smoke. "That's very interesting. I mean the Freudian interpretation of the game. I had no idea chess had anything to do with such unpleasant things."

Muñoz, his head slightly to one side, seemed absorbed in his own thoughts.

"It's usually the father who teaches the child his first moves in the game. And the dream of any son who plays chess is to beat his father. To kill the king. Besides, it soon becomes evident in chess that the father, or the king, is the weakest piece on the board. He's under continual attack, in constant need of protection, of such tactics as castling, and he can only move one square at a time. Paradoxically, the king is also indispensable. The king gives the game its name, since the word 'chess' derives from the Persian word *shah* meaning king, and is pretty much the same in most languages."

"And the queen?" asked Julia.

"She's the mother and the wife. In any attack on the king, she provides the most efficient defence. The queen is the piece with the best and most effective resources. And on either side of the king and the queen is the bishop: the one who blesses the union and helps in the fight. Not forgetting the Arab *faras*, the horse that crosses the enemy lines, the knight. In fact, the problem existed long before Van Huys painted his *Game of Chess*; men have been trying to solve it for fourteen hundred years."

Muñoz paused, and seemed about to say more, but instead of words, what appeared on his lips was that brief suggestion of a smile.

"Sometimes," he said at last, as if it were an enormous effort to formulate his thoughts, "I wonder if chess is something man invented or if he merely discovered it. It's as if it were something that has always been there, since the beginning of the universe. Like whole numbers."

As if in a dream, Julia heard the sound of a seal being broken and, for the first time, she was properly aware of the situation: a vast chessboard embracing both past and present, Van Huys and herself, even Álvaro, César, Montegrifo, the Belmontes, Menchu and Muñoz. And she suddenly felt such intense fear that she had to make an almost physical effort not to express it out loud. The fear must have shown in her face because both César and Muñoz gave her a worried look.

"I'm all right," she said, shaking her head as if that might help calm her thoughts. Then she took from her pocket the list of different levels that existed in the painting, according to Muñoz's first interpretation. "Have a look at this."

Muñoz studied the sheet of paper and passed it to César without comment.

"What do you think?" asked Julia.

César was hesitant.

"Most disturbing," he said. "But perhaps we're being too literary about it." He glanced again at Julia's diagram. "I can't make up my mind whether we're all racking our brains over something really profound or something absolutely trivial."

Julia didn't reply. She was staring at Muñoz. He placed the piece of paper on the table, took a pen from his pocket and added something and passed it back to her.

"Now there's another level," he said in a worried voice. "You're at least as involved as any of the others."

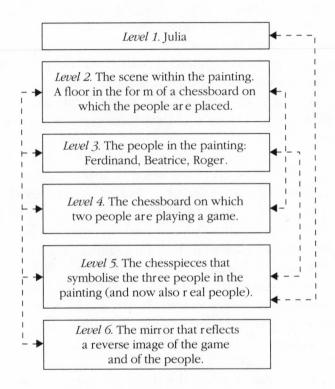

"That's what I thought," said Julia.

"Level 6 is the one that contains all the others." Muñoz pointed to the list. "Whether you like it or not, you're there in it too."

"That means," said Julia, looking at him with wide-open eyes, "that the person who may have murdered Álvaro, the same one who sent us that card, is playing some kind of mad chess game. A game in which not only I, but we, all of us, are pieces. Is that right?"

There was no sadness in Muñoz's face, only a sort of expectant curiosity, as if fascinating conclusions could be drawn from what she'd just said, conclusions he would be only too happy to comment on.

"I'm glad," he replied at last, and the diffuse smile returned to his lips, "that you've both finally realised that."

Menchu had made herself up with millimetric precision and had chosen her clothes to calculated effect: a short, very tight skirt and an extremely elegant black leather jacket over a cream sweater that emphasised her bosom to an extent that Julia instantly decried as "scandalous". Perhaps foreseeing this, Julia had opted that afternoon for an informal look, choosing to wear moccasins, jeans, a suede bomber jacket and a silk scarf. As César would have said, had he seen them parking Julia's Fiat outside Claymore's, they could easily have passed for mother and daughter.

Menchu's perfume and the sound of her high heels preceded them into an office with walls of fine wood, a huge mahogany table, and ultramodern lamps and chairs, where Paco Montegrifo advanced to kiss the hand of each of them, smiling the trademark smile that displayed his perfect teeth, a flash of white against his bronzed skin. They sat in armchairs offering a splendid view of the valuable Vlaminck that dominated the room; Montegrifo sat beneath the painting itself, on the other side of the table, with the modest air of someone who deeply regretted being unable to provide them with a better view, a Rembrandt, perhaps. At least that could have been the implication behind the intense look he gave Julia, once he'd cast an indifferent eye over Menchu's ostentatiously crossed legs. Or perhaps a Leonardo.

He lost no time in getting down to business once his secretary had served coffee in china cups from the East India Company, coffee that Menchu sweetened with saccharin. Julia took hers black, bitter and very hot and drank it in small sips. By the time she'd lit a cigarette – Montegrifo leaning impotently across the vast table with his gold lighter – he'd already outlined the situation. And Julia had to admit that he could certainly not be accused of beating about the bush.

At first sight, the situation seemed crystal-clear: Claymore's regretted that they were unable to accept Menchu's conditions as regards equal shares in the profits from the Van Huys. Menchu should know that the owner of the painting, Don – Montegrifo calmly consulted his notes – Manuel Belmonte, with the agreement of his niece and her husband, had decided to cancel the agreement made with Doña Menchu Roch and transfer all rights in the Van Huys to Claymore and Co. All of this, he added, was set out in a document, authenticated by a notary public. Montegrifo gave Menchu a look of deep regret, accompanied by a worldly sigh.

"Do you mean to say," said a shocked Menchu, her cup rattling in its saucer, "that you're threatening to take the painting away from me?"

Montegrifo looked at his gold cuff links as if it were they who had uttered some unfortunate remark and tugged fastidiously at his starched cuffs.

"I'm afraid we already have," he said in the contrite tone of someone regretting having to pass on to a widow the bills left by her dead husband. "However, your original percentage of the profits on the auction price remains the same; minus expenses of course. Claymore's does not wish to deprive you of anything, only to avoid the abusive conditions that you, my dear lady, tried to impose." He slowly took out his silver cigarette case and placed it on the table. "Claymore's simply sees no reason for an increase in your percentage. And that's that."

"No reason?" Menchu glanced towards Julia in despair, expecting indignant exclamations of solidarity. "The reason, Montegrifo, is that, thanks to research carried out by us, the painting will vastly increase in price. Isn't that reason enough?"

Montegrifo looked at Julia, making it silently and courteously plain that he did not for a minute include her in this sordid bit of horse-trading. Turning back to Menchu, his eyes hardened.

"If the research that the two of you have carried out" – that "two of you" made it absolutely clear what he thought of Menchu's talent for research – "increases the price of the Van Huys, it will automatically increase the percentage of the profits you agreed to with Claymore's." He allowed himself an affable smile before turning away from Menchu again and looking at Julia. "As for you, the new situation in no way affects your interests. Quite the contrary. Claymore's," he said, and the smile he gave her left no doubt as to exactly who in Claymore's, "considers your handling of the affair to have been exemplary. So we'd like you to continue your restoration work on the picture. You need have no worries at all about the financial aspect."

"And may one know," Menchu said, and her lower lip, as well as the hand holding the coffee cup, was trembling now, "how it is that you're so well informed about the painting? Because Julia may be a little naive, but I can't imagine that she'd pour out her life story to you over a candlelit supper. Or did she?"

That was a low blow, and Julia opened her mouth to protest. Montegrifo, however, calmed her with a gesture.

"Look, Señora Roch, when I took the liberty of putting some proposals of a professional nature your friend a few days ago, she chose the elegant option of simply saying that she would think about it. The details about the state of the painting, the hidden inscription and so on, were kindly supplied to us by the niece of the owner. A charming man, by the way, Don Manuel. And I must say that he was most reluctant to withdraw responsibility for the Van Huys from you. A loyal man, it would seem, for he also demanded, indeed he insisted, that no one but Julia should touch the painting until the restoration work was done. In all these negotiations my alliance, my tactical alliance, if you like, with Don Manuel's niece has proved very useful. As for Señor Lapeña, her husband, he raised no further objections once I'd mentioned the possibility of an advance."

"Another Judas," said Menchu, almost spitting the words out.

"I suppose," he said, shrugging, "you could call him that. Although other names also spring to mind."

"I've got a signed document too, you know," protested Menchu.

"I know. But it's an unauthenticated agreement, whereas mine was made in the presence of a notary public, with the niece and her husband as witnesses and all kinds of guarantees that include a deposit as security on our part. If I may use an expression Alfonso Lapeña used as he signed our agreement, it's a whole new ball game, my dear lady."

Menchu leaned forwards in a way that made Julia fear that the cup of coffee her friend had in her hand might just end up all over Montegrifo's immaculate shirt front, but she merely placed it on the table. She was bursting with indignation, and, despite all the careful make-up, her anger added years to her face. When she moved, her skirt rode up still further, and Julia, embarrassed, regretted being there with all her heart.

164

"And what will Claymore's do," asked Menchu in a surly tone, "if I decide to take the painting to another auctioneer?"

Montegrifo was contemplating the smoke spiralling from his cigarette.

"Frankly," he said, and he seemed to give the matter serious thought, "I'd advise you not to complicate matters. It would be illegal."

"I could also sue the lot of you and tie you up in a court case that would drag on for months, putting a stop to your auctioning the painting. Have you considered that?"

"Of course I have. But you'd come off worst." Montegrifo smiled politely. "As you can imagine, Claymore's has very good lawyers at its disposal. You risk losing everything. And that would be a great pity."

Menchu gave a tug at her skirt as she stood up.

"All I have to say to you" – and her voice cracked, overwhelmed by anger – "is that you're the biggest son of a bitch I've ever set eyes on."

Montegrifo and Julia also stood up, she upset, he in complete control of himself.

"I can't tell you how much I regret this scene," he said calmly to Julia. "I really do."

"So do I." Julia looked at Menchu, who was at that moment throwing her bag over her shoulder with the determined gesture of someone slinging on a rifle. "Couldn't we all be just a bit more reasonable?"

Menchu glared at her.

"You can be reasonable, if you like, seeing you're so taken with this swindler, but I'm getting out of this den of thieves."

Her high heels click-clacked fast and furiously away. Julia remained where she was, not knowing whether or not to follow her.

"A woman of character," Montegrifo said.

Julia turned towards him, still uncertain.

"She's just invested too many hopes in the painting. Surely you can understand that."

"Oh, I do understand." He gave a conciliatory smile. "But I can't allow her to blackmail me."

"But you plotted behind her back, conspired with the niece and her husband. I call that playing dirty."

Montegrifo's smile grew broader. That's life, he seemed to be saying. He looked at the door through which Menchu had departed.

"What do you think she'll do now?"

Julia shook her head.

"Nothing. She knows she's lost the battle."

"Ambition, Julia, is a perfectly legitimate feeling," Montegrifo said after a moment. "But where ambition's concerned, the only sin is failure. Triumph automatically presupposes virtue." He smiled again, this time into space. "Señora Roch tried to get involved in something that was too big for her . . . Let's say" – he blew a smoke ring and let it float up to the ceiling – "that she just wasn't big enough for her ambitions." His brown eyes had grown hard, and Julia realised that behind his rigorous mask of politeness, Montegrifo was a dangerous adversary. "I trust she will cause us no further problems," he continued, "because that would be a sin that would have to be punished. Do you understand? Now, if you don't mind, let's talk about our painting."

Belmonte was alone in the house, and he received Julia and Muñoz in the drawing room, sitting in his wheelchair near where *The Game of Chess* used to hang. The solitary nail and the mark left on the wall created a pathetic air of domestic desolation, of despoliation. Belmonte, who had followed the direction of his visitors' gaze, smiled sadly.

"I didn't want to hang anything else there just yet," he explained, "not for the moment." He raised one bony hand and waved it in a gesture of resignation. "It's difficult to get used to . . ."

"I understand," said Julia with genuine sympathy.

The old man nodded slowly.

"Yes, I know you do." He looked at Muñoz, doubtless hoping for a show of equal understanding from him, but Muñoz remained silent, looking at the empty wall with inexpressive eyes. "I've always thought you were an intelligent young woman, right from the very first day." He looked at Muñoz. "Wouldn't you agree, sir?"

Muñoz slowly shifted his eyes away from the wall to the old man and nodded slightly, without saying a word. He seemed immersed in remote thoughts.

"As for your friend," Belmonte said, and he seemed to be embarrassed, "I'd like you to explain to her . . . that I really had no choice."

"Don't worry. I understand. And Menchu will too."

"I'm so glad. They put a lot of pressure on me. Señor Montegrifo made a good offer too. He also undertook to give maximum publicity to the painting's history." He stroked his ill-shaven chin. "And, I must confess, that did influence me somewhat," he sighed softly, "that and the money."

Julia pointed to the record player.

"Do you play Bach constantly, or is it just a coincidence? I heard that record the last time I was here."

"The *Musical Offering*?" Belmonte seemed pleased. "I often listen to it. It's so complex and ingenious that every now and then I still find something unexpected in it." He paused, as if recalling something. "Were you aware that there are certain musical themes that seem to sum up a whole life? They're like mirrors you can peer into and see yourself reflected. In this composition, for example, a theme emerges expressed in different voices and different keys; indeed, sometimes at different speeds, with inverted tonal intervals, or even back to front." He leaned on the arm of his wheelchair. "Listen. Can you hear it? It begins with a single voice that sings the theme, and then a second voice comes in, starting four tones higher or four tones lower, and that becomes a secondary theme. Each of the voices enters at its own particular time, just like different moments in a life. And when all the voices have come into play, the rules come to an end." He gave Julia and Muñoz a broad, sad smile. "As you see, a perfect analogy of old age."

Muñoz pointed at the wall.

"That nail," he said rather abruptly, "also seems to symbolise a lot of things."

Belmonte looked attentively at Muñoz and nodded slowly.

"That's very true," he confirmed with another sigh. "And sometimes I find myself looking at the place where the picture was and I seem to see it there still. It isn't there, but I see it. After all these years, I still have it up here." He tapped his forehead. "The people, the exquisite detail. My favourite parts were always the landscape you can see through the window and the convex mirror on the left, reflecting the fore-shortened figures of the players."

"And the chessboard," said Muñoz.

"Yes, and the chessboard. I often used to reconstruct the position of the pieces on my own chessboard, especially at the beginning, when I inherited it from my poor Ana."

"Do you play?" asked Muñoz casually.

"I used to. Now I hardly ever do. But the truth is, it never occurred to me that you could play that game backwards." He paused, tapping his hands on his knees. "Playing backwards. It's odd. Did you know that Bach was very keen on musical inversions? In some of his canons he inverts the theme, elaborating a melody that jumps down a pitch every time the original theme jumps up. The effect can seem strange, but when you get used to it, you find it quite natural. There's even a canon in the *Musical Offering* that's played the opposite way round from the way it's written." He looked at Julia. "I think I told you before that Johann Sebastian was an inveterate joker. His work is full of tricks. It's as if every now and then a note, a modulation or a silence were saying to you: 'I've hidden a message in here: find it.' "

"As in the painting," said Muñoz.

"Yes. With the difference that music doesn't consist of images, the positioning of chess pieces or, in this case, of vibrations in the air, but of the emotions that those vibrations produce in the brain of each individual. You'd run into serious problems if you tried to apply to music the investigatory methods you used to solve the game in the painting. You'd have to find out which particular note provoked which emotional effect. Or which combinations of notes. Doesn't that strike you as much more difficult than playing chess?"

Muñoz thought about it carefully.

"I don't think so," he said at last. "Because the general laws of logic are the same for everything. Music, like chess, follows rules. It's all a question of working away at it until you isolate a symbol, a key." One half of his mouth seemed to twist into a smile. "Like the Egyptologists' Rosetta Stone. Once you have that, it's just a question of hard work and method. And time."

Belmonte blinked mockingly.

"Do you think so? Do you really think that all hidden messages can be deciphered? That it's always possible to reach an exact solution just by the application of method?"

"I'm sure of it. Because there's a universal system, general laws that allow one to demonstrate what is demonstrable and to discard whatever is not."

168

The old man made a sceptical gesture.

"Forgive me, but I really can't agree with you there. I think that all the divisions, classifications, categorisations and systems that we attribute to the universe are fictitious, arbitrary. There isn't one that doesn't contain within it its own contradiction. That's the opinion of an old man with some experience of these things."

Muñoz shifted a bit in his seat and looked round the room. He didn't seem very happy with the turn the conversation had taken, but Julia had the impression that he didn't want to change the subject either. She knew he was not a man to waste words and concluded that he must be after something. Perhaps Belmonte was one of the chess pieces Muñoz was studying in order to solve the mystery.

"That's arguable," Muñoz said at last. "For example, the Universe is full of demonstrable infinites: prime numbers, the combinations in chess."

"Do you really think so? That everything is demonstrable, I mean? Allow me to say, as the musician I once was, or, rather, despite all this," he indicated his useless legs with a kind of calm disdain, "as the musician I still am, that every system is incomplete. That demonstrability is a much weaker concept than truth."

"The truth is like the perfect move in chess: it exists, but you have to look for it. Given enough time, it's always demonstrable."

Hearing that, Belmonte smiled mischievously.

"I would say, rather, that the perfect move you talk about, whether you call it that or whether you call it the truth, may exist. But it can't always be demonstrated. And that any system that tries to do so is limited and relative. Try sending my Van Huys to Mars or to Planet X, and see if anyone there can solve your problem. I'd go further: send them the record you're listening to now or, to make it still harder, break the record and send them the pieces. What meaning will it contain then? And since you seem so keen on exact laws, I'd remind you that the angles of a triangle add up to one hundred and eighty degrees in Euclidian geometry, but to more in elliptic geometry and to less in hyperbolic. And that's because there is no one system, there are no universal axioms. Systems are disparate even within themselves. Do you enjoy resolving paradoxes? It isn't only music, painting or, I imagine, chess that are full of them." He picked up pencil and paper from the

169

table, wrote a few lines and showed them to Muñoz. "Have a look at that, will you?"

The chess player read it out loud:

"The sentence I am now writing is the one that you are now reading." He looked at Belmonte in surprise. "So?"

"That's all there is. That sentence was written by me a minute and a half ago and you read it only forty seconds ago. That's to say, my writing and your reading correspond to different moments in time, but on that piece of paper 'now' and 'now' are undoubtedly the same 'now'. Therefore, on the one hand the sentence is true, but on the other hand it lacks all validity. Or is it the concept of time that we're failing to take into account? Don't you think that's a good example of a paradox? I can see you have no answer to it. Well, you'll find the same problem with the enigmas posed by my Van Huys or by anything else. Who's to say that your solution to the problem is the correct one? Your intuition and your system? Fine, but what superior system can you count on to demonstrate that your intuition and your system are valid? And what other system can you call on to corroborate those two systems? As a chess player, I imagine you'll find these lines interesting."

Pausing between each line, Belmonte recited:

> The player too is captive of caprice
> (The words are Omar's) on another ground
> Where black nights alternate with whiter days
>
> God moves the player, he in turn the piece.
> But what god beyond God begins the round
> Of dust and time and sleep and agonies?

"The world is just one vast paradox," the old man concluded. "And I defy you to prove the contrary."

Julia glanced at Muñoz and saw that he was shaking his head slightly, and his eyes had grown dull again. He seemed disconcerted.

Filtered by the vodka she'd drunk, the music – gentle jazz with the volume turned down to a tenuous murmur that seemed to blossom from the shadowy corners of the room – surrounded her like a warm caress, soft and soothing, that was transformed into calm lucidity. It was as if everything, night, music, shadows, even the comfortable feeling of the arm of the leather sofa under her neck, blended into a perfect harmony; everything, down to the tiniest object in the room, down to the most fleeting of her thoughts, had found its precise place in her mind and in space, fitting with geometrical exactitude into her perceptions and her consciousness.

Nothing, not even the gloomiest of memories, could have shattered the calm that reigned in her spirit. It was the first time she'd managed to recover that sense of balance, and she plunged into it with absolute abandon. Not even the ring of the telephone, as it announced one of those threatening, by now almost familiar, silences, could break the spell. With her eyes closed, moving her head gently to the rhythm of the music, Julia allowed herself a warm, secret smile. At times like this it was so easy to live in peace with oneself.

She opened her eyes lazily. In the shadows, the polychromed face of a Gothic virgin was smiling too, her gaze lost in the stillness of the centuries. Leaning against the table leg, on the paint-stained Shiraz carpet, was a painting in an oval frame, its layer of varnish only half removed, a romantic Andalusian landscape, nostalgic and peaceful, that depicted the river in Seville flowing quietly past leafy green banks, with a ship and some trees in the background. And in the middle of the room – in the midst of sculptures, frames, bronzes, paintings, bottles of solvent, canvases, a half-restored baroque Christ, art books piled up next to records and ceramics – at the strange intersection, random but undeniable, of lines and perspectives, *The Game of Chess* presided solemnly over the orderly disorder reminiscent of an auction room or an antiques shop. The dim glow from the hallway cast a narrow rectangle of pale light on the painting, enough to bring the surface to life and for every detail, although steeped in deceptive chiaroscuro, to be clearly visible from where Julia was reclining, her feet and legs bare below her baggy black woollen sweater. Rain was pattering on the skylight but the radiators kept out the cold.

The golden letters of the newly uncovered inscription gleamed from the shadows. It had been a difficult, painstaking task, interrupted often to photograph each phase of the process as she removed the top layer of copper resinate and as the orpiment of the Gothic lettering was gradually revealed, five hundred years after Pieter Van Huys had covered it up, the better to conceal the mystery.

Now it was there before her: *Quis necavit equitem*. Julia would have preferred leaving the inscription hidden beneath the original layer of pigment, given that the X-rays proved its existence. Montegrifo, however, had insisted on uncovering it; according to him, it would excite the morbid curiosity of clients. Soon the painting would be open to the gaze of everyone: auctioneers, collectors, historians. The discreet privacy it had enjoyed until now, apart from its brief spell in the Prado, would be over for ever. Soon *The Game of Chess* would come under the scrutiny of experts; it would become the subject of polemical debates, and newspaper articles would be written about it as well as erudite theses and specialised texts such as the one she was preparing. The old Flemish master, its creator, could never have imagined that his painting would achieve such fame. And should Ferdinand Altenhoffen ever learn of it, his bones would doubtless tremble with pleasure beneath his dusty gravestone in the crypt of some abbey in Belgium or France. His name would at last be cleared, and a few lines in the history books would have to be rewritten.

She looked at the painting. Almost all of the top layer of oxidised varnish was gone, and with it the yellowish surface that had dulled its colours. Unvarnished and with the inscription uncovered, there was a luminosity about it and a perfection of colour that was apparent even in the near darkness of the room. The outlines of the figures could be seen in all their extreme precision, perfectly clear and succinct, and the sense of balance that characterised the domestic scene – paradoxically domestic, thought Julia – was so typical of a certain style and period that the painting was sure to fetch an astonishing price.

Paradoxically domestic: the phrase was exactly right. Nothing about the two serious gentlemen playing chess or the lady by the window dressed in black, reading, her eyes lowered, a demure expression on her face, would lead one to suspect the drama that lay coiled beneath the surface, like the twisted root of a lovely plant.

She studied the profile of Roger de Arras as he leaned over the chessboard, absorbed in the game, a game in which he was already dead. The steel gorget and the leather cuirass made him look like the soldier he once was, like the warrior whose insigne he had worn (perhaps

dressed in burnished armour like that worn by the knight riding alongside the Devil) when he had escorted her to the nuptial bed to which
she was destined by reasons of state. Julia could imagine Beatrice clearly
– still a virgin, younger than she appeared in the painting, before bitterness had etched lines about her mouth – peeping out between the
curtains of the litter, a maid by her side, and admiring the gallant
gentleman whose fame went before him: her future husband's best
friend, still a young man, who, having fought beneath the fleur-de-lys
of France against the lion of England, had sought peace by the side of
his childhood companion. And Julia imagined Beatrice's wide blue eyes
meeting, just for a moment, the calm, weary gaze of the knight.

It was impossible that the two of them were never united by anything
more than that one look. For some obscure reason, by some inexplicable
twist of the imagination – as if the hours spent working on the painting
had spun a mysterious connecting thread between her and that fragment
of the past – Julia contemplated the scene in the Van Huys painting
with the familiarity of one who had experienced every detail of the story
alongside the characters depicted in it. The mirror on the wall in the
picture reflecting the foreshortened figures of the two chess players also
contained her, in the same way that the mirror in *Las Meninas* reflected
the king and queen as they watched – was it from inside or outside the
picture? – the scene being painted by Velázquez, or just as the mirror
in *The Arnolfini Double Portrait* reflected the presence and the meticulous
gaze of Jan Van Eyck.

The flame from the match as she lit a cigarette dazzled her for a
moment, hiding *The Game of Chess* from her view until, gradually, her
retina readjusted to the scene again, to the people and the colours. She
herself had always been there – she was sure of that now – right from
the beginning, ever since Pieter Van Huys first imagined that moment,
even before he had begun the careful preparation of calcium carbonate
and animal glue with which to impregnate the wood before he started
painting.

Beatrice, Duchess of Ostenburg, a touch of melancholy in her eyes
intent on her book – perhaps prompted by a mandolin played by a page
outside at the foot of the wall – remembers her youth in Burgundy, her

hopes and dreams. Above the window framing the pure blue Flanders sky, a stone St George plunges his lance into the dragon writhing beneath his horse's hooves. It does not escape the implacable eye of the painter observing the scene — nor that of Julia observing the painter — that time has blunted the tip of St George's lance, and where his right foot, no doubt once wearing a sharp spur, used to stand out in sharp relief, there is only a broken stump. This St George, putting the vile dragon to death, is not only half-armed, with his stone shield worn away by time, but also lame. Perhaps that only makes the figure of the knight all the more touching, reminding Julia, by a curious transposition of ideas, of the martial pose of a lead soldier.

She's reading, this Beatrice of Ostenburg, who, by reason of lineage and family pride and despite her marriage, never really stopped being Beatrice of Burgundy. And she's reading a strange book, whose binding is decorated with silver studs, and with a silk ribbon to mark her page, a book whose chapter headings are exquisite brightly coloured miniatures by the master of the *Coeur d'Amour épris*, a book entitled *Poem of the Rose and the Knight*, which, although the author is officially anonymous, everyone knows was written almost ten years before, in the French court of King Charles Valois, by an Ostenburg gentleman called Roger de Arras:

> Lady, the same dew
> that at break of day
> lays on the roses
> in your garden hoarfrost,
> falls, on the field of war,
> like teardrops,
> upon my heart,
> upon my eyes, upon my sword.

Sometimes those eyes, which have the luminous clarity of Flemish eyes, leave her book and look up at the two men playing chess at the table. Her husband is leaning on his left elbow, his fingers distractedly playing with the insigne of the Golden Fleece that his uncle by marriage, the late Philip the Good, sent him as a wedding present, which he wears about his neck, on the end of a heavy golden chain. Ferdinand of Ostenburg cannot decide on his next move; he reaches out a hand towards a piece, touches it, changes his mind, and looks apologetically into the calm eyes of Roger de Arras, whose lips curve in a courteous smile. "Touching a piece is the same as moving it, sir," those lips murmur with just a touch of friendly irony, and a slightly embarrassed Ferdinand moves the piece he touched, because he knows that his opponent is not just a courtier, but his friend. He shifts on his stool, feeling vaguely happy, for he knows that it is no bad thing to have someone who, from time to time, reminds him that there are some rules even princes must abide by.

The notes from the mandolin drift up from the garden into another window, not visible from there, the window of the room where Pieter Van Huys, court painter, is preparing an oak panel, made up of three sections his assistant has just glued together. The old master is not sure yet what use to make of it – perhaps a religious subject that has been in his mind for a while now: a young Virgin, almost a child, shedding tears of blood as she gazes, grief-stricken, at her empty lap. But, after due consideration, Van Huys shakes his head and emits a discouraged sigh. He knows he will never paint that picture. No one would understand its true meaning, and in the past he's had his fair share of problems with the Inquisition; his weary limbs would not withstand another encounter with the rack. With paint-encrusted fingernails, he scratches his bald head beneath his woollen beret. He's becoming an old man and he knows it; he has too few practical ideas and too many vague phantasms in his mind. To exorcise them he closes his tired eyes. When he opens them again, he sees the oak panel still there, waiting for the idea that will bring it to life. In the garden someone is still playing the mandolin; some lovesick page no doubt. The painter smiles to himself and, after dipping a brush into a clay pot, he applies the primer in thin layers, up and down, following the grain of the wood. Now and then he looks out of the window, and his eyes fill with light. He feels grateful for the oblique ray of sunlight that warms his old bones.

Roger de Arras has just made a remark in a low voice, and the Duke is laughing, in a good mood now, for he's just taken a knight. Beatrice of Ostenburg, or of Burgundy, is finding the music unbearably sad. She's on the point of asking one of her maids to have the player stop, but she doesn't, for she hears in its notes an exact echo, a perfect harmony of the pain flooding her heart. The music mingles with the friendly murmurings of the two men playing chess, and she finds a heartbreaking beauty in the poem whose lines tremble in her fingers. Born of the same dew that covers the rose and the knight's sword, there is a tear in her blue eyes when she looks up and meets Julia's gaze, watching in silence from the shadows. And she thinks that the gaze of that dark-eyed Italianate young woman is only a reflection in the dim surface of some distant mirror of her own gaze, fixed and anguished. Beatrice of Ostenburg, or of Burgundy, feels as if she were outside the room, on the other side of a pane of dark glass, from where she observes herself sitting beneath the mutilated St George, next to a window framing a blue sky that contrasts with the black of her dress. And she knows that no amount of confession will ever wash away her sin.

X

The Blue Car

"That was a dirty trick," said Haroun . . .
"Show me another . . . one that is honest."
Raymond Smullyan

BENEATH THE BRIM of his hat, César arched a peevish eyebrow as he swung his umbrella and looked about with the disdain, tempered by the most exquisite boredom, in which he usually entrenched himself when reality confirmed his worst fears. The Rastro, it must be said, did not look terribly welcoming that morning. The grey sky threatened rain, and the owners of the stalls set up along the streets occupied by the market were taking precautions against a possible downpour. In some places, walking became a tortuous process of dodging people and skirting the canvas and grimy plastic with which the stalls were hung.

"In fact," he said to Julia, who was looking at a pair of battered brass candlesticks displayed on a blanket on the ground, "this is a complete waste of time. I haven't found anything decent here for ages."

This wasn't quite true, and Julia knew it. From time to time, thanks to his expert eye, César would unearth from the pile of discarded junk in the old market – drawn from that vast cemetery of dreams swept out into the street on the tide of many an anonymous shipwreck – some forgotten pearl, some tiny treasure that chance had chosen to conceal from the eyes of others: an eighteenth-century crystal tumbler, an antique frame, a diminutive porcelain *objet d'art*. Once, in a shabby little shop selling books and old magazines, he'd found two beautiful chapter headings delicately and skilfully illuminated by some nameless thirteenth-century monk, which, once restored by Julia, he had sold for a small fortune.

They slowly made their way to the upper part of the market, to the short row of buildings with peeling walls and gloomy inner courtyards connected by alleyways with wrought-iron gates, that were home to those specialist antiques shops more or less worthy of the name – although César wore a look of prudent scepticism when he spoke of them.

"What time did you arrange to meet your dealer?"

César shifted his umbrella – a very expensive piece with a beautifully turned silver grip – to his other hand, pushed up his cuff and studied the face of his gold watch. He was looking very elegant in a light brown felt hat with broad brim and silk band, a camel's-hair coat draped over his shoulders and a handsome cravat at the open neck of his silk shirt. He always dressed perilously close to the limits of good taste, though without ever overstepping the mark.

"In about fifteen minutes."

They browsed amongst the stalls. Under César's mocking gaze, Julia picked up a painted wooden plate showing a yellowing landscape rather crudely done, a rural scene with an ox cart moving down a path edged by trees.

"Surely you're not going to buy that, my dear?" César said, enjoying his own disapproval. "It's revolting. Aren't you even going to haggle?"

Julia opened her shoulder bag and took out her purse, ignoring César's protests.

"I don't know what you're complaining about," she said as the plate was being wrapped for her in a few pages from an illustrated magazine. "You've always said that people, *comme il faut*, never discuss the price of anything: you pay on the nail and walk away with your head held high."

"That rule doesn't apply here." César, looking about with an air of professional detachment, wrinkled his nose at the plebeian sight of junk-laden stalls. "Not when you're dealing with people like this."

Julia put the package into her bag.

"Even so you might have had the decency to buy it for me. When I was a child, you bought me anything I fancied."

"I spoiled you horribly when you were a child. Anyway, I refuse to pay good money for trash like that."

"You're getting mean in your old age, that's your problem."

"Be silent, viper!" The brim of his hat cast a shadow over his face as he bent to light a cigarette outside a shop crammed with dusty old dolls. "One more word and I write you out of my will."

Julia watched him climbing the flight of steps as he left for his meeting. He did so with great dignity, keeping the hand that held the ivory cigarette holder slightly raised, and wearing the half-disdainful, half-bored air of one who does not expect to find very much at the end of the road, but who, for aesthetic reasons, takes pains to walk that road as elegantly as possible. Like a Charles Stuart climbing to the scaffold almost as if he were doing so as a favour to the executioner, with his already rehearsed "Remember" on his lips and in the hope that he would be beheaded in profile, as he appeared on the coins struck in his image.

Clutching her bag, as a precaution against pickpockets, Julia threaded her way amongst the stalls. There were too many people in that part of the market, so she decided to go back to the steps and the balustrade overlooking the square and the market's main street, where people were milling about beneath endless rows of awnings and plastic sheets.

She had an hour before meeting César again, in a small café on the square, between a shop selling nautical instruments and a second-hand clothes shop that specialised in army surplus. Below the balustrade, sitting on the edge of a stone fountain full of fruit peel and empty beer cans, a young man with long blond hair and a poncho was playing Andean melodies on a rudimentary flute. She listened to the music as she let her gaze drift over the market. After a while she went back down the steps and stopped at the shop window full of dolls. Some were clothed, others were naked; some were dressed in picturesque peasant costumes or complicatedly romantic outfits complete with gloves, hats and parasols. Some represented girls and others grown women. The features of some were crude, others were childish, ingenuous, perverse. Their arms and hands were frozen in diverse positions, as if surprised by the cold wind of all the time that had passed since their owners abandoned or sold them, or died. Girls who became women, thought Julia – some beautiful, some plain, who had loved or perhaps been loved – had once caressed those bodies made of rags, cardboard and porcelain. Those dolls had survived their owners. They were dumb, motionless witnesses whose imaginary retinas still retained images of scenes long since erased from the memories of the living: faded pictures sketched amongst mists of nostalgia, intimate moments of family life,

179

children's songs, loving embraces, as well as tears and disappointments, dreams turned to ashes, decay and sadness, perhaps even to evil. There was something unbearably touching about that multitude of glass and porcelain eyes that stared at her unblinking, full of the Olympian knowledge that only time possesses, lifeless eyes embedded in pale wax or papier-mâché faces, above dresses so darkened by time that the lace edgings looked dull and grubby. And then there was the hair, some combed and neat, some dishevelled, real hair – the thought made her shiver – that had belonged to real women. By a melancholy association of ideas, a fragment of a poem surfaced in her mind, one that she'd heard César recite long ago:

> If they had kept all the hair
> of all the women who have died . . .

She found it hard to look away from the window, the glass of which reflected the heavy grey clouds darkening the city. And when she did turn round, ready to walk on, she saw Max, wearing a heavy navy blue jacket, his hair, as usual, tied back in a ponytail. He was looking down the steps as if fleeing from someone whose proximity troubled him.

"What a surprise!" he said, and gave her that handsome, wolfish smile that so enchanted Menchu. They exchanged a few trivial remarks about the unpleasant weather and the number of people at the market. He gave no explanation for his presence there, but Julia noticed that he seemed jumpy, slightly furtive. Perhaps he was expecting Menchu, since he mentioned that they'd arranged to meet near there, some complicated story about cheap frames which, once restored – Julia had often done it herself – could be used to set off canvases on display at the gallery.

Julia didn't like Max, and she attributed to this the discomfort she always felt with him. Quite apart from the nature of his relationship with her friend, there was something that displeased her, something she'd sensed the first moment they met. César, whose fine, feminine intuition was never wrong, used to say that, beautiful body aside, there was an indefinable, mean-spirited quality about Max that surfaced in his crooked smile and in the insolent way he looked at Julia. Max's gaze could never be held for long, but whenever Julia forgot it and then looked back at him again, she would find his gaze stubbornly fixed on her, crafty and watchful, evasive yet insistent. It wasn't one of those vague glances, like Paco Montegrifo's, that wander about before calmly returning to rest once more on the object or person claiming his attention; it was the kind of glance that turns into a stare when the person thinks no one is looking and grows shifty the moment he feels he's being observed. "It's the look of someone intent, at the very least, on stealing your wallet," César had said once about Menchu's lover. Julia had simply responded to César's spiteful remark with a disapproving frown, but she had to admit that he was absolutely right.

There were other murky aspects to him. Julia knew that those glances contained something more than mere curiosity. Confident of his physical attraction, Max often behaved, in Menchu's absence or behind her back, in a fashion that was both calculated and suggestive. Any doubts she'd had about that had been dispelled during a party at Menchu's house, in the early hours of the morning. Conversation had been flagging, and her friend had left the room to get more ice. Leaning towards the low table where the drinks were, Max had picked up Julia's glass and raised it to his lips. That would have meant little if he hadn't then replaced it on the table, looked at her, licked his lips and smiled with cynical regret that circumstances prevented him intruding further upon her person. Needless to say, Menchu was completely unaware of this, and Julia would have cut out her tongue rather than report something that would merely have sounded ridiculous when put into words. So she had adopted the only attitude she could with Max: an evident disdain on occasions when she found speaking to him unavoidable and a deliberate arm's-length chilliness whenever they met face to face without witnesses, as now, in the Rastro.

"I don't have to meet Menchu until later," he said, dangling before her that self-satisfied smile she so detested. "Do you fancy a drink?"

She looked at him hard then shook her head slowly, pointedly.

"I'm waiting for César."

Max knew full well that he was no favourite of César's.

"Pity," he murmured. "We don't often get the chance to meet like this. On our own, I mean."

Julia merely arched her eyebrows and looked around as if César were about to appear at any moment. Max followed the direction of her gaze and shrugged.

"I've arranged to meet Menchu over there in half an hour, by the statue of the soldier. If you want to, we could meet for a drink later on." He left a long meaningful pause before adding: "The four of us."

"I'll see what César says."

She watched him as he walked off into the crowd, his broad shoulders swaying, until he'd disappeared from view. As on other occasions, she was left with the uncomfortable feeling of having been unable just to let things be, as if, despite her rejection of his offer, Max had again managed to violate her inner self. She was irritated with herself, although she didn't know quite what she should have done. There were times, she thought, when she would give anything to be strong enough simply to punch Max in his handsome, self-satisfied stud's face.

She wandered amongst the stalls for about a quarter of an hour before going to the café. She tried to distract herself with the comings and goings about her, with the voices of the sellers and the people round the stalls, but to no avail. Once she'd forgotten Max, the painting, and Álvaro's death, the game of chess returned like an obsession, posing unanswerable questions. Perhaps the invisible player was also near at hand, in the crowd, watching her as he planned his next move. She looked about suspiciously and pressed her leather bag to her, the bag containing César's pistol. It was all terribly absurd, or perhaps it was the other way round, absurdly terrible.

The café had a wooden floor and old wrought-iron-and-marble tables. Julia ordered a cold drink and sat next to a misty window, trying not to think about anything, until César's blurred silhouette appeared in the street outside. She went out to meet him, in search of consolation, as seemed only fitting.

"You get lovelier by the minute," said César, affecting an admiring tone and standing ostentatiously in the middle of the street, with his hands on his hips. "How ever do you manage it, my dear?"

"Don't be silly," she said, taking his arm with a feeling of infinite relief. "It was only an hour ago that I left you."

"That's what I mean, Princess." César lowered his voice as if he were whispering secrets. "You're the only woman I know capable of becoming more beautiful in the space of sixty minutes. If I knew how you did it, we could patent it. Really."

"You're an idiot."

"And you, my dear, are gorgeous."

They walked down the street towards Julia's car. Along the way, César brought her up to date on the success of the operation he'd just conducted: a *Mater dolorosa* which, to a fairly undiscerning buyer, could be safely attributed to Murillo and a Biedermeier writing desk signed and dated in 1832 by Virienichen, a bit battered but authentic, and nothing that a good cabinet-maker couldn't put to rights. Two genuine bargains acquired at a very reasonable price.

"Especially the writing desk, Princess." César was swinging his umbrella, delighted with the deal he'd made. "As you know, there's a certain social class, blessings be upon them, who cannot live without a bed that once belonged to Empress Eugénie or the desk where Talleyrand signed his perjuries. Well, now there's a new bourgeois class of *parvenus* who, in their attempts to emulate them, feel they simply have to have a Biedermeier as the supreme symbol of their triumph. They come to you and ask you straight out, without specifying whether they want a table or a desk; what they want is a Biedermeier whatever the cost and whatever it is. Some even believe blindly in the historical existence of poor Mr Biedermeier and are most surprised when they see that the piece of furniture is actually signed by someone else. First, they give me a disconcerted smile, then they nudge each other and immediately ask if I haven't got another Biedermeier, a real one." César sighed, no doubt deploring the difficult times in which he lived. "If it wasn't for their chequebooks, I can assure you that I'd be tempted to send a few of them *chez les grecs*."

"I seem to remember that on occasion that's exactly what you have done."

César sighed again, with a pained grimace.

"That's my daring side, my dear. Sometimes my character just gets the better of me; it's the scandalous old queen in me, I suppose. A bit like Dr Jekyll and Mr Hyde. Just as well hardly anyone these days speaks decent French."

They reached Julia's car, parked in an alley, just as she was telling him about her encounter with Max. The mere mention of the name was enough to make César frown.

"I'm only glad I didn't see him, the pimp," he remarked crossly. "Is he still making treacherous propositions?"

"Nothing serious. I suppose that deep down he's afraid Menchu would find out."

"That's where it would hurt the little rat. In the wallet." César walked round the car towards the passenger door. "Look at that! They've slapped a fine on us."

"They haven't, have they?"

"Oh, yes, they have. It's stuck under the windscreen wiper." Irritated, he banged the ground with his umbrella. "I don't believe it. Right in the middle of the Rastro and the police spend their time giving out fines instead of doing what they should be doing, arresting criminals and other riffraff. It's a disgrace!" He repeated it loudly, looking about him defiantly: "An absolute disgrace!"

Julia removed the empty aerosol can someone had placed on the bonnet of the car and picked up the piece of paper, which was in fact a small card, about the size of a visiting card. Then she stood utterly still, thunderstruck. The shock must have shown on her face, because César, alarmed, hurried round to her side.

"You've gone quite pale, my dear. What's wrong?"

When she spoke, she didn't recognise her own voice. She felt a terrible desire to run away to some warm, secure place where she could hide her head and close her eyes and feel safe.

"It isn't a fine, César."

She held out the card, and César uttered a word no one would expect to hear from him. Because there, in a now all too familiar format, someone had typed the sinisterly laconic characters:

Pa7 x Rb6

As she stood, stunned, she felt as if her head were spinning. The alley was deserted. The person nearest to it was a seller of religious images, who was sitting on a wicker chair on the corner, about twenty yards from them, watching the people walking past the merchandise she'd laid out on the ground.

"He was here, César. Don't you see? He was *here*."

She realised that there was fear in her words but not surprise. Now – and the realisation came in waves of infinite despair – she was not afraid of the unexpected, her fear had become a kind of gloomy sense of resignation, as if the mystery player and his close, threatening presence were becoming an irremediable curse under which she would have to live for the rest of her life. Always supposing, she thought with lucid pessimism, that she had much life left to live.

Ashen, César was turning the card round and round. He could barely speak for indignation:

"The swine . . . the blackguard."

Julia's thoughts were suddenly distracted from the card. What claimed her attention was the empty can she'd found on the bonnet. She picked it up, feeling, as she bent to do so, as though she were moving through the mists of a dream. But she was able to concentrate long enough on the label to understand what it was. She shook her head, puzzled, before showing it to César.

"What's that?" he asked.

"An aerosol for repairing flat tyres. You stick it in the valve and the tyre inflates. It's got a sort of white paste in it that repairs the puncture from inside."

"What's it doing here?"

"That's what I'd like to know."

They checked the tyres. There was nothing odd about the two on the left. Julia walked round the car and checked the two on the right, which also seemed fine. But just as she was about to drop the can on the ground, she noticed that the valve on the back tyre was missing its cap. In its place was a bubble of white paste.

"Someone's pumped up the tyre," said César, after staring at the empty container. "Perhaps it was punctured."

"It wasn't when we parked it," said Julia, and they looked at each other, full of dark presentiments.

"Don't get in," said César.

The seller of religious images had seen nothing. There were always a lot of people around and, besides, she was busy with her own affairs, she explained, laying out sacred hearts, statuettes of San Pancracio and sundry virgins. As for the alley, she wasn't sure. A couple of locals had been past in the last hour, possibly a few other people.

"Do you remember anyone in particular?" César had taken off his hat and was bending towards the seller, his overcoat over his shoulders and his umbrella under his arm. The image of a perfect gentleman, the woman must have thought.

"I don't think so." She wrapped her woollen shawl more tightly round her and frowned as if struggling to remember. "There was a lady, I think. And a couple of young men."

"Do you remember what they looked like?"

"Just young men, you know the type: leather jackets and jeans . . ."

An absurd idea flitted across Julia's mind. The limits of the impossible had, after all, broadened considerably in the last few days.

"Did you see someone in a navy blue jacket? A man about thirty with his hair in a ponytail?"

The seller did not remember having seen Max. She'd noticed the woman, though, because she'd stopped for a moment as if she were going to buy something. She was blonde, middle-aged and well-dressed. But she couldn't imagine her breaking into a car; she wasn't the type. She was wearing a raincoat.

"And dark glasses?"

"Yes."

César looked at Julia gravely.

"It's not even sunny today," he said.

"I know."

"It could have been the same woman who delivered the documents." César paused and his eyes hardened. "Or Menchu."

"Don't be ridiculous."

César shook his head, glancing at the people walking past.

"No, you're right. But you yourself thought it might be Max."

"Max . . . is different." Her face darkened as she looked down the street, as though Max or the blonde in the raincoat might still be around. What she saw froze the words on her lips and shook her with the force of a blow. There was no woman answering the description, but amongst the awnings and the plastic sheeting of the stalls was a car, parked near the corner. A blue car.

From where she was standing, Julia couldn't tell if it was a Ford or not, but the jolt of emotion she felt propelled her into action. To César's surprise, she left the seller of religious images, walked a little way along the pavement and then, skirting a couple of stalls, stood staring over at the corner, on tiptoe in order to get a better look. It was a blue Ford, with smoked-glass windows. Thoughts crowded into her head. She couldn't see the numberplate, but there had been too many coincidences that morning: Max, Menchu, the card on the windscreen, the empty spray can, the woman in the raincoat and now the car that had become a key element in her nightmare. She was conscious that her hands were trembling and she thrust them into her pockets at the same moment she felt César's presence behind her.

"It's the car, César. Do you know what that means? Whoever it is, is inside."

César didn't say anything. He slowly took off his hat, perhaps thinking it inappropriate for whatever might happen next, and looked at Julia. She had never loved him so much as she did then, his lips pressed together, his chin up, his blue eyes narrowed and in them a rare glint of steel. The thin lines of his meticulously shaven face looked tense; his jaw muscles twitched. His eyes seemed to say that, man of impeccable manners with little inclination for violence he might be, but he was no coward. At least not where his princess was concerned.

"Wait for me here," he said.

"No. Let's go together. You and me." She looked at him tenderly. Once, when she was a child, she'd kissed him playfully on the mouth. At that moment she felt an impulse to do so again; but this wasn't a game they were playing now.

She put her hand in her bag and cocked the derringer. Very calmly, César put his umbrella under his arm, went over to one of the stalls and, as if he were selecting a walking stick, grabbed a huge iron poker.

"May I?" he said, pressing the first note he found in his wallet into the astonished stallholder's hand. He then looked serenely at Julia again and said: "Just this once, my dear, allow me to go first."

They set off towards the car, using stalls as cover. Julia's heart was beating hard when she at last got a glimpse of the numberplate. There was no doubt about it: a blue Ford, smoked-glass windows and the letters TH. Her mouth was dry, and she had an uncomfortable feeling in her stomach as if it had contracted in upon itself. That, she said to herself quickly, was what Captain Peter Blood used to feel before boarding an enemy ship.

They reached the corner, and everything happened fast. Someone inside the car lowered the driver's window to toss out a cigarette. César dropped his umbrella and his hat, raised the poker and walked round to the left side of the car, prepared, if necessary, to kill the pirates or whoever was inside. Julia, her teeth gritted and the blood pounding in her temples, started to run. She took the pistol out and stuck it through the window before the driver had time to wind it up again. In front of her pistol appeared an unknown face: a young man with a beard, who was staring at the gun with terrified eyes. The man in the passenger seat jumped when César wrenched opened the door, the iron poker raised threateningly above his head.

"Get out! Out!" shouted Julia, almost beside herself.

His face deathly pale, the man with the beard raised his hands with his fingers wide, in a gesture of supplication.

"Calm down, Señorita!" he stammered. "For God's sake, calm down! We're the police."

"I recognise," said Inspector Feijoo, clasping his hands together on his office desk, "that so far we haven't been terribly efficient in this matter . . ."

He smiled placidly at César, as if the police's lack of efficiency was justified. Since we're in sophisticated company, his look seemed to say, we can allow ourselves a certain amount of constructive self-criticism.

But César seemed ill-disposed to accept this.

"That," he said disdainfully, "is one way of describing what others would call sheer incompetence."

It was clear from Feijoo's crumbling smile that César's remark was the last straw. His teeth appeared beneath the thick moustache, biting his lower lip and he began an impatient drumming on the desk with the end of his cheap ballpoint. César's presence meant that he had no option but to tread carefully, and all three of them knew why.

"The police have their methods."

These were empty words, and César grew impatient, cruel. The fact that he had dealings with Feijoo didn't mean that he had to be nice to him, still less when he'd caught him in some funny business.

"If those methods consist of having Julia followed while some madman out there is on the loose, sending anonymous messages, I would rather not say what I think of such methods." He turned towards Julia, then back to the policeman. "I can't believe that you consider her to be a suspect in the death of Professor Ortega. Why haven't you investigated me?"

"We have." Feijoo was piqued by César's impertinence, and had to bite back his anger. "The fact is, we investigated everyone." He turned up his palms, accepting responsibility for what he was prepared to acknowledge had been a monumental blunder. "Unfortunately, these things do happen in this job."

"And have you found out anything?"

"I'm afraid not." Feijoo reached inside his jacket to scratch an armpit and shifted uncomfortably in his seat. "To be perfectly honest, we're back at square one. The pathologists can't agree on the cause of Álvaro Ortega's death. If there really is a murderer at large, our only hope is that at some point he makes a mistake."

"Is that why you've been following me?" asked Julia, still furious. She was clutching her bag in her lap. "To see if I make a mistake?"

The Inspector looked at her grimly.

"You shouldn't take it so personally. It's purely routine. Just police tactics."

César arched an eyebrow.

"As a tactic it doesn't strike me as being either particularly promising or particularly efficient."

Feijoo gulped down the sarcasm. At that moment, thought Julia with wicked delight, he must be deeply regretting any illicit dealings he'd had with César. All it needed was for César to open his mouth in a few opportune places and, with no direct accusations being made and with no official paperwork involved, in the discreet way that things tend to be done at a certain level, the Inspector would find himself ending his career in a gloomy office in some far-flung police department, as a pen-pusher with no prospect of extra income.

"I can only assure you," he said at last, when he'd managed to digest some of the rancour which, as his face plainly revealed, was still stuck in his gullet, "that we will continue our investigations." He seemed to remember something, reluctantly. "And of course the young lady will be put under special protection."

"Don't bother," said Julia. Feijoo's humiliation was not enough to make her forget her own. "No more blue cars, please. Enough is enough."

"It's for your own safety, Señorita."

"As you see, I can look after myself."

The policeman looked away. No doubt his throat still hurt from the bawling out he'd given the two policemen for letting themselves be surprised. "Idiots!" he'd screamed at them. "Bloody amateurs! You've really dropped me in the shit this time and, believe me, you're going to suffer for it!" César and Julia had heard it all while they were waiting in the corridor at the police station.

"As for that . . ." he began now, after waging what had obviously been a hard battle in his mind between duty and convenience, and crumbling before the weightier demands of the latter. "Given the circumstances, I don't think that . . . I mean that the pistol . . ." He swallowed again before looking at César. "After all, it is an antique, not a modern weapon in the real sense of the word. And you, as an antiques dealer, have the correct licence." He looked down at the desk, doubtless remembering the last piece, an eighteenth-century clock, for which, only weeks before, César had paid him a good price. "For my part, and I'm speaking here for my two men involved as well . . ." Again he gave that treacherous, conciliatory smile. "I mean that we're prepared to overlook certain details of the matter. You, Don César, may reclaim your derringer as long as you promise to take better care of it in future. As for you, Señorita, keep us informed of any new developments and, of course, phone us at once if you have any problems. As far as we're concerned, there never was any gun. Do I make myself clear?"

"Perfectly," said César.

"Good." His concession over the gun seemed to give Feijoo some sort of moral advantage, so he appeared more relaxed when he spoke to Julia. "As for the tyre on your car, I need to know if you want to make a complaint."

She looked at him, surprised.

"A complaint? Against whom?"

The Inspector waited before replying as if hoping that Julia would guess his meaning without recourse to words.

"Against a person or persons unknown," he said. "On a charge of attempted murder."

"Álvaro's, you mean?"

"No, yours." His teeth appeared beneath his moustache again. "Because whoever is sending you those cards has something more serious than chess on his mind. You can buy an aerosol like the one used to fill your tyre, once he'd let the air out, in any shop selling spare parts. Except that this particular aerosol was topped up with a syringeful of petrol. That, with the gas and the plastic stuff already in the container, becomes highly explosive above certain temperatures. You would only have had to drive a few hundred yards for the tyre to heat up sufficiently to produce an explosion immediately underneath the petrol tank. The car would have burst into flames with both of you inside." He was smiling with evident malice, as if his telling them that was a minor act of revenge. "Isn't that terrible?"

Muñoz arrived at César's shop an hour later, his ears sticking out above his raincoat collar and his hair wet. He looked like a scrawny stray dog, Julia thought as she watched him shaking off the rain at the door. He shook Julia's hand, an abrupt handshake, without warmth, a simple contact that committed him to nothing, and greeted César with a nod of the head. Doing his best to keep his wet shoes away from the carpet, he listened unblinkingly to what had happened in the Rastro, moving his head every now and then in a vaguely affirmative gesture, as if the story about the blue Ford and César's poker held no interest for him whatsoever. His dull eyes only lit up when Julia took the card out of her bag and placed it before him. Minutes later he had laid out his small chess set, which recently he'd never been without, and was intent on studying the latest position of the pieces.

"What I don't understand," Julia said, looking over Muñoz's shoulder, "is why the empty spray can was left on the bonnet. We were bound to see it there. Unless the person who did it had to leave in a hurry."

"Perhaps it was just a warning," suggested César from his leather armchair beneath the stained-glass window. "A warning in the worst possible taste."

"It was a lot of trouble to go to though, wasn't it? Preparing the aerosol, letting the air out of the tyre and then pumping it up again. Not to mention the fact that she risked being seen while she was doing it . . . It's pretty ridiculous," she added, "but have you noticed how I'm referring to our invisible player in the feminine? I can't stop thinking about the mystery woman in the raincoat."

"Perhaps we're going too far," said César. "When you think about it, there must have been dozens of blonde women in raincoats in the Rastro this morning. Some might have been wearing dark glasses. But you're right about that empty can. Leaving it right there on the car, in full view. Really grotesque."

"Not so grotesque perhaps," said Muñoz, and they both looked at him. Sitting on a stool, with the small chessboard laid out on a low table, he was in his shirtsleeves, which had been shortened with a tuck just above the elbow. He'd spoken without raising his head from the chess pieces. And Julia, who was by his side, saw at one corner of his mouth that indefinable expression she'd come to know well, halfway between silent reflection and the suggestion of a smile, and she knew he'd managed to decipher the latest move.

He reached out a finger to the pawn on square a7, without touching it.

"The black pawn that was on square a7 takes the white rook on b6," he said, showing them the situation on the board. "That's what our opponent says on the card."

"And what does that mean?" asked Julia.

"It means that he's declined to make another move which, in a way, we were afraid he might. I mean, taking the white queen on e1 with the black rook on c1. That move would inevitably have involved an exchange of queens." He glanced up from the pieces and gave Julia a worried look. "With all that that would imply."

Julia opened her eyes wide.

"Do you mean he's declined to take *me*?"

Muñoz's face remained ambivalent.

"You could interpret it like that." He studied the piece representing

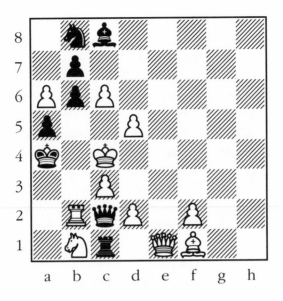

the white queen. "And, if that's the case, what he's saying to us is: 'I'm quite capable of killing, but I'll only do it when I want to.'"

"Like a cat playing with a mouse," murmured César, striking the arm of his chair. "The man's an utter villain!"

"The man or woman," Julia said.

César clicked his tongue.

"No one's saying that the woman in the raincoat, if she was the one in the alley, acted on her own. She might be someone's accomplice."

"Yes, but whose?"

"That's what I'd like to know, my dear."

"Anyway," said Muñoz, "if you forget the woman in the raincoat and concentrate on the card, you might reach a different conclusion about the personality of our opponent." He looked at each of them in turn before pointing to the board, as if he considered it a waste of time to seek answers anywhere but there. "We know he has a twisted mind, but it turns out that he's also extremely smug. He, or she, is also arrogant. He's playing with us." He indicated the board again, urging them to study the position of the pieces. "Look, in practical terms, in pure chess terms, taking the white queen would have been a bad move. White would have had no option but to accept the exchange of queens, taking the black queen with the white rook on b2, and that would leave Black in a very bad position. Black's only way out then would have been to move the black rook from e1 to e4, threatening the white king. But the latter would have protected himself simply by moving the white pawn from d2 to d4. Then, seeing the black king surrounded by enemy pieces, with no possible help, checkmate would have been inevitable. Black would lose the game."

"Do you mean," asked Julia, "that all that business with the can left on the car and the threat to the white queen is just a bluff?"

"It wouldn't surprise me in the least."

"But why?"

"Because our enemy has chosen the move I would have made in his place: taking the white rook on b6 with the pawn that was on a7. That eases White's pressure on the black king, who was in an extremely difficult position." He shook his head admiringly. "I told you he was a good player."

"And now?" asked César.

Muñoz passed a hand across his forehead and looked at the board thoughtfully.

"Now we have two options. Perhaps we should take the black queen, but that would force our opponent to carry out an exchange of queens," he said, looking at Julia, "and I don't like that. We don't want to force him to do something he's already decided against." He shook his head again as if the black and white pieces confirmed his thoughts. "The odd thing is that he knows that's how we'll think, which has its advantages, because I see the moves he makes and sends to us, whereas he can only imagine mine. Yet he can still influence them. Up until now, we've been doing what he wants us to do."

"Have we any choice?" asked Julia.

"Not so far. But later we might."

"So what's our next move?"

"We move our bishop from f1 to d3, threatening his queen."

"And what will he or she do?"

Muñoz paused before answering. He sat unmoving before the board, as if he hadn't heard the question.

"In chess too," he said at last, "there's a limit to the forecasts one can make. The best possible move, or the most probable one, is the one that leaves one's opponent in the least advantageous position. That's why one way of estimating the expediency of the next move consists simply in imagining that move has been made and then going on to analyse the game from your opponent's point of view. That means falling back on your own resources, but this time putting yourself in your enemy's shoes. From there, you conjecture another move and then immediately put yourself in the role of your opponent's opponent, in other words, yourself. And so on indefinitely, as far ahead as you can. By that, I mean that I know where I've got to, but I don't know how far he's got."

"According to that reasoning," Julia said, "isn't he most likely to choose the move that will do most damage to us?"

Muñoz scratched the back of his neck. Then, very slowly, he moved the white bishop to square d3, placing it near the black queen. He seemed absorbed in deep thought while he analysed the new situation.

"One thing I'm sure of," he said at last, "is that he's going to take another of our pieces."

XI

❦

Analytical Approaches

> Don't be silly. The flag is impossible,
> hence it can't be waving. The wind is waving.
> *Douglas R. Hofstadter*

THE SOUND OF THE TELEPHONE made her jump. Unhurriedly, she removed the solvent-soaked plug of cotton from the corner of the painting on which she was working – a stubborn bit of varnish on a tiny area of Ferdinand of Ostenburg's clothing – and put the tweezers between her teeth. Then she looked distrustfully at the telephone by her feet on the carpet, wondering if, when she picked it up, she would once again have to listen to one of those long silences that had become the norm over the last couple of weeks. At first she'd just held the phone to her ear without saying anything, waiting impatiently for some noise, even if only breathing, that would indicate life, a human presence, at the other end, however disquieting that might be. But she found only a void, without even the dubious consolation of hearing the click of the phone being put down. It was always the mystery caller – male or female – who held out longest. Whoever it was simply stayed there, listening, showing no sign of haste or concern about the possibility that the police might be tapping the phone to trace the call. The worst thing was that the person who telephoned her had no idea that he was safe. Julia had told no one about the calls, not even César or Muñoz. Without quite knowing why, she felt ashamed of them, humiliated by the way they invaded her privacy, invaded the night and the silence she had so loved before the nightmare began. It was like a ritual violation, without words or gestures, repeated every day.

When the phone had rung for the sixth time, she picked it up, and was relieved to hear Menchu's voice at the other end. Her relief lasted only a moment, however, for Menchu was extremely drunk. Perhaps, Julia thought with some concern, she had something stronger than alcohol in her blood. Raising her voice to make herself heard above the buzz of conversation and music, half of her phrases stumbling into incoherence, Menchu told Julia that she was at Stephan's and then recounted some confused story involving Max, the Van Huys and Paco Montegrifo. Julia didn't understand, and when she asked her friend to explain again what had happened, Menchu burst into hysterical laughter. Then she hung up.

The air was heavy, cold and damp. Shivering inside her cumbersome three-quarter-length leather coat, Julia went down to the street and hailed a taxi. The lights of the city slid across her face in flashes as she nodded now and again in response to the taxi driver's unwanted chatter. She leaned her head back on the seat and closed her eyes. Before leaving, she'd switched on the electronic alarm and locked the security door, turning the key twice in the lock. At the downstairs door she couldn't help casting a suspicious glance at the grid next to her bell, afraid of finding another card there. But she found nothing. The invisible player was still pondering his next move.

There were a lot of people at Stephan's. The first one she recognised was César, sitting on a sofa with Sergio. The young man was nodding, looking charming, his tousled blond hair over his eyes, as César whispered something to him. César was sitting with his legs crossed, smoking. The hand holding the cigarette rested on his knee; he waved the other in the air as he spoke, close to his protégé's arm but never quite touching it. As soon as he saw Julia, he got up and came to meet her. He didn't seem surprised to see her there at that hour, with no make-up on and wearing jeans.

"She's over there," he said, pointing to the interior of the club with a neutral look on his face that revealed, nonetheless, a certain amused anticipation. "On one of the sofas at the back."

"Has she been drinking a lot?"

"Like a fish. And I'm afraid she's oozing white powder from every orifice. She's been making suspiciously frequent visits to the Ladies; she can't need to pee that often." He regarded the ash on his cigarette and gave a wicked smile. "She made a scene a while ago at the bar: she slapped Montegrifo. Can you imagine, my dear? It was really" – he savoured the idea like a connoisseur, before uttering the word out loud – "delicious."

"And Montegrifo?"

César's expression became cruel.

"Fascinating, darling, verging on the divine. He left in that stiff, dignified way of his, with a very attractive blonde on his arm, a bit common but well-dressed. She was *so* embarrassed, the poor thing, as well she might be. You couldn't really blame her." He smiled with intense malice. "I have to admit, Princess, that the chap has style. He took the slap very coolly, without batting an eyelid, like tough guys in the films. A very interesting man, that auctioneer of yours. I must admit he behaved impeccably. Cool as a cucumber."

"Where's Max?"

"I haven't seen him tonight, I'm sorry to say." Again that perverse smile appeared. "Now that really would have been fun. The icing on the cake."

Leaving César, Julia walked into the club. She greeted several acquaintances without stopping to talk, and saw her friend Menchu sitting slumped on a sofa, alone. Her eyes were glazed, her short skirt was hitched up and she had a grotesque tear in one leg of her tights. She looked ten years older.

"Menchu."

She looked at Julia, barely recognising her. Mumbling incoherently, she shook her head and let out the short, uncertain laugh of the drunk.

"You missed it," she said after a moment, her voice slurred. "That bastard – standing right there he was, half his face bright scarlet." She pulled herself up and rubbed her reddened nose, oblivious to the inquisitive, scandalised looks of people at nearby tables. "Stupid arrogant sod."

Julia felt everyone's eyes on her; she could hear muttered comments and she blushed.

"Do you think you can manage to stand up and get out of here?"

"I think so. But first, I must just tell you . . ."

"Tell me later. Let's go."

Menchu struggled to her feet, clumsily pulling down her skirt. Draping Menchu's coat over her shoulders, Julia got her to walk towards the door in a relatively dignified manner. César came over to them.

"Everything OK?"

"Yes. I think I can manage."

"Are you sure?"

"Yes. I'll see you tomorrow."

Out in the street Menchu swayed, and someone yelled an obscenity at her from the window of a passing car.

"Take me home, Julia. Please."

"Yours or mine?"

Menchu looked at her as if she had some difficulty recognising her. She was moving like a sleepwalker.

"Yours," she said.

"What about Max?"

"It's all over with Max. We had a row. It's finished."

They got a taxi and Menchu hunched up in the back seat. Then she burst into tears. Julia put an arm around her trembling shoulders. The taxi stopped at a traffic light and a brilliant shop window lit up Menchu's ravaged face.

"I'm sorry. I'm a . . ."

Julia felt embarrassed, uncomfortable. It was just grotesque. Damn Max, she said to herself. Damn the lot of them.

"Don't be silly," she said, interrupting.

She saw the taxi driver observing them curiously in his rear-view mirror, and when she turned back to Menchu she caught an unusual look in her eyes, a brief flash of unexpected lucidity, as if there was still a place inside untouched by the fumes of alcohol and drugs. She was surprised to see something of infinite depth, of dark significance. It was a look so inappropriate to the state Menchu was in that Julia felt disconcerted. When Menchu spoke, her words were even stranger.

"You don't understand anything," she said, shaking her head in pain, like a wounded animal. "But whatever happens . . . I want you to know . . ."

She stopped abruptly, as if biting back the words, and her gaze became lost once more in the shadows, leaving Julia perplexed. It was too much for one night. All she needed now, she thought, feeling a vague apprehension that augured no good, was to find another card by the entry bell.

*   *   *

But there was no card that night, and she could devote herself to looking after Menchu, who seemed to be moving in a fog. Julia gave her two cups of coffee before putting her to bed. Feeling like a psychiatrist seated by her couch, she gradually managed, with great patience, to reconstruct out of the incoherent babblings exactly what had happened. At the worst possible moment, Max, ungrateful Max, had got it into his head to go off on a trip, some stupid story about a job in Portugal. She was having a bad time and his going off like that seemed a selfish dereliction of duty. They'd argued, and instead of resolving the problem in bed, as they usually did, he'd slammed the door on her. Menchu didn't know if he intended to come back or not, but she didn't give a damn either way. Determined not to be alone, she'd gone to Stephan's. A few lines of coke had helped to clear her head, leaving her in a state of aggressive euphoria. With Max forgotten, she sat in her corner drinking very dry martinis and eyeing a gorgeous guy who'd noticed her. Then the mood of the night suddenly changed. Unfortunately for Paco Montegrifo, he turned up too, accompanied by one of those bejewelled bitches he was seen with from time to time. The matter of the percentages was still fresh in her mind and she thought she detected a certain irony in the way he greeted her. As they say in novels, it was like a knife being turned in the wound. She delivered a single slap, thwack, a real humdinger, that caused a great stir amongst the clientele. A huge uproar ensued, end of story. Curtain.

Julia put a blanket over Menchu and sat by her for a while. She finally got to sleep at about two in the morning. Sometimes she flailed about and uttered unintelligible words, her lips pressed together, her hair all over her face. Julia looked at the lines around her mouth and lips, at the black smudges where tears and sweat had made her make-up run. It gave her a pathetic look: the look of an ageing courtesan after a bad night. No doubt César would have drawn some scathing conclusion, but Julia didn't feel like thinking about César. She found herself praying to life to give her the necessary spirit of resignation to grow old with dignity when her turn came. It must be terrible, at the moment of shipwreck, not to have a solid raft on which to save oneself. She realised that Menchu was old enough to be her mother, and felt ashamed at the thought, as if in some way she'd taken advantage of her friend's sleep in order to betray her.

She drank what remained of her coffee, cold now, and lit a cigarette. The rain was once more beating down on the skylight, the sound of solitude, she thought sadly. It reminded her of that other rainy night, a year ago, when she'd ended her relationship with Álvaro and knew that something had broken inside her for ever, like a faulty mechanism beyond repair. And she knew too that, from then on, the bittersweet solitude that filled her heart would be her one sure companion as she walked what roads were left for her to follow, beneath a heaven in which the gods were slowly dying amidst great gales of laughter. That night she had crouched beneath the shower, steam curling about her like scalding mist, her tears mingling with the water falling in torrents on her drenched hair and her naked body. That clean, warm water had washed Álvaro away a year before his physical and definitive death. And by one of those strange ironies of which Fate is so fond, that was how Álvaro had ended his life, in a bathtub, with his eyes wide open and his neck broken, beneath the shower, beneath the rain.

She dismissed the memory, saw it vanish, amongst the shadows in her studio. Then she thought about César and moved her head slowly to the rhythm of a melancholy, imaginary music. At that moment, she would have liked to lean her head on his shoulder, close her eyes and breathe in the delicate smell of tobacco and myrrh that she'd known since she was little, the smell that meant César. And to relive with him all those stories in which you knew beforehand there would be a happy ending. How far away they seemed, those days of happy endings, incompatible with any kind of mature lucidity! It was hard sometimes to look at herself in the mirror and know that she was in eternal exile from Never-Never-Land.

She switched off the light and sat on the carpet in front of the Van Huys, seeing the people in the picture in her imagination and hearing the distant rumble of the tides of their lives washing around the game of chess that had lasted throughout time and space and still continued to be played – like the slow, implacable mechanism of a clock that has defied the centuries – a game whose outcome no one could foresee. Then she forgot about everything – about Menchu, about her nostalgia for time past – and instead felt a now familiar shiver run through her, a shiver of fear, which was also obscurely, unexpectedly consoling. A kind of morbid expectancy. Like when she was a child and sat curled up against César to hear a new story. Perhaps Captain Hook had not disappeared into the mists of the past after all. Perhaps now he was simply playing chess instead.

When she woke up, Menchu was still asleep. She dressed with a minimum of noise, left a set of keys on the table and went out, carefully locking the door behind her. It was almost ten o'clock, and the rain had given way to a murky mix of fog and smog that blurred the grey outlines of the buildings and made the cars driving along seem ghostly, the reflections from their headlights fragmenting on the asphalt into infinite points of light that wove an atmosphere of luminous unreality about her as she walked along with her hands in the pockets of her raincoat.

Belmonte received her in his wheelchair, in the room with the mark left by the Van Huys. The inevitable Bach was playing on the gramophone and Julia wondered, as she took the dossier out of her bag, if the old man put it on deliberately each time she visited. He expressed regret at the absence of Muñoz, the mathematician-cum-chess-player, as he called him with an irony that did not go unnoticed, and carefully read the report Julia had brought, which gave all the historical facts about the painting, Muñoz's final conclusions regarding the enigma of Roger de Arras, photographs of the different phases of the restoration work and the colour brochure, just printed by Claymore's, giving details of the painting and the auction. He gave occasional satisfied nods and sometimes glanced up at Julia before immersing himself once more in the report.

"Excellent," he said when he'd finished and closed the dossier. "You're a remarkable young woman."

"It wasn't just me. As you know, a lot of people have worked on this . . . Paco Montegrifo, Menchu Roch, Muñoz . . ." She hesitated. "We also consulted art experts."

"You mean the late Professor Ortega?"

Julia looked at him, disconcerted.

"I didn't know you knew about that."

The old man gave a sly smile.

"Well, as you see, I do. When his body was found, the police got in touch with my niece, her husband and me. An inspector came to see me; I don't remember his name . . . He had a big moustache and he was fat."

"His name is Feijoo, Inspector Feijoo." Julia looked away, embarrassed. Damn, she thought, useless bloody police. "But you didn't say anything about this last time I was here."

"I was waiting for you to tell me. If you didn't, I assumed you must have your reasons."

There was a note of reserve in his voice, and Julia understood that she was on the point of losing an ally.

"I thought . . . I mean, I'm sorry, really I am . . . I was afraid I might upset you with such news. After all, you . . . ."

"Do you mean because of my age and my state of health?" Belmonte clasped his bony freckled hands over his stomach. "Or were you concerned that it might influence the fate of the painting?"

Julia shook her head, not knowing what to say. Then she smiled and shrugged, with an air of confused sincerity which, as she perfectly well knew, was the only response that would satisfy the old man.

"What can I say?" she murmured, sure that she'd hit the target when Belmonte also smiled, accepting the climate of complicity she was offering him.

"Don't worry. Life is difficult and human relationships even more so."

"I can assure you that . . ."

"You don't have to assure me about anything. We were talking about Professor Ortega. Was it an accident?"

"I think so," Julia lied. "At least, so I understand."

The old man looked at his hands. It was impossible to know whether he believed her or not.

"It's still terrible . . . don't you think?" He gave her a long, serious look in which vague disquiet was apparent. "That sort of thing, by which I mean death, always shocks me a little. And at my age it ought to be the other way round. It's odd how, against all logic, one clings to life in inverse proportion to the quantity of life one has left to look forward to."

For a moment, Julia was on the point of entrusting him with the rest of the story: the existence of the invisible player, the threats, the dark feelings weighing her down, the curse of the Van Huys, whose mark, an empty rectangle beneath a nail, watched over them from the wall like an evil omen. But that would mean providing explanations she didn't feel strong enough to embark upon. She was also afraid of alarming the old man still further, and needlessly.

"There's no need to worry," she lied again, with aplomb. "That's all under control. Like the painting."

They smiled at each other, but it was forced this time. Julia didn't know whether Belmonte believed her or not. He'd leaned back in his wheelchair and was frowning.

"There was something about the painting that I wanted to tell you." He stopped and thought a little before going on. "The other day, after you and your chess-playing friend visited me, I was thinking about the Van Huys. Do you remember our discussion about a system being necessary in order to understand another system and that both would need a superior system, and so on indefinitely? And the Borges poem about chess and which god beyond God moves the player who moves the chess pieces? Well, I think there is something of that in this painting. Something that both contains itself and repeats itself, taking you continually back to the starting point. In my opinion, the real key to interpreting *The Game of Chess* doesn't follow a straight line, a progression that sets out from one beginning. Instead, this painting seems to go back again and again, as if turned in upon itself. Do you understand what I mean?"

Julia nodded, listening intently to his words. What she'd just heard was a confirmation of her own intuition, but expressed in logical terms and spoken out loud. She remembered the list she had made, amended by Muñoz to six levels containing each other, of the eternal return to the starting point, of the paintings within the painting.

"I understand better than you might think," she said. "It's as if the painting were accusing itself."

Belmonte was puzzled.

"Accusing itself? That goes some way beyond my idea." With a slight lift of his eyebrows, he dismissed her apparently incomprehensible remark. "I was talking about something else." He pointed to the gramophone. "Listen to Bach."

"We always do."

Belmonte gave her a conspiratorial smile.

"I hadn't planned to be accompanied by Johann Sebastian today, but I decided to evoke him in your honour. It's the French Suite No. 5, and you'll notice that this composition consists of two halves, each of which is repeated. The tonic note of the first half is G and it ends in the key of D. All right? Now listen. Just when it seems that the piece has finished in that key, that trickster Bach suddenly makes us jump back to the beginning, with G as tonic again, and then slides back again to D. And, without our knowing quite how, that happens again and again. What do you think?"

"I think it's fascinating." Julia was following the musical chords intently. "It's like a continuous loop. Like those paintings and drawings by Escher, in which a river flows along, then becomes a waterfall and inexplicably goes back to the beginning. Or the staircase that leads nowhere, only back to the start of the staircase itself."

Belmonte nodded, satisfied.

"Exactly. And it's possible to play it in many keys." He looked at the empty rectangle on the wall. "The difficulty, I suppose, is to know where to place oneself in those circles."

"You're right. It would take a long time to explain, but there is something of that going on in the painting. Just when it seems the story has ended, it starts again, but goes off in another direction. Or apparently in another direction. Because perhaps we never actually move from the spot we're in."

Belmonte shrugged.

"That's a paradox to be resolved by you and your friend the chess player. I lack the necessary information. As you know, I'm only an amateur. I wasn't even capable of guessing that the game could be played backwards." He gave Julia a long look. "Unforgivable of me really, considering what I've just said about Bach."

Julia pondered these new and unexpected interpretations. Threads from a ball of wool, she was thinking. Too many threads for one ball.

"Apart from the police and me, have you had any other visits recently from anyone interested in the painting? Or in chess?"

The old man took a while to reply, as if trying to ascertain what lay behind the question.

"Neither the one nor the other. When my wife was alive, people often came to the house. She was more sociable than me. But since I was widowed I've kept in touch with only a few old friends. Esteban Cano, for example. You're too young to have known him when he was a successful violinist. But he died, two years ago now. The truth is that my small circle of friends has gradually been disappearing." He gave a resigned smile. "There's Pepe, a good friend. Pepín Pérez Giménez, retired like me, who still goes to the club and drops by from time to time to have a game of chess with me. But he's nearly seventy and gets terrible migraines if he plays for more than half an hour. He was a great chess player once. And there's my niece."

Julia, who was taking out a cigarette, stopped. When she moved again, she did so very slowly, as if any excited or impatient gesture might cause what she'd just heard to vanish.

"Your niece plays chess?"

"Lola? Yes, very well." The old man gave an odd smile, as if he regretted that his niece's virtues did not extend to other areas of her life. "I taught her to play myself, years ago; but she outgrew her teacher."

Julia was trying to remain calm. She forced herself to light her cigarette calmly and exhaled two slow clouds of smoke before she spoke again. She could feel her heart beating fast.

"What does your niece think about the painting? Did she approve of you selling it?" A shot in the dark.

"She was very much in favour of it. And her husband was even keener." There was a bitter note in the old man's voice. "No doubt Alfonso has already worked out on which number of the roulette wheel he's going to place every last cent he gets from the Van Huys."

"But he hasn't got it yet," Julia pointed out.

The old man held her gaze and a hard light appeared in his pale, liquid eyes, but it was rapidly extinguished.

"In my day," he said with unexpected good humour and only placid irony in his eyes now, "we used to say you shouldn't count your chickens before they're hatched."

"Has your niece ever mentioned anything mysterious about the painting, about the people in it or the game of chess?"

"Not that I remember. You were the first one to talk about that. For us, it had always been a special painting, but not extraordinary or mysterious." He looked thoughtfully at the rectangle on the wall. "Everything seemed very obvious."

"Do you know if, before or at the time when Alfonso introduced you to Menchu Roch, your niece was negotiating with someone else?"

Belmonte frowned. That possibility seemed to displease him greatly.

"I certainly hope not. After all, the painting was mine." The expression on his face was astute and full of a knowing mischief. "And it still is."

"Can I ask you one more question, Don Manuel?"

"Of course."

"Did you ever hear your niece and her husband talk about consulting an art historian?"

"I don't think so. I don't recall them doing it, and I think I'd remember something like that." Suspicion had resurfaced in his eyes. "That was Professor Ortega's job, wasn't it? Art history. I hope you're not trying to insinuate . . ."

Julia realised she'd gone too far, so she produced one of her best smiles.

"I didn't necessarily mean Álvaro Ortega, but any art historian. It's not such an odd idea that your niece might have been curious to know the value of the painting, or to find out its history."

Belmonte looked at the backs of his freckled hands with a reflective air.

"She never mentioned it. And I think she would have, because we often talked about the Van Huys. Especially when we used to replay the game the people in the painting are playing. We played it forwards, of course. And do you know something? Although White appears to have the advantage, Lola always won with Black."

She walked aimlessly about in the fog for almost an hour, trying to put her ideas in order. The damp air left droplets of moisture on her face and hair. She passed the Palace Hotel, where the doorman, in top hat and gold-braided uniform, was sheltering beneath the glass canopy, wrapped in a cloak that made him look like someone out of nineteenth-century London, in keeping with the fog. All that was missing, she thought, was a horse-drawn carriage, its lantern dimmed by the grey mist, out of which would step the gaunt figure of Sherlock Holmes, followed by his faithful companion, Watson. Somewhere in the murk the sinister Professor Moriarty would be watching. The Napoleon of crime. The evil genius.

Lately she seemed to have come across far too many people who played chess. And everyone had excellent reasons for their links with the Van Huys. There were too many portraits inside that wretched painting.

Muñoz: he was the only person she'd met *since* the mystery began. When she couldn't sleep, when she was tossing and turning in her bed, he was the only one she did not connect with the nightmare images. Muñoz was at one end of the ball of wool and all the chess pieces, all the other characters, were at the other. But she couldn't even be sure of him. She had indeed met him *after* the mystery began, but *before* the story had gone back to its starting point and begun again in a different key. It was impossible even to know with absolute certainty that Álvaro's death and the existence of the mystery player were part of the same movement.

She stopped, feeling on her face the touch of the damp mist wrapped about her. When it came down to it, the only person she could be sure óf was herself. That was all she had to go on with, that and the pistol she still carried in her bag.

She made her way to the chess club. There was sawdust in the hallway, umbrellas, overcoats and raincoats. It smelled of damp, of cigarette smoke, and had the unmistakable atmosphere of places frequented exclusively by men. She greeted Cifuentes, the director, who rushed obsequiously to meet her, and, as the murmurs provoked by her appearance in the club died down, searched amongst the chess tables until she spotted Muñoz. He was concentrating on a game, sitting motionless as a sphinx, with one elbow on the arm of his chair, his chin resting on the palm of that hand. His opponent, a young man with thick glasses, kept licking his lips and casting troubled glances at Muñoz, as if he were afraid that at any moment the latter might destroy the complicated king's defence which, to judge by his nervousness and his look of exhaustion, it had cost him an enormous effort to construct.

Muñoz seemed his usual calm, absent self; rather than studying the board, his motionless eyes seemed to be merely resting on it. Perhaps he was immersed in those daydreams of which he had spoken to Julia, a thousand miles away from the game taking place before his eyes, while his mathematical mind kept weaving and unweaving infinite, impossible combinations. Around them, a few onlookers were studying the game apparently with more interest than the players themselves. From time to time, they mumbled comments or suggested moving this or that piece. What seemed clear, given the tension around the table, was that they expected Muñoz to make some decisive move that would sound the death knell of the young man in glasses. That justified the nervousness of the latter, whose eyes, magnified by the lenses, looked at his adversary like a slave in the amphitheatre at the mercy of the lions, pleading for clemency from an omnipotent emperor in purple.

At that moment, Muñoz looked up and saw Julia. He stared at her for several seconds as if he didn't recognise her, then came to slowly, with the look of someone waking from a dream or returning from a long journey. His face brightened as he made a vague gesture of welcome. He glanced back at the board, to see if things there were still in order, and, not hastily or as if he were merely improvising, but as the conclusion of a long reasoning process, moved a pawn. A disappointed murmur arose around the table, and the young man in glasses looked across at him, first with surprise, then like a prisoner whose execution has been cancelled at the last moment, and then with a satisfied smirk.

"That makes it a draw," remarked one of the onlookers.

Muñoz, who was getting up from the table, shrugged.

"Yes," he replied, without looking at the board. "But if I'd moved bishop to queen 7 it would have been checkmate in five moves."

He went over to Julia, leaving the others to study the move he'd just mentioned. Discreetly indicating the group around the table, Julia said in a low voice:

"They must really hate you."

Muñoz put his head on one side and his expression could as easily have been interpreted as a distant smile or a look of scorn.

"I suppose so," he replied, picking up his raincoat. "They tend to gather like vultures, hoping to be there when someone finally tears me limb from limb."

"But you let yourself be beaten . . . That must be humiliating for them."

"That's the least of it," he said, but there was no smugness or pride in his voice, just a kind of objective contempt. "They wouldn't miss one of my games for anything."

Opposite the Prado, in the grey mist, Julia brought him up to date regarding her conversation with Belmonte. Muñoz heard her out without comment, not even when she told him about the niece's interest in chess. He seemed indifferent to the damp weather as he walked slowly along, listening carefully to what Julia said, his raincoat unbuttoned and the knot of his tie half undone as usual, his head bent and his eyes fixed on the scuffed toes of his shoes.

"You asked me once if there were any women who play chess," he said at last. "And I told you that, although chess is essentially a masculine game, there are some reasonable women players. But they are the exception."

"The exception that proves the rule, I suppose."

Muñoz frowned.

"No. You're wrong there. An exception doesn't prove anything; it invalidates or destroys any rule. That's why you have to be very careful with inductive reasoning. What I'm saying is that women *tend* to play chess badly, not that *all* women play chess badly. Do you understand?"

"I understand."

"Which doesn't detract from the fact that, in practice, women have little stature as chess players. Just to give you an idea: in the Soviet Union, where chess is the national pastime, only one woman, Vera Menchik, was ever considered to have reached grand master level."

"Why is that?"

"Maybe chess requires too much indifference to the outside world." He paused and looked at Julia. "What's this Lola Belmonte like?"

Julia considered before answering.

"I don't know how to describe her really. Unpleasant. Possibly domineering. Aggressive. It's a shame she wasn't there when you were with me the other day."

They were standing by a stone fountain crowned by the vague silhouette of a statue that hovered menacingly above their heads in the mist. Muñoz ran his hands over his hair and looked at his damp palms before rubbing them on his raincoat.

"Aggression, whether externalised or internalised," he said, "is characteristic of many players." He smiled briefly, without making it clear whether he considered himself to fall outside that definition or not. "And the chess player tends to be someone who's frustrated or oppressed in some way. The attack on the king, which is the aim in chess, that is, going against authority, would be a kind of liberation from that state. From that point of view the game could be of interest to a woman." The fleeting smile crossed his lips again. "When you play chess, people seem very insignificant from where you're sitting."

"Have you detected something of that in our enemy's games?"

"That's a difficult question to answer. I need more information. More moves. For example, women tend to show a predilection for bishop mates." Muñoz's expression grew animated as he went into details. "I don't know why, but those pieces, with their deep, diagonal moves, possibly have the most feminine character of all the pieces." He gestured as if he didn't give much credence to his words and were trying to erase them from the air. "But until now the black bishops haven't played an important role in the game. As you know, we have lots of nice theories that add up to nothing. Our problem is just the same as it is on a chessboard: we can only formulate imaginative hypotheses, conjectures, without touching the chess pieces."

"Have you come up with any hypotheses? Sometimes you give the impression that you've reached conclusions that you don't want to tell us about."

Muñoz tilted his head a little, as he always did when confronted by a difficult question.

"It's a bit complicated," he replied after a brief pause. "I have a couple of ideas in my head but my problem is just what I've been saying. In chess you can't prove anything until you've moved, and then it's impossible to go back."

They started walking again, between the stone benches and the blurry hedges. Julia sighed gently.

"If someone had told me that one day I'd be tracking a possible murderer with the help of a chessboard, I'd have said he was stark, staring mad."

"I told you before that there are many links between chess and police work." Muñoz's hand moved chess pieces in the void. "Even before Conan Doyle, there was Poe's Dupin method."

211

"Edgar Allan Poe? Don't tell me he played chess too."

"Oh, yes, he was a very keen player. There was an automaton known as Maelzel's Player which almost never lost a game. Poe wrote an essay about it around 1830. To get to the bottom of the mystery he developed sixteen analytical approaches and concluded that there must be a man hidden inside the automaton."

"And is that what you're doing? Looking for the hidden man?"

"I'm trying to, but that doesn't guarantee anything. I'm not Poe."

"I hope you succeed. It would certainly be to my advantage. You're my only hope."

Muñoz shrugged and said nothing for a while.

"I don't want you to get your hopes up," he said after they'd walked on a little further. "When I began playing chess, there were times when I felt sure I couldn't lose a single game. Then, in the midst of my euphoria, I was beaten, and that failure set my feet firmly back on the ground." He screwed up his eyes as if he could make out someone ahead of them in the fog. "There's always someone better than you. That's why it's useful to keep yourself in a state of healthy uncertainty."

"I find it terrible, that uncertainty."

"You have reason to. However fraught a game becomes, each player knows that it's a bloodless battle. After all, he consoles himself, it is only a game . . . But that's not so in your case."

"And you? Do you think *he* knows about your role in this?"

Muñoz looked evasive again.

"I don't know if he knows who I am. But he must know that there's someone capable of interpreting his moves. Otherwise, the game would make no sense."

"I think we should pay Lola Belmonte a visit."

"I agree."

Julia looked at her watch.

"Since we're near my place, why don't you come up for coffee? Menchu's staying with me, and she should be awake by now. She has a few problems."

"Serious problems?"

"So it seems, and last night she was behaving very strangely. I'd like you to meet her . . . Especially now."

They crossed the avenue, dazzled by car headlights.

212

"If I find out that Lola Belmonte is behind this whole thing," Julia said unexpectedly, "I'll kill her with my bare hands."

Muñoz looked at her, surprised.

"Assuming that my theory of aggression is correct," he said, and she saw that he was observing her with new respect, "you'd make an excellent player if you ever decided to take up chess."

"I already have taken it up," Julia replied, peering rancorously at the shadows drifting by her in the fog. "I've been playing for some time now, and I don't enjoy it one bit."

She put her key in the security lock and turned it twice. Muñoz was waiting by her side on the landing. He'd taken off his raincoat and folded it over his arm.

"It'll be a mess," she said. "I didn't have time to tidy up this morning."

"Don't worry. It's the coffee that matters."

Julia went into the studio and raised the large ceiling blind. The foggy brightness from outside slipped into the room, dusting the air with a grey light that left the farthest corners of the room in shadow.

"Still too dark," she said and was about to switch on the light when she saw the look on Muñoz's face. With a sudden feeling of panic, she followed the direction of his gaze.

"Where have you put the painting?" he asked.

Julia didn't reply. She felt as though something had burst inside her, deep inside, and she stood utterly still, her eyes wide, staring at the empty easel.

"Menchu," she murmured finally, feeling as if everything were spinning about her. "She warned me about this last night, only I couldn't see it."

Her stomach contracted and she felt the bitter taste of bile in her mouth. Absurdly, she glanced at Muñoz and then ran towards the bathroom, but, feeling faint, stopped and leaned against the doorway of her bedroom. That was when she saw Menchu. She was lying on her back on the floor at the foot of the bed. The scarf that had been used to strangle her was still around her neck. Her skirt was pulled grotesquely up to her waist, and the neck of a bottle had been thrust into her vagina.

XII

Queen, Knight, Bishop

I'm not playing with lifeless black and white
pawns. I'm playing with flesh-and-blood human beings.
E. Lasker

THE JUDGE didn't order the body to be taken away until seven o'clock, by which time it was dark. All afternoon the house had been filled with the comings and goings of policemen and court officials, with flashlights flickering in the hallway and in the bedroom. At last, they carried Menchu out on a stretcher, zipped up inside a white plastic cover, and all that remained of her was the silhouette drawn in chalk on the floor by the indifferent hand a policeman, the one who'd been driving the blue Ford when Julia drew her pistol on him in the Rastro.

Inspector Feijoo was the last to leave; he'd stayed on for nearly an hour to complete the statements made earlier by Julia and Muñoz, and also by César, who had come as soon as he heard the news. The policeman, who'd never been near a chessboard in his life, was patently bewildered. He kept looking at Muñoz as if at some bizarre animal, but nodded with wary gravity at the latter's technical explanations, every now and then turning to César and Julia as though wondering whether this were just some huge practical joke concocted by the three of them. Occasionally, he jotted down notes, tugged at his tie and gave another uncomprehending glance at the typewritten characters on the card found by Menchu's body. Muñoz's interpretation of the symbols had merely succeeded in giving Feijoo a splitting headache. What really interested him, apart from the oddness of the whole situation, were details about the quarrel Menchu and her boyfriend had had the previous evening. This was because – as policemen sent to investigate had reported back during the afternoon – Máximo Olmedilla Sánchez, twenty-eight years old, single and a male model by profession, was nowhere to be found. Furthermore, two witnesses, a taxi driver and the porter in the building opposite, had seen a young man answering his description leaving Julia's building between twelve and twelve-fifteen that day. According to the pathologist's first report, Menchu Roch had been strangled, from the front, having first been dealt a mortal blow to the throat, between eleven and twelve. The detail of the bottle in the vagina – a large bottle of Beefeater gin, almost full – to which Feijoo made repeated and extremely crude reference (revenge for all that chess nonsense his three inter-viewees had thrown at him), he interpreted as concrete evidence, in the sense that everything pointed to a crime of passion. After all, the mur-dered woman – he'd frowned and put on a suitably grave face, making it clear that people generally get what they deserve – was, as both Julia and César had just explained, not a person of irreproachable sexual morality. As to how this murder was linked to the death of Professor Ortega, the connection was obvious, given the disappearance of the painting. He ventured a few more explanations, listened attentively to the replies that Julia, Muñoz and César gave to his further questions, and finally said good-bye, after arranging to see them at the police station the following morning.

"As for you, Señorita, you've nothing more to worry about." He paused on the threshold, with the dignified expression of a public official fully in charge of the situation. "We know who we're looking for now. Good night."

When she'd closed the door, Julia leaned back against it and looked at her two friends. She had dark shadows under her now dry eyes. She'd cried a lot, out of grief and rage, tormented by her own impotence. Immediately after finding Menchu's body she'd wept, quietly in front of Muñoz, then, when César had arrived, looking pale and harassed, with the horror of the news evident on his face, she'd embraced him as she had when she was a child, her tears had become sobs, and she'd lost all control, clinging to César, who could only murmur futile words of consolation. It wasn't just her friend's death; it was, she said, her voice breaking as hot tears streamed down her face, the unbearable tension of the last few days, the humiliating certainty that the murderer was playing with their lives with absolute impunity, confident that he had them at his mercy.

At least the police interrogation had had one positive effect: it had restored her to a sense of reality. The stubborn stupidity with which Feijoo refused to see the obvious, the false affability with which he'd accepted – without understanding anything, without making the slightest attempt to understand – the detailed explanations they'd given him about what was going on, had reinforced her belief that she had nothing to hope for from that direction. The phone call from the officer dispatched to Max's and the discovery of the two witnesses had confirmed Feijoo in his idea, typical of the police, that the simplest motive is usually the most likely. The chess story was, of course, interesting, something that would doubtless fill out the details of the incident. But as far as the substance of the matter went, it was purely anecdotal. The detail of the bottle proved it. Pure criminal pathology. "Because, despite what you read in detective novels, Señorita, appearances are never deceptive."

"There's no doubt about it now," said Julia as the Inspector could be heard going down the stairs. "Álvaro was murdered, like Menchu. Someone's obviously been after the painting for a long time."

Muñoz, standing by the table, was looking at the piece of paper on which, the moment Feijoo had left, he'd noted down the contents of the card found by the body. César was sitting on the sofa where Menchu had spent the night, staring in stupefaction at the empty easel. When he heard Julia speak, he shook his head.

"It wasn't Max who did it," he said. "There is absolutely no way an imbecile like him could have thought all this up."

"But he was here. At least in the building."

César bowed before the evidence, but without much conviction.

"There must be someone else involved. If Max was, so to speak, the hired help, someone else was pulling the strings." He slowly raised one hand and tapped his forehead with his index finger. "Someone with brains."

"The mystery player. And now he's won the game."

"He hasn't won it yet," said Muñoz, and they turned towards him in surprise.

"He's got the painting," Julia pointed out. "If that isn't winning . . ."

There was a gleam of absorbed fascination in Muñoz's eyes; their

216

dark pupils seemed to see, beyond the four walls of the room, the mathematical meeting in space of complex combinations.

"With or without the painting, the game goes on," he said, and showed them the paper:

. . . Q x R

Qe7? – Qb3+

Kd4? – Pb7 x Pc6

"This time," he added, "the murderer doesn't suggest one move, but three." He went over to his raincoat and took out his pocket chess set. "The first is obvious: Q x R, the black queen takes the white rook. The taking of the white rook represents Menchu Roch's murder, just as, in this game, the white knight symbolised your friend Álvaro and, in the painting, Roger de Arras." Muñoz arranged the pieces on the board as he talked. "Therefore, so far in this game, the black queen has taken only two pieces. And in reality," he glanced at César and Julia, who'd gathered round to study the board, "each of those two pieces represents a murder. Our opponent identifies himself with the black queen; when another black piece takes a white piece, as happened two moves back when we lost the first white rook, nothing happened. At least, not as far as we know."

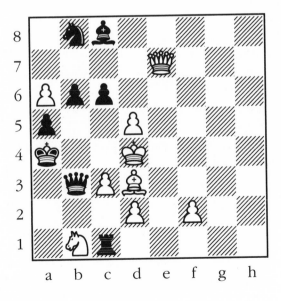

Julia pointed to the paper.

"Why have you put question marks by the next two moves by White?"

"I didn't put them there. They were on the card; the murderer has foreseen what we will do next. I assume those signs to be an invitation for us to make those moves. 'If you do this, I'll do this', he's saying to us. And if we do that" – he moved some pieces – "the game would look like this.

"As you can see, there have been important changes. Having taken the rook on b2, Black foresaw that we would make the best possible move we could, that is, move our white queen from square e1 to e7. That gives us an advantage: a diagonal line of attack threatening the black king, who is already fairly limited in his movements by the presence of the white knight, bishop and pawn nearby. Assuming that we would make the move we've just made, the black queen moves up from b2 to b3 to support the king and to threaten the white king with check. The latter has no alternative but to withdraw to the square to his right, as in fact we have done, fleeing from c4 to d4, out of reach of the queen."

"That's the third time he's had us in check," said César.

"Yes. And one could interpret that in several ways. It could be a case of third time lucky, for example, since the third time he has us in check the murderer steals the painting. I think I'm beginning to understand him a little. Including his peculiar sense of humour."

"What next?" asked Julia.

"Black then takes our white pawn on c6 with the black pawn that was on b7. That move is protected by the black knight on b8. Then it's our turn to move, but our opponent makes no suggestion on the card. It's as if he's saying that what we do next is up to us, not up to him."

"And what are we going to do?" asked César.

"There's only one good option: to keep playing the white queen." He looked at Julia as he said this. "But playing the queen also means we risk losing her."

Julia shrugged. All she wanted was for it to be over, whatever the risks might be.

"The queen it is then."

César was leaning over the board, his hands behind his back, as if he were subjecting the questionable quality of a piece of antique china to particularly close scrutiny.

"That white knight, the one on b1, doesn't look too safe either," he said in a low voice, addressing Muñoz. "Wouldn't you agree?"

"I know. I doubt Black will let him stay there much longer. His presence, threatening Black's rearguard, provides the main support for an attack by the white queen. There's the white bishop on d3 too. Both of those pieces near the queen could prove decisive."

The two men looked at each other in silence, and Julia saw a current of sympathy grow between them that she'd not seen before. It was like the Spartans' resigned solidarity in the face of danger at Thermopylae, when they heard the distant sound of the Persian chariots approaching.

"I'd give anything to know which of the chess pieces we are," remarked César, arching an eyebrow. His lips curved. "I'd really rather not be that horse."

Muñoz raised a finger.

"It's a knight, remember. That's a much more honourable name."

"I'm not worried about the name." César studied the piece with a worried expression. "He looks as if he's in a spot of danger there, that knight."

"I agree."

"Is it you or me, do you think?"

"No idea."

"I confess I'd rather take the part of the bishop."

Muñoz put his head on one side, thoughtfully, without taking his eyes off the board.

"Me too. He's in a safer position than the knight."

"That's what I meant, my dear."

"Well, I wish you luck."

"And the same to you. And the last one to leave turn out the lights."

A long silence followed, which Julia broke, addressing Muñoz.

"Since it's our turn to play, what's our next move? You mentioned the white queen . . ."

Muñoz gave a desultory glance at the board. All the possible combinations had already been analysed in his mind.

"At first I thought of taking the black pawn on c6 with our pawn on d5, but that would give our opponent too much of a breathing space. So we'll move our queen from e7 to e4. We have only to move our king next time and we have the black king in check. Our first check."

This time it was César who moved the white queen, placing her on the corresponding square, next to the king. Julia noticed that, despite his apparent calm, his fingers were trembling slightly.

"That's it," nodded Muñoz. And the three of them looked again at the board.

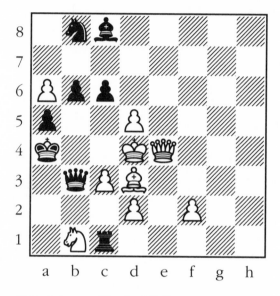

"And what will 'he' do next?" asked Julia.

Muñoz crossed his arms, without taking his eyes off the chessboard, and stood thinking. When he replied, she knew that he hadn't been considering the move, only whether or not he should put it into words.

"He has several options," he said vaguely. "Some are more interesting than others. And more dangerous too. From this point on, the game branches off in several directions. There are at least four possible variants. Some would involve us in a long and complex game, which might well be his intention. With others the game could be over in four or five moves."

"Which do you think?" asked César.

"I'll reserve judgment on that for the moment. It's Black's turn to move now."

He picked up the pieces, folded the board and returned it to his raincoat pocket. Julia looked at him with some curiosity.

"It's odd, what you said a while ago. I mean about the murderer's sense of humour. When you said that, you'd begun to understand it. Do you really find some humour in all of this?"

"You could call it humour, or irony if you prefer," he said. "But our enemy's taste for puns is undeniable." He placed one hand over the piece of paper on the table. "There's something you may not have realised. Using the symbols Q x R, the murderer links the death of your friend with the rook taken by the black queen. Menchu's surname was Roch, wasn't it? And that word, like 'rook', has its origins in the word 'rock'."

"The police called this morning." Lola Belmonte gave Julia and Muñoz a sour look, as if she held them directly responsible for that intrusion. "This is all . . ." She searched unsuccessfully for the word, turning to her husband for help.

"Most unpleasant," said Alfonso, who then immersed himself once more in his blatant contemplation of Julia's bosom. It was clear that, police or no police, he had only just got out of bed. The dark circles under his still puffy eyes emphasised his habitual air of dissipation.

"It was worse than that." Lola Belmonte had at last found the word she wanted and leaned her bony form forwards in her chair. "It was *ignominious*. Do you know So-and-so? Anyone would think *we* were the criminals."

"And we're not," said her husband with ironic seriousness.

"Don't be stupid." Lola Belmonte gave him a spiteful look. "This is a serious conversation."

Alfonso gave a short laugh.

"It's a waste of time. All that matters is that the painting's disappeared and with it our money."

"My money, Alfonso," said Belmonte, from his wheelchair, "if you don't mind."

"Just a manner of speaking, Uncle."

"Well, be more accurate in future."

Julia stirred the contents of her cup. The coffee was cold, and she wondered if the niece had served it like that on purpose. They'd turned up unexpectedly in the latter part of the morning on the pretext of keeping the family informed of events.

"Do you think the painting will be found?" asked the old man. He'd received them dressed casually in sweater and slippers but with a friendliness that made up for the niece's sullen scowl. He was disconsolate now. The news of the theft and of Menchu's murder had come as a great shock to him.

"The matter is in the hands of the police," said Julia. "I'm sure they'll find it."

"I understand there's a black market for works of art. And that they could sell it abroad."

"Yes, that's true, but the police have photographs. I gave them several myself. It won't be easy to get it out of the country."

"I can't understand how they got into your apartment. The police told me that there's a security lock and an electronic alarm."

"It could have been Menchu who opened the door. The chief suspect is Max, her boyfriend. There are witnesses who saw him leaving by the street door."

"We've met the boyfriend," said Lola. "He came here with her one day. A tall, good-looking young man. Too good-looking, I thought . . . I hope they catch him quickly and give him what he deserves. For us" – she looked at the empty space on the wall – "the loss is irreparable."

"At least you can claim the insurance money," said her husband, smiling at Julia. "Thanks to the forethought of this lovely young woman . . ." He seemed suddenly to remember, and his face grew appropriately grave. "Although, of course, that won't bring your friend back."

Lola Belmonte gave Julia a spiteful look.

"That would have been the last straw if, on top of everything else, they hadn't insured it." She stuck out a scornful lower lip. "But Señor Montegrifo says that, compared with the price it would have got at auction, the insurance money is a pittance."

"Have you spoken to Paco Montegrifo already?" asked Julia.

"Yes. He phoned early this morning. He almost got us out of bed with the news. That's why we were fully informed when the police got here. He's such a gentleman." The niece looked at her husband with ill-concealed rancour. "I always said this business got off to a bad start."

Alfonso made a gesture of washing his hands of the matter.

"Poor Menchu's offer was a good one," he said. "It's not my fault if subsequently things got complicated. Besides, Uncle has always had the final say." He looked at Belmonte with exaggerated respect. "Isn't that so?"

"I'm not so sure about that," said the niece.

Belmonte looked at Julia over the top of the cup he'd just raised to his lips, and she caught in his eyes the self-contained gleam she knew well by now.

"The painting is still in my name, Lolita," he said, after carefully drying his lips on a crumpled handkerchief. "For good or ill, stolen or not, it's my concern." When his eyes met Julia's again, there was genuine sympathy in them. "As for this young lady" – he smiled encouragingly, as if it were she who was in need of cheering up – "I'm sure her part in all this has been irreproachable." He turned to Muñoz, who had not as yet opened his mouth. "Wouldn't you agree?"

Muñoz was slumped in an armchair, his legs stretched out and his fingers interlaced beneath his chin. When he heard the question, he blinked a little and put his head on one side, as if they'd interrupted him in the middle of a complicated meditation.

"Undoubtedly," he said.

"Do you still believe that any mystery is decipherable using mathematical laws?"

"I certainly do."

That short exchange reminded Julia of something.

"There's no Bach today," she said.

"After what happened to your friend and the disappearance of the painting, it's not a day for music." Belmonte seemed lost in thought and then he smiled enigmatically. "Anyway, silence is just as important as organised sound. Wouldn't you agree, Señor Muñoz?"

For once, Muñoz was in agreement.

"Absolutely," he remarked with renewed interest. "I think it's rather like photographic negatives. The background, which has apparently not been exposed, contains information too. Is that what happens with Bach?"

"Of course. Bach uses negative spaces, silences that are as eloquent as notes, tempi and syncopations. Do you cultivate the study of empty spaces within your logical systems?"

"Naturally. It's like changing your point of view. Sometimes it's like looking at a garden which, when viewed from one place, has no apparent order, but which, viewed from another perspective, is laid out with geometric regularity."

"I'm afraid," said Alfonso, giving them a mocking look, "it's too early in the day for me to cope with such scientific talk." He got up and walked over to the bar. "A drink, anyone?"

No one replied. With a shrug, he prepared himself a whisky, went across to the sideboard and stood leaning on it as he raised his glass to Julia.

"A garden, eh? I like it," he said and took a sip of his drink.

Muñoz, who appeared not to have heard the remark, was looking at Lola Belmonte now. Rather like a hunter lying in wait, only his eyes seemed alive, with that thoughtful, penetrating expression Julia had come to know well, the only sign that behind the façade of apparent indifference there was an alert spirit watching events in the outside world. He's about to pounce, Julia thought with considerable satisfaction, drinking a little of her cold coffee in order to disguise the knowing smile on her lips.

"I imagine," said Muñoz slowly, addressing Lola, "that it's been a hard blow for you too."

"Of course it has." Lola gave her uncle an even more reproachful look. "That picture is worth a fortune."

"I didn't mean just the economic aspect of the matter. I believe you used to play the game shown in the picture. Are you a keen player?"

"Fairly."

Her husband raised his whisky glass.

"She plays very well. I've never managed to beat her." He winked and took a long drink. "Not that that means much."

Lola was looking at Muñoz with some suspicion. She had, thought Julia, an air that was at once prudish and rapacious, exemplified by her excessively long skirts, her bony, clawlike hands and the steady gaze underlined by an aquiline nose and aggressive chin. Julia noticed that the tendons on the backs of Lola's hands kept tensing and untensing as if full of repressed energy. A nasty piece of work, Julia thought, an embittered, arrogant woman. It wasn't hard to imagine her spreading malicious gossip, projecting onto others her own complexes and frustrations. A blocked personality, oppressed by her circumstances, whose only reaction to external authority was, in chess terms, to attack the king; cruel and calculating, she was out to settle a score with something or someone, with her uncle, with her husband, perhaps. Possibly with the whole world. The painting could be the obsession of a sick, intolerant mind. And those slender, nervous hands were certainly strong enough to kill with a blow to the back of the neck, to strangle somebody with a silk scarf. Julia had no difficulty imagining her in dark glasses and a raincoat. She couldn't, however, establish any link between her and Max. That would be taking things to absurd extremes.

"It's quite unusual," Muñoz was saying, "to meet a woman who plays chess."

"Well, I do." Lola Belmonte seemed wary, defensive. "Do you disapprove?"

"On the contrary. I'm all for it. You can do things on the chessboard that in practice, in real life I mean, are impossible. Don't you agree?"

A look of uncertainty flickered across her face.

"Maybe. For me it's just a game. A hobby."

"A game for which you have some talent, I believe. I still say that it's unusual to meet a woman who can play chess well."

"Women are perfectly capable of doing anything. Whether they're allowed to is another matter, of course."

Muñoz gave a small, encouraging smile.

"Do you prefer playing Black? They tend to be limited to defensive play. It's generally White who takes the initiative."

"What nonsense! I don't see why Black should just sit back and let things happen. That's like being a wife stuck at home." She glanced scornfully at her husband. "Everyone takes it for granted that it's the man who wears the trousers."

"Isn't that true?" asked Muñoz, the half-smile still on his lips. "For example, in the game in the painting, the initial position seems to favour White. The black king is under threat. And, at first, the black queen can do nothing."

225

"In that game, the black king doesn't count at all; it's the queen who has to do all the work. It's a game that's won with queen and pawns."

Muñoz reached into his pocket and drew out a piece of paper.

"Have you ever played this variant?"

Visibly disconcerted, Lola Belmonte looked first at him and then at the piece of paper he put in her hand. Muñoz let his eyes wander about the room until, as if by chance, they came to rest on Julia. The glance she returned to him said, "Well played," but the chess player's expression remained utterly inscrutable.

"Yes, I think I have," said Lola after a while. "White either takes a pawn or moves the queen next to the king ready for check in the next move." She looked at Muñoz with a satisfied air. "Here White has chosen to move its queen, which seems the right thing to do."

Muñoz nodded.

"I agree. But I'm more interested in Black's next move. What would you do?"

Lola narrowed her eyes suspiciously. She appeared to be looking for ulterior motives. She returned the piece of paper to Muñoz.

"It's some time since I played that game, but I can remember at least four variants: the black rook takes the white knight which leads to an uninspiring victory for White based on pawns and queen. Another possibility, I think, is knight takes pawn. Then there's bishop takes pawn. The possibilities are endless. But I don't see what this has to do with anything."

"But what would you do," asked Muñoz implacably, ignoring her objection, "to ensure a Black victory? I'd like to know, as one player to another, at which point Black gains the advantage."

Lola Belmonte looked smug.

"We can play the game any time you like. Then you'll find out."

"I'd love to and I'll take you up on that. But there is a variant you haven't mentioned, perhaps because you've forgotten it. A variant that involves an exchange of queens." He made a brief gesture with his hand, as if clearing an imaginary board. "Do you know the one I'm referring to?"

"Of course. When the black queen takes the pawn that's on d5, the exchange of queens is inevitable." As she said this, a cruelly triumphant look flickered across her face. "And Black wins." Her bird-of-prey eyes looked disdainfully at her husband before turning to Julia. "It's a shame you don't play chess, Señorita."

"What do you think?" asked Julia, as soon as they were out in the street.

Muñoz cocked his head slightly to one side. His lips were pressed tightly together and his gaze wandered absently over the faces of the people they passed. Julia noticed that he seemed unwilling to reply.

"Technically," he said at last, "it could have been her. She knows all the game's possibilities and she plays well too. Very well, I'd say."

"You don't seem convinced."

"It's just that there are certain details that don't fit."

"But she comes close to the idea we have of *him*. She knows the game in the painting inside out. She has enough strength to kill a man or a woman, and there's something unsettling about her, something that makes you feel uncomfortable in her presence." She frowned, searching for the word that would complete the description. "She just seems such a nasty person. What's more, for some reason I can't understand, she feels a particular antipathy towards me. And that's despite the fact, if we're to take what she says seriously, that I'm what a woman should be: independent, with no family ties, with a certain amount of self-confidence . . . Modern, as Don Manuel would say."

"Perhaps that's exactly why she hates you. For being what she would like to have been but couldn't. I don't remember much about those stories you and César are so keen on, but I seem to recall that the witch ended up hating the mirror."

Despite the grim circumstances, Julia burst out laughing.

"That's quite possible. It never occurred to me."

"Well, now you know." Muñoz had managed a half-smile. "You'd better avoid eating apples for a few days."

"And I have my princes. You and César. Bishop and knight. Isn't that right?"

Muñoz wasn't smiling any more.

"This isn't a game, Julia," he said. "Don't forget that."

"I won't," she said and took his arm. Almost imperceptibly, Muñoz tensed. He seemed uncomfortable but she kept hold of his arm as they walked. In fact, she'd come to admire this strange, awkward and taciturn man. Sherlock Muñoz and Julia Watson, she thought, suddenly full of immoderate optimism that only faded when she remembered Menchu.

"What are you thinking about?" she asked Muñoz.

"About the niece."

"Me too. The truth is, she's exactly what we're looking for. Although you don't agree."

"I didn't say that she might not be the woman in the raincoat, just that I don't see her as the mystery chess player."

"But there are things that fit perfectly. Doesn't it strike you as odd that such a mercenary woman, only a few hours after the theft of an extremely valuable painting, should suddenly forget her indignation and start calmly talking about chess?" Julia let go of Muñoz's arm and looked at him. "She's either a hypocrite or chess means much more to her than you'd think. Either way, it looks suspicious. She could have been pretending all along. She'd had more than enough time since Montegrifo phoned to prepare what you would call a line of defence, working on the assumption that the police would question her."

Muñoz nodded.

"She could indeed. After all, she *is* a chess player. And a chess player knows how to make use of certain resources. Especially when it comes to getting out of compromising situations."

He walked on for a while in silence, studying the tips of his shoes. Then he looked up and shook his head.

"I still don't think it's her," he said at last. "I always thought that I would feel something special when I came face to face with 'him'. But I didn't feel anything."

"Has it occurred to you that perhaps you idealise the enemy too much?" asked Julia. "Couldn't it be that, disillusioned with the reality of the situation, you simply won't accept the facts?"

Muñoz's narrowed eyes were devoid of expression.

"It *had* occurred to me," he murmured, looking at her in his opaque way. "I don't reject that as a possibility."

Despite Muñoz's laconic reply, Julia knew there was something else. In his silence, in the way he put his head on one side and looked without seeing her, lost in hermetic thoughts that only he was privy to, she felt certain that something else, which had nothing at all to do with Lola Belmonte, was going round in his head.

"Is there something else?" she asked, unable to contain her curiosity. "Did you find out something in there you haven't told me about?"

Muñoz declined to reply.

They dropped by César's shop to tell him the details of the interview. He was waiting for them impatiently and rushed to greet them as soon as he heard the bell on the shop door.

"They've *arrested* Max. This morning, at the airport. The police phoned half an hour ago. He's at the police station in Paseo del Prado, Julia. And he wants to see you."

"Why me?"

César shrugged, as if to say that, whilst he might know a lot about blue Chinese porcelain or nineteenth-century painting, the psychology of pimps and criminals in general was not one of his specialities, thank you very much.

"What about the painting?" asked Muñoz. "Do you know if they've found it?"

"I doubt it very much." César's blue eyes revealed a glimmer of concern. "I think that's precisely the problem."

Inspector Feijoo did not seem pleased to see Julia. He received her in his office but neglected to invite her to sit down. He was obviously in a filthy mood and he came straight to the point.

"This is all a little irregular," he said brusquely, "seeing that we're dealing here with someone supposedly responsible for two murders. But he insists that he will make no proper statement until he's spoken to you. And his lawyer" – he paused, as if about to spit out exactly what he thought of lawyers – "agrees."

"How did you find him?"

"It wasn't difficult. Last night we issued his description to everyone, including border crossings and airports. He was identified this morning at passport control in Barajas airport as he was about to board a flight to Lisbon with a false passport. He didn't put up any resistance."

"Has he told you where the painting is?"

"He hasn't said anything at all." Feijoo raised one plump, stubby finger. "Oh, except that he's innocent. But that's a phrase we often hear; it's pretty much par for the course. But when I showed him the statements the taxi driver and the porter had made, he crumpled, and just kept asking for a lawyer. And that was when he demanded to see you."

He accompanied her out of the office and along the corridor to a door where a uniformed policeman was standing guard.

"I'll be here if you need me. He insisted on seeing you alone."

They locked the door behind her. Max was sitting on one of the chairs placed on either side of a wooden table in the middle of a windowless room with dirty padded walls. It was completely bare of any other furniture. Max was wearing a rumpled sweater over an open-necked shirt, and his hair, no longer caught back in a ponytail, was dishevelled, a few locks hung loose over his eyes. His hands, resting on the table, were handcuffed.

"Hello, Max."

He looked up and stared at her. He had dark circles under his eyes from lack of sleep and he seemed uncertain, as if he had reached the end of a long, vain enterprise.

"At last, a friendly face," he said with heavy irony, and indicated the other chair.

Julia offered him a cigarette, which he lit avidly, moving his face close to the lighter she held out.

"Why did you want to see me, Max?"

His breathing was fast and shallow. He was no longer a handsome wolf, but a rabbit cornered in its burrow, listening to the sound of the ferret getting nearer and nearer. Julia wondered if the police had beaten him, but he didn't seem to have any bruises. They don't beat people up any more, she said to herself. Not any more.

"I wanted to warn you," he said.

"Warn me?"

"She was already dead, Julia," he said in a low voice. "I didn't do it. When I got to your apartment, she was already dead."

"How did you get in? Did she open the door?"

"I've told you; she was already dead . . . the second time."

"The second time? You mean there was a first?"

Max leaned his elbows on the table, resting his unshaven chin on his thumbs, and let the ash fall from his cigarette.

"Hang on," he said with infinite weariness. "It's best if I start at the beginning." He raised the cigarette to his lips again, half-closing his eyes against the smoke. "You know how badly Menchu took that business with Montegrifo. She was pacing round her house like a caged animal, muttering all kinds of insults and threats. 'They've robbed me!' she kept shouting. I managed to calm her down, and we talked it over. The idea was mine."

"What idea?"

"I have contacts with people who can get almost anything out of the country. I suggested that we steal the Van Huys. At first she went crazy, hurling abuse at me and talking about your friendship. Then she saw that it wouldn't actually hurt you. Your responsibility was covered by the insurance, and as for your share of the profits . . . well, we'd find a way of compensating you later on."

"I always knew you were a son of a bitch, Max."

"Maybe I am, but that's beside the point. The important thing is that Menchu agreed to my plan. She had to get you to take her home with you. Drunk or high on drugs . . . To be honest, I never thought she'd do it as well as she did. The next morning, I was to phone and see if everything was ready. So that's what I did, and I went over there. We wrapped up the painting to camouflage it and I took the keys Menchu gave me. I was to park the car in the street and come up again to pick up the Van Huys. The plan was that after I left with the painting, Menchu would stay behind to start the fire."

"What fire?"

"In your apartment." Max laughed mirthlessly. "That was part of the plan. I'm sorry."

"You're sorry!" Julia thumped the table in stunned indignation. "Good God, you have the nerve to tell me you're sorry!" She looked at the walls and then at Max. "You must both have been completely mad to think up something like that."

"We were perfectly sane, actually, and nothing would have gone wrong. Menchu would have faked some kind of accident, a discarded cigarette, for example. And with the amount of solvents and paint in your apartment . . . We'd decided that she should stay there until the last minute and then leave, choking on the smoke, hysterical and calling for help. Before the firemen managed to get there, half the building would be in flames." He made a face of crude apology and regret. "Everyone would assume that the Van Huys had gone up in flames along with everything else. You can imagine the rest. I'd sell the painting in Portugal to a private collector we were already negotiating with . . . In fact, the day we met in the Rastro, Menchu and I had just seen the middleman. As for the fire, Menchu would have accepted responsibility; but since she was your friend and it was an accident, the charges wouldn't have been that serious. A charge brought by the owners, perhaps, but nothing more. What delighted her most, she said, was the thought of Montegrifo's face when he found out."

Julia, incredulous, shook her head.

"Menchu wasn't capable of doing something like that."

"Menchu, like all of us, was capable of anything."

"God, you're a bastard, Max."

"At this stage, what *I* am isn't terribly important." Max's face took on a look of defeat. "What does matter is that it took me quite a while to bring the car round and park it in your street. The fog was really thick and I couldn't find a parking place. That's why I kept looking at my watch; I was worried you might turn up any minute. It must have been about quarter past twelve when I went upstairs again. I didn't ring. I opened the door with the key. Menchu was in the hall, lying on her back, with her eyes wide open. At first I thought she must have fainted out of sheer nervousness, but when I knelt down by her side I saw the bruise on her throat. She was dead, Julia, and she was still warm. I panicked. I knew that if I called the police, I'd have a hell of a lot of explaining to do. So I threw the keys on the floor, closed the door and went racing down the stairs. I couldn't think. I spent the night in a pension, absolutely terrified. I didn't sleep a wink. Then in the morning, at the airport . . . Well, you know the rest of the story."

"Was the painting still in the house when you found Menchu dead?"

"Yes. That was the only thing I noticed apart from her. It was on the sofa, wrapped up in newspaper and tape, just as I'd left it." He gave a bitter laugh. "But I didn't have the guts to take it with me. I was in enough trouble already."

"You say Menchu was in the hall? Yet she was found in the bedroom. Did you see the scarf round her neck?"

"There was no scarf. She had nothing round her neck, and her neck was broken. She'd been killed by a blow to the throat."

"And the bottle?"

"Don't you start on about that bloody bottle. All the police keep asking me is why I stuck that bottle up Menchu's cunt. I swear I don't know what they're talking about." He put what remained of his cigarette to his lips and inhaled deeply, nervously, giving Julia a suspicious look. "Menchu was dead, that's all. Killed by a single blow and nothing else. I didn't move her. I was only there for about a minute. Someone else must have done that afterwards."

"Afterwards? When? According to you, the murderer had already left."

Max frowned, trying to remember.

"I don't know." He seemed genuinely confused. "Perhaps he came back later, after I left." Then he turned pale as if he'd just realised something. "Or perhaps . . ." Julia saw that his cuffed hands were trembling. "Perhaps he was still there, hidden. Waiting for you."

They'd decided to share the work. While Julia visited Max and subsequently recounted the story to the Inspector, who listened to her without even trying to disguise his scepticism, César and Muñoz made enquiries amongst the neighbours. The three of them met in an old café in Calle del Prado in the evening. Max's story was scrutinised from all angles during a prolonged discussion round the marble table, the ashtray overflowing and the table crowded with empty cups. They leaned towards each other, like conspirators, talking in low voices.

"I believe Max," concluded César. "What he says makes sense. After all, the story about stealing the painting is just the sort of thing he'd do. And I can't believe he was capable of doing the rest . . . The bottle of gin *was* too much, my dears. Even for a man like him. On the other hand, we know that the woman in the raincoat was also around. Lola Belmonte, Nemesis or whoever she turns out to be."

"Why not Beatrice of Ostenburg?" asked Julia.

César looked at her reprovingly.

"I find that kind of joke completely uncalled for." He shifted nervously in his seat, looked at Muñoz, whose face was a blank, and then, half-joking, half-serious, held up his hands, as if warding off ghosts. "The woman who was prowling round your building was flesh and blood. At least I hope she was."

He had discreetly interrogated the porter in the building opposite, whom he knew by sight. From him, César had found out a few useful facts. For example, around twelve, just when he was finishing sweeping the hallway, the porter had seen a tall young man, his hair in a ponytail, come out of the front door of Julia's building and walk up the street to a car parked by the kerb. Shortly afterwards – and César's voice grew hoarse with sheer excitement, as it did when he was recounting some high-class bit of social tittle-tattle – perhaps half an hour later, when the porter was taking in the rubbish bin, he'd passed a blonde woman wearing dark glasses and a raincoat. César lowered his voice as he said this, looking around apprehensively, as if the woman might be sitting at one of the nearby tables. The porter, it seems, didn't get a good look at her because she was walking up the street, in the same direction as the young man. Nor could he say with certainty that the woman had come out of Julia's front door. He'd simply turned round with the rubbish bin in his hand and there she was. No, he hadn't told the policemen who questioned him that morning because they hadn't asked him about that. He wouldn't have thought of it, the porter confessed, scratching his head, if Don César hadn't asked him. No, he didn't notice if she was carrying a large package. He'd just seen a blonde woman walking along the street. And that was that.

"The street," said Muñoz, "is full of blonde women."

"All wearing dark glasses and a raincoat?" commented Julia. "It could have been Lola Belmonte. I was with Don Manuel at the time. And neither she nor her husband was at home."

"No," said Muñoz, "by midday you were already with me, at the chess club. We walked for about an hour and got to your apartment about one o'clock." He looked at César, whose eyes responded with a flicker of mutual intelligence that did not go unnoticed by Julia. "If the murderer was waiting for you, he must have had to change his plans when you didn't turn up. So he took the painting and left. Perhaps that saved your life."

"Why did he kill Menchu?"

"Perhaps he wasn't expecting to find her there and eliminated her as

234

an inconvenient witness," Muñoz said. "The move he'd planned might not have been queen takes rook. It's possible it was all a brilliant improvisation."

César raised a shocked eyebrow.

"Calling it 'brilliant' is a bit much, my dear."

"Call it what you like. Changing the move like that, on the spur of the moment, coming up with an instant variant appropriate to the situation and placing the card with the corresponding notation next to the body . . ." The chess player reflected on this. "I had a chance to have a look at it. The note was even typed, on Julia's Olivetti, according to Feijoo. And there were no fingerprints. Whoever did it acted with great calm, but also with speed and efficiency. Like a machine."

Julia suddenly remembered Muñoz, hours before, while they waited for the police to come, kneeling by Menchu's corpse, not touching anything and saying nothing, studying the murderer's visiting card as coolly as if he were sitting before a chessboard at the Capablanca Club.

"I still don't understand why Menchu opened the door."

"Because she thought it was Max," suggested César.

"No," said Muñoz. "He had the key, which we found on the floor when we arrived. She knew it wasn't Max."

César sighed, turning the topaz ring round and round on his finger.

"I'm not surprised the police are hanging onto Max for all they're worth," he said, sounding demoralised. "There aren't any other suspects. And at this rate, soon there won't be any more victims left either. If Señor Muñoz continues to stick strictly to his deductive systems, it's going to end up – I can see it now – with you, my dear Muñoz, surrounded by corpses, like the final act of *Hamlet*, and being forced to the inevitable conclusion: 'I am the only survivor, therefore, according to strict logic, discounting all impossible suspects, that is, those who are already dead, the murderer must be me . . .' and then giving yourself up to the police."

"That's not necessarily so," said Muñoz.

"That you're the murderer? Forgive me, my dear friend, but this conversation is beginning to sound dangerously like a dialogue in a madhouse. I never for one minute thought . . ."

"I don't mean that." The chess player was studying his hands, holding his empty cup. "I'm talking about what you said a moment ago: that there are no more suspects."

"You don't mean," murmured Julia, "that you've got someone else in mind?"

Muñoz looked at her for a long time. Then he clicked his tongue, put his head a little to one side and said:

"Possibly."

Julia protested and begged him to explain, but neither she nor César could get a word out of him. Muñoz was gazing absently at the empty stretch of table between his hands, as if he could see in the marbled surface the mysterious moves of imaginary chess pieces. From time to time the vague smile, behind which he shielded himself when he preferred not to be drawn into things, would drift across his lips like a fleeting shadow.

XIII

❧

The Seventh Seal

In the fiery gap he had seen
something unbearably awesome,
the full horror of the abysmal depths
of chess.   *Vladimir Nabokov*

"NATURALLY," Paco Montegrifo said, "this regrettable incident will
not affect our agreement."

"Thank you."

"There's no need to thank me. We know you had nothing to do with
what happened."

The director of Claymore's had gone to visit Julia at the workshop
in the Prado, taking advantage, he said when he turned up there
unexpectedly, of an interview with the director of the museum with a
view to their buying a Zurbarán commended to his company. He'd
found her in the middle of injecting an adhesive made from glue and
honey into an area of incipient flaking on a triptych attributed to Duccio
di Buoninsegna. Julia, who was not in a position to stop what she was
doing, greeted Montegrifo with a hurried nod of her head while she
pressed the plunger of the syringe to inject the mixture. The auctioneer
seemed delighted to have surprised her *in flagrante* – as he said, at the
same time bestowing on her his most brilliant smile. He'd sat down on
one of the tables to watch her.

Julia felt uncomfortable and did her best to finish what she was doing
quickly. She protected the treated area with water-repellent paper and
placed a bag filled with sand on top, taking care to mould it carefully
to the surface of the painting.

"A marvellous piece of work," said Montegrifo, indicating the

237

painting. "About 1300, isn't it? The Master Buoninsegna, if I'm not mistaken."

"That's right. The museum acquired it a few months ago." Julia looked critically at the results of her labours. "I've had some problems with the gold leaf along the edge of the Virgin's cloak. In some places it's been lost completely."

Montegrifo leaned over the triptych, studying it with a professional eye.

"It's still a magnificent effort," he said when he'd finished examining it. "Like all your work."

"Thank you."

The auctioneer gave her a look of deepest sympathy.

"Although, naturally," he said, "there's no comparison with our dear Flanders panel."

"Of course not. With all due respect to the Duccio."

They both smiled. Montegrifo tugged at his immaculate shirt cuffs to ensure that the required inch was showing below the sleeves of his navy blue double-breasted jacket, enough to reveal the gold cuff links bearing his initials. He was wearing a pair of impeccable grey trousers and, despite the rainy weather, his black Italian shoes gleamed.

"Do you have any news of the Van Huys?" Julia asked.

The auctioneer adopted an expression of elegant melancholy.

"Alas, no." Although the floor was strewn with sawdust, paper and splashes of paint, he made a point of dropping the ash from his cigarette in the ashtray. "But we're in contact with the police. The Belmonte family have put me in charge of all negotiations." The look on his face was one that managed simultaneously to praise the owners' good sense in doing so and regret that they had not done so before. "The paradoxical thing, Julia, is that if *The Game of Chess* ever does turn up, this whole unfortunate series of events will send the price sky high."

"I'm sure it will. But, as you said, that's if it ever does turn up."

"You don't seem very optimistic."

"After what I've been through the last few days, I don't really have much reason to be."

"I understand. But I have faith in the police investigation. Or in luck.

And if we do manage to recover the painting and put it up for auction, I can assure you it will be a real event." He smiled as if he had a marvellous present for her in his pocket. "Have you read *Art and Antiques*? They've dedicated five colour pages to the story. We've had endless phone calls from specialist journalists. And the *Financial Times* is doing an article on it next week. By the way, some of those journalists asked to be put in touch with you."

"I don't want any interviews."

"That's a shame, if you don't mind my saying so. Your reputation is your livelihood. Publicity can only increase your professional standing."

"Not that kind of publicity. After all, the painting was stolen from my apartment."

"We're trying to gloss over that fact. You're not to blame, and the police report leaves no doubt about that. Everything points to your friend's boyfriend having handed over the painting to an unknown accomplice. That's their main line of enquiry. I'm sure it will turn up. It wouldn't be easy to export a painting as famous as the Van Huys illegally. At least, not in theory."

"I'm glad you're so confident. That's what I call being a good loser. Good sportsmanship, I think they call it. I'd have thought that the theft would have been a real blow to your company."

Montegrifo put on a pained expression. Doubt is most hurtful, his eyes seemed to say.

"As indeed it is," he replied, looking at Julia as if she'd done him an injustice. "In fact I had a lot of explaining to do at our head office in London. But such problems are always cropping up in this business. Still, it's an ill wind . . . Our branch in New York has discovered another Van Huys: *The Money Changer of Louvain.*"

"The word 'discovered' strikes me as a bit excessive. It's a well-known painting, it's been catalogued. It belongs to a private collector."

"You're well-informed, I see. What I meant to say is that we're in negotiations with the owner. He considers that now is the moment to get a good price for his painting. My colleagues in New York have managed to get in before our competitors."

"Congratulations."

"I thought we might celebrate." He looked at the Rolex on his wrist. "It's almost seven o'clock now, so how about coming out to supper with me? We need to discuss your future work with us. There's a poly-chrome statue of San Miguel, seventeenth-century Indo-Portuguese, that I'd like you to have a look at."

"That's very kind of you, but I'm still rather upset. My friend's death, the matter of the painting . . . I wouldn't be very good company tonight."

"As you wish." Montegrifo took her refusal with resigned gallantry and without losing his smile. "If you like, I'll phone you early next week. Would Monday be all right?"

"Fine." Julia held out a hand and he clasped it gently. "Thanks for dropping in."

"It's always a pleasure to see you, Julia. If you need anything" – he gave her a long look, full of meanings she couldn't quite decipher – "and I mean anything, whatever it might be, don't hesitate to call me."

He left, turning at the door to give her one last, brilliant smile. Julia spent another half hour on the Buoninsegna before putting away her things. Muñoz and César had insisted that she not go home for a few days, and César had again offered her his house; but Julia had remained steadfast, simply changing the security lock. Stubborn and immovable, as César had described her with some annoyance during one of his many phone calls to check that everything was all right. As for Muñoz, Julia knew, because César had let it slip, that both of them had spent the night after the murder keeping watch near her building, numb from the cold, with only a thermos of coffee and a flask of brandy (which César had had the foresight to bring with him) for company. Swaddled in overcoats and scarves, they consolidated the odd friendship which, by force of circumstance, these two very different personalities had struck up around Julia. When she found out, she forbade them to repeat the episode, promising in exchange that she wouldn't open the door to anyone and that she would go to sleep with the derringer underneath her pillow.

She saw the gun when she was putting her things in her bag and she brushed the cold chrome-plated metal with the tips of her fingers. It was the fourth day since Menchu's death with no cards or phone calls. Perhaps, she said to herself without conviction, the nightmare has ended. She draped a linen cloth over the Buoninsegna, hung her overalls in a cupboard and put on her raincoat. The watch on the inside of her left wrist said it was quarter to eight.

She was just going to put out the light when the phone rang.

She put the receiver down and stood holding her breath, suppressing the desire to run as far away as possible. A shiver, a breath of icy air down her spine, made her tremble violently, and she had to lean on the table to recover. She couldn't take her eyes off the phone. The voice she'd just heard was unrecognisable, asexual, like the voice ventriloquists give to their creepy articulated dummies. A voice with shrill notes in it that had pricked her skin with a stab of blind terror.

"Room 12, Julia." Silence and muffled breathing, perhaps because a handkerchief was covering the mouthpiece. "Room 12," the voice had said again. "Brueghel the Elder," it added after another silence. There was a short, dry, sinister laugh and the click of the phone being put down.

She tried to put her scattered thoughts in order and not let panic take over. César had told her once that when ducks were flushed out by beaters for the benefit of hunters' rifles, it was the frightened ones who were always the first to fall. César. She picked up the phone and dialled his shop and then his home number, but got no answer. She had no success with Muñoz either. She would have to fend for herself, and she trembled at the thought.

She took the derringer out of her bag and cocked it. At least that way, she thought, she could be as dangerous as the next person. Again the words César had spoken to her as a child surfaced. There are exactly the same things in a room at night as there are in the daytime; it's just that you can't see them.

Pistol in hand, she went out into the corridor. At that hour the building was deserted apart from the security guards making their rounds, but she didn't know where to find them. She had to go down three flights of stairs which formed a sharp angle with a broad landing on each floor. Lights cast a bluish penumbra there, in which could be made out dark paintings, the marble banister and busts of Roman patricians watching from their niches.

She took off her shoes and put them in her bag. The chill from the floor seeped through the soles of her feet and into her body. This night's adventure might end up giving her a monumental head cold. She stopped now and then to peer over the banister, though without seeing or hearing anything suspicious. At the bottom she had to make a choice. One route, through several rooms set up as restoration workshops, would lead her to a security door through which, using her electronic card, she could get out to the street near Puerta Murillo. The other route, at the end of a narrow corridor, would take her to a door that led into the museum itself. It was usually closed but never locked before ten o'clock at night, when the guards made their final inspection of the annexe.

She stood at the bottom of the stairs, the gun in her hand, considering the two possibilities. She could either get out as fast as possible or find out what was going on in Room 12. The second option would involve an unpleasant trek of six or seven minutes through the deserted building. Unless, on the way, she was lucky enough to meet the guard in charge of that wing, a young man who, whenever he found Julia working in the studio, would buy her coffee from the vending machine and joke about what nice legs she had, assuring her that they were the main attraction at the museum.

What the hell, she said to herself, after all, she had once killed pirates. If the murderer was there, it was a good opportunity, perhaps the only one, to meet him face to face. She, being a sensible duck, was watching out of the corner of her eye; meanwhile in her right hand she held eighteen ounces of chrome metal, mother-of-pearl and lead which, when fired at a short distance, could easily reverse the roles in this unusual hunting trip.

Flaring her nostrils as if trying to sniff out the direction danger might come from, she gritted her teeth and called up in her aid all the rage contained in her memories of Álvaro and Menchu, and the decision not to be just a frightened pawn on a chessboard, but someone quite capable, given the opportunity, of demanding an eye for an eye and a tooth for a tooth. If he, whoever he was, wanted to find her, then he would, be it in Room 12 or in hell.

She went through the inner door, which, as expected, was unlocked. The security guard must have been far away, for the silence was absolute. She walked down an aisle of disquieting shadows cast by marble statues, who watched her pass with blank, motionless eyes, and continued through the room containing medieval retables, of which, amongst the dark shadows they made on the walls, she could make out only the occasional dull gleam of the gilt and gold leaf backgrounds. To the left, at the end of that long aisle, she saw the small staircase that led to the rooms containing early Flemish paintings, amongst them Room 12.

She paused on the first step, peering with extreme caution into the dark. The ceiling was lower there, and the security light allowed a better view of the details. In the blue penumbra, the colours of the paintings had turned to monochrome. She could make out Van der Weyden's *Descent from the Cross*, almost unrecognisable in the shadows. In the unreal darkness it took on an air of sinister grandeur, revealing only its palest colours, the figure of Christ and the face of his mother, fainting, her fallen arm parallel with the dead arm of her son.

There was no one there, apart from the people in the paintings, and most of them, hidden in the dark, seemed locked in a long sleep. Distrusting the apparent calm, troubled by the presence of so many images created by the hands of men who had all died hundreds of years ago, images that seemed to be watching her from their old frames on the walls, Julia reached the door leading into Room 12. Her throat was dry but she could not swallow. She glanced over her shoulder again but could see nothing suspicious. Conscious of the knot of tension in her jaw muscles, she took a deep breath before going into the room as she'd seen people in films do: grasping the gun in both hands, pointing into the shadows, her finger on the trigger.

There was no one there, and Julia felt an immense, intoxicating sense of relief. The first thing she saw, its colours muted by the shadows, was the dazzling nightmare of Bosch's *The Garden of Delights*, which took up most of one wall. She leaned against the opposite wall, her breath blurring the glass protecting Dürer's self-portrait. With the back of her hand she wiped away the sweat from her forehead before going over to the wall at the far end of the room. As she walked, the shapes and the lighter tones of Brueghel's painting began to emerge. That painting had always held a peculiar fascination for her. The tragic tone that informed every brush stroke, the eloquence of the innumerable figures shaken by the mortal, inexorable breath, the many scenes that made up the macabre whole, had for many years stirred her imagination. The feeble blue light from the ceiling illuminated the skeletons bursting in hordes from the bowels of the earth, in a vengeful, all-destroying wind; the distant fires silhouetting the black ruins on the horizon; the wheels of Tantalus in the distance, spinning atop their poles, next to the skeleton who stands with sword raised, about to bring it down on the neck of the blindfolded prisoner kneeling in prayer; in the foreground, the king surprised in the middle of the feast, the lovers oblivious even at the final hour, the smiling skeleton beating the drums of Judgment Day; and the knight who, trembling with terror, still has courage enough to make one last gesture of valour and rebellion, and unsheathes his sword, ready to fight for his life in one last hopeless battle.

The card was there, stuck in the frame just above the gilt plate on which, Julia knew, were the four sinister words that form the title of the painting: *The Triumph of Death*.

When she reached the street, it was pouring with rain. The light from the Isabelline street lamps lit up the curtains of water that burst in torrents out of the darkness and beat on the paving stones. The puddles were spattered by fat drops of rain, splintering the reflections of the city into a furious coming and going of lights and shadows.

Julia lifted her face to the rain and let it run freely over her hair and face. Her cheekbones and lips grew taut in the cold and her wet hair clung to her face. She buttoned her raincoat at the neck and walked between the hedges and stone benches indifferent to the rain and the dampness invading her shoes. The images in the Brueghel painting were still engraved on her retina; the terrifying medieval tragedy still danced before her eyes. And in it, amongst the men and women submerged by the avalanche of avenging skeletons exploding out of the earth, she could clearly see the characters from the other picture: Roger de Arras, Ferdinand Altenhoffen, Beatrice of Burgundy. In the middle distance, she could even see the lowered head and resigned face of old Pieter Van Huys. Everything came together in that one definitive scene, where, regardless of how the dice fell, the last dice thrown on the card table of the Earth, beauty and ugliness, love and hatred, good and evil, hard work and profligacy would all meet their end. Julia had also seen herself in the mirror, which reproduced with pitiless clarity the breaking of the

Seventh Seal of the Apocalypse. She was the young woman with her back to the scene, absorbed in her daydreams, mesmerised by the music played on a lute by a grinning skeleton. In that sombre landscape there was no room now for pirates and hidden treasure, all the Wendys were being dragged away, kicking and screaming, by the legion of skeletons; Cinderella and Snow White, their eyes wide with terror, could smell the sulphur, and the little tin soldier, Roger de Arras, like St George without his dragon, stood with his sword half out of its sheath, unable to help them now. He had enough to do lunging vainly into the void, a mere point of honour, before joining hands, like everyone else, with the fleshless hands of Death, who was drawing them all in to join his macabre dance.

The headlights of a car lit up a telephone booth. Julia scrabbled for some coins in her bag, moving as if in a dream. Mechanically, her drenched hair dripping into the earpiece, she dialled the numbers of César and Muñoz without getting a reply. She leaned her head against the glass and placed between her lips, numb with cold, a damp cigarette. Standing with her eyes closed, she let the smoke curl about her until the tip began to burn the skin between her fingers and she dropped it. As the rain beat down monotonously, she knew, with a disconsolate feeling of infinite tiredness, that this was only a fragile truce, which could not protect her from the cold, the lights and the shadows.

She had no idea how long she stood there. At one point she put the coins in the telephone again and dialled a number, Muñoz's this time. When she heard his voice, she seemed to come slowly to her senses, as if returning from a long journey, a journey through time and herself. With a serenity that grew as she spoke, she explained what had happened. Muñoz asked what the card said, and she told him: B x P, bishop takes pawn. There was silence at the other end of the line. Then Muñoz, in a strange voice she'd never heard before, asked where she was. When she told him, he said she was not to move; he'd be there as soon as possible.

Fifteen minutes later, a taxi drew up by the telephone booth, and Muñoz opened the door and told her to get in. Julia ran out into the rain and dived into the car. As the taxi drove off, Muñoz removed her soaked raincoat and placed his own around her shoulders.

"What's going on?" she asked, shivering.

"You'll find out soon enough."

"What does bishop takes pawn mean?"

The fleeting lights outside slid across Muñoz's frowning face.

"It means," he said, "that the black queen is about to take another piece."

Julia blinked, stunned by this news. She grasped Muñoz's hand with her two frozen hands and looked at him in alarm.

"We must warn César."

"We've still got time," replied Muñoz.

"Where are we going?"

"To Penjamo. One j two aitches."

It was still raining heavily when the taxi pulled up outside the chess club. Muñoz opened the door without letting go of Julia's hand.

"Come on," he said.

She followed him meekly up the steps to the hall. There were still a few players at the tables, but Cifuentes, the director, was nowhere in sight. Muñoz led her straight to the library. There, amongst trophies and diplomas, were glass-fronted shelves lined with a few hundred books. Letting go of Julia's hand, he slid open one of the glass doors and took down a fat leatherbound volume. On the spine, in gold letters darkened by use and time, a puzzled Julia read: *Chess Weekly. Fourth quarter.* The year was illegible.

Muñoz put the book on the table and turned the yellowing pages of cheap paper. Chess problems, analyses of games, information about tournaments, old photographs of smiling winners in white shirt, tie and suits and haircuts of the period. He stopped at a double-page spread of photographs.

"Look at them carefully," he told Julia.

She bent over the photos. They were of poor quality and all showed groups of chess players posed for the camera. Some held cups or certificates. She read the headline: SECOND JOSÉ RAÚL CAPABLANCA NATIONAL TROPHY.

"I don't understand," she murmured.

Muñoz pointed at one of the photos. In the group of boys, two were holding small trophies; the other four were staring solemnly at the camera. At the bottom of the photo were the words: FINALISTS IN THE JUNIOR LEAGUE.

"Do you recognise anyone?" asked Muñoz.

Julia studied the faces one by one. Only a face on the far right seemed faintly familiar. It belonged to a boy of fifteen or sixteen. His hair was brushed back and he was wearing a jacket and tie and a black armband on his left arm. He was looking at the camera with calm, intelligent eyes, in which she thought she could see a glint of defiance. Then she recognised him. When she pointed at him with her finger, her hand was shaking, and when she looked up at Muñoz, he nodded.

"Yes," he said, "that's our invisible player."

XIV

❧

Drawing-room Conversation

"I found it only because I was looking for it."
"What? You mean you were expecting to find it?"
"I thought it not unlikely."
                    Sir Arthur Conan Doyle

THE LIGHT ON THE STAIRS wasn't working, and they went up in the dark, Muñoz first, guiding himself with his hand on the banister. When they reached the landing, they stood in silence, listening. They heard no sound inside, but there was a line of light beneath the door. Julia couldn't see her companion's face in the darkness, but she knew Muñoz was looking at her.

"There's no going back now," she said in response to his unasked question. The only reply she got was Muñoz's calm breathing. She felt for the bell and pressed it once. Inside, its noise faded to a distant echo.

It was a while before they heard the slow approach of footsteps. The steps paused for a moment, then continued, moving still more slowly and getting nearer, until they stopped completely. The lock turned for what seemed an age and then at last the door opened, casting a momentarily dazzling rectangle of light on them. Julia looked at the familiar figure silhouetted against the soft light, thinking that this was one victory she did not want.

He stepped aside to let them pass, appearing unperturbed by their unexpected visit. The only outward sign was a somewhat disconcerted smile Julia glimpsed as he closed the door behind them. On the heavy walnut-and-bronze Edwardian coatstand, a raincoat, hat and umbrella were still dripping.

He led them down a long corridor with a high, exquisitely coffered ceiling and walls adorned with nineteenth-century landscape paintings

248

from Seville. He went on ahead of them, turning round every so often with the attentiveness of a good host. In vain, Julia sought some hint of that other personality she now knew lay hidden in him, like a ghost that had always floated between them and whose presence she would never again be able to ignore. Despite the light of reason seeping into the corners of her doubts, despite the facts that fitted together now like the smooth-edged pieces of a jigsaw and projected onto the images in *The Game of Chess* the outlines, in light and shade, of the other tragedies that were now superimposed on the one symbolised in the Flemish painting – despite all that and her sharp awareness of the pain which, little by little, was replacing her initial stupor, Julia was incapable of hating the man walking ahead of them, half-turning with solicitous courtesy, elegant even in private, in a blue silk dressing gown over well-cut trousers, a scarf knotted in the open neck of his shirt, his hair, slightly wavy at the back of the neck and at the temples, immaculate, his eyebrows arched in the expression of indifference proper to an ageing dandy but which, in Julia's presence, had always been softened by the sad, sweet, tender smile that hovered now at the corners of his pale, thin lips.

None of them said anything until they reached the large drawing room with its high ceiling decorated with classical scenes. Julia's favourite, until that night, had always been the scene depicting Hector in a shining helmet bidding farewell to Andromache and her son. The room, whose walls were covered with tapestries and paintings, contained César's most prized possessions, those which he had chosen to keep for himself, no matter what price was offered for them. Julia knew them all as if they were her own: the silk-upholstered Empire sofa, on which Muñoz, his face set in an expression of stony seriousness, his hands in his raincoat pockets, hesitated to sit even though César urged him to do so; the bronze statuette of a fencing master signed by Steiner, its swordsman erect and handsome, his proud chin lifted, dominating the room from his pedestal on the late eighteenth-century Dutch writing desk at which, for as long as Julia could remember, César had always written his letters; the Regency corner cabinet containing a beautiful collection of chased silver that he himself polished once a month; the Lord's Anointed ones, his favourite paintings: a *Young woman* attributed to Lorenzo Lotto, a very beautiful *Annunciation* by Juan de Soreda, a sinewy *Mars* by Luca Giordano, a melancholy *Eventide* by Thomas Gainsborough; the collection of English porcelain; the carpets, tapestries and fans. These were pieces whose individual histories César had carefully compiled, collating every last fact about style, provenance and genealogy, to form a private collection so personal, so closely bound by his own aesthetic taste and character that he seemed to be part of the essence of each and every one.

Muñoz had remained standing, affecting a calm, silent exterior, although something about him, perhaps the way his feet were positioned on the edge of the carpet or the way his elbows stuck out above the hands thrust into his pockets, indicated that he was on the alert, ready to confront the unexpected. For his part, César was looking at him with dispassionate, courteous interest, only now and then turning to look at Julia, as if, because she was at home there, it was up to Muñoz, the only stranger in the house, to explain his reasons for turning up so late at night. Julia, who knew César as well as she knew herself – she made an instant mental correction: whom until that night *she had thought* she knew as well as herself – had seen, the moment César opened the door, that he understood their visit implied something more than just a call on their third comrade in the adventure. Beneath his attitude of friendly forbearance, she recognised, in the way he smiled and in the innocent expression in his clear blue eyes, cautious expectation and a touch of amusement. It was the same look with which, when he'd held her on his knees, he would wait for her to say the magic words, the answers to the childish riddles she loved him to set her: It looks like gold, it is not silver . . . Or: What is it that goes on four legs in the morning, two legs at noon and three legs in the evening? . . . And, the best of all: The distinguished lover knows the name of the lady and the colour of her dress . . .

And yet on this strange night, in the diffuse light cast through the parchment shade of the English lamp with a base in the form of a book press, which lent strange foreshortenings and shadows to other objects, César paid little attention to her. It was not that he was avoiding her eyes, for when he looked at her he held her gaze, frankly and directly, albeit only briefly, as if between them there were no secrets, as if everything between the two of them would already have been given an answer, precise, convincing, logical and definitive, perhaps the answer to all the questions she had asked throughout her life. But, for the first time, Julia did not feel like listening. Her curiosity had been fully satisfied when she had stood before Brueghel the Elder's *Triumph of Death*. She didn't need anyone now, not even him. And this had happened before Muñoz opened an old volume on chess and pointed out to her one of the photographs. Her presence here tonight, in César's home, was motivated strictly by curiosity, aesthetic curiosity, César would have said. Her duty was to be present, simultaneously protagonist and chorus, actor and audience for the most fascinating of classical tragedies. They were all there: Oedipus, Orestes, Medea and her other old friends. After all, the performance was in her honour.

Yet it was unreal. Julia sat on the sofa, crossed her legs and placed one arm along the back. The two men stood in front of her, and so formed a composition very similar to that in the vanished painting. Muñoz, on the left, stood on the edge of an ancient Pakistani carpet, whose faded threads accentuated its beautiful reds and ochres. The chess player – now they were *both* chess players, thought Julia with perverse satisfaction – had not removed his raincoat. He was looking at César, his head a little to one side, with that Holmesian expression that lent him a peculiar dignity. But he was not looking at César with the smugness of a victor. There was no animosity, nor even, given the circumstances, justifiable apprehension, only tension in his eyes and the twitching muscles in his jaw. That, in Julia's judgment, was due to the fact that Muñoz was now studying the *real appearance* of the enemy after working for so long only with his *ideal appearance*. He was doubtless going over old mistakes, reconstructing moves, judging intentions. It was the stubborn, absent expression of one who, having won a game by a series of brilliant moves, is concerned only to work out how the hell his opponent had managed to snatch away one pawn from some irrelevant and forgotten square.

César stood on the right and, with his silvery hair and silk dressing gown, he looked like an elegant figure in a turn-of-the-century comedy: calm and distinguished, conscious that he owned the two-hundred-year-old carpet on which Muñoz was standing. Julia watched him draw from a pocket a pack of gold-tipped cigarettes and fit one into his ivory holder. The scene would be engraved for ever on her memory: the backdrop of darkly gleaming antiques, the slender classical figures painted on the ceiling; and, standing face to face, the ageing dandy, elegant and ambivalent in appearance, and the thin, shabby man in the crumpled raincoat, looking at each other in silence, as if waiting for someone, possibly the prompter hidden behind one of the pieces of period furniture, to give the cue to begin the final act.

From the moment Julia had noticed something familiar about the face of the young man staring into the photographer's camera with all the seriousness of his fifteen or sixteen years, she had guessed that the final act would be more or less like this and how it would end. She looked at her two favourite characters as she sat on César's comfortable sofa and let her thoughts drift lazily. She would never have got such a perfect seat in a theatre. Then a memory came back to her, a recent memory. She'd already had a glance at the script. It had been only a few hours before, in Room 12 of the Prado: the painting by Brueghel, beating drums providing a background to the annihilating breath of the inevitable, sweeping away as it passed the last blade of grass on earth, and everything subsumed into one last, gigantic pirouette, into the sound of a loud belly laugh from some drunken god recovering from an Olympian hangover somewhere behind the blackened hills, the smoking ruins and the glow of the fires. Pieter Van Huys, that other Fleming, the old master of the court of Ostenburg, had explained it all too, in his own way, perhaps with more delicacy and subtlety, more hermetic and sinuous than the brutal Brueghel, but with the same aim. In the end all paintings were paintings of the same painting, just as all mirrors gave the reflection of the same reflection, and all deaths were the death of the same Death:

> 'Tis all a Chequer-board of Nights and Days
> Where Destiny with Men for Pieces plays . . .

She murmured these words to herself, looking at César and at Muñoz. Everything was ready. They could begin. The yellow light from the English lamp created a cone of brightness that wrapped itself about the two main characters. César inclined his head a little and lit his cigarette. As if that were the signal for the dialogue to start, Muñoz nodded slightly and spoke:

"I hope you have a chessboard to hand, César."

Not the most brilliant of openings, thought Julia, nor even the most appropriate. An imaginative scriptwriter would doubtless have come up with some better words to place in Muñoz's mouth. But, she thought disconsolately, the writer of the tragicomedy was, after all, as mediocre as the world he'd created.

"I don't think a chessboard will be necessary," replied César, and with that the dialogue improved. Not because of the words, but because of the tone, which was perfect, particularly that hint of boredom César gave to the phrase. It was a tone typical of him, one he might use were he observing a distant scene from a garden chair, a wrought-iron one painted white, with a very dry martini in one hand. César had his decadent poses down to a fine art, as he did his homosexuality, his perversity, and Julia, who had loved him for that too, could appreciate the value of that rigorous, precise attitude, so perfect in every detail. And the most fascinating thing was that he had been deceiving her for twenty years. Although, to be fair, the person responsible for the deceit was not him, but her. Nothing had changed in César. Now he was feeling no remorse or disquiet for what he'd done. She knew this with absolute certainty. He appeared to be as distinguished and correct as he had when Julia heard from his lips beautiful stories about lovers and warriors, about Long John Silver, Wendy, Lagardère, Sir Kenneth, the Knight of the Couchant Leopard. Yet he was the one who had dumped Álvaro under the shower, rammed a bottle of gin between Menchu's legs. Julia savoured her own bitterness. If he is himself, she thought, and it's clear that he is, then the one who has changed is me. That's why I see him differently tonight, with altered eyes: I see a blackguard, a fraud and a murderer. And yet I'm still here, hanging on his every word, fascinated. In a few seconds, instead of telling me a tale of adventures in the Caribbean, he's going to tell me that he did it all for me or some such thing. And I'll listen to him, as I always have, because this is better than all César's other stories. It surpasses them all in imagination and horror.

She removed her arm from the back of the sofa and leaned forwards a little, not wanting to miss the slightest detail of the scene. That movement seemed the signal to resume the dialogue. Muñoz, his hands in his pockets, his head on one side, looked at César.

"Just clarify something for me," he said. "After the black bishop takes the white pawn on a6, White decides to move his king from d4 to e5,

253

discovering the check of the white queen on the black king. What should Black do next?"

César's eyes seemed to be smiling independently of his impassive features.

"I don't know," he replied after a moment. "You're the master, my dear. You should know."

Muñoz made one of his vague gestures, as if brushing aside the title César had bestowed on him.

"I insist," he said slowly, dragging out the words, "on knowing the authorised version."

César's lips became infected by the smile that until then had been restricted to his eyes.

"In that case, I would protect the black king by placing the bishop on c4." He looked at Muñoz with courteous solicitude. "Does that seem right to you?"

"Then I'll take that bishop," Muñoz said, almost rudely, "with my white bishop on d3. And then you'll have me in check with your knight on d7."

"I'll do no such thing, my friend." César held his gaze unflinchingly. "I don't know what you're talking about. And this is no time to play charades."

Muñoz frowned and looked stubborn.

"You'll have me in check on d7," he insisted. "Stop play-acting and concentrate on the board."

"Why should I?"

"Because you have very few escape routes now. I avoid that check by moving the white king to d6."

César sighed when he heard this, and his blue eyes rested on Julia. In the dim light, they seemed extraordinarily pale, almost colourless. After placing his cigarette holder between his teeth, he nodded twice, with a slight look of regret on his face.

"Then, I'm sorry to say" – and he did indeed seem put out – "I would have to take the second white knight, the one on b1." He looked at Muñoz contritely. "A pity, don't you think?"

"Yes. Especially from the knight's point of view." Muñoz bit his lower lip. "And would you take it with the rook or with the queen?"

"With the queen, naturally." César seemed offended. "There *are* certain rules . . ." He left the phrase hanging in the air with a gesture of his right hand. A fine, pale hand, on the back of which could be seen the bluish ridges of his veins, a hand that Julia now knew was capable of killing, perhaps initiating the lethal blow with the same elegant gesture.

Then, for the first time since they'd arrived, Muñoz smiled, that vague, distant smile that never meant anything, that was a response to his strange mathematical reflections rather than to the surrounding reality.

"In your place I would have played queen to c2, but that's of no importance now," he said in a low voice. "What I'd like to know is how you were thinking of killing me."

"Don't talk nonsense," replied César, and he seemed genuinely shocked. Then, as if appealing to Muñoz's sense of politeness, he made a gesture in the direction of the sofa where Julia was sitting, though without looking at her. "There's a young lady present . . ."

"At this point," remarked Muñoz, the smile still there at one corner of his mouth, "the young lady is, I imagine, as curious as I am. But you didn't answer my question. Were you thinking of resorting again to the tactic of a blow to the throat or the back of the neck or were you saving a more classical ending for me? I mean poison, a dagger or something like that . . . How would you put it?" He glanced up at the paintings on the ceiling, seeking some appropriate phrase. "Ah, yes, something 'Venetian'."

"I would have said 'Florentine'," César corrected him, punctilious as always, although not without a certain admiration. "I had no idea you had a sense of irony about such matters."

"I don't," replied Muñoz. "Not at all." He looked at Julia and pointed at César. "There he is: the man who enjoys the trust of both king and queen. If you want to fictionalise the thing, he's the plotting bishop, the treacherous Grand Vizier who conspires in the shadows because he is, in fact, the Black Queen in disguise."

"It would make a marvellous soap opera," remarked César mockingly, clapping his hands in slow, silent applause. "But you haven't told me what White would do after losing the knight. Frankly, my dear, I can't wait to find out."

"Bishop to d3, check. And Black loses the game."

"That easy, eh? You frighten me, my friend."

"Yes, that easy."

César considered this while he removed what remained of his cigarette from the holder and placed it in an ashtray, having first delicately removed the ash.

"Interesting," he said and slowly, so as not to alarm Muñoz unnecessarily, went over to the English card table next to the sofa. After turning the small silver key in the lock of a chest veneered in lemonwood, he took out the dark, yellowing pieces of a very old ivory chess set that Julia had never seen before.

"Interesting," he repeated. His slender fingers with their manicured nails arranged the pieces on the board. "The situation, then, would be like this."

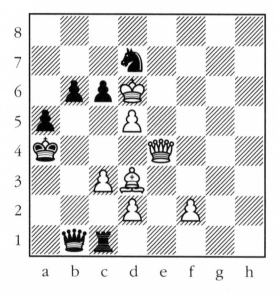

"Exactly," said Muñoz, who was looking at the board from a distance. "The white bishop, when it withdraws from c4 to d3, allows a double check: white queen on black king and the bishop itself on the black queen. The king has no alternative but to flee from a4 to b3 and to abandon the black queen to her fate. The white queen will provide another check on c4, forcing the enemy king to retreat, before the white bishop finishes off the queen."

"The black rook will take that bishop."

"Yes, but that's not important. Without the queen, Black is finished.

256

What's more, once that piece disappears from the board the game loses its *raison d'être*."

"You may be right."

"I am right. The game, or what's left of it, is decided by the white pawn on d5, which, after taking the black pawn on c6, will advance, with no one to stop it, until it is promoted. That will happen within six or, at most, nine moves." Muñoz put a hand into one of his pockets and drew out a piece of paper covered with pencilled jottings. "These, for example."

Pd5 x Pc6	Ktd7 – f6
Qc4 – e6	Pa5 – a4
Qe6 x Ktf6	Pa4 – a3
Pc3 – c4+	Kb2 – c1
Qf6 – c3+	Kc1 – d1
Qc3 x Pa3	Rb1 – c1
Qa3 – b3+	Kd1 x Pd2
Pc6 – c7	Pb6 – b5
Pc7 – c8 . . .	(Black resigns)

César picked up the piece of paper and very calmly studied the chessboard, his empty cigarette holder clamped between his teeth. His smile was that of a man accepting a defeat that was already written in the stars. One after another he moved the pieces until they represented the final situation:

"You're right. There's no way out," he said at last. "Black loses."

Muñoz's eyes shifted from the board to César.

"Taking the second knight," he murmured in an objective tone, "was a mistake."

César shrugged, still smiling.

"After a certain point Black had no choice. You could say that Black was also a prisoner of his mobility, of his natural dynamic. That knight rounded off the game." For a moment Julia caught in César's eyes a flash of pride. "In fact, it was almost perfect."

"Not in chess terms," said Muñoz dryly.

"Chess? My dear friend" – César made a disdainful gesture in the direction of the chess pieces – "I was referring to something more than

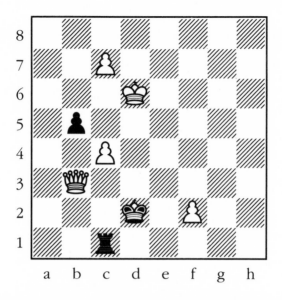

a simple chessboard." His blue eyes grew dark, as if a hidden world were peering out from beneath their surface. "I was referring to life itself, to those other sixty-four squares of black nights and white days of which the poet speaks. Or perhaps it's the other way round, perhaps it should be white nights and black days. It depends on which side of the player we choose to place the image . . . on where, since we're talking in symbolic terms, we place the mirror."

Julia felt that his words were addressed to her.

"How did you know it was César?" she asked Muñoz, and César seemed startled. Something suddenly changed in his attitude, as if Julia, by giving voice to and sharing Muñoz's accusation, had broken a vow of silence. His initial reserve disappeared at once, and his smile became a bitter, mocking grimace.

"Yes," he said to Muñoz, and that was his first formal admission of guilt, "tell her how you knew it was me."

Muñoz turned his head a little towards Julia.

"Your friend made a couple of mistakes." He hesitated for a second over the exact sense of his words and then glanced towards César, possibly in apology. "Although I'm wrong to call them 'mistakes', because he always knew exactly what he was doing and what the risks were. Paradoxically, *you* made him give himself away."

"I did? But I hadn't the slightest idea until . . ."

César shook his head, almost sweetly, Julia thought, frightened of her feelings.

"Our friend Muñoz is speaking figuratively, Princess."

"Please, don't call me Princess." Julia didn't recognise her own voice. It sounded strangely hard. "Not tonight."

César looked at her for a few moments before nodding his assent.

"All right." He seemed to find it difficult to pick up the thread. "What Muñoz is trying to explain is that your presence in the game provided him with a contrast by which to observe the intentions of his opponent. Our friend is a good chess player, but he's turned out to be a much better sleuth than I expected. Not like that imbecile Feijoo, who sees a cigarette end lying in an ashtray and deduces, at most, that someone's been smoking." He looked at Muñoz. "It was bishop to pawn instead of queen to pawn d5 that put you on the alert, wasn't it?"

"Yes. Or at least it was one of the things that made me suspicious. On his fourth move, Black passed up a chance to take the white queen, which would have decided the game in his favour. At first I thought he was just playing cat and mouse, or that Julia was so necessary to the game that she couldn't be taken or murdered until later. But when our enemy, you, chose bishop to pawn instead of queen to pawn d5, a move that would inevitably have meant an exchange of queens, I realised that the mystery player had never had any intention of taking the white queen, that he was even prepared to lose the game rather than take that step. And the link between that move and the spray can left on Julia's car in the Rastro, that presumptuous 'I could kill you but I won't', was so obvious that I no longer had any doubts: the threats to the white queen were all a bluff." He looked at Julia. "Because, throughout this whole episode, you were never in any real danger."

César nodded as if what was being considered were not his actions but those of a third party about whose fate he cared nothing.

"You also realised," he said, "that the enemy was not the king but the black queen."

Muñoz shrugged.

"That wasn't difficult. The connection with the murders was obvious: only those pieces taken by the black queen symbolised real murders. I applied myself to studying the moves of that one piece and I drew some interesting conclusions. For example, her protective role as regards Black's play in general, which extended even to the white queen, her main enemy, and which she nevertheless respected as if the latter were sacred. The proximity of the white knight, myself, the two pieces on adjacent squares, almost like good neighbours, yet the black queen chose not to use her poisonous sting on him until later, when there would be no alternative." He was looking at César with opaque eyes. "At least I have the consolation of knowing that you would have killed me without hatred, even with a certain finesse and fellow feeling, with an apology on your lips, asking for my understanding. That you were driven purely by the demands of the game."

César made a theatrical, eighteenth-century gesture with his hand and bowed his head, grateful for the apparent precision of Muñoz's analysis.

"You're absolutely right," he said. "But tell me, how did you know you were the knight and not the bishop?"

"Thanks to a series of clues, some minor and others more important. The decisive one was the symbolic role of the bishop, which, as I mentioned before, is the piece that enjoys the trust of both king and queen. You, César, played an extraordinary role in all this: white bishop disguised as black queen, acting on both sides of the board. And that very condition is what brought about your downfall, in a game which, curiously enough, you started precisely for that reason, to be beaten. And you received the *coup de grâce* from your own hand: the white bishop takes the black queen, Julia's antiquarian friend betrays the identity of the invisible player with his own game, like the scorpion stinging itself with its own tail. I can assure you that it's the first time in my life I've ever witnessed a suicide on the chessboard carried out to such perfection."

"Brilliant," said César, and Julia couldn't tell if he was referring to Muñoz's analysis or to his own game. "But tell me something. In your judgment, how would you interpret that identification of mine with both the black queen and the white bishop?"

"I imagine that a detailed explanation would take us all night and the ensuing discussion several weeks. I can only speak now of what I saw revealed on the chessboard, and that was a split personality: evil, César, in all its blackness. Your feminine side, do you remember? You asked me once for an analysis: someone hemmed in and oppressed by his surroundings, defiant in the face of authority, hostile and homosexual impulses. All of that was embodied beneath the black dress of Beatrice of Burgundy, in other words, the queen of chess. And in opposition to that, as different as day from night, was your love for Julia. Your other side which is just as painful to you: the masculine side, with certain modifications; the aesthetic side embodied in your chivalrous attitudes; what you wanted to be and were not. Roger de Arras embodied not in the knight but in the elegant white bishop. What do you think?"

César was pale and motionless, for the first time in her life, Julia saw him paralysed by surprise. Then, after a few moments that seemed an eternity, filled only by the ticking of a wall clock marking the passing of that silence, César finally managed a faint smile, at one corner of his bloodless lips. But it was mechanical, a way of confronting the implacable dissection of his personality that Muñoz had cast into his face, like someone throwing down a gauntlet.

"Tell me about the bishop," he said in a hoarse voice.

"Since you ask me to, I will." Muñoz's eyes were lit now by the decisive brilliance of his moves. He was repaying his opponent for all the doubts and uncertainties the latter had put him through at the board; it was his professional revenge. And when she realised this, Julia knew that at some point in the game Muñoz must have thought he was going to lose. "The bishop, with its deep, diagonal movement," he said, "is the chess piece that best embodies homosexuality. Yes, you gave yourself another magnificent part as the bishop protecting the helpless white queen, the bishop who, in the end, in a moment of sublime resolution planned right at the start, deals a mortal blow to his own obscure condition and offers up to his adored white queen a masterly and terrifying lesson. I saw all that only gradually, as I slowly put my ideas together. But you didn't play chess. At first that prevented my suspicions from centring on you. And even when I was almost certain, that was what disconcerted me. The game plan was too perfect for a normal player, and inconceivable even in a keen amateur. In fact, that still troubles me."

"There's an explanation for everything," replied César. "But I didn't mean to interrupt you, my dear. Go on."

"There's not much more to say. At least not here, tonight. Álvaro Ortega was killed by someone he perhaps knew, but I wasn't completely

261

sure about that. However, Menchu Roch would never have opened the door to a stranger, especially in the circumstances described by Max. In the café the other night, you said there were almost no suspects left, and you were right. I tried to approach it analytically, in successive stages. Lola Belmonte wasn't my opponent; I knew that as soon as I met her. Nor was her husband. As for Don Manuel Belmonte, his odd musical paradoxes gave me plenty of food for thought . . . But the suspect was someone unbalanced. His chess-playing side, if I may put it like that, was not up to it. Besides, he was an invalid, which ruled out the violent actions perpetrated against Álvaro and Menchu. A possible combination of uncle and niece, bearing in mind the blonde woman in the raincoat, didn't stand up to detailed analysis either: why would they steal something that was theirs already? As for Montegrifo, I made some enquiries, and I know that he has no links with chess whatsoever. Besides, Menchu would never have opened the door to him either that morning."

"So that left only me."

"As you know, when one has eliminated the impossible, whatever remains, however improbable, must be the truth."

"Of course I remember, my dear. And I congratulate you. I'm glad to see that I did not misjudge you."

"That's why you chose me, isn't it? You knew that I would win the game. You wanted to be beaten."

With an obliging little smile, César indicated that it was now a matter of no importance.

"I did indeed expect to be beaten. I called on your good offices because Julia needed a guide in her descent into hell . . . Because this time I had to concentrate on playing the role of the Devil. She needed a companion. So I gave her one."

Julia's eyes flashed when she heard that. Her voice sounded metallic.

"You weren't playing at being the Devil, but at being God. Dealing out good and evil, life and death."

"It was your game, Julia."

"You're lying. It was yours. I was just a pretext."

César gave her a reproving look.

"You haven't understood anything, my dear. But that doesn't matter any more. Look in any mirror; perhaps you'll agree with me then."

"You can keep your mirrors, César."

He was genuinely hurt, like a dog or a child unjustly treated. The dumb reproach, overflowing with absurd loyalty, gradually faded from his eyes, and all that remained was an absorbed, almost tearful gaze, staring into space. Slowly he moved his head and looked again at Muñoz.

"You haven't yet told me," he said, and he seemed to have difficulty recovering the tone he had used before when talking to Muñoz, "how you set the trap that finally made your inductive theories fit the facts. Why have you come to see me with Julia tonight, and not yesterday, for example?"

"Because yesterday you hadn't declined for the second time to take the white queen. Also because until this afternoon I hadn't found what I was looking for: a bound volume of chess magazines for the fourth quarter of 1945. There's a photograph of the finalists in a junior chess tournament in it, and you're there, César, your name and surname are on the following page. What surprises me is that you weren't a winner. It also puzzles me that after that there's no mention of you as a chess player. You never played in public again."

"There's something I don't understand," said Julia. "Or, to be exact, there's something else, apart from all the many things I don't understand in all this madness. I've known you for as long as I can remember, César. I grew up with you, and I thought I knew every corner of your life. But you never once mentioned chess. Never. Why?"

"That's a long story."

"We've got time," said Muñoz.

It was the last game in the tournament, with only a few pieces left on the board. Opposite the platform on which the finalists were playing, a few spectators were following the moves as a judge wrote on a panel on the wall, between a portrait of General Franco and a calendar – the date was 12 October 1945 – above the table on which stood the gleaming silver cup intended for the winner.

The young boy in the grey jacket fiddled nervously with the knot of his tie and looked despairingly at the black pieces on the board. The last few moves of his opponent's methodical, implacable game had manoeuvred him relentlessly into a corner. It wasn't that White had a brilliant game plan, it was simply a question of slow progress starting with a solid initial defence – the King's Indian defence – and getting the upper hand purely and simply by waiting patiently and exploiting his opponent's mistakes. An unimaginative game that risked nothing had, for precisely that reason, sabotaged every attempt at an attack on his king by Black, whose forces were now scattered, incapable of helping each other, or even of providing obstacles to the advance of the two white pawns, which, taking turns to move, were about to be promoted.

The eyes of the boy in the grey jacket were dull with weariness and shame. The knowledge that his game was superior, more daring and brilliant than that of his opponent, could not console him for his inevitable defeat. His fifteen-year-old's imagination, extravagant and fiery, the extreme sensitivity of his spirit and the lucidity of his thought, even the almost physical pleasure he felt when he moved the varnished wooden chessmen elegantly across the board, creating on the black and white squares a delicate network that he considered to be of almost perfect beauty and harmony, all seemed sterile now, sullied by the crude satisfaction and disdain evident on his opponent's face: a sallow-skinned lout with small eyes and coarse features whose only strategy had been to wait prudently, like a spider in the centre of his web, a strategy of unspeakable cowardice.

So this too was chess, thought the boy playing Black. In the final analysis, it was the humiliation of undeserved defeat, with the prize going to those who risk nothing. That was what he felt at that moment, seated for a game that was not merely a foolish set of moves, but a mirror of life itself, of flesh and blood, life and death, heroism and sacrifice. Like the proud knights of France at Crécy, undone in the midst of empty victory by the Welsh archers of the King of England, he had seen the attacks made by his knights and bishops, moves that were daring and deep, like the splendid, glittering blows of a sword, one crash after the other, like heroic but futile waves, against the phlegmatic immobility of his opponent. And that hated piece, the white king, on the other side of his insurmountable barrier of plebeian pawns, observed from a safe distance, with as much scorn as that reflected on the face of the White player, the discomfort and impotence of the solitary black king, incapable of helping his remaining faithful pawns, who were engaged in á hopeless battle, an agonising free-for-all.

On that pitiless battleground of cold black and white squares there was no room for honour in defeat. Defeat wiped out everything, destroying not only the loser but also his imagination, his dreams, his self-esteem. The boy in the grey jacket leaned his elbow on the table, cradled his forehead in the palm of his hand and closed his eyes, listening as the sound of clashing weapons died slowly away in the valley flooded with shadows. Never again, he said to himself. Just as the Gauls conquered by Rome refused ever to speak of their defeat, he too, for the rest of his life, would refuse to remember his, and sterility of victory. He would never again play chess. And, with luck, he would be able to wipe it from his memory, just as the names of dead Pharaohs were removed from all the monuments.

Opponent, judge and spectators were awaiting his next move with ill-disguised irritation, for the game had gone on for far too long. The boy took one last look at his besieged king and, with a sad feeling of shared solitude, decided that all that remained for him to do was to commit one last merciful act and give him a worthy death at his own hand, thus avoiding the humiliation of being boxed in like a fugitive dog. He reached out his hand and, in a gesture of infinite tenderness, slowly upended the defeated king and laid him lovingly down on the empty square.

XV

❧❧❧

Queen Ending

What I did originated a lot of sin,
as well as passion, dissension, vain words –
not to mention lies – in myself,
in my antagonist or in both. Chess drove me
to neglect my duties to God and to men.
The Harleyan Myscellany

WHEN CÉSAR'S LOW VOICE STOPPED, he gave an absent smile
and slowly turned his eyes from some indeterminate spot in the room
to the ivory chess set on the table. Then he shrugged, as if to say, "Well,
no one gets to choose his own past."

"You never told me about that," Julia said, and the sound of her voice
seemed an absurd intrusion.

César paused before replying. The light from the parchment
lampshade lit only half his face, leaving the other half in shadow. The
effect accentuated the lines around his eyes and mouth, emphasised his
aristocratic profile, his fine nose and chin, like the effigy on an antique
medal.

"I could hardly tell you about something that didn't exist," he murmured softly, and his eyes, or perhaps just the dull gleam of his eyes in
the penumbra, rested on Julia's. "For forty years I applied myself carefully to the task of believing that to be the case." There was a mocking
edge to his voice now, no doubt directed at himself. "I never played
chess again, not even alone. Never."

Julia shook her head, finding it all very hard to believe.

"You're sick."

He gave a short, humourless laugh.

"You disappoint me, Princess. I hoped that you at least would not

266

resort to clichés." He looked thoughtfully at his ivory cigarette holder. "I assure you I'm completely sane. How else could I have constructed with such meticulous detail this whole beautiful story?"

"Beautiful?" She looked at him in stupefaction. "We're talking about Álvaro and about Menchu . . . Beautiful story?" She shuddered with horror and disgust. "For God's sake! What the hell are you talking about?"

César held her gaze, unmoved, and then turned to Muñoz as if for support.

"There are . . . aesthetic aspects," he said, "there are some extraordinarily original factors that can't be dismissed in such a superficial way. The chessboard isn't just black and white. There are higher planes, from which you can view events. Objective planes." He gave them a look of sudden and apparently sincere pain. "I thought you'd both realised that."

"I know what you mean," remarked Muñoz. He had not moved from his position, and his hands were still in the pockets of his crumpled raincoat. At one corner of his mouth, the vague smile had appeared again, indefinable and distant.

"You do, do you?" exclaimed Julia. "What do *you* know about it?"

She clenched her fists indignantly, holding in the breath that echoed in her ears like that of an animal at the end of a long run. But Muñoz did not react, and Julia noticed that César gave him a quiet look of gratitude.

"I was right to choose you," he said. "And I'm glad I did."

Muñoz didn't respond. He simply glanced around at the paintings, the furniture, the objects in the room and nodded slowly, as if he were drawing mysterious conclusions. After a few moments he indicated Julia with a lift of his chin.

"I think she deserves to know the whole story."

"So do you, my dear," added César.

"Yes, I do. Although I'm here only in the role of witness."

There was no note of censure or menace in his words. It was as if the chess player were maintaining some absurd neutrality. An impossible neutrality, thought Julia, because, sooner or later, there will come a point when words will run out and we'll have to make a decision.

However, numbed by a sense of unreality she couldn't shake off, she felt that that moment still seemed far off.

"Let's begin, then," she said, and when she heard herself speak, she found with unexpected relief that she was regaining her lost composure. She gave César a hard look. "Tell us about Álvaro."

César nodded.

"Yes, Álvaro," he repeated in a low voice. "But first I should mention the painting." A look of sudden annoyance crossed his face, as if he'd neglected some point of elementary courtesy. "I haven't asked if you'd like a drink or anything . . . Unforgivable of me. Would you like something?"

No one replied. César went over to the old oak chest he used as a drinks cabinet.

"The first time I saw that painting was when I was in your apartment, Julia. Do you remember? They'd delivered it a few hours before, and you were like a child with a new toy. For almost an hour I watched while you studied it in minute detail, explaining to me the techniques you thought you'd use to make it, and I quote, the most beautiful piece of work you'd ever done." As he spoke, César selected a narrow tumbler of expensive cut glass and filled it with ice, gin and lemon juice. "I was surprised to see you so happy, and the truth is, Princess, I was happy too." He turned round with the glass in his hand and, after a cautious taste, seemed satisfied with it. "But what I didn't tell you then . . . Well, even now it's hard to put into words. You were delighted with the beauty of the image, the balance of the composition, the colour and the light. I was too, but for different reasons. That chessboard, the players and the pieces, the lady reading by the window, aroused a dormant echo of my old passion. Believing it to be completely forgotten, I felt it return like a bolt from the blue. I was simultaneously feverish and terrified, as if I'd felt the breath of madness on my cheek."

César fell silent, and the half of his mouth lit by the lamp curved into a wickedly intimate smile, as if he now found special pleasure in savouring that memory.

"It wasn't just a matter of chess," he continued, "but a deep, personal sense of the game as a link between life and death, between reality and dream. And while you, Julia, were talking about pigments and varnishes, I was barely listening, surprised by the tremor of pleasure and exquisite

268

anguish running through my body as I sat next to you on the sofa and looked not at what Pieter Van Huys had painted on that Flemish panel but at what that man, that genius, had in mind while he was painting."

"And you decided that you had to have it."

César looked at Julia with an expression of ironic reproof.

"Don't oversimplify things, Princess." He took a brief sip of his drink and smiled at her as if begging her indulgence. "What I decided, very suddenly, was that it was absolutely vital that I give full rein to my passion. It's not for nothing that one lives as long as I have. Doubtless that's why I understood at once, not the message, which, as we discovered later, was in code, but the certain truth that the painting contained some fascinating and terrible enigma. Think of it: perhaps the enigma would, at last, prove me right."

"Right?"

"Yes. The world is not as simple as people would have us believe. The outlines are vague; it's the details that count. Nothing is black and white; evil can be a disguise for good or beauty and vice versa, without one thing necessarily excluding the other. A human being can both love and betray the object of that love without diminishing the reality of his or her feelings. You can be father, brother, son and lover all at the same time; victim and executioner . . . You can choose your own examples. Life is an uncertain adventure in a diffuse landscape, whose borders are continually shifting, where all frontiers are artificial, where at any moment everything can either end only to begin again or finish suddenly, for ever and ever, like an unexpected blow from an axe. Where the only absolute, coherent, indisputable and definitive reality is death. Where we are only a tiny lightning flash between two eternal nights, and where, Princess, we have very little time."

"What has that got to do with Álvaro's death?"

"Everything has to do with everything else." César raised a hand, asking for patience. "Besides, life is a succession of events that link with each other whether one wants them to or not." He held his glass up to the light and peered at the contents as if the rest of his thought process might be found floating there. "Then – I mean that day, Julia – I decided to find out everything I could about the painting. And, like you, the first person I thought of was Álvaro. I never liked him, neither when you were together nor afterwards, with the important difference that I never forgave the wretch for having made you suffer the way he did . . ."

"That was my business," Julia said, "not yours."

"You're wrong. It was mine too. Álvaro had occupied a position that I never could. In a way . . ." he hesitated for a moment and gave a bitter smile, "he was my rival. The only man capable of taking you away from me."

"It was all over between him and me. It's absurd to relate the two things."

"Not that absurd. But let's not discuss it further. I hated him, and that's that. Naturally, that isn't a reason to kill anyone. If it were, I can assure you I wouldn't have waited so long before doing it. This world of ours, the world of art and antiquities, is a very small one. Álvaro and I had had professional contact now and then; it was inevitable. Our relationship could not be termed friendly, of course, but sometimes money and self-interest make strange bedfellows. The proof is that, when faced by the problem of the Van Huys, you yourself went straight to him. So I also went to see him and I asked him to write a report on the painting. I didn't expect him to do it for the love of art, of course. I offered him a reasonable sum of money. Your ex, God rest him, was always an expensive boy. Very expensive."

"Why didn't you say anything to me about this?"

"For various reasons. The first was that I didn't want to see you start a relationship with him again, not even professionally. You can never guarantee that there aren't some embers still burning beneath the ashes. But there was something else. The painting had to do with very personal feelings." He pointed to the ivory chess set on the card table. "It had to do with a part of me that I believed I had renounced for ever, a corner of myself to which no one was allowed access, not even you, Princess. That would have meant opening the door to matters that I would never have had the courage to discuss with you." He looked at Muñoz, who was holding himself aloof from the conversation. "I imagine our friend here could enlighten you on the subject. Isn't that right? Chess as a projection of the ego, defeat as a frustration of libido and other such deliciously murky things. Those long, deep moves diagonally across the board that the bishops make." He ran the tip of his tongue round the edge of his glass and shuddered slightly. "Oh, well. I'm sure old Sigmund would have had plenty to say on the subject."

He sighed in homage to his own ghosts, then raised his glass slowly in Muñoz's direction.

"I still don't understand," insisted Julia, "what all this has to do with Álvaro."

"Not very much, at first," César acknowledged. "I just wanted a simple little report on the history of the painting. Something for which, as I said, I was prepared to pay well. But things got complicated when you decided to consult him too. That wasn't a serious problem in principle. For Álvaro, showing a praiseworthy professional discretion, refrained from telling you about my interest in the painting, since I'd specifically asked that it remain top secret."

"But didn't he find it odd that you were researching the painting behind my back?"

"Not at all. Or if he did, he didn't say anything. Perhaps he thought I wanted to give you a surprise, by providing you with some new facts. Or perhaps he thought I was playing a trick on you." César pondered seriously. "Now I think of it, he would have deserved to be killed just for that."

"He did try to warn me. He said something about the Van Huys being very fashionable lately."

"A villain to the end," remarked César. "By giving you that simple warning, he covered himself as regards you, without upsetting me. He kept us both happy: he took the money and kept open the possibility of reviving tender scenes from yesteryear." He arched one eyebrow and gave a short laugh. "But I was telling you what happened between Álvaro and me." He peered into his glass again. "Two days after my talk with him, you came and told me about the concealed inscription. I tried to hide it as best I could, but the effect on me was like an electric shock. It confirmed my feeling about the existence of some mystery. I knew that it would increase the value of the Van Huys, and I remember telling you as much. That, together with the history of the painting and its characters, would open possibilities that at the time I thought would be marvellous: you and I would share in the research and solve the enigma together. It would be like the old days, you see, like hunting for buried treasure, but a real treasure this time. And it would mean fame for you, Julia. Your name in specialist magazines, in art books. As for me . . . let's just say that I was satisfied with that. But involving myself in the game also meant a complex personal challenge. One thing is certain, ambition had nothing to do with it at all. Do you believe me?"

"I believe you."

"I'm glad. Because only then will you be able to understand what happened next." César clinked the ice in his glass, and the noise seemed to help him order his memories. "When you left, I phoned Álvaro, and we arranged that I would see him at midday. I went with no evil intentions, and I confess that I was trembling with pure excitement. Álvaro told me what he'd learned. I saw, with satisfaction, that he knew nothing about the hidden inscription. Everything went swimmingly until he started talking about you. Then, Princess, the whole atmosphere changed completely."

"In what sense?"

"In every sense."

"I mean what did Álvaro say about me?"

César shifted in his chair, apparently embarrassed, before he gave his reluctant reply.

"Your visit had made a big impression on him. Or at least that's what he implied. I saw that you'd stirred up old feelings in a most dangerous way, and that Álvaro wouldn't mind at all if things were to go back to the way they were." He paused and frowned. "Julia, you simply can't imagine how that irritated me. Álvaro had ruined two years of your life, and there I was, sitting opposite him, listening to his brazen plans to erupt into your life again. I told him, in no uncertain terms, to leave you in peace. He looked at me as if I were an interfering old queen, and we began to argue. I'll spare you the details, but it was most unpleasant. He accused me of sticking my nose in where it wasn't wanted."

"And he was right."

"No, he wasn't. You mattered to me, Julia. You matter to me more than anything in the world."

"Don't be absurd. I would never have got together again with Álvaro."

"I'm not so sure about that. I know how much that wretch meant to you." He smiled wryly into space, as if Álvaro's ghost, rendered inoffensive now, were there. "While we were arguing, I felt my old hatred for him well up in me. It went to my head like one of your hot vodka toddies. It was, my dear, a hatred I don't recall ever having felt before; a good, solid hatred, deliciously 'Latin'. I stood up, and I think I lost control, because I hurled abuse at him, using the select vocabulary of a fishwife, which I reserve for very special occasions. At first, he seemed surprised by my outburst. Then he lit his pipe and laughed in my face. He said it was my fault that his relationship with you had ended. That I was to blame for your never having grown up. My presence in your life, which he described as unhealthy and obsessive, had clipped your wings. 'And the worst thing,' he added with an insulting smile, 'is that, deep down, you're the one Julia's always been in love with, because you symbolise the father she never knew . . . And that's why she's in the mess she's in now.' Having said that, Álvaro put one hand in his pocket, gave a few puffs on his pipe and peered at me through the smoke. 'Your relationship,' he concluded, 'is nothing more or less than a case of unconsummated incest. It's just lucky you're a homosexual.' "

Julia closed her eyes. César left his final words floating in the air and had retreated into silence. When, ashamed and embarrassed, she'd gathered enough courage to look at him again, he gave a dismissive shrug, as if what he was about to say was not his responsibility.

"With those words, Princess, Álvaro signed his death warrant. He went on smoking in the chair opposite me but, in fact, he was already dead. Not because of what he'd said – after all, his opinion was as valid as anyone else's – but because of what it revealed to me about myself. It was as if he'd pulled back a curtain which, for years, had separated me from reality. Perhaps because it confirmed ideas that I'd kept locked away in the darkest corner of my mind, never allowing myself to cast the light of reason and logic on them."

He stopped, as if he'd lost the thread of what he was saying and looked hesitantly at Julia and at Muñoz. At last, with an ambiguous smile, simultaneously perverse and shy, he raised his glass to his lips to take a sip of gin.

"I had a sudden inspiration. And then, wonder of wonders, a complete plan revealed itself, just the way it happens in fairy tales. Each and every one of the pieces that had been floating randomly about found its exact place, its precise meaning. Álvaro, you, me, the painting. It fitted in too with my shadow side, with all the distant echoes, the forgotten feelings, the dormant passions. In those few seconds everything was laid out before me, like a giant chessboard on which each person, each idea, each situation found its corresponding symbol in a chess piece, found its exact place in time and space. That was a Game with a capital G, the great game of my life. And of yours. Because it was all there, Princess: chess, adventure, love, life and death. And at the end of it, there you stood, free of everything and everyone, beautiful and perfect, reflected in the bright mirror of maturity. You had to play chess, Julia; that much was certain. You had to kill us all in order, at last, to be free."

"Good God."

César shook his head.

"God has nothing to do with it. I can assure you that when I went over to Álvaro and struck him on the back of the neck with the obsidian ashtray that was on the table, I no longer hated him. That was nothing but a rather unsavoury part of the plan. Irritating but necessary."

He studied his right hand with some curiosity. He seemed to be weighing the capacity to inflict death contained in his long, pale fingers with their manicured nails, which at that moment were holding, with elegant indolence, his glass of gin.

"He dropped like a stone," he concluded in an objective tone, once he'd finished examining his hands. "He fell without even a groan, with his pipe still clenched between his teeth. Once he was on the floor, I made sure he was well and truly dead with another blow, rather better judged. After all, if a job's worth doing, it's worth doing well. The rest you know already: the shower and everything else were just artistic touches. *Brouillez les pistes*, Arsène Lupin used to say. Although Menchu, God rest her, would doubtless have attributed the saying to Coco Chanel. Poor thing." He drank a sip of gin to Menchu's memory. "Anyway, I wiped my fingerprints off with a handkerchief and took the ashtray with me, just in case, throwing it into a rubbish bin some miles away. I know I shouldn't say so, Princess, but for a novice's my mind worked in an admirably criminal way. Before leaving, I picked up the report on the painting that Álvaro had intended delivering to you, and I typed the address on an envelope."

"You also picked up a handful of his white index cards."

"No, I didn't actually. That was an ingenious touch, but it only occurred to me later. There was no way I could go back for them, so I bought some identical cards in a stationer's. But first I had to plan the game; each move had to be perfect. What I did do, was to make sure that you got the report. It was vital that you knew everything there was to know about the painting."

"So you resorted to the woman in the raincoat."

"Yes. And here I must make a confession. I've never gone in for cross-dressing, it doesn't interest me in the least. Sometimes, especially when I was young, I used to dress up just for fun, as if it was Carnival time. But I always did it alone, in front of the mirror." César's face wore the roguish, self-indulgent look of someone evoking pleasant memories. "When it came to getting the envelope to you, I thought it would be amusing to repeat the experience. A whim really, a sort of challenge, if you want to think of it in more heroic terms. To see if I was capable of deceiving people by playing at telling a kind of truth or a part of it. So I went shopping. A distinguished-looking gentleman buying a rain-coat, a handbag, low-heeled shoes, a blond wig, stockings and a dress doesn't arouse suspicion if he does it in the right way, in one of those big department stores full of people. The rest was achieved by a good shave and some make-up, which, I confess without embarrassment now, I did already have. Nothing over the top, of course. Just a discreet touch of colour. No one suspected a thing at the courier's. And I must say I found it an amusing experience . . . instructive, too."

He gave a long, studiedly melancholy sigh. Then his face clouded over.

"In fact," he added, and his tone was less frivolous now, "that was what you could call the playful part of the affair." He gave Julia an intense look, as if he were choosing his words carefully for the benefit of a more serious and invisible audience, on whom he believed it impor-tant to make a good impression. "The *really* difficult bit came next. I had to guide you both towards solving the mystery, that was the first part of the game, and towards the second part, which was much more dangerous and complicated. The problem lay in the fact that, officially, I didn't play chess. We had to progress together in our investigation of the painting, but my hands were tied when it came to helping you. It was horrible. I couldn't play against myself either; I needed an opponent, someone of stature. So I had no alternative but to find a Virgil to guide

275

you on the adventure. He was the last piece I needed to place on the board."

He finished his drink and put the glass on the table. Then he dabbed carefully at his lips with a silk handkerchief he drew from the sleeve of his dressing gown. At last he looked across at Muñoz and gave him a friendly smile.

"That was when, after due consultation with my neighbour Señor Cifuentes, the director of the Capablanca Club, I decided to choose you, my friend."

Muñoz nodded, just once. If he had any thoughts on that dubious honour, he refrained from voicing them.

"You never doubted that I would win, did you?" he said in a low voice.

César doffed an imaginary hat, in ironic salute.

"No, never," he agreed. "Quite apart from your talent as a chess player, which was apparent the moment I saw you in front of the Van Huys, I was prepared, my dear, to provide you with a series of juicy clues, which, if correctly interpreted, would lead you to uncover the second enigma: the identity of the mystery player." He gave a satisfied click of his tongue, as if savouring some delicious morsel. "I must admit you impressed me. To be honest, you still do. It's that way you have, so peculiar to you, of analysing each and every move, of gradually discounting all the unlikely hypotheses. I can only describe it as masterly."

"I'm overwhelmed," remarked Muñoz expressionlessly, and Julia couldn't tell if his words were intended sincerely or ironically.

César threw back his head and gave a silent, theatrical laugh of pleasure.

"I must say," he added with an ambivalent, almost coquettish look on his face, "that the feeling of being gradually cornered by you became genuinely exciting, really. Something . . . almost physical, if you'll allow me that word. Although, admittedly, you're not exactly my type." He remained absorbed in thought for a few moments, as if trying to decide exactly how best to categorise Muñoz, but then appeared to abandon the attempt. "With the final moves I realised that I was becoming the only possible suspect. And you knew that I knew . . . I don't think I'd be wrong in saying that it was from that moment that we began to draw closer to each other. Wouldn't you agree? The night we spent sitting on a bench opposite Julia's building, keeping watch with the aid of my flask of cognac, we had a long conversation about the psychological characteristics of the murderer. By then, you were almost sure I was your opponent. I listened with rapt attention as you explained, in response to my questions, the relationship of the known hypotheses on the pathology of chess. Except one, of course. One that you didn't mention until today but which, nevertheless, you were perfectly aware of. You know which one I mean."

Muñoz nodded, a calm, affirmative gesture. César pointed at Julia.

"You and I know, but she doesn't. Or at least not everything. We should explain it to her."

Julia looked at César.

"Yes," she said, feeling tired and irritated with both of them. "Perhaps you'd better explain what you're talking about, because I'm beginning to get thoroughly fed up with all this bloody matiness."

Muñoz kept his eyes fixed on César.

"The mathematical aspect of chess," he replied, unaffected by Julia's ill humour, "gives the game a very particular character, something that specialists would define as anal sadistic. You know what I mean: chess as a silent battle between two men, evocative of terms such as aggression, narcissism, masturbation . . . and homosexuality. Winning equals conquering the dominant father or mother, placing oneself above them. Losing equals defeat, submission."

César raised one finger, demanding attention.

"Unless, of course," he pointed out politely, "*that* is the real victory."

"Yes," said Muñoz. "Unless victory consists precisely in demonstrating the paradox: inflicting defeat upon oneself." He looked at Julia for a moment. "You were right in what you said to Belmonte: the game, like the painting, was accusing itself."

César gave him a surprised, almost joyful, look.

"Bravo," he said. "Immortalising oneself in one's own defeat; isn't that it? Like old Socrates when he drank the hemlock." He turned towards Julia with a triumphant air. "Our dear friend Muñoz knew all this days ago, Princess, but didn't say a word to anyone, not even to you or me. Finding myself conspicuous by my absence in my opponent's calculations, I modestly assumed that he must be on the right track. In fact, once he'd talked to the Belmontes and could finally discount them as suspects, he had no further doubts about the identity of the enemy. Am I right?"

"You are."

"May I ask you a rather personal question?"

"Ask and you'll find out."

"What did you feel when you finally hit on the correct move, when you knew it was me?"

Muñoz thought for a moment.

"Relief," he said. "I would have been disappointed if it had been someone else."

"Disappointed to have been wrong about the identity of the mystery player? I wouldn't want to exaggerate my own merits, but it wasn't that obvious, my friend. Several of the characters in this story weren't even known to you, and we've been together only a couple of weeks. You had only your chessboard to work with."

"You misunderstand me," replied Muñoz. "I wanted it to be you. I liked the idea."

Julia was looking at them, incredulity written on her face.

"I'm so glad to see you two getting along so well," she said sarcastically. "If you like, later on we can all go out for a drink, pat each other on the back and tell each other what a laugh we've all had over this." She shook her head, as if trying to recover some sense of reality. "It's incredible, but I feel as if I were in the way here."

César gave her a look of pained affection.

"There are some things you can't understand, Princess."

"Don't call me Princess! Besides, you're quite wrong. I understand it all perfectly. And now it's my turn to ask you a question. What would you have done that morning in the Rastro, if I hadn't noticed the spray can and the card and I'd just got into that car with its tyre made into a bomb and started the engine?"

"That's ridiculous." César seemed offended. "I would never have let you."

"Even at the risk of betraying yourself?"

"Of course. You know that. Muñoz said so earlier. You were never in any danger. That morning everything was planned down to the last detail: the disguise ready in the poky little room with its two separate doors, which I've been renting as a storeroom, my appointment with the dealer, a real appointment that I dealt with in a matter of minutes . . . I got dressed as fast as I could, walked to the alleyway, fixed the tyre, left the card and put the empty spray can on the bonnet. Then I stopped by the woman selling images to make sure she'd remember me, returned to the storeroom and, after a change of clothes and make-up, went off to meet you at the café. You have to admit my timing was impeccable."

"Sickeningly so."

César gave her a reproving look.

"Don't be vulgar, Princess." He looked at her with an ingenuousness that was remarkable for its utter sincerity. "Using ghastly adverbs like that will get us nowhere."

"Why take such pains to terrify me?"

"It was an adventure, wasn't it? There had to be a hint of menace in the air. Can you imagine an adventure from which fear is absent? I couldn't tell you the stories that used to thrill you as a child, so I invented the most extraordinary adventure I could imagine. An adventure that you would never forget as long as you lived."

"Of that you can be sure."

"Mission accomplished, then. The struggle between reason and mystery, the destruction of the ghosts ensnaring you. Not bad, eh? And add to that the discovery that Good and Evil are not clearly delimited like the black and white squares on a chessboard." He looked at Muñoz before giving an oblique smile, as if in reference to a secret to which both were privy. "All the squares, my dear, are grey, tinged by the awareness of Evil that we all acquire with experience, an awareness of how sterile and often abjectly unjust what we call Good can turn out to be. Do you remember Settembrini, the character I so admired in *The Magic Mountain*? He used to say that Evil is the shining weapon of reason against the powers of darkness and ugliness."

Julia was intently watching César's face. At certain moments it appeared that only half of his face was speaking, the visible half or the half in shadow, the other there only as witness. And she wondered which of the two was more real.

"That morning when we attacked the blue Ford I really loved you, César."

Instinctively, she addressed the illuminated half of his face, but the reply came from the half that was plunged in shadow:

"I know you did. And that justifies everything. I didn't know what that car was doing there either. I was as intrigued by it as you were. Perhaps more so, for obvious reasons. No one, if you'll forgive the rather lugubrious joke, had invited it to the funeral." He shook his head gently at the memory. "I must say that those few yards, you with your pistol and me with my pathetic poker, and our attack on those two imbeciles, before we found out they were actually Inspector Feijoo's henchmen" – he gestured as if he couldn't find words to express his feelings – "were absolutely marvellous. I watched you walking straight at the enemy, brows furrowed, teeth clenched, as brave and terrible as an avenging fury. In addition to excitement, I felt genuine pride. There's a woman with real character, I thought, admiringly. If you'd been a different kind of person, unstable or fragile, I would never have put you to such a test. But I was sure you would emerge from this a new woman, harder and stronger."

"Don't you think the price for that was rather high? Álvaro, Menchu . . . you yourself."

César seemed to search his memory, as if it were an effort to remember the person Julia was referring to. "Ah, yes, Menchu," he said at last, and frowned. "Poor Menchu, caught up in a game that was much too complex for her. Though, if you'll forgive the immodesty, her case was a brilliant bit of improvisation. When I phoned you first thing that morning, to see how everything had worked out, Menchu answered and said you weren't there. She seemed in a hurry to hang up, and now we know why. She was waiting for Max to carry out their absurd plan to steal the painting. I knew nothing about it, of course. But as soon as I put the phone down, I knew what my next move should be: Menchu, the painting. Half an hour later I rang the bell, in the guise of the woman in the raincoat."

At this point, César looked amused, as if trying to get Julia to see the oddly funny side of the situation he was describing.

"Princess," he continued, arching one eyebrow, "I always told you that you should get one of those spy holes in your door – very useful if you want to know who's calling. Menchu might not have opened the door to a blonde woman in dark glasses. But all she heard was César's voice telling her he had an urgent message from you. She had no alternative but to open the door, and she did." He turned his hands palm up, as if in posthumous apology for Menchu's mistake. "I imagine that at that moment she thought her plan with Max was about to be ruined, but her concern turned to surprise when she saw a strange woman standing on the doorstep. I just had time to see the startled look in her eyes before giving her a punch in the throat. She died without knowing who her killer was, I'm sure. I shut the door and set about preparing everything. Then – and this I didn't expect – I heard the sound of a key turning in the lock."

"Max," said Julia unnecessarily.

"Indeed. It was the handsome pimp, who, as I learned later, when he told you the whole story at the police station, was making his second call of the morning, in order to take the painting away before Menchu set fire to your apartment. An absolutely ridiculous plan, by the way, but typical of Menchu and that fool."

"It could have been me at the door. Did you think of that?"

"I must confess that when I heard the key in the lock, I thought it was you."

"And what would you have done? Punched me in the throat too?"

He looked at her again with the pained expression of one unjustly used.

"Such a question," he said, looking for an appropriate response, "is both cruel and monstrous."

"Really?"

"Yes, really. I don't know exactly how I would have reacted. But the fact is, I felt lost, and all I could think of was to hide. I ran into the bathroom and held my breath, trying to come up with a way of getting out of there. But nothing would have happened to you. The game would simply have ended halfway through. That's all."

Julia stuck out her lower lip, feeling words burning in her mouth.

"I don't believe you, César. Not any more."

"Whether you believe me or not, my dear, doesn't change a thing." He made a resigned gesture, as if the conversation were beginning to weary him. "At this stage it really doesn't matter. What counts is that it wasn't you, but Max. I heard him saying: 'Menchu, Menchu'. He was terrified, but he didn't dare cry out, the villain. I'd calmed down by then. I had a dagger in my pocket, the Cellini you've often seen. And if Max had begun sniffing round the rooms, he would have encountered that knife in the most stupid way possible, right in his heart, suddenly, before he could say a word. Luckily for him, and for me, he didn't have the courage but chose instead to run off. Such a hero."

He paused and sighed, but not boastfully.

"He owes his life to that, the cretin," he added, getting up from his chair. Once on his feet, he looked at Julia and Muñoz, both of whom were watching him, and wandered round the room, the carpets muffling his footsteps.

"I should have done what Max did and run away as fast as I could, since, for all I knew, the police could have been about to arrive. But what we might call my artistic honour got the better of me, and I dragged Menchu into the bedroom and . . . well, you know what happened. I rearranged the décor a bit, certain that Max would get the blame. It took five minutes."

"Why did you have to do that with the bottle? It was completely unnecessary. Disgusting and horrible."

César tutted. He'd paused before one of the paintings hanging on the wall, *Mars* by Luca Giordano, and was looking at it as if he expected the god, encased in the gleaming metal of his anachronistic medieval armour, to provide an answer.

"The bottle," he murmured without turning to face them, "was a complementary detail. A final inspirational touch."

"It had nothing to do with chess," Julia pointed out, and her voice had the cutting edge of a razor. "More of a settling of accounts . . . with all women."

César turned slowly round to her. His eyes this time neither begged indulgence nor hinted at irony; they were, instead, distant, inscrutable.

"Then," he said at last, in an absent tone and as if he hadn't heard what Julia had said, "I used your typewriter to type out the next move, picked up the painting wrapped up by Max and left with it under my arm. And that was that."

He'd been speaking in a neutral voice, as if the conversation was no longer of any interest to him. But Julia was far from considering the matter closed.

"But why kill Menchu? You could come and go in my apartment

whenever you wanted. There were a thousand other ways of stealing the painting."

That comment brought a spark of life back into César's eyes.

"I see, Princess, that you're determined to give the theft of the Van Huys an exaggerated importance. In fact, it was just another detail. Throughout this whole affair I did some things simply because they complemented others. The icing on the cake, if you like," he said, struggling to find the right words. "There were several reasons Menchu had to die: some are irrelevant now and others aren't. Let's say they go from the purely aesthetic, and that's how our friend Muñoz made his astonishing discovery of the link between Menchu's surname and the rook that was taken, to other deeper reasons. I'd organised everything to free you from pernicious ties and influences, to cut your links with the past. Unfortunately for her, Menchu, with her innate stupidity and vulgarity, was one of those links, as was Álvaro."

"And who gave you the power over life and death?"

César gave a Mephistophelian smile.

"I did, all on my own. And forgive me if that sounds impertinent." He seemed suddenly to recall the presence of Muñoz. "As regards the rest of the game, I didn't have much time. Muñoz was like a bloodhound sniffing out my trail. A few more moves and he would point the finger at me. But I knew our dear friend wouldn't intervene until he was absolutely certain. On the other hand, he was sure by then that you weren't in any danger. He's an artist too, in his way. That's why he let me continue, while he looked for proofs that would confirm his analytical conclusions. Am I right, friend Muñoz?"

Muñoz's only reply was to nod slowly. César had gone over to the small table on which the chess set stood. After observing the pieces for a while, he delicately picked up the white queen, as if it were made of fragile glass, and looked at it for a long time.

"Yesterday evening," he said, "while you were working in the studio at the Prado, I got to the museum ten minutes before it closed. I hung about in the rooms on the ground floor and planted the card on the Brueghel painting. Then I went to have a coffee to while away the time before I could phone you. That was all. The only thing I couldn't foresee was that Muñoz would dust off that old chess magazine in the club library. I had forgotten its existence."

283

"There's something that doesn't make sense," Muñoz said suddenly, and Julia turned to him, surprised. He was staring at César with his head on one side, an inquisitive light shining in his eyes; it was the way he looked when he was concentrating on the chessboard, tracking a move that didn't quite satisfy him. "You're a brilliant chess player; on that we agree. Or, rather, you have the ability to be one. Nevertheless, I don't believe you have the ability to play this game the way you did. The combinations were too perfect, inconceivable for someone who hasn't been near a chessboard in thirty-five years. In chess, what counts is practice and experience. That's why I'm sure you've been lying to us. Either you've played a lot during these years, alone, or someone helped you. I hate to wound your vanity, César, but I'm sure you had an accomplice."

A long dense silence followed these words. Julia was looking at them both, disconcerted, unable to believe what Muñoz had said. But just when she was about to shout that it was all utter nonsense, she saw that César, whose face had frozen into an impenetrable mask, had finally arched one ironic eyebrow. The smile that then appeared was a grimace of recognition and admiration. He sighed deeply, crossed his arms and nodded.

"My friend," he said slowly, dragging out the words, "you deserve to be something more than an obscure weekend chess player in a local club." He threw out his right hand as if to indicate the presence of someone who'd been there with them all the time, in a shadowy corner of the room. "I do, in fact, have an accomplice, although in this case he can consider himself quite safe from any reprisals on the part of Justice. Would you like to know his name?"

"I was hoping you'd tell me."

"Of course I will, since I don't believe my betrayal will harm him much." He smiled, more broadly. "I hope you won't feel offended, my esteemed friend, that I kept this small source of satisfaction to myself. Believe me, it affords me great pleasure to know that you didn't find out absolutely everything. Can't you guess who he is?"

"I can't, and I'm sure it's no one I know."

"You're right. His name is Alfa PC-1212. He's a personal computer with a complex chess programme with twenty levels of play. I bought it the day after killing Álvaro."

284

For only the second time since she'd known him, Julia saw a look of amazement on Muñoz's face. The light in his eyes had gone out and his mouth hung open in astonishment.

"Haven't you got anything to say?" asked César, observing him with amused curiosity.

Muñoz gave him a long look but didn't answer. After a while, he looked across at Julia.

"Give me a cigarette, will you," he said in a dull voice.

She offered him the pack, and he turned it around in his fingers before taking out a cigarette and putting it to his lips. Julia proffered a lit match, and he inhaled the smoke slowly, deeply, filling his lungs. He seemed to be a million miles from there.

"It's hard to take, isn't it?" said César, laughing softly. "All this time you've been playing against a simple computer, a machine with no emotions or feelings. I'm sure you'll agree with me that it's a delicious paradox, a perfect symbol of the times we live in. Maelzel's prodigious player had a man hidden inside, according to Poe. Do you remember? But times change, my friend. Now it's the automaton that hides inside the man." He held up the yellowing ivory queen he had in his hand and showed it, mockingly. "And all your talent, imagination and extra-ordinary capacity for mathematical analysis, dear Señor Muñoz, have their equivalent on a simple plastic diskette that fits in the palm of a hand, like the ironic reflection in a mirror that shows us only a caricature of what we are. I'm very much afraid that, like Julia, you will never be the same after this. Although in your case," he acknowledged with a reflective smile, "I doubt if you will gain much from the change."

Muñoz still said nothing. He merely stood with his hands in his raincoat pockets again, the cigarette hanging from his lips, his inexpress-ive eyes half closed against the smoke. He looked like a parody of a shabby detective in a black-and-white movie.

"I'm sorry," said César, and he seemed sincere. He returned the queen to the board with the air of someone about to draw a pleasant evening to a close and looked at Julia.

"To finish," he said, "I'm going to show you something."

He went over to a mahogany escritoire, opened one of its drawers and took out a fat sealed envelope and the three porcelain figurines by Bustelli.

"You win the prize, Princess." He smiled at her with a glint of mischief in his eyes. "Once again you've managed to find the buried treasure. Now you can do with it what you like."

Julia regarded the figurines and the envelope suspiciously.

"I don't understand."

"You will in a minute. During these last few weeks I've also had time to concern myself with your interests. At this moment, *The Game of Chess* is in the best possible place: a safe-deposit box in a Swiss bank, rented by a limited company that exists only on paper and has its headquarters in Panama. Swiss lawyers and bankers are rather boring people but very proper, and they ask no questions as long as you respect the laws of their country and pay their fees." He placed the envelope on the table, near Julia. "You own seventy-five per cent of the shares in that limited company, the deeds of which are in the envelope. Demetrius Ziegler, a Swiss lawyer and an old friend you've heard me mention before, has been in charge of this. No one, apart from us and a third person, of whom we will speak later, knows that for some time the Pieter Van Huys painting will remain where it is, out of sight in that safe-deposit box. Meanwhile, the story of *The Game of Chess* will have become a major event in the art world. The media and specialist magazines will exploit the scandal for all it's worth. We foresee, at a rough estimate, a value on the international market of several million . . . dollars, of course."

Julia looked at the envelope and then at César, perplexed and incredulous.

"It doesn't matter what value it reaches," she murmured, pronouncing the words with some difficulty. "You can't sell a stolen painting, not even abroad."

"That depends to whom and how," replied César. "When everything's ready – let's say in a few months – the painting will come out of its hiding place in order to appear, not at public auction, but on the black market for works of art. It will end up hanging, in secret, in the luxurious mansion of one of the many millionaire collectors in Brazil, Greece or Japan, who hurl themselves like sharks on such valuable works, either in order to resell them or to satisfy private passions to do with luxury, power and beauty. It's also a good long-term investment, since in certain countries there's a twenty-year amnesty on stolen works of art. And you're still so deliciously young. Isn't that marvellous? Anyway, you won't have to worry about that. What matters now is that, in the next few months, while the Van Huys embarks on its secret journey, the bank account of your brand-new Panamanian company, opened two days ago in another worthy Zurich bank, will be richer to the tune of some millions of dollars. You won't have to do anything, because someone will have taken care of all those worrying transactions for you. I've made quite sure of that, Princess, especially as regards the vital loyalty of that person. A loyal mercenary, it must be said. But as good as any other; perhaps even better. Never trust disinterested loyalties."

"Who is it? Your Swiss friend?"

"No. Ziegler is an efficient, methodical lawyer but he doesn't know much about art. That's why I went to someone with the right contacts, with no scruples whatsoever and expert enough to move easily in that complicated subterranean world. Paco Montegrifo."

"You're joking."

"I don't joke about money. Montegrifo is a strange character, who, it should be said, is a little in love with you, although that has nothing to do with the matter. What counts is that he is simultaneously an utter villain and an extraordinarily gifted individual, and he'll never do anything to harm you."

"I don't see why not. If he's got the painting, he'll be off like a shot. Montegrifo would sell his own mother for a watercolour."

"Undoubtedly, but he can't do that to *you*. In the first place, because Demetrius Ziegler and I have made him sign a quantity of documents that have no legal value if made public, since the whole matter constitutes a flagrant breach of the law, but which are enough to show that you have nothing whatsoever to do with all this. They'll also serve to implicate him if he talks too much or plays dirty, enough for him to have every police force in the world after him for the rest of his life. I'm also in possession of certain secrets whose publication would damage his reputation and create serious problems for him with the law. To my knowledge, Montegrifo has, amongst other things, on at least two occasions undertaken to remove from the country and sell illegally objects that are designated part of our national heritage, objects that came into my hands and which I placed in his as intermediary: a fifteenth-century reredos attributed to Pere Oller and stolen from

Santa María de Cascalls in 1978 and that famous Juan de Flandes that disappeared four years ago from the Olivares collection. Do you remember?"

"Yes, I do. But I never imagined that you . . ."

César shrugged indifferently.

"That's life, Princess. In my business, as in all businesses, unimpeachable honesty is the surest route to death from starvation. But we weren't talking about me, we were talking about Montegrifo. Of course, he'll try to keep as much money for himself as he can; that's inevitable. But he'll remain within certain limits that won't impinge upon the minimum profit guaranteed by your Panamanian company, whose interests Ziegler will guard like a Dobermann. Once the business is finished, Ziegler will automatically transfer the money from the limited company's bank account to another private account, whose number only you will have. He will then close the former in order to cover our tracks, and destroy all other documents apart from those referring to Montegrifo's murky past. Those he will keep in order to guarantee you the loyalty of our friend the auctioneer. Though I'm sure that, by then, such a precaution will be unnecessary . . . By the way, Ziegler has express instructions to divert a third of your profits into various types of safe, profitable investments in order both to launder that money and to guarantee you financial security for the rest of your life, even if you decide to go on the most lavish of spending sprees. Take any advice he gives you, because Ziegler is a good man whom I've known for more than twenty years: honest, Calvinist and homosexual. He will, of course, be equally scrupulous about deducting his commission plus expenses."

Julia, who had listened without moving a muscle, shuddered. Everything fit perfectly, like the pieces of some incredible jigsaw puzzle. César had left no loose ends. She gave him a long look, and walked about the room, trying to take it in. It was too much for one night, she thought as she stopped in front of Muñoz, who was watching her impassively. It was perhaps too much even for one lifetime.

"I see," she said, turning back to César, "that you've thought of everything. Or almost everything. Have you also considered Don Manuel Belmonte? You may think it a trifling detail, but he is the owner of the painting."

"I have considered that. Needless to say, you could always suffer a praiseworthy crisis of conscience and decide not to accept my plan. In that case, you have only to inform Ziegler and the painting will turn up in some suitable place. It will upset Montegrifo but he'll just have to put up with it. Then, everything will remain as before: the scandal will have increased the painting's value, and Claymore's will retain the right to auction it. But should you take the sensible path, there are plenty of arguments to salve your conscience: Belmonte gets rid of the painting for money, so, once you've excluded the painting's sentimental value, there remains its economic worth. And that's covered by the insurance. Besides, there's nothing to stop you from anonymously donating whatever compensation you consider appropriate. You'll have more than enough money to do so. As for Muñoz . . ."

"Yes," said Muñoz, "I'm curious to know what you have in store for me."

César gave him a wry look.

"You, my dear, have won the lottery."

"You don't say."

"Oh, but I do. Foreseeing that the second white knight would survive the game, I took the liberty of linking you, on paper, with the company, with twenty-five per cent of the shares, which will, amongst other things, permit you to buy yourself some new shirts and to play chess in the Bahamas if you fancy it."

Muñoz raised a hand to his mouth and what remained of his cigarette. He looked at it briefly and very deliberately dropped it on the carpet.

"That's very generous of you," he said.

César looked at the dead stub on the floor and then at Muñoz.

"It's the least I can do. I have to buy your silence in some way, and, besides, you've more than earned it. Let's just say it's my way of making up for the nasty trick I played on you with the computer."

"Has it occurred to you that I might refuse to participate in all this?"

"Of course. You are, after all, an odd sort. But that's not my affair any more. You and Julia are now associates, so you can sort it out between you. I have other things to think about."

"That leaves you, César," said Julia.

"Me?" He smiled – painfully, Julia thought. "My dear Princess, I have many sins to purge and little time to do it in." He indicated the sealed envelope on the table. "There you have a detailed confession, explaining the whole story from start to finish, apart, of course, from our Swiss arrangement. You, Muñoz and, for the moment, Montegrifo, come out of it clean. As for the painting, I explain its destruction in great detail, along with the personal and sentimental reasons that drove me to it. I'm sure that after a learned examination of my confession, the police psychiatrists will happily label me a dangerous schizophrenic."

"Do you intend going abroad?"

"Certainly not. The only thing that makes having a place to go to desirable is that it gives you an excuse to make a journey. But I'm too old for that. On the other hand, I don't much fancy prison or a lunatic asylum. It must be rather awkward with all those well-built, attractive nurses giving you cold showers. I'm afraid not, my dear. I'm fifty years old and no longer up to such excitement. Besides, there is one other tiny detail."

Julia looked at him gravely.

"What's that?"

"Have you heard" – César gave an ironic smile – "of something called acquired something or other syndrome, which seems to be horribly fashionable these days? Well, I am a terminal case. Or so they say."

"You're lying."

"Not at all. That's what they called it: terminal, like some gloomy Underground station."

Julia closed her eyes. Everything around her seemed to fade away, and in her mind all that remained was a dull, muffled sound, like that of a stone falling into a pool. When she opened them again, her eyes were full of tears.

"You're lying, César. Not you. Tell me you're lying."

"I'd love to, Princess. I assure you I'd like nothing better than to tell you that it's all been a joke in the worst possible taste. But life is quite capable of playing such tricks on one."

"How long have you known?"

César brushed the question aside with a languid gesture of his hand, as if time had ceased to matter to him.

"Two months, more or less," he said. "It began with the appearance of a small tumour in my rectum. Rather unpleasant."

"You never said anything to me."

"Why should I have? If you'll forgive the indelicacy, my dear, I've always felt my rectum was strictly my business."

"How much longer have you got?"

"Not much. Six or seven months, I think. And they say the weight simply falls off you."

"They'll send you to a hospital then. You won't go to prison. Nor even to a lunatic asylum, as you put it."

César shook his head calmly.

"I won't go to any of those places, my dear. Can you imagine anything more horrible when dying of something so vulgar? Oh, no. Definitely not. I refuse. I at least claim the right to give my exit a personal touch. It must be dreadful to take with you as your last image of this world an intravenous drip hanging over your head, with your visitors tripping over your oxygen tank." He looked at the furniture, the tapestries and the paintings in the room. "I prefer to give myself a Florentine death, amongst all the objects that I love. A discreet, gentle exit is better suited to my tastes and my character."

"When?"

"In a while. Whenever you two are kind enough to leave me alone."

Muñoz was waiting in the street, leaning against the wall with his raincoat collar turned up. He seemed absorbed in secret thoughts, and when Julia appeared at the door and came over to him, he didn't at first look up.

"How's he going to do it?" he asked.

"Prussic acid. He's got a flask of it that he's had for ages." She smiled bitterly. "He says a bullet would be more heroic, but it would leave him with an unpleasantly surprised look on his face. He prefers to die looking his best."

"I understand."

"There's a telephone box near here, around the corner." She looked at Muñoz absently. "He asked us to give him ten minutes before calling the police."

They set off along the pavement side by side, beneath the yellow light of the street lamps. At the end of the deserted street, the traffic lights were changing from green to amber to red. The light illuminated Julia's face, marking it with deep, fantastic shadows.

"What do you think you'll do now?" asked Muñoz. He spoke without looking at her, keeping his gaze fixed on the ground ahead of him. She shrugged.

"That depends on you."

Then Julia heard Muñoz laugh. It was a profound, gentle laugh, slightly nasal, that seemed to bubble up from deep inside him. For a fraction of a second, she had the impression that it was one of the characters in the painting, and not Muñoz, who was laughing at her side.

"Your friend César is right," Muñoz said. "I do need some new shirts."

Julia ran her fingers over the three porcelain figurines – Octavio, Lucinda and Scaramouche – that she was carrying in her raincoat pocket, along with the sealed envelope. The cold night air dried her lips and froze the tears in her eyes.

"Did he say anything else before you left him alone?" asked Muñoz.

" '*Nec sum adeo informis* . . . I'm not so very ugly. I saw myself recently, reflected in the waters along the shore, when the sea was calm.' " It was just like César to quote Virgil when she turned at the door to take in at a glance the chiaroscuro drawing room, the dark tones of the old paintings on the walls, the faint gleam, filtered by the parchment lampshade, on the surface of the furniture, the yellowing ivory, the gold on the spines of the books. And César standing against the light in the middle of the room, his features impossible to make out; a clear, slim silhouette like the effigy on a medal or an antique cameo, his shadow falling, almost brushing Julia's feet, on the red and ochre arabesques of the carpet. And the chimes that sounded at the same instant she closed the door, as if it were the stone slab of a tomb. It was as if everything had been foreseen long before, and each of them had conscientiously performed the role assigned in the play that had finished on the chessboard at that exact hour, five centuries after the first act, with the mathematical precision of the black queen's final move.

"No," she murmured in a low voice, feeling the image moving slowly off, sinking into the depths of her memory. "No, he didn't really say much else."

Muñoz looked up, like a thin, ungainly dog sniffing the dark sky above their heads, and he smiled with wry affection.

"It's a pity," he said. "He'd have made an excellent chess player."

The sound of her footsteps echoes in the empty cloister, beneath the vaulted roof already plunged in shadow. The final rays of the setting sun fall almost horizontally, filtered through the stone shutters, staining red the convent walls, the empty niches, the ivy leaves turned yellow by the autumn curling about the capitals of the columns, the monsters, warriors, saints, mythological beasts that support the grave, Gothic arches surrounding the garden invaded by weeds. The wind howls outside, warning of the cold northern weather that always precedes winter, whirling up the side of the hill, where it shakes the branches of the trees and draws from the gargoyles and the eaves of the roof the boom of centuries-old stone; it sets the bronze bells in the tower swaying and, above them, a creaking, rusty weathervane points obstinately south, a south that is perhaps luminous, distant and inaccessible.

The woman dressed in mourning stops by a mural eaten away by time and damp. Only a few fragments of the original colours remain: the blue of a tunic, the ochre outline of a figure; a hand cut off at the wrist, one index finger pointing up at a nonexistent sky, a Christ whose features meld into the crumbling plaster of the wall; a ray of sun or of divine light, with no origin or destination, suspended between heaven and earth, a segment of yellow light absurdly frozen in time and space, which the years and the weather have gradually worn away, until one day it will be extinguished or erased, as if it had never even been there. And an angel with no mouth and a frown like that of a judge or an executioner, of whom one can only make out, amongst what remains of the paint, a pair of wings stained with lime, a fragment of tunic and the vague shape of a sword.

The woman dressed in mourning lifts the black veils that cover her face and looks for a long time into the eyes of the angel. For eighteen years she has stopped here every day at the same hour and she sees the ravages of time gnawing away at what remains of that painting. She has watched it disappear little by little, as if afflicted by a leprosy that tears off lumps of flesh, that blurs the figure of the angel, so that it blends with the dirty plaster of the wall, with the damp that causes the colours to blister, that cracks and fragments the images. Where she lives there are no mirrors. They are forbidden by the order she entered, or that perhaps she was obliged to enter. Like the painting on the wall, her memory contains more and more blanks. She has not seen her own face for eighteen years, and for her that angel, who doubtless once possessed a beautiful face, is the only external reference to the effect of passing time on her own features: peeling paint instead of wrinkles, blurred outlines instead of ageing skin. In the occasional moments of lucidity that arrive like waves licking the sands of a beach, moments to which she clings, desperately trying to fix them in her confused, ghost-ridden memory, she seems to recall that she is fifty-four years old.

From the chapel comes a chorus of voices, the sound muffled by the thickness of the walls, voices singing the praises of God before going to the refectory. The woman dressed in mourning has permission not to attend certain services and at that hour they allow her to walk alone, like a dark, silent shadow, in the deserted cloister. A long rosary of dark wooden beads hangs from her belt, a rosary she has not touched for some time. The distant religious singing becomes confused with the whistling of the wind.

When she starts walking again and reaches the window, the dying sun is just a bright smudge of red in the distance, beneath leaden clouds coming from the north. At the foot of the hill there is a broad grey lake that glitters like steel. The woman rests her thin, bony hands on the ledge of a lancet window – again, as on every evening, her memories pitilessly return – and she feels how the cold from the stone rises up her arms and approaches, slowly, dangerously, her worn-out heart. She is seized by a terrible fit of coughing that shakes her fragile body undermined by the damp of so many winters, tortured by seclusion, solitude and intermittent memories. She no longer hears the songs from the chapel or the sound of the wind. Now it is the sad, monotonous music of a mandolin that emerges from the mists of time, and the harsh autumnal horizon vanishes before her eyes to form, as if in a painting, another landscape: a gentle undulating plain and in the distance, silhouetted against the blue sky as if painted by a fine brush, the slender outline of a belfry. And suddenly she seems to hear the voices of two men sitting at a table, the echo of laughter. And she thinks that if she turns round, she will see herself sitting on a stool with a book in her lap, and that when she looks up, she will see the gleam of a steel gorget and an insigne representing the Golden Fleece. And an old man with a grey beard will smile at her while, brush in hand, he paints on an oak panel, with the quiet skill of his profession, the eternal image of that scene.

For an instant, the wind rips asunder the covering of clouds, and a final gleam of light, reverberating across the waters of the lake, illuminates the woman's ageing face, dazzles her eyes, which are clear and cold and almost lifeless. Then, as the light dies, the wind seems to howl louder still, stirring the black veils that flap about her like the wings of a crow. She feels again that sharp pain gnawing at her, inside, near her heart, a pain that paralyses half her body and that nothing can alleviate. It freezes her limbs, her breath.

The lake is nothing but a dull smudge in the shadows. And the woman dressed in mourning, whom the world knew as Beatrice of Burgundy, knows that the winter advancing from the north will be her last. And she wonders if, in the dark place to which she is heading, there will be enough mercy to erase from her mind the final shreds of memory.

La Navata, April 1990